A
Map of
the World

Also by Jane Hamilton:

THE BOOK OF RUTH

A
Map of
the World

Jane Hamilton

ANCHOR BOOKS
A DIVISION OF RANDOM HOUSE, INC.
New York

First Anchor Books Edition, June 1995

Special thanks to master cartographer Katy Seeley, and to the National Endowment for the Arts, and to the Ragdale Foundation, where much of this book was written.

The author gratefully acknowledges permission to quote from the following:

The Poems of W. B. Yeats: A New Edition, edited by Richard J. Finneron. Copyright 1940 by Georgie Yeats, renewed 1968 by Bertha Georgie Yeats, Michael Butler Yeats, and Anne Yeats. Used by permission.

Little House in the Big Woods by Laura Ingalls Wilder. Reprinted by permission of HarperCollins. Copyright renewed 1960 by Roger MacBride. Little House is a registered trademark of HarperCollins.

Poems of Gerard Manley Hopkins. Oxford University Press. Used by permission.

Book Design by Gretchen Achilles

Library of Congress Cataloging-in-Publication Data

Hamilton, Jane, 1957–
    A map of the world / by Jane Hamilton. — 1st Anchor
Books ed.
        p.   cm.
    I. Title.
    1. Dairy farms—Middle West—Fiction.   2. Farm life—Middle West—Fiction.   3. Children—Death—Fiction.   4. Middle West—Fiction.   5. Drowning—Fiction.   I. Title.
PS3558.A4427M36   1995b
813'.54—dc20   95-3001
                                                                            CIP

ISBN 0-385-72010-6

www.anchorbooks.com

Printed in the United States of America
10 9 8 7 6 5

For STEVEN SHAHAN
with love and thanks.

And for ELIZABETH WEINSTEIN
also with love, and with thanks in each day
all the way back to B-34.

Alice

Chapter One

———

I USED TO THINK if you fell from grace it was more likely than not the result of one stupendous error, or else an unfortunate accident. I hadn't learned that it can happen so gradually you don't lose your stomach or hurt yourself in the landing. You don't necessarily sense the motion. I've found it takes at least two and generally three things to alter the course of a life: You slip around the truth once, and then again, and one more time, and there you are, feeling, for a moment, that it was sudden, your arrival at the bottom of the heap.

I opened my eyes on a Monday morning in June last summer and I heard, somewhere far off, a siren belting out calamity. It was the last time I would listen so simply to a sound that could mean both disaster and pursuit. Emma and Claire were asleep and safe in their beds, and my own heart seemed to be beating regularly. If the barn was out the window, clean, white, the grass cropped as close as a golf course, the large fan whirring in the doorway, then my husband Howard was all right. I raised up to take a look. It was still standing, just as I suspected it would be. I had never said out loud a little joke I used to say to myself now and again: Everywhere that barn goes, Howard, you are sure to be close behind. He was a philosophical and poetical farmer who bought Golden Guernseys because he both liked their color and the way "Golden Guernsey" floated off his tongue. It was secondary that the breed was famous for their butterfat. I worried about his choice when we bought the farm because I was certain that poetry is almost never rewarded. Now, in my more charitable moods, I wonder if our hardworking, God-fearing community members punished us for something as intangible as whimsy. We would not have felt eccentric in a northern city, but in Prairie Center we were perhaps outside the bounds of the collective imagination.

The ambulances were streaking down the highway while I lay in bed in our farmhouse, in what used to be a very small town called Prairie Junction. Three years before they had built a greyhound racetrack outside of the city limits, a facility which has brought so many business and goods and services to the area the governing body voted to change the name of the new, improved version of our town to Prairie Center. Even people who lived there could never remember where they were.

I wondered if a building was burning down, if there was a car accident at the perilous intersection, or a baby coming early in one of the subdivisions. Our range of disaster in that town was fairly limited, but we were due for something, certainly. The last rain had come at the beginning of April and now, at the first of June, all but the hardiest mosquitoes had left their papery skins in the grass. It was already seven o'clock in the morning, long past time to close the windows and doors, trap what was left of the night air, slightly cooler only by virtue of the dark. The dust on the gravel had just enough energy to drift a short distance and then collapse on the flower beds. The sun had a white cast, as if shade and shadow, any flicker of nuance, had been burned out by its own fierce center. There would be no late afternoon gold, no pale early morning yellow, no flaming orange at sunset. If the plants had vocal cords they would sing their holy dirges like slaves.

I often had the fanciful thought that the pond would save us; it would be the one thing that would postpone our deaths by scorching as the climate of our part of the world changed. We were going to spend the long summer months ahead thinking always of the relief of our own unspoiled waters. Most afternoons our daughters, Emma and Claire, and I, and occasionally Howard, farmer, husband, and father, would walk the thirty yards down the wooded path to the jewel of the property, the clear water gurgling up from a spring into a seven-acre pond. There were no leeches, no film or scum or snapping turtles, no monstrous vestiges from the Cretaceous Age lurking in the depths. There, under the blazing sun, were cool, clean ripples spreading from their mysterious source and fanning to the shore, while trout circled beneath.

I needed to get out of bed. Howard, in his quiet, sissing voice, soothing as a dove, had told me to sleep in, but I should have been up to help him, should have woken hours earlier. I lay still and took another minute to smell: I smelled the warm, sweet, all-pervasive smell of silage, as well as the sour dirty laundry spilling over the basket in the hall. I could pick out the acrid smell of Claire's drenched diaper, her sweaty feet, and her hair crusted with sand. The heat compounded the smells, doubled the fragrance. Howard always smelled and through the house his scent seemed always to be warm. His was a musky smell, as if the source of a muddy river, the Nile or the Mississippi, began right in his armpits. I had grown used to thinking of his smell as the fresh man smell of hard work. Too long without washing and I tenderly beat his knotty arms with my fists. That morning there was alfalfa on his pillow and cow manure embedded in his tennis shoes and the cuffs of his coveralls that lay by the bed. Those were sweet reminders of him. He had gone out as one shaft of searing light came through the window. He had put on clean clothes to milk the cows.

I knew just then, in a brief glimmer of truth, that the stink and mess, the frenetic dullness of farming, our marriage, the tedium of work and love—all of it was my savior. Half the world seemed to be scheming to escape husbands or wives, but I was planted firmly enough, striving, always striving, to take root. I was sure that that morning our family was connected by a ribbon of pure, steaming, binding, inviolable stench, going from room to room and out to the barn. I was so far from my mistakes of the school year, never considering in the freedom of summer that my winter's missteps could strain our vigorous bonds.

At breakfast I was putting out bowls when Claire banged her spoon on the table and announced, "I'm going to die when you do."

"What?" I said, once in a voice roughly an octave lower than usual, and then again in my normal register. "What?" What had possessed Claire, three years old, to say such a thing, other than the terrible force of our doomsayer genes? Or was she prescient? Did she see before her our wrecked car, the Jaws of Life working in vain to extract what was left of us? In any case, I wasn't paying strict attention that morning; I didn't think about my five-year-old daughter, Emma, requiring milk in her red plastic cup so that she could pour her own milk over her cereal. In all innocence I poured the unpasteurized, completely homogenized milk from our cows straight from the blue pitcher into Emma's bowl.

"WHAT ARE YOU DOING?"

"Christ," I said under my breath.

Emma's shrieks made our one crystal vase rattle and the blood pound in my head. She was flailing in her chair as if she'd been inadequately electrocuted. I knew from experience that there was not going to be any quick consolation for my transgression. "Emma, Emma, Emma," I said, wishing I could somehow teach her to take the smaller blows of life in stride. It was possible my blunder would start a chain reaction that might last a full morning, one tantrum after the next, each round going off when we least expected it.

"Why did you do that?" she sobbed. She was the child who was frequently on the verge of hysteria, the tears right under her lids waiting to fall. She was so often unhappy about what she didn't have or was about to receive. We led a hectic life, and she had a darling baby sister who had stolen some of her thunder, but even so her tantrums were excessive, indeed violent. They frightened me. They seemed to be about so much more than the protocol I had not observed. "Emma, I'm sorry," I said. "I wasn't thinking. Did I ever tell you about Aunt Kate's chicken pitcher that clucked when it was empty?" Of course I had told her about the chicken. I had told her about the magical porcelain pitcher countless times and she usually interrupted, begging for one just like it. "If you want to start over," I said, "I'd be glad to fill your cup with milk and begin again."

She threw her head back and groaned. My dispensation meant nothing. Her skin was already so brown that when she spread her fingers in her woe the little webs between were white as pearl. Her face, stretched to the limit with exaggerated heartbreak, was red and blotchy. I wasn't sure I could bear a day like that one was sure to be, and I slammed my hands down on the table, saying, with such exquisite self-control I felt as if I was singing, "Emma, if you need to scream and cry and carry on you may go sit on the chair in the hall."

"Why," Emma heaved, "did you do that to me?"

"I did not do anything to you," I explained, with emphasis on every word. "I will count to three, and if you are still in a temper you will go to the chair." That was the procedure my neighbor Theresa used with great success to discipline her children. I counted. Emma remained seated during the punctuated and fractionated count from zero to three. Even after I was done, absolutely no place to go after three, I waited, giving her the chance to bolt. In the end there was nothing to do but lift her under her arms and drag her away. She kicked and tossed her head back and forth, snarling and spitting. She could be a torment, a humiliation, at nearly six years of age carrying on as if she was preparing for the role of Helen Keller. I didn't know how the calm and deep wellspring of mother love could sustain itself through years of such storms. I hated her being so unreasonable and so fierce in her anger. She didn't have any right to be angry!

There was a black chair in the hall that had been set there for those occasions, and when I forced her onto the worn seat she dug her fingernails into my arm and pulled down so that blood sprang up from the scratches. "Stay there," I growled. I stumbled back into the kitchen and set the timer for five minutes. My hands were shaking. I looked at my arm, at the three bloody tracks. Emma's rage was as perfect an anger as I could think of, flowing spontaneously on a moment's notice from the depth of her being, where a careful accounting of justice, swift as light, must take place. I could have cried at the terror of it, the surprise, the strength of her fury; I could have cried because I knew that I was responsible for her anger; I wanted to cry most of all because I had wanted to right my own wrongs, to raise a loving family, and I had instead produced a hellion. A hellion! She would pursue us through our lives, fueled by rage, crashing into the nursing home where I would sit slumped over in a wheelchair, to give me a piece of her mind. Emma, more than anyone I had ever known, made me think in outlandish terms, in measurements that occasionally extended through to eternity. I covered the scratch with my other hand. "What did you say a minute ago?" I asked Claire, who was sitting straight in her chair peeling the stickers off the bananas. Her short sleek, dark hair was molded around her head like a close-fitting cap.

"I forget," was all. Our daughters had forged their roles early on with our unwitting complicity: Emma, the bad. Claire, the good. Emma had come hard into this world. "Who are you?" we had hardly dared to ask as she miraculously sucked and burped and moved her bowels. "Where did you come from?" We had stood over her waiting for her, our creation, to find her hands, to sit; we begged her to walk, to use the shape sorter properly, to say our names. We wanted to know she was normal and secretly hoped she was quite a bit above average. We were so careful, buying her skid-proof socks and a bike helmet for the goat cart. At night Howard and I fell asleep discussing her intelligence and her remarks. Claire was the blessed second child, nothing more than a baby, someone who had come to live at our house, who would grow up in her own time, her achievements more often than not overlooked in the confusion of getting to work, scratching up meals, finding clean clothes.

When the timer rang, Emma marched into the kitchen, climbed on her chair, turned her bowl over, and then dropped it to the floor, a look of triumph on her tearstained face. The bowl smashed. I fetched the broom, without missing a step, as if the scene had been choreographed, swept up the broken porcelain and then walked out into the yard, slamming the kitchen door behind me with all my might. She had been sitting so peacefully on the black chair, not because she was obedient, but because she had been hatching her plot.

Outside, the air smelled as if it had been cooked, as if it had been altered by the heat and was no longer life sustaining.

"Don't leave me!" Emma shouted from the porch.

I did not direct my answer to her. I was cupping my hand over the yellow cat's face while it went wild with the prospect of near suffocation. During the next tantrum I would have to tell Emma that I was going to count to infinity, that I would give her that much time to compose herself. I was hissing, shaking the poor cat as I lectured him, when Howard said, "What are you doing, Alice?"

He was standing in the doorway of the milk house, wearing his rubber overalls and his rubber boots, each the length of a basset hound.

The open buckles on the boots and the metal hooks on the overalls jangled when he moved. I felt a rush of admiration for him, in his stiff, clattery suit that on anyone else would have looked oafish. Because he himself was commanding he gave even a rubbery old hillbilly getup dignity.

"What am I doing?" I asked myself, prying the cat's claws from my shirt. "I'm about to suffocate this cat instead of our daughter, that's all," I said, snorting, as if I'd made a joke. Without saying, he'd know I meant Emma.

"I'll be in soon, as soon as I can." He turned and shuffled into his barn. His overalls were pulled too tight in the back and had the beguiling effect of the wicked schoolboy's trick known as Chinese laundry.

"I'm handling it fine, Howard, I really think I am." I sometimes felt dismayed because he didn't seem to trust me the way he should have. "I'm pretty sure I'm doing the right thing," I said under my breath, "strangling the cat instead of Emma."

I had always suspected that deep down Howard was able to slip into a phone booth, shed his rubber overalls right down to a blue body suit, and then take off into the sky, scooping up the children with one strong arm before he made off to a land where milk naturally flows in the rivers. He has always been capable. This is my fondest image from his childhood: Howard, nine years old, is in his back yard in Minneapolis, setting up battalions of toy soldiers and then digging the firecrackers into the ground, lighting them, and exploding his armies. The noise, the smoke, the destruction, are not only thrilling, but beautiful. I can so well imagine the pleasure he would have gotten from being the master planner. In his family album he always has the same crew cut and he doesn't smile. He was a solemn boy who was taught that life is both important and nice. When I first knew him he believed in irresistible notions as the result of living in a neighborhood brimming with Lutherans. He believed that God gave people certain gifts and that if you used them appropriately you'd travel the path that was there expressly for you. His Maker was organized, just like his mother. For Howard, life was never ridiculous; humans, at heart, were not even remotely foolish.

I could see him disappearing through the inner door to the milking parlor. "Don't rush yourself," I called, dropping the cat. "Theresa is bringing her girls over so we'll be fine without your—" I was thinking the words, "model of control."

The night before, our neighbors, Dan and Theresa, had come for dinner with their children. And in our yard, in the spot where I stood, Howard had thrown the glow-in-the-dark ball up in the air, the four little girls fluttering like bats, rising and falling, barely visible in the dark. The luminous ball, a strange glowing green, bounced in the grass and the littlest girl, Lizzy, clapped and shouted, "Moon. Moon. Moon."

When I got to the house, Claire was dutifully eating her cereal. Emma sat in her chair sucking on a strand of her stringy hair. "Someone forgot to feed me breakfast," she choked.

"I'd like some now," I said. "Would you rather I ate here with you, so we could talk about our day, or should I take the tray out to the porch, where there is peace and quiet?"

"Here," Emma said. "Could I please have something to eat?"

"Certainly." I smiled a tight, close-lipped smile at my reformed daughter. Welcome back, I wanted to say. We will tread so carefully, so lightly, so you will not go off again.

"Tell me," she said, "exactly what the plan is."

The farm is surrounded by housing tracts now. Even so, on our swatch of land, looking across the rye, I occasionally had the feeling that all of the wide sky could be seen from our porch. Because of poor drainage and the whim of two stubborn town fathers, the land we owned was locked into agricultural zoning for time immemorial, or until money or new blood could forcibly change the rules. When we bought the farm it was the cheapest four hundred acres we could find. Although there were problems with standing water and rotting outbuildings there was the allure of varied topography, of marsh and woods and gentle hills. After we'd moved, every parcel around us fell prey to what has long been heralded as progress. From our sanctuary of woods and oats we looked out to garage doors painted with iridescent geese flying off to a better land, and black satellite dishes standing like lunar ornamental shrubs. When we walked to a place Howard called "the Highest Point on the Earth" we could see in the distance the square steel-and-glass complex with its black windows where the greyhounds race. I've never been, but I think of it as a silent sport, the menacing dogs galloping noiselessly around and around the track, the spectators standing up to shout and nothing coming from their mouths.

We were, even under normal circumstances, outsiders, far more than the city dwellers who came to the subdivisions for the country life. First of all, it was common knowledge in Prairie Center—the kind of knowledge that one acquires by the simple act of respiration—that we had no business moving into a place that had been in the Earl family for three generations. After Maynard Earl died there was no relation who was willing to carry on the dairy tradition. Although ours was not Howard's exact dream farm, it was four hundred acres for the price of two, had a solid house with a dry basement and three good floors, and it wasn't too far away from an elementary school. Not least of all, the barn was in good repair, with a new roof and recent structural improvements. After the building boom he spent a fair amount of energy going out into the night, making blinders with his hands at each side of his head, and finding a place where he could look and see the dark. "I need to know there's a patch of wild space," he said once.

I can think of any number of reasons why people feared us. The wheels were set in motion that first week when Lloyd, an old friend of Howard's, came rattling into town in a silver-green Thunderbird. One side of his car had been knocked out and replaced with a kitchen door. We didn't stop to think that a person of African descent in their midst might frighten and then enrage the natives of Prairie Junction. And Lloyd wasn't someone whom we could very well hide or disguise. His brown skin gleamed and his head was covered with long, dirty-looking dreadlocks. He loped instead of walked, as if the day would wait for him to catch up with it. He could fix anything, and did that summer, making miracles from rusty old parts that had no memory of their purpose. True Midwesterners, our new neighbors were polite about their revulsion. They didn't burn our lawn or egg our house. Lloyd stayed with us for two months, during which time no one spoke to us, or offered a friendly word, or welcomed us with a potted plant or a casserole. It was as if we didn't exist, not only that first summer, but for years after. I noticed the little things, how the bank tellers were falling over each other with their "Have a nice day," and then I'd come up to the window and they'd suddenly be all business. Howard never believed what I repeatedly told him, that those bank ladies used to turn away from me and file their nails, or they'd slap a Next Window sign down on the counter just when I'd come forward, or they'd go to their coin machine and do up hundreds of dollars worth of pennies while I stood waiting. We were labeled from the first as that hippie couple who had the—the help.

Later there were the usual problems that came with farming in what was becoming suburbia: Undisciplined dogs bolted from their owners and hours later came panting home from our chicken yard with bloodied teeth; teenagers plundered and pillaged and copulated in the outbuildings; occasionally neighbors complained about the smell of manure and the noise of machinery. Very few seemed to make the connection between the sustaining white liquid they poured on their breakfast cereal and Howard's clattering, stinking enterprise across the way.

Despite the encroachment, Howard often felt, and I did, too, that we were living in a self-made paradise on the last dairy farm in Prairie Center. Before dawn and then at night, before supper, I frequently helped Howard with the chores. In the morning I'd leave the girls asleep in their beds and go out into the cold night. The barn blocked the subdivision lights and gave us the sense as we walked hand and hand to our work that we were the only two people awake, certainly in Prairie Center, and perhaps farther afield too: the county, the state, the face of the earth. I loved that feeling, that we were alone. The routine was much like waitressing, cleaning counters and setting tables, and serving, and then wiping up afterward. We had our supply wagon in the aisle and Howard and I went from cow to cow, first cleaning off the udders with an iodine solution and then drawing off a milk sample, and attaching the milking machine.

After chores in the summer I tried my best to be a good farm wife, to live up to Howard's expectations. We grew an enormous garden and there were literally days, breakfast, dinner, and supper, when we could boast that everything we were putting into our mouths had come from our own land. I made butter in the food processor, the girls and I put up strawberries and apple jelly and tomatoes and sweet corn and dilly beans and watermelon pickles. In hay season, "threshing time," Howard called it, I drove the tractor with the bailer behind it as it swept up the alfalfa and compressed it into bundles, and then of all things, expertly tied knots around the bales. I could never get over the fact that the poor old rusted 1949 McCormick baler knew exactly how to tie a knot.

From September to June, five mornings a week, I had the job of school nurse at Blackwell Elementary. It was as if I stepped into another skin when I put on my white polyester pants and my pink shirt and my stethoscope. In my school cubicle, the day always began with the dirty, smelly boy who never got breakfast and had chronic stomachaches, followed by those who had forgotten to take their Ritalin. There were seasons of head lice and influenza, chicken pox and bronchitis—the long line of wheezing children waiting to get their cough syrup. Several afternoons a week I traveled to the neighboring townships with a team of nurses, took my place behind a screen in the municipal buildings, and administered immunizations to howling babies and small children. We were widely known as "the shot ladies" and we inspired fear wherever we went. Howard and I were going to be in debt for possibly longer than we were planning to live. Shortly after we moved, almost six years before, I had cast about for a profession which I could take up after a brief and inexpensive course of study. It was my mother-in-law, Nellie, who suggested nursing at first, and then insisted I go back to school, and finally provided the funds for my degree. A nurse herself, she assured me that I would find great satisfaction in tending the sick. It took a year and some months at the technical college in Blackwell to become a licensed practitioner nurse.

On school mornings, after chores, I carted the girls off to a baby-sitter, so that I could sit at my desk brandishing tongue depressors. Leading a split life is what most everyone does, nothing extraordinary about it. And yet, it sometimes seemed as if an unnamed and terrifying thing was chasing behind me just about to sink its teeth into my calves. This was life, I supposed, running and running and running, and realizing along the way that the phantom was getting closer and also that I was losing my socks, my white polyester pants, my pink shirt, my head scarf, that my clothes were separating from my body and flapping off in the wind.

When June came each year I hung my uniform in the back of the closet. Every Monday in the summer my neighbor Theresa and I took turns caring for all of our children. Theresa also had two daughters, each a year younger than Emma and Claire. When it was Theresa's turn to baby-sit I dropped the girls up at the subdivision and ran home as fast as I could. I refused to see the ruins of my housekeeping: the ruptured, the overripe, the filthy. I did not hear Howard's call for assistance. I used to take the tape player out on the upstairs porch and pull down the shades, and then I'd dance to the Hungarian, Bulgarian, Scandinavian, and Rumanian music I had recorded in high school. I would bow to myself and curtsey, and put my hands on my imaginary partner's shoulders. I could dance for hours and not notice that any time had passed, feeling the happiness all the way up my throat, and afterward I could go and so peacefully drive tractor or pull weeds or hand the appropriate tool to Howard as he lay prostrate under some great broken machine.

Out of the twenty families in the subdivision on the hill, Dan and Theresa Collins were my only friends. I had an intimacy with Theresa that I had never expected to have with anyone. I could walk in the door at her house and call, "Yoo-hoo," just the way Laura Petrie and her pop-eyed Millie used to do back in the Golden Age. I always took care to wipe my feet and check my hands and fingernails. When I was sure I was clean I put the copper kettle on for coffee and sat down at the oiled butcher-block table to wait. There were equal measures of comfort and amusement in our communications; I think it is safe to say that we delighted in one another. She used to laugh at my stories until she wept, and I tried to take her sound advice to heart. The quality of our friendship seemed to me to be heaven-sent, something that I had received not in direct relation to any deed performed. At first I thought it a windfall, free of charge. "Make yourself at home," Theresa always used to sing out from upstairs. Like a nervous suitor her saying so every time made me wonder if the instruction on some day might suddenly change.

On that Monday morning last summer it was my turn to watch the children. Just as Theresa arrived in the driveway with her girls, Audrey and Lizzy, Emma ran into the bathroom and slammed the door. "Don't let anyone come in here while I'm on the toilet," she called.

I didn't answer.

"DON'T YOU DARE LET ANYONE COME IN. DO YOU HEAR?"

Theresa opened the screen door with her foot and came into the kitchen with her arms full of clothes, and the diaper bag, and her two-year-old Lizzy, and a box of pea pods. "Can you use any of this?" she asked. "I'm under here, I really am."

Theresa had a round face framed by black curls, octagonal tortoise-shell glasses, and blue eyes with lashes so long and dense and curly they looked as if they scraped against her lenses when she blinked. Her glasses were often halfway down her nose, pushed by the sheer force of her eyelashes. Her unadulterated Irish Catholic skin was faintly freckled and almost translucent across her cheeks. She had dimples and native sweetness which miraculously had not been tempered by her work for social service agencies. She grew up in Prairie Junction when there were seven working dairy farms surrounding the village, went off to seek her fortune as a therapist in Chicago, and then came home to the subdivision called Vermont Acres. Howard and I used to be privately scornful of their development that has a creaking, rough-hewn covered bridge at the main entrance and streets that are all named after New England states.

"Here are the diapers and the swimming suits, and a change of clothes, and Lizzy's blanket and Audrey's doll. These clothes are just some odds and ends my mother got at a rummage sale. You can use the peas, can't you?" She bent her knees and set Lizzy down, and one by one unloaded the things onto the table. Lizzy had had the good fortune to inherit her mother's eyes and skin, and her father's long legs. She toddled off into the living room.

"Hi, Liz," I called, but she was already on her way.

"I've got to run because I'm meeting Mom in town for coffee. You will not believe this," she said, coming to me and grabbing my forearm. "We've heard that Uncle Emmett is going to introduce his secret illegitimate daughter at the family picnic. You know about her—my God, we've all known about her for years, but we've never admitted it. I think it's a blessing, that he's going to be able to get it off his chest, but my poor mother is so traumatized—she ate an entire Sara Lee cheesecake last night."

"No!" I said, moving away, brushing my hand over the scratch marks Emma had made at breakfast.

"Did you hurt yourself?" Theresa asked, peering through my fingers at my wound.

"No, no," I said, "I spoiled Emma's world irrevocably first thing this morning by pouring milk into her cereal bowl, instead of letting her do it herself. I thought for a minute a cobra had bitten her foot off, but it was only a mistake I was in the process of making."

Theresa wrinkled her brow, not quite sure how the marks on my arm related to the cereal bowl, and then she laughed, saying, "I know, I know."

No, I wanted to say. You don't know. Audrey and Lizzy are never as bad as Emma.

"I'll tell you everything later," she said, going out and closing the screen door. She went a few steps into the yard and then she turned around and called into the house, "Bye, Audrey. Bye, Lizzy."

"MOM," Emma shouted from the bathroom. "I need you in here."

I went directly to her aid only to find her sitting on the toilet studying a catalogue. "Emma," I said, "could you please ask me in a calmer way? I'm afraid I don't have much patience this morning, and I don't want to spend this nice time acting like an old witch. Please ask me in a calm way, and I'd be happy to help you."

I leaned back against the wall wondering how she was ever going to be civilized enough to go to kindergarten.

"Could you please help me, Mom?" she asked. "Is Audrey here?"

"Yes," I said, as I adjusted the criscrossing bathing suit straps, something she could have done herself. "Lizzy and Audrey are both in the living room, and in a little while, if we can all achieve some kind of radiant serenity, or at least get you out of the bathroom in one piece, we'll go swimming. Now, go behave yourself, *please,* while I finish clearing the table."

This was my plan: I would walk down the lane. The simplest thing in the world. The girls would run ahead, until they got to the edge of the pond, just about to fling themselves in the four-inch shallows, and then they'd stop short, test the water, say how cold it was. They'd play with their buckets and shovels and boats in a sand pile, and wade up to their thighs watching the minnows swim around their feet. I was going to get myself wet and then stretch out with my chin on my hands. I was going to lie exposed, heedless of the dangerous sun. The girls would find endless amusement with four pails of water and seven acres of water and pretty soon the morning would be over.

First I put the milk away and then I climbed down the basement ladder to get some homemade butter from the freezer. When I'd gotten the plastic tub I could still hear the girls playing in the living room so I went straight upstairs to get my swimming suit. I thought I had thrown it over the chair in the bedroom, but I didn't see it. We hadn't swum in a day or two and I wasn't sure where I had left it last. I walked to the storage room to look out to the clothesline. In Theresa's house this would never happen. Their refrigerator was the size of a barn and was equipped on the outside with juice spigots hanging down like goat tits. There were oak drawers and shelves built into the walls, one drawer in the kitchen solely for pens, sorted by color. I don't know what prompted me to look in the dresser in the hall, an unlikely place to stash a swimming suit in summer. I yanked the drawer open to the chaos of old shoes, pens and bolts, masking tape, and moth-eaten sweaters and my map, my map of the world.

I hadn't thought about my map for years. I took out the sheaf of papers and knelt down, spread them on the floor, ran my fingers over the lime-green forests, the meandering dark blue rivers, the pointy lavender mountain ranges. I had designed a whole world when I was a child, in secret. I had made a series of maps, one topographical, another of imports and exports, another highlighting mineral deposits, animal and plant species, another with descriptions of governments, transportation networks, and culture centers. My maps had taken over my life for months at a time; it was where I lived, the world called Tangalooponda, up in my room, my tray of colored pencils at my side, inventing jungle animals, the fish of the sea, diplomats and monarchs. Although there were theoretical people in my world, legions of them, all races and creeds, when I imagined myself in Tangalooponda I was always alone, composed and serene as an angel in the midst of great natural beauty. I remembered that ideal solitude as I squatted on the floor last summer, and I laughed at my young foolishness.

I carefully rolled up the maps and put them in the back of the drawer. I stood, thinking, until I remembered that I'd hung the suit in the shower, the logical place after all. I left the dresser drawer open and looked. Yes, it was there, in a puddle clogging the drain, along with a melting bar of soap. I picked up the soap and the suit. The soap I carefully placed on the filmy ledge. I went over to the sink and rinsed the suit in cold water, and then first wrung out the bodice, and then the skirt. It was a suit that had been designed to obscure as much of the body as possible without losing its integrity as a swimming costume. It had been one of the more peculiar presents my mother-in-law had given me. I wrapped the thing in a towel, set it on the floor, and stepped on it to get it as dry as possible. At the moment I couldn't think of anything more uncomfortable than putting on a cold wet suit, even on a hot Monday morning. Finally I picked up the towel with the suit inside, walked down the hall, and took the stairs one at a time to the living room.

Emma and Audrey were feeding their dolls at the blue plastic table. Claire was sitting on a stool putting pennies in her mouth.

"Claire," I cried, throwing the towel aside, kneeling down and fishing in her mouth, "You know better than that! What's wrong with you?"

I began picking up the money that was on the floor and in Claire's lap. "I like them," Claire said.

"I know you do," I said, "but they're not to eat. They'll hurt you." I shouldn't have said, what's wrong with you? That was a terrible thing to say to anyone. "You're a good smart girl," I told her, "but money isn't food." I looked up to see if anyone had choked on coins and died.

"Where's Lizzy?" I said, to no one in particular.

No one answered.

"Lizzy?" I called. I paused to reach between my legs and pull a hanging thread from the back of my shorts. It was tickling my calf. "Did you see where she went, Claire?"

She shook her head, her straight black hair flouncing from side to side. The older girls were under the table, whispering. "Emma," I said, "make sure Claire doesn't put pennies in her mouth while I look for Lizzy, will you please?" Emma was jeering at me. I would have liked to pound her. I lifted my hand and brought it down on my own thigh and then I picked up Claire and started through the house. "You're heavy, Claire, too heavy for me to lug around."

"I know," Claire said. "I like pennies because they taste cold."

"Oh Christ," I was about to say, but I remembered that Howard had recently given me a short talking to about swearing in front of the children. "Lizzy, where are you?" I bellowed. "Make a squeak noise." We looked in the utility closet and the pantry, the bathroom and Howard's office. We went upstairs. We peeked in the closets expecting her to be crouching with her hands at her face. It was only when we came back downstairs to the kitchen that I noticed the wide open screen door. I stopped because my feet suddenly felt like two flabby pink erasers. I knew what I had to do. If you are on an airplane you are supposed to give air to yourself and your own kind before you help someone else. "Do not move," I said, turning on the TV, putting Claire directly in front of "The Frugal Gourmet."

"Do not leave this house," I ordered. And then I was out the door and across the garden, down the wooded lane to the pond. I suspect that when animals, a deer or a fox, run from their predators, they are governed by a keen intelligence. They do not waste their movements, and because they know the depth of the woods, the breadth of a field, they flee anticipating the curve of the land, the perfectly situated thicket. I ran like a blind person, stumbling over my own heavy limbs.

When I came to the clearing I couldn't see past the single glaring point of sunlight, dancing on the water. I put my hand to my forehead, to make a visor, and still it took me a minute to find the pink seersucker bottom just beneath the surface, about fifteen feet from the beach.

When I am forced to see those ten minutes as they actually were, when I look clearly, without the scrim of half-uttered prayers and fanciful endings, I am there, tall and gangly and clumsy and slow, crying out unintelligibly, splashing through the water to Lizzy. I had nothing of a hero's elegance or pace. As I moved I was thinking, She's fine! She's fine! People don't really drown in shallow places—that's an old wives' tale! She's probably looking for minnows or stones or snails so far from the shore.

I pulled her up and slung her over my shoulder, tripping through the water, screaming then, screaming for help. I didn't know how to make enough noise, to be heard. I was shrieking with so much force I felt as if I might split, and yet all the world was placid, still. The leaves in the trees hung limp like palsied hands. I lay Lizzy on her back, that was right, and then I tilted her chin and put my ear to her cold chest, and tried to listen.

It was impossible to hear anything but the noise of myself, panting and dripping, and the bamming of my own sturdy heart. Lizzy's skin was rubbery, her face the gray of an old carp, her lips dark as blueberries. Her wide, unblinking eyes were the color of mud. I opened my mouth and screeched again. I'm sure I felt for her pulse before I tore her jump suit and began pumping wildly on her chest; if I was remembering, I couldn't think, I did it just as if the twenty-four-pound two-year-old girl with a chest as insubstantial as a moth were a full-grown adult, although you were supposed to use one hand instead of two. You were to ventilate every —I didn't know exactly. CPR was scientific and specific! They kept changing the rules because their understanding of the human body was growing more and more detailed and complete. I stopped pumping to give air to Lizzy. I am a licensed practitioner nurse, and I could not remember how to do CPR properly. I had never had to actually resuscitate a living or dead person and I had not had the refresher course since the year before. Children at school did not fall into sinks and drown; they did not have heart failure. Howard was at my side, his hand on my back for an instant. I kept my mouth to Lizzy's mouth. I couldn't recall the cycle and the numbers and yet my hands and my mouth were pumping and forcing air down Lizzy's throat, of their own accord.

I don't remember stopping or looking or breathing until a man in navy pants hauled me up and pushed me to Howard. I could see now, that the ambulance was in the lane, that the paramedics were as thick as thieves.

"What happened?" Howard was shaking my shoulders. "What's happening? How is she?"

In all the time that has passed we have never once talked about those moments, when I called and called, and he heard me and came running, and saw, and went back to the house, phoned the rescue squad, waited for their arrival, held the girls at bay. I do not know if I tried to resuscitate Lizzy for five minutes or five hours. The scene is always with me, shimmering in the distance. When I least expect to have to look I find myself seeing: It shines right in my eyes, the pond, the lifeless girl on the ground, Howard standing over me. He hadn't shaved yet, and his hat was covered with bits of clover. He had white creases around his eyes, where the sun had been unable to penetrate. Take Howard's nose or eyes or chin and tack it on any matinee idol and his movie career would be ruined. Still, the cumulative effect of all of his irregular features is a handsome man. I love how he looks. In those days he was rugged and tanned, belying the fact that he is unusually sentimental. I thought him an alarmingly good person, solid, beautifully silent, thinking, working through problems and ideas, his mind humming with thought.

Lizzy seemed to be dead. But she couldn't be, with her eyes open. She couldn't have died in our pond. Emma used to stare at the wall at night. She didn't know enough to close her eyes and go to sleep.

"Tell me, Alice. Say something."

I put my hand to my mouth and bit down hard across my second and third fingers. Without moving my lips I said, "She'll be fine."

The men would save Lizzy. They would find her pulse with no trouble because they were calm and well trained. Howard shook me, trying, I thought afterward, to shake the truth from me.

"Don't," I cried. I didn't want to tell him, had to get out of his clutches.

"We need to call Dan," he said.

He meant that I should. "I know, I will," I panted. Anything to wrench myself from his grip.

"If she's hurt—"

"I'll call him," I puffed, "I'll go now." I was already tearing past the ambulance in the lane, running and tripping.

Audrey and Emma were standing on the porch, watching me come. The song, "Cruella Deville" was drifting from our bedroom window, from the tape recorder, along with Claire's piping voice. I had never gotten around to closing up the house.

I knew what I had to do first. The air was no good for breathing. It stung, like the dry, pricking heat in a sauna. I thought of tall Dan, Lizzy's father, with his stomach rolling over his swim suit, and his maroon and blue–framed glasses. City Dan, whose claim to fame was building a dairy exhibit for the museum in Blackwell, "the Dairy Shrine," it was called, to commemorate the dairy industry that had once been so strong in the southern part of the state. Dan made birthday cakes for the family, and canned bushels of sweet corn to the music of his favorite CD, *The Great Ladies of Jazz*. Lizzy had run to the pond and splashed in. It had felt good on her hot feet and she kept running and then she was pedaling and pedaling. She tried to grab hold of the water, pawing for the metal bar, a ladder rung, her mother, but there was nothing. She clutched and flailed. She opened her mouth to cry "Mama." Her lungs filled with water and she sank. Maybe she saw the great white light and felt the intoxicating warmth of God, like some say happens before death. She sank. The trout that Howard had stocked in the pond swam along through the dark water. They noticed Lizzy out of the corner of their eyes. They had inherited the knowledge of that look, and they knew it by heart.

Dan, with his crooked smile, would come to the house and stab me with his pocket knife. I put my hands to my face and whispered, "Lizzy, don't do this." I fumbled with the phone, trying to make the sticky rotary dial turn.

"Dan Collins," he said, before the first ring was complete, as if he was sitting in his office waiting for a thing he feared.

"Dan." A choking noise came up my throat and went down the receiver.

"Hello? Is someone there?"

I didn't want to tell him, wouldn't tell him, would make something up. I put my head against the dirty kitchen window. I saw myself taking Lizzy from Theresa, instead of the box of pea pods, the rummage sale clothes, and the diaper bag. After Theresa goes I latch the door. There we are looking out from the screen, out to the yard and the lane, where Lizzy wants to go if I would only let her down. Emma shouts from the bathroom while I stand at the door and stand at the door, breathing in the unbearable sweetness of Lizzy's sweaty head.

Chapter Two

THE MORNING LIZZY FELL into the pond stretched through three calendar days. In the hospital, in the lounge that had no windows, there was no signal to distinguish day from night except the sound of the meal carts coming and going, the smell of eggs, or broth, or breaded veal cutlets. Now and then, with the need to mark time, I listened for a change in the steady hum of the fluorescent lights. I thought I might hear a clue about where we were in the circadian cycle. When there was no fluctuation, I put my ear to the carpeted wall, straining for the night sound of crickets, the possible day sound of cicadas. It was too early for cicadas, I knew, and yet it was hot enough to perhaps fool an insect that lived most of its life underground as a nymph, as a sightless mass of white protoplasm. I clutched my ribs to warm myself as the chill air blew up from the basement heating ducts, up from what I assumed was the archetypal morgue with its neat rows of surgical tables, cold gray feet sticking out from the sheets with labels around the toes. Time and seasons were for others, for bankers and bus drivers, teachers and storekeepers. We would wait. We would wait, hour after hour in the subzero maroon-and-blue enclosure, with a rubber plant for oxygen.

On the way to the hospital the sheriff asked me how many minutes

Lizzy had been missing. I couldn't think how long I had dug in the freezer for the butter, how long I had looked at my map of the world, how long I'd called through the house. Was it possible that I'd been moving through the brittle heat in slow motion, without realizing, and that it had actually taken me hours to find my suit? As I called for Lizzy I had been thinking of Claire, wondering if Claire had swallowed pennies, if her stomach was like the tiled bottom of a wishing pool that is littered with coins. I had no idea how long I had labored above Lizzy's clammy chest. I knew, with a certainty I didn't often feel, that Lizzy had been dead. Then, by the pond, the paramedics had performed a wondrous mechanical feat, something quite like the jump start. They had given Lizzy life again, and to us they gave a dazzling hope. Doctors could fix everything, they could and they would, and it was wildly impossible that they wouldn't have her up and about in a day or two. I was sure they would revive her, despite the fact that medicine had failed to save my mother and my Aunt Kate and my father. The staff would rise to the occasion for a two-year-old because there was so much at stake.

"Ah, Ma'am, how long was she missing?" the sheriff had had to ask again.

Ten minutes? Could it have been longer? I turned to him and whispered, "Seven?"

I was told to stay in the lounge when we got to the hospital. I remember glancing across the room and noticing Robbie Mackessy's mother. Robbie was a kindergartner at Blackwell Elementary, one of the few children who paid regular visits to the nurse's office. He was frequently sick, because of his mother, I thought, because of her negligence. She was leafing through a magazine looking, not at the print, but at me. She was squinting, as if she couldn't stand to have her eyes wide open, to see all of me at once. I should have known then, that we were as good as tumbling down a hill, that at some point far off we would come to the bottom, broken and finally at rest. It was her ugly mouth, her sneer, that made me feel like crying. My hair was still dripping down my back and my wet T-shirt clung to my stomach and defined my breasts: And I didn't have graceful little button nipples. They were circles the size of small saucers, with the pimply skin of a plucked chicken. I crossed my arms over my chest and found I was shivering uncontrollably, that it was cold, cold like the meat locker where Howard took the lamb carcasses.

What had Claire said to me at breakfast, about wanting to die together, at the same time? I could think of any old thing in that lounge because the doctors would fix Lizzy and then we could go home. I had sometimes been on the verge of believing that Claire had had other lives, although I'm not anywhere near the sort who is prone to Tarot cards or herbal remedies, or astrological charts. Still, Claire more than her sister, knew things that I doubt anyone had taught her. She was quick to understand the natural order and the rules of society. It was tempting to think of her in foreign lands, with strange parents and an array of siblings, riding a camel down the avenue, speaking a language that is long since dead. I could think of anything, anything at all. Theresa always reported that the girls got along so well when they were at her house. I'm no good at mothering, I had said to myself, more often than I cared to admit. I didn't feel that I had instincts to guide me. I liked Theresa's children, of course I did, but I was always at a loss when I had them, our children and hers, four of them, together on Monday mornings. First one demanded a glass of milk, and then another, and then the next and the next, and then one of them spilled and the others followed. They'd want the modeling clay, and five minutes later the watercolors and a pretzel and more milk. They outnumbered me, and to tell them all no, and to listen to them carry on about their hunger and thirst was not worth it. I poured the milk. I told myself on those Mondays that I wouldn't look at the clock. I tried to build a beautiful and impressive structure out of blocks, but one of them would smash the tower and trip and bump her head and need a Band-Aid, and then her blanket, which couldn't be found in the mess. In the end there the five of us were, glazed, licking our wounds in front of the television.

The doctor would come through the door soon, I knew, and tell me that Lizzy was drinking a bit of broth, that she was tired and ready to go home. He might ask me if the parents had been notified, or if it wasn't easier for me to take her back, drop her at Vermont Acres. The trip to the hospital wouldn't amount to anything more than an outing. The brain, with its folds and wrinkles, its inscrutable network, as heavy as granite, was resilient. Lizzy hadn't been missing for more than a heartbeat. It had seemed a long time, to be sure, but it probably hadn't been more than a minute or two. Everything would be fine; I was sure it would be fine. The rescue squad and the emergency room would cost a fortune, but we would pay. Maybe Howard could ask his mother in just the right way, to lend us the money. Nellie was unpredictable at best, but if Howard could make her think something was her own idea she was often only too happy to write a generous check. We could have the hospital bill paid by the end of the month. Lizzy, understandably, wouldn't want to come over to our house for a while. We couldn't very well put a fence around the pond, so it was for the best if she stayed at home. Next year she would be able to follow directions and learn to swim enough to paddle, and blow bubbles under water.

I ducked, head to my knees, because I could hear someone running down the ramp in the section that had not yet been carpeted. Theresa's white sandals with the small heels made a bright clacking noise. She and Dan were pounding down the ramp. When they hit the carpet the sound stopped. There wasn't a trace for a minute. As they advanced I could hear the whisper of their exertion, and as they came closer I could make out the anguish in their breathlessness. They tore past me, to the nurse who was waiting to take them through the stainless-steel doors of the emergency room. The doors swung behind them and then banged and vibrated and glinted, catching the light from the ceiling. In the flickering steel I could see Lizzy's pink-and-white seersucker bottom bobbing in the sunlight. I began to pray, without thinking, without realizing. I was doubled over, my clenched hands to my cheeks, my eyes shut tight, knowing by some unexercised impulse how to assume a beseeching posture. Although I had had very little practice, the prayer, as crude as an old stick, was surely the genuine article. I could feel the words, feel them crawling on their hands and knees through my hollow bones, clamoring and shouting.

As for religion, I was dimly aware that I had no more tools than a child, and in addition I had the obstruction of skepticism. And yet there was the gaunt old man with a white, flowing beard and soft, blue, one-hundred-percent cotton robes, the kind that has been professionally dis-tressed, draped around his shoulders. Behind my closed eyes He was holding a staff and looking down upon me with His brows furrowed. He pointed his long index finger to Lizzy alive. Look, he seemed to be saying, Look at her playing in the grass, rising and falling, fluttering and clapping.

She was just beginning to speak in short sentences. She was at the juncture in her babyhood when it was possible she knew everything worth knowing. She understood the texture of her family; she understood territory and rage and love, although she couldn't say much more than *ball* and *moo, I want, pretty girl,* and *bad dog.* As her language shaped her experience and limited her ideas, she would probably lose most of her wisdom for a time. Watching my own children grow had reinforced for me the notion of Wordsworth's, that a child's knowledge of infinity escapes him as the years pass, perhaps, I thought, through a little pinprick at the nape of their necks. Lizzy, at two, was on the brink, between stations. It was tempting to think that if only they could speak, infants could take us back to their beginning, to the force of their becoming; they could tell us about patience, about waiting and waiting in the dark.

When I heard the word "Alice," it took me a minute to receive it, to understand, to jerk up. I stumbled into Theresa's midriff. She had her jaw set in such a way that I recovered myself without embracing her. "What?" I cried. Her curls were plastered to her forehead in circles and her glasses were teetering at the end of her nose. She looked, with her feet far apart, her knees slightly bent, and her splayed hands at chest level, as if she was bracing herself, waiting for some great weight to be hurled in her direction. I stood six inches away, flapping my arms at my side.

"She's breathing about ten respirations a minute," she said. "It's slow. Dr. Hildebrand from Children's Hospital just happened to be visiting this morning and he recommends keeping her here. He says he doesn't know what sort of"—she looked up into the neon Exit sign—"brain activity there is, but the next few hours will—"

She was speaking as if we always met each other and began comparing the children's oxygen intake. Our small-town hospital was civilized, a place where babies were carried full term and then born, where prostates were mended, and tonsils removed only when necessary. Children didn't go brain dead in the newly remodeled facility with track lighting and carpet on the walls.

Of all things I blurted, "We were having a chaotic morning. Emma was on the toilet screaming, and I thought Lizzy had gone right into the living room. I—I was in the bathroom for just a minute, and when I came out and looked around she wasn't there."

"I told Lizzy you were going to take her swimming, that you were going to the pond." She pushed her glasses up and held the bridge to her nose. In a high, thin voice she said, "I told her she was a good swimmer."

Now was the moment for me to prove my valor and goodness. Theresa had turned her back and was covering her face, protecting her skin from the scratchy upholstery. I wanted to hold her somehow, and then say just the thing, so that she would look back years from now at that desperate time in the hospital and remember my line. Four or five words that had made all the difference; five words which demonstrated remarkable insight. When Lizzy was well Theresa might ask me how I had known, how I had been able to be wise at a time like that.

I put my cold hand on her shoulder. "It will be fine," wouldn't do, because there was no telling. Her back was rising and falling fitfully. To steady myself, I pictured Howard's size-thirteen rubber boots with the buckles jangling. When Theresa sat up I was going to plow in, take her in my arms. I waited, with my hand on her. I waited until an enormous woman, dark, glowering like a bull, went to the reception desk and beat on the little service bell. Robbie MacKessy's mother had gone without my noticing. The newcomer ripped open a family-size foil bag of corn chips and started eating them. It is probably not possible to eat corn chips quietly, but she certainly made no attempt to be discreet. "Let's . . ." Theresa began, wiping her face with her tissue and walking away toward the lobby.

There was art on the wall, as well as carpet. There was a marble fountain that began in the mezzanine and trickled down a path like a staircase, with ferns on either side. Theresa and I had taken a tour together at the hospital open house, after the renovation. We had studied the renderings, made by local artists, one after the next: the murky police station, Dan's own Dairy Shrine, the Kiwanis lodge, the old schoolhouse, several churches, and the first freestanding Kentucky Fried Chicken restaurant in a strip mall in the state. We had been rude and arrogant, secure in our good health and superior knowledge. It hadn't occurred to me that I might someday feel culpable even for a thing as seemingly insignificant as passing judgment on local art. In my life I had felt stunned before; I have known how the paintings in a room, the dishes on the shelf, the peaches on the table, how everything comes into relief and looks clear, sharp, against your own emptiness. When we got on the elevator we stood side by side staring at the numbers on the digital panel, as if we expected to read something besides 1 and 2 and 3, as if we expected a truth to be divulged in midair. I took a deep breath and smelled the cucumber soap Theresa ordered by the pallet from a company in St. Louis. It was such a familiar smell, a fragrance that evoked not a hospital elevator, but home, the children, mornings at coffee.

"Am I allowed here?" I whispered, tagging behind her through the doors of the intensive care unit. She didn't hear me. She had wanted to find me, to tell me and show me, so it made sense for me to follow; it was what she meant. There was ringing and buzzing and beeping coming from every door down the hall. Dan was in room 309, at the far end of the bed, and Reverend Nabor, from the Presbyterian Church in town, was at the foot, his hands folded, his head bowed. Lizzy's little body was there too, after all, underneath a tangle of blue tubing. The machines supporting her were hissing and clicking, the goods running up her nose and down her throat, into the veins in her arms. She'll be fine, I said to myself again. The doctor from Milwaukee was an expert and medical technology sublime. There will be a burst of smoke, dense, thick smoke—the machine will make it—and when it clears Lizzy will be whole, awake, unencumbered, looking at our pained faces with surprise.

I'm sure it sounds strange at best, and hardhearted at worst, but I found myself at the side of the bed, concentrating all of what was abject fear into the straightforward loathing of the good Reverend Joseph Nabor. I thought I heard him say something about rain upon the earth, sending waters upon the fields. He came to Theresa then with his hairy hands outstretched, palms down, like a sleepwalker. He took hold of her arms. It was common knowledge that he himself was continuously in mortal peril, that great bearded man who had such acute asthma he had trouble getting through his sermon without the aid of a nebulizer. He spoke so softly I couldn't hear his words, but I could feel what he was saying from the tilt of his head, a ministerial tilt, a tilt which was supposed to convey both humility and authority. Theresa was a Catholic, for God's sake. She didn't need a Protestant with asthma to lead her through an unfamiliar prayer.

Dan had his eyes fixed on Lizzy's face. He was stroking a small patch on her calf, the one place on her body that wasn't taken up with tubing, the one place he was allowed to touch.

SIT UP, LIZZY. I clapped my hand over my mouth. I wasn't sure if I had shouted or if the noise was inside my head. No one looked at me and still I didn't know if it was their failure to register the sound or my inability to make the noise. I didn't know if I should stand or sit, stay or leave, wait with my eyes closed or open, offer a word, hold still, or move. I wanted to shout at Dan, too. SAY SOMETHING, DAN, OLD MAN. TALK TO ME. I stared at the floor, at the tiles, because Lizzy now looked nothing like herself.

When the Reverend finished with Theresa he came to me. He was twenty-eight years old, just out of school. I didn't like him, didn't want to take his outstretched hand. He was acting a part, putting on airs he hadn't earned, wearing a solemnity beyond his years. He had privately tried to negotiate a land deal with the McDonald Corporation when he first came to Prairie Center several months before. He had proposed selling a wooded area along the highway, part of the fifteen acres behind the church cemetery, for a restaurant and playland. We had stumbled into a prayer about waters upon the fields because it was the only passage he had memorized at seminary, or else he had come directly from a meeting on drought relief and it was fresh in his mind. I could see that he was going to try to comfort me by leading me through a few Bible verses. "You will be in need of the Lord's help," he declared.

I'm afraid I had a momentary and reckless urge to laugh, to belt out, "You can say that again, Joe." I withdrew my hand and turned to the bed to once more find Lizzy, the Lizzy who would soon be well. The tubes were flooding her with nourishment: air and waters that might possibly, with some assistance from the supernatural, convey Lizzy herself, what was spirit and potential, back into the heart and brain.

Reverend Nabor took me firmly by the elbow and led me away. I thanked him and sat down in the lounge chair outside the intensive care unit. Right away I put my head in my hands and prayed. I would pray all day and all night: I would pray for as long as it took, and after it was over as well. I would become a devout follower of Reverend Nabor, waiting in the wings to take over the readings when he became short of breath.

I prayed for the rest of the day, with only one lapse, one short length of time when my mind wandered. I implored the old man, Lord God. I said Please and Please and Please, like a child who isn't disciplined enough to stop asking. It was all I could think to say, begging He who I hadn't until that very morning considered, much less believed in His amazing powers. I was saying Please when I remembered the fortune cookie I'd gotten two weeks before, at the Chinese restaurant in Blackwell. I had pulled the strip of paper from the inside of the cookie and read, "Happiness is illusion. Pain is reality."

I remembered saying to Howard, "This is dessert?" His fortune said, "We come only to sleep, only to dream." I protested then, saying that I should have gotten his fortune. I told him that I'd been having dreams about being one of his sixty beautiful Golden Guernseys with a big wet brown nose, dewy eyes, and that he of course patted my rump with a special twang.

"It's hard to imagine what you'd be like as a cow," Howard had said, slowly, thoughtfully. "What part of your personality is most cowlike. You might be too skittery. I might have to ship you—"

"You wouldn't ship me! You wouldn't."

"Okay, all right, I wouldn't. You're right."

We were celebrating birthdays and anniversaries, killing our birds with one stone. Howard noted matter-of-factly that the chunks of beef, water chestnuts, and pea pods tasted as if they had been marinated in bath water. The Chinese husband and wife cook and waitress team were so happy to have customers we already felt guilty for not ever coming back. Howard had combed his thick black hair for possibly the first time since our fifth anniversary. We were the only diners in the restaurant and I felt sure I could detect romance. I imagined a romance meter maid coming along in her narrow little cart, her white wand shooting out to mark our legs with yellow chalk. We were well within the bounds of adequate feeling for a married couple of six years.

Howard was leaning toward me, first describing Claire sitting in the hay chute holding two wild kittens by the neck, and then Emma hitching the dog up to the old goat cart, getting the ride of her life. He smiled as he wiped the steam from the window with his hand. I was slightly drunk on one bottle of beer. I laughed out loud, burped, and got hiccups in swift succession. Our children were marvelous and not even Howard's beef or my lukewarm salty Chicken Almond Ding with one or two almonds in a gray-green slurry could dampen our enthusiasm.

"I wonder if a kid like Robbie MacKessy thinks that pain is the only reality," Howard had said after I opened my fortune and read, "Happiness is illusion. Pain is reality."

I didn't like the idea that Happiness was nothing more than a phantom. I looked through the circle that Howard had cleared on the window, and I saw, all the way back, to the time when my father took me to Bolyston, Ohio, to see the Gem of Egypt. It was a giant earth-moving machine, an absolutely colossal machine, used for surface coal mining. It stood fifteen stories high, with pulleys the size of Ferris wheels, and rigging and scaffolding as glorious as the Golden Gate Bridge. It had a claw that could move 150 cubic yards of dirt in one bite. In one or two passes the Gem of Egypt could wipe out an entire coal town. The company my father worked for had made the pulleys and the machine was his pride and joy. When I started to run toward it, my father yanked me back by the collar and shouted, "What's the matter with you?" When I didn't answer, he shook me. "I said, what's the matter with you?"

I finally managed to say, "I want to climb on it—and wave to you."

He took me under my arms and lifted me up. I was ten years old, much too old for that sort of thing. As far as I could remember he had never held me before. I started to scream and then stuffed my hands in my mouth. It was my father's unspoken rule that I wasn't to cry for any reason. He lifted me up and up, so I could see the Gem. "It's bigger than the goddamn Parthenon," my father used to say, as if the Parthenon was a standard unit of measurement. Being three feet taller didn't appreciably change my perspective, and I couldn't really concentrate on it anyway, because I was on his shoulders. They were sharp and I couldn't help noticing that he had dandruff, huge pieces in his brown hair like pussy willows growing along a stalk. Still, I knew that I would never forget that moment—it, the happiness, was stronger than almost anything I could think of, like the terrible blinding glare of sun on fresh deep snow.

"What are you thinking about?" Howard had asked that night at the restaurant.

"What?" In my experience people didn't ask such a question unless their love was brand-new. "I was just remembering more of my cow dream," I lied. "It was such a stressful night's work, dreaming that dream. I was being brought in from the pasture to the milking parlor and prodded into a stanchion. My name was there on the board, everything you needed to know: GARDNER FRANCES KATHRYN GOODWIN ALICE." I ticked them off on my fingers. "Gardner from my father, Frances from my mother, Kathryn from my aunt, who raised me, Goodwin from you, the sperm donor, Alice for myself. I was a fine milker, really. I would have been superb but it was impossible to chew the grain, locked in the stanchion because you were watching me—"

"You weren't thinking that Alice, were you? You looked so peaceful just a minute ago—"

"You're right, Howard," I had said. "You're right! Isn't it awful"—I stabbed a piece of chicken with my chopstick—"that we know each other so well we can't even have a little fantasy in private? I was thinking about our strange, lonesome wedding and the warty-headed whatever his name Justice was. Remember what he said about our deep knowledge of one another? We knew nothing about each other! Maybe, actually, we still don't. Sometimes I think I know the bone-grinding routine of our life, that that's all I know, up to milk cows, in for breakfast, out to the—"

"Alice," he had said, shaking his head, "let's just love each other. Did you ever think it's as simple as that?"

It wasn't nearly as simple as that—was it? Could it be? "I know, I know," I said, leaning over to massage my calf. "I'm talking about— Christ, my leg is knotted up—"

"You're making it worse," he had said in his calm and mature sixty-head-of-cattle farmer voice. I was curled over, clutching my leg. "Try to sit up and relax." The pain was turning the bend in my knee, traveling along my thigh, en route to my stomach. "Relax, Alice. You're making it worse."

We had had to go home early. I lay in the hot water in the bath that night absently stroking my irreproachably relaxed calf, thinking about

Emma, who had been the reason for our marriage. Emma had been no hardier than a peach *in utero,* but she had had the power to force us to become a family, to buy the farm at Prairie Junction. She would have been happy in a drawer or a box, and we had gone and got married, bought four hundred acres, a barn, several outbuildings, and a three-story house. She had forced us to go beyond knowing each other deeply, beyond loving each other: She had impelled us to make a life.

I had felt the charley horse coming on again, and I sank down into the tub. As I got older and older and then died somehow or other, I knew I would feel excruciating pain that was only a part of ordinary deterioration. There would be the chronic pain of aching joints, a broken hip, gallbladder surgery, the malignant lump in my breast—the sorts of trials that people endure day in and out. At thirty-two I had the occasional shadow of mistrust. I could imagine, as the years went on, my body becoming something outside of myself, something to cheer on, an old friend who is huffing up the hill on a bicycle. Still, I hoped that there would be no pain so great that it could blot out the time I sat on my father's shoulders looking at the extraordinary, the magnificent, the gorgeous Gem of Egypt, dwarfing all of mankind.

Howard had come into the bathroom with a candle. He had turned off the light and undressed and climbed into the tub, displacing so much water it rose to my chin. It seemed, just then, like a summer to rejoice in the heat. It was so good of him to think that a rumpus in the bathtub would be fun, so good of him to walk straight in, with a candle, and without saying a word, put his hand on my head, stroke my hair. I moved up to make room for him. It had been a dry spell, as I had told Theresa recently, and who was to blame the hungry farmwife if one quiet night she had pulled a can of store-bought whipped cream out of her bathrobe pocket and squirted some froth on the dairy farmer's privates? Theresa and I had howled out on the porch, trading the secrets of our marriage beds. I hadn't taken into consideration how cold the whipped cream would feel, and so I had been surprised when Howard ran squealing like a pig into the hallway. He had tried to be good humored but he couldn't stand the thought of my spending money on a dairy product when I could skim our own cream off the milk pail.

I had so often been in awe of the luck which had led me to him years before in Ann Arbor, Michigan. That night in the tub I was thankful for Howard, thankful for the prospect of renewal. Although it was cramped in the deep but short bathtub on claws, although I was in danger of being impaled on the faucet at several points in the tumult, I was grateful, all the same.

I was sitting with my eyes shut, in the hospital lounge, remembering that night in the bathtub, when the elevator bell rang and Howard stepped out onto the newly washed floor. "How is she?" he asked, sitting down, putting his arm around me. I could hear his heart beating. I tried resting my cheek on the metal snap of his shirt pocket. Howard was the most potent man in Wisconsin. I had smelled him in my stupor from the lounge on the third floor when he was out in the parking lot, I was sure of it now.

"Her eyelids fluttered this afternoon," I said. I had been alert then, coming up for air after a strenuous supplication. Dan had come from room 309 shouting for Theresa. It was possible, I thought, that Howard would make the miracle take place. The power of smell would bring Lizzy back into herself.

"What does it mean?" Howard asked.

I shook my head. I wanted to wake up to find Emma and Claire in the next room. I would scream at them for pulling each other's hair, and we would resume our happy life. I would have recklessly given away anything to find that I had only slipped into another dimension, like Scrooge did every Christmas Eve. I was in a preview of the possible future and when I got back to earth and turned over several new leaves, all would be well. The fluttering eyelids might or might not be meaningless, according to the rumors that had circulated in the lounge.

I had admired Howard from the start because of his beauty and the way he stood back quietly, both observing and not judging, a remarkable combination, I had thought. He was everything my father wasn't. He wept at movies, he loved auctions and thrift stores for their antiques, and he occasionally made a comment out of the blue that was killingly funny, well worth the wait. He knew about things: He knew how matches were made, what to do if a swarm of bees landed in a tree, how to bandage a wound, start a fire, make a candle, kill something for dinner. If he said he did something twenty times or twice, or one thousand times, it was accurate. He didn't ever stretch the truth or embellish. It was his code, to be scrupulously honest. I had thought there was no occasion to which he could not rise.

"Howard," I whispered into his shirt snap. "What am I going to do?"

He rubbed his hand over his freshly shaven chin. "What happened?"

I tried to swallow but my tongue felt thick and bristly, like a Brillo pad. "I don't—" I could hardly stand the feel of what was my tongue against the roof of my mouth. "I don't know."

He pulled me hard against his chest. That was comforting. Being held so firmly you couldn't injure anything. I could imagine spending the rest of my numbered days on the hospital sofa. The second time I had crashed the car into the stone planter by the garage he had said in his owner-of-the-manor voice, "Alice, you're going to have to tell me what happened." He was waiting. It was his nature to move, to work, to produce. He was going to wait for me for a while. "I don't know what I'm going to do," I said after a minute. "It happened so fast, while Emma was in the bathroom." I realized, as the words came past my teeth, that I had edited out the time I had spent in the basement and upstairs. "Where are Emma and Claire?" I asked. "How are they?"

"I called Nellie," Howard said.

His face was like a Cro-Magnon's. He was all crags, and he had shaggy eyebrows, a looming forehead; he would have looked wonderful in a cave painting. He would have been a Cro-Magnon celebrity, on the cover of Cro-Magnon *People,* the most handsome, nearly modern man of the year. His eyes were set too close together. It made a person feel cross-eyed just to look into them. Howard's mother, Nellie, had come from St. Paul, Minnesota, eight hours away. She had come because it was a real emergency. I rested in the thought of how repulsive I found Reverend Joseph Nabor. I pictured him calling his mother when he got home and telling her what a job he had done helping the sick, the bereaved, and the criminal, when he himself could hardly breathe.

Howard was saying something about going to eat. I couldn't make my way to the cafeteria, couldn't sit down to eat banana cream pie while Lizzy battled to get well. I couldn't, didn't want to, and he was pulling me up, hardly waiting while I slipped on my flip flops. When we passed the broad open doors of the intensive care unit I faltered, broke away from Howard, had to stand and look. This was not something in my imagination. It was not one of the dreadful things I worried about, not an Uzi stickup or the sun glaring through the great big ozone hole. There, surrounding Lizzy's bed, were all of Theresa's prodigious Catholic family: sisters, brothers, mother and father, grandmothers, aunts and uncles, great-uncles and cousins. There were so many of them they were spilling out into the hall—they were at the hospital instead of making coleslaw and potato salad for the family picnic tomorrow. They were encircling the bed, holding hands, praying together. They were saying every single prayer, from the first Hail Mary to the last novena. Five out of eight of Theresa's siblings could certifiably be excommunicated from the Church —she had told me elaborate stories about each of their sins. They had fornicated, blasphemed, committed adultery. And what had Theresa said about the Uncle's secret illegitimate daughter? She was probably the one with the short skirt and the dangerous-looking platform sandals.

I should go straight to the relatives, I knew, and let them see me in my abundant shame and misery. I was going to get pushed down the chute into the white flames of hell and I would tell them right out that I deserved to burn and burn. I didn't ordinarily censor my thoughts, but I would, from now on, blot out what was bullheaded and extreme. They were gathered around the bed of the child, chanting and praying, believing for the moment, committing themselves, just as I had, to eternal belief and purity of heart and mind, if only the one, the most important error could be rectified. No one beckoned. No one broke away from the circle to invite us into the room. Dan looked up and did not seem to recognize us.

We sat in the lounge for two more nights and two more days. Howard left only to milk, to return with a fresh, piquant smell on his tennis shoes. We closed our eyes at night, leaning against each other, listening to the world moving up and down the hall on wheels. The laundry baskets were on wheels, the scales, the I.V. poles, the respirators, the meal trays, the beds, the chairs, the dressers, the bedside tables. Nothing was rooted to the floor. The nurses seemed weightless, like birds, flying down the hall, their cushioned shoes barely touching the ground. They were as swift as they could be, considering the ringing bells and gravity and the time of night.

Other families came to wait out their calamities. We stood by as they formed their own communities within the space of the lounge. I sat at the end of the sofa watching Lizzy's door. Periodically the obese woman rose up and asked for our attention. "Let us bow our heads," she began.

Chapter Three

WHEN I USED TO grieve for my mother, and later for my Aunt Kate, I told myself that although they were certainly as dead as they were ever going to be they were still mine, that they inhabited my interior world, which was at least as noisy and various as life itself. From early on I valued the gift of memory above all others. I understood that as we grow older we carry a whole nation around inside of us, places and ways that have disappeared, believing that they are ours, that we alone hold the torch for our past, that we are as impenetrable as stone. Memory still seems a gift to me and I hold tight to those few things that are forever gone and always a part of me, while the new life, the changing view, streams by. Theresa, I feel sure, has been able to achieve the healthy balance between cherishing what was and forging ahead. Howard has made the last several years a blank. Sometimes I think he tries to trick himself into believing that Prairie Center was an impossible and foolish fancy, that we fell asleep in a field of poppies shortly after we met, and were out cold for six years. When we woke we found ourselves in a surprising and yet inevitable location. If I mention Lizzy, he has to stop and stare at his shoes and then he shakes himself, as if he has had to dig back into a dream to remember our friends' daughter.

At the hospital, Theresa's oldest sister organized the family so that there were always six or seven people in the prayer circle. Those off duty brought food and pillows, shuttled Grandma to and fro, gave back rubs, and made phone calls to relatives out of state. Theresa's youngest sister cried outside of room 309, not for Lizzy at that moment, but because at nineteen she was still the baby and couldn't do anything right. She had brought the wrong order from the Chinese restaurant: one grease-stained shopping bag with twelve cartons of sweet and sour pork, six cartons of rice, and twenty-four fortune cookies. The girl had so much misery in her face, her mascaraed tears running into her mouth, that Howard had taken off to the end of the hall to look out the window at the heating plant.

Hour after hour I sat, confessing my fundamental unworthiness to God. I was going to try to do much better, was going to put all my strength into forcing love into my heart. If only I had more Shakespeare on my tongue, more than a few lines knocking around; if only I could rise up, climb on the end table and with nothing but verbal wizardry rout the angels from their warrens. I had so little, no complete poems or Bible verses lounging in my brain like firemen on cots, waiting for the disaster. I could only get as far as, "Do not go gentle into that good night," and "No worst, there is none. Pitched past pitch of grief."

The only thing I had that was close to religion was the weekly pilgrimage Aunt Kate and I used to make to the international folk-dance group in Hyde Park, at first glance, nowhere near the Judeo-Christian path to the divine. Much as I tried to concentrate on Lizzy, what was not only her bone and flesh, but also what was the pure stuff of her soul, I couldn't help drifting, occasionally, going back to Hyde Park, dancing, swirling around and around with my Aunt Kate. Every Friday night the oddest assortment of people gathered in Ida Noyes Hall and executed dances from the world over. The leader pulled out meticulously catalogued records from pink metal boxes and carefully guided the needle to the chosen band. That was our church, our communion. My Aunt Kate tried in vain to teach me to forgive the men in their thirties still fighting acne, who stepped on my feet and were always popping up to ask for the next dance. Most of them had spent far too long in a lab, feeding, I thought, out of their Petri dishes instead of eating a decent meal now and again. Aunt Kate used to answer my complaints about so and so's bad breath by saying, "Yes, my dear, it's dreadful, like an old goat—but be kind, be merciful."

"Have you been praying?" I asked Howard, as we were adjusting the pillows on the hospital sofa. We were preparing to rest in the lounge again, for the second night. I wouldn't go home, couldn't bear the thought of Nellie's inquisition, couldn't stand the idea of waiting in the midst of everyday life. It was one thing to wait stubbornly, to hold out in the rarefied atmosphere of the hospital lounge, a place where, like purgatory, we accounted for our sins and hoped for mercy. I needed to devote myself to the waiting; I had no interest in trying to pass the time with mindless chores and food and people. Howard had only just returned from the farm. It was past ten o'clock and everyone else had pulled up stakes and gone to sleep in their own beds.

"Have I been saying what?" he said, trying a position flat on his back, finding it unsatisfactory, and turning over. He twisted his mouth to one side and felt his bristly cheek. "What if Lizzy doesn't get better?"

"What?" I said.

"What I mean," he whispered, "is what if nothing happens?"

I had told Emma and Claire over the telephone that I was staying at the hospital to help Lizzy get well. Howard was looking at me without flinching and I could see plainly in his eyes, Dan and Theresa moving the tubes and machines home, Lizzy forever suspended between life and death. She would lie in the living room; the girls would think of her as someone on the order of Snow White when they visited. She would grow and they would roll her from side to side every day, so that she would wear evenly. She would be ugly and ungainly as a preteen and beautiful again at sixteen. She would menstruate and never be bothered. Years would pass and the family might gather in the living room without even thinking about Lizzy's presence, taking the sleeping child for granted. Every now and then they might think she had heard; on Christmas Day Dan would say grace in the dining room and he would mention how much they loved Lizzy, and out of the corner of her eye Theresa would see the girl move her head and look at them, and then turn back to sleep.

I clutched Howard's forearm as if he too had seen. "I'll visit her every day," I brayed. "I'll stay with her while Theresa goes to the grocery store, the library, the therapist, I swear I'll—" Theresa and I, at seventy-five, our husbands long dead, would sit and wait by the side of the gray-haired woman who had never woken.

Time went on, unbroken by usual mealtimes and sunsets and ablutions. It was Howard who finally wondered if all the novenas and Hail Marys weren't serving to usher Lizzy into the next world. I shook my head and told him, No. It could not be true that there was nothing behind her eyelids. The doctor had put her through a series of tests to evaluate brain activity in relation to eye responses. At the first, apparently, she did not have even the most primitive reflexes. Lizzy's pupils did not react to light. She didn't sneeze when her nostrils were tickled, up inside, with a Kleenex. It could not be true that she was like an egg that has been blown out. I wasn't always sure there was any such thing as a soul to begin with, if there was an essence that was independent of our bodies, and that doubt made it all the more difficult to think of a little soul. Was Lizzy's soul like a bird with its wings clipped, inside that bloated body, growing quiet and still, and then closing its eyes? Or had it flown out, up and up, days before, when she began to sink in the pond?

Dr. Hildebrand dispensed his diagnoses gradually, until the final decision seemed to be a mutual one made by him and Reverend Nabor and Dan and Theresa. They were going to let her go. The family filed into the lounge late the third night. The nurse took a wooden rocking chair into Lizzy's room, with braided circles tied to the seat and the back. In the lounge we all sat trying not to look into the unit, at the window with the curtain drawn, and the closed door, where, somehow, impossibly, a life was coming to an end. Mrs. Clark, the prayer leader, swished her behind in her seat, her preamble to rising, but her daughter reached for her hand and kept her down.

In room 309 the nurse took the I.V. out of Lizzy's arm, the tube from her nose, switched off the respirator, the heart monitor, removed the blood pressure band, and the catheter. Dan lifted Lizzy out of the bed and took her to the rocking chair. His shoulders were at his ears. He rocked her a little. Theresa kneeled on the floor and put her head on Lizzy's lap.

They could touch her anywhere they wanted now. They talked to her, and believed that her reason had returned, that she could now hear and understand. Dan counted to himself while Lizzy took breaths first twelve seconds apart, and fourteen, and eighteen, and twenty. They waited, bent over her, but no next breath came.

Chapter Four

———

HOWARD'S MOTHER NELLIE HAD not only occupied Emma and Claire for three days, but she also had baked bread and pies and cookies, made two pans of chicken and broccoli casserole, as well as miscellaneous food-stuffs: several different Jell-Os, dips, her secret garlic salad dressing. When we got home that night of Lizzy's death, the fan in the living room was blowing the hot air in circles. Howard wondered if the fires of hell could be any hotter than the present temperature of our own kitchen. I said I didn't know, it felt pretty hot, but hell was probably in a different league, that it—

"Never mind," he had said.

In bed we closed our eyes over a veil of tears and lay awake. It was no use trying to sleep and well before dawn I slipped down the creaking stairs. Out of long habit I went over, opened the refrigerator, and stood motionless in front of its maw. The light had burned out weeks ago and it was all a darkness. The green glow of the digital microwave clock on the far counter, as soft as candlelight, illuminated the room. When I shifted my weight from my right to my left foot the raspberry Jell-O on the bottom shelf, with banana and pineapple chunks embedded inside, caught the light and seemed to wink. Howard had told me that the church ladies were distributing food to the Collinses, that Nellie had carefully marked our Tupperware with masking tape and an indelible ink pen and then taken several dishes over to the church kitchen.

He had not said a word on the way home. When we were just inside he asked me when the funeral was going to be, as if he expected me to have learned something between the car door and the threshold. I had gaped at him, my eyes wide and mouth slack, like a dolt, and of all things, I had laughed. I couldn't think where it was I wanted to be, where I could go to feel steady. The lingering smell of fresh bread, the abundance of food made from scratch, the sink scrubbed clean, the place mats that had been cleared off the table and stacked neatly in a pile on the cold wood stove, the saltshaker filled to the brim—every one of those details made me feel a stranger in my own kitchen. Life is nourishment, Nellie seemed to be saying with her food. Here is life!

I went out to the porch and sat on the swing. Heat lightning flashed in the distance and lit up the sky for an instant, before I had time to see. There were so many miracles at work: that a blossom might become a peach, that a bee could make honey in its thorax, that rain might someday fall. For Lizzy there would be no more miracles. I thought then about the seasons changing, and in the gray of the night I could almost will myself to see the azure sky, the gold of the maple leaves, the crimson of the ripe apples, the hoarfrost on the grass. Lizzy somehow suddenly belonged to the earth. We would want to look at the beauty, trying to see through her eyes, and yet at the same time she was the air, the flower, perhaps even the moon now. All we could do, the only act left to us, was to look.

When I woke up two hours later I was still on the swing outside. I had slumped over and slept, my cheek resting on the scoop of the garden trowel. Howard's rusted, stained T-shirts were hung up, shirt after shirt, on the clothesline. I wondered if I had hung them out. There wasn't a cloud in the sky and the birds were chirping sweetly in the lilac bush by the feeder. I pulled myself up into a patch of pale light. It was another perfect morning. The green was slowly burning out of the grass and the dried ends would prick my feet if I walked across the lawn. The swallow in the nest in the far corner of the porch looked at me with distrust, I could tell, as if he thought I might run for him and crush him in my hand.

I remember realizing that if I had ever felt rooted, it was nothing more than wishful thinking on my part. I had been simpleminded to think that I had come to a point of repose. The bottom, the solid ground of the world, had gone out beneath my feet.

I went upstairs, stepping carefully around the loose boards that groaned, to Emma's room. Maybe this was home, I thought, this one small room with a bed and a dresser in it. There were feathers on the floor from a doll quilt, dried-out Magic Markers with no caps in sight, pennies hidden in the pile of the rug. I sat on the bed and looked at Emma. She was not going to be especially pretty, a fact that had now and again pained me. She had thin blond hair, a pug nose, and small eyes with sparse lashes. I used to kiss my children at night, holding dear their untroubled lives. It was the short time of grace, the time before a sorrow would teach them the ways of the world.

Emma looked like a different child in sleep, with her mouth shut and her folded hands at her chin. Although she had unnerved me from the start, at birth, because she was so clearly her own person, I felt as time went on that I knew her, that I would always know her better than she could ever know herself. I understood her before she had a concept of herself, and that knowledge, of her habits and proclivities, I would keep like a secret cache. I had washed her day after day, moving my hands over her smooth skin dotted with little golden hairs, skin that for years hadn't had a single mole on it. I wanted to think, despite my better judgment, that whatever befell her—marriage, divorce, childbirth, disappointment, and triumph—I would know her. She sniffled and screwed up her eyes as she slept. I touched her hair and I was so glad, so glad that it wasn't she who had drowned. It struck me that my girls would be safe because they had statistics on their side: No more than one child per neighborhood died in a given length of time. We had sacrificed Lizzy for the safety of all the others. Emma was free of danger for now, free to go to kindergarten where she would learn to sit in a circle and cut and paste and make rude noises on her forearm. She would have the chance to go through the long, dark tunnel of public education, and graduate in a long, white gown, and go on to the college we could afford. I wondered what she'd been told about Lizzy. I tried to be quiet, but I couldn't keep from wailing into the extra pillow on the bed.

"Grammie gave me a new bracelet." She had half risen up, was resting her head on her fists, elbows bent, staring at me.

"That's nice," I whispered.

"It's rhinestones," she said, "what princesses wear."

I had never cried so hard in my life, and Emma didn't want to notice. It was as if that was how I greeted her every morning, crying. Crying because I didn't feel I had a right to be in her room anymore, crying because I had inadvertently fouled our own nest.

The visitation and funeral took place two days after Lizzy's death, in the evening, at the Presbyterian Church in Prairie Center. Dan loved the small town church where every Sunday he put on his black robe, came through the minister's door to the pulpit, and took his place at the organ. He only knew how to use eight pedals but he got by. He had donated a life-size cow from the Dairy Shrine for the crèche that went on the lawn at Christmastime, which he kindly stored in his garage during the off-season.

We were eating at 4:45 when Nellie asked Howard what he was going to wear to the funeral.

He had just taken a bite of muffin, and when he said, "My navy blue sport coat," crumbs went flying in all directions.

"Look at Daddy!" Claire squealed.

It took a full minute for Nellie to mentally roam through Howard's wardrobe and come to the worn corduroy sport coat she had purchased for him when he was sixteen.

"You don't mean the one you had in high school," she said, tittering at the absurdity of the suggestion.

"Yep," Howard said.

When she managed to close her mouth, she cleared her throat, braced both hands on the table, threw her head back, stuck her pointed chin out, and from that great height looked down upon him. "Honey," she declared, "you cannot wear corduroy when it is one hundred degrees." She straightened up, and with all the vigor of a sergeant strode to her room. She was back again before we could guess her order. "Go buy yourself a suit," she said, slapping a blank check down on the table. "You ought to own one—and then you'll have it for occasions like this."

Were there going to be more occasions just like this? And could an exceptionally tall and slim person purchase a suit on short notice?

"Do you know what I could do with the—hundred or so dollars it's going to cost?" Howard said with no trace of irritation in his voice. "I could get a better—"

"Don't be silly. You'll want a suit when Emma graduates from high school, from college, and gets married."

She had no idea what moved her son. He was always silly, wasn't he? First of all, he was under the impression that he could buy a suit for one hundred dollars, and second, he got up at 4:30 every morning because he longed to get out to the barn and milk animals the size of the Parthenon. Nellie was sure that Howard would soon outgrow his fantasy about the dairy farm, that that dream life of his wasn't too much different than a boy spending hours moving a tractor around in the sandbox, making his own engine noises. A person could get by without depriving a cow of what was rightfully hers; we could all drink calcium-fortified orange juice and soy milk. My ears burned, my cheeks felt hot when I thought too much about her. I couldn't forgive her for the way she treated Howard— as if she thought he was begging for candy. *Okay, sweetheart, here's one hundred thousand dollars for your farm. Don't eat it in one sitting or you'll get a tummyache.* She had the wicked habit of generously giving and then chiding us for not using the money wisely. Sometimes she literally threw cash at us, and other times we felt we would have to get down on our knees and beg to get a nickel out of her. I should have been grateful, inwardly and outwardly, for her occasional spontaneous showers. No matter how much I prepared myself, how well I thought I had steeled myself against her, against my own irritation, I was always amazed, as if for the first time, by her little speeches, her slights, her apparently careless generosity that later implied a condition or two.

Howard was adept at concealing his exasperation, but I knew him well enough to understand that the steady gaze he now turned on me was his way of pleading for help. I shrugged my shoulders and pushed my plate back. She wanted him to look nice. Her son was going to smell of manure and have a dirty face at church; he wasn't going to put his best foot forward and no one would know what a good, smart boy he was. I could see the worry in her puckered face. Her son's wife was a disgrace, and he wasn't going to look as if he was separate from her. Nellie was tired, and she was growing old. To her credit she had said very little about Lizzy's death, and giving her the benefit of the doubt, the suit business was probably her way of trying to make it all right for us. I did feel a little bit sorry for her. He had already jeopardized the cows' productivity and comfort by milking two hours earlier, so why not oblige her? "I'll drive," I said to Howard. And to Nellie I murmured, "We'll find him something presentable."

On the way to town I couldn't keep from saying my usual line: "Someday we have to stop taking her money."

"I know." It was characteristic of him to speak in monosyllables when there might be an argument.

At the men's store in Blackwell, Hutchin's, conveniently open late on Fridays, Howard tried on three suits, all of which were big around the middle and too short in the sleeves. Although he is color blind he picked out a respectable gray-and-green ensemble. "This isn't pink, is it?" he whispered. The saleswoman reminded him that he needed shoes and a tie, a shirt and socks. She winked at me as if to say, We are on the same side. We have a mutual interest in dressing the senseless mannequin. When it dawned on her that something was wrong with me, that I was feeble-minded or deaf, she turned her back and addressed Howard as if she had only just recognized his genius for matching socks to ties.

We sat for fifteen minutes scratching our legs and thumbing through the *Reader's Digest*s while the suit was being altered. The seamstress lived right around the corner and was called from her supper for the emergency. For all our bad luck there was a speck of good fortune. I found a fashion magazine with a scratch-and-sniff perfume ad and applied the strip vigorously to my wrists. After a while Howard began playing his front tooth with his fingernail and tapping his foot on the hardwood floor. Finally he got up and burst into the back room where the woman sat doubled over, her nose in the hem of the pants. From his pocket he took the needle he had used to sew up the back end of the cow with the prolapsed uterus that afternoon. "I can fix it with a neat slip stitch," he said. "No need to worry. I took an upholstery class in college."

The startled seamstress had a forehead the size of Mount Rushmore. It was astonishing that a person could have such little eyes, an acorn of a mouth, hardly any hair, and yet so much forehead. I couldn't help staring, thinking how you'd have to be careful coming around the corners with a forehead like that, how easy it would be to wham into the icebox or the kitchen cupboard.

"We're short on time," Howard was explaining. "Should have been there a half hour ago."

At 6:15 the suit was finished. He paid a terrific sum, carefully writing the figures on Nellie's check, and then he went into the dressing room to put on his finery. He emerged, silent, looking down, as if he couldn't believe that anything below his neck was still his own body. I stood back marveling at him, at the handyman, who didn't care how he looked, who had little use for daily personal hygiene, and there he was ravishing in his suit. It was only June and his face was tanned to a deep brown. His teeth were blindingly white, dangerous to look at, like an eclipse. It was impossible not to admire him, hard not to want to do something to contain that kind of beauty—drink him, ingest him, sneak into his shirt and hide for the rest of one's natural life. After six years of marriage he had the power to occasionally render me weak in the knees.

"Did you see the forehead on that seamstress?" I cried, outside on the pavement. "I've never seen such a cranium—"

He grabbed my arm and we both stopped. "Alice," he said, "why do you always notice the strangest things? Why can't you ever pick out one good quality about someone?"

It wasn't his habit to criticize openly, and his judgments always rattled me. I saw the good in people, I was sure I did. Didn't I? I opened my mouth to defend myself, but he said, "Just don't talk about it." He went around to his side of the car, muttering to himself as he opened the door. I heard him say, "I'd like this to be over and done."

The suit escapade had temporarily distracted me from the purpose of the evening, it was true, and now I remembered, with what felt like the force of a lead pipe coming straight down on my skull. He was right. How could I be so much of this world, to think of someone's forehead when we had a hurdle before us that was going to require our best social skills, our firmest fortitude.

"I'm sorry," I said. "I'm very sorry."

There was a line halfway around the church when we pulled over to the side of the road. The lot was overflowing and the somber deacons were directing the cars to double park. It was seven o'clock in the evening and the sun bore down with the intensity of noon. I remember how frightened I was, seeing all of the bright cars, the hot metal and glass catching the light like water. No one in the line had the strength to fan themselves or flick the gnats away. Everything was blistering, stale, as if we were being held inside a balloon. Most of the women near us were wearing nylon stockings and their dresses were sticking to their legs. I felt faint, just being next to them, and I whispered to Howard, "These people are going to have heatstrokes."

"Don't say anything," Howard snapped. "Just don't talk."

I looked down the hill into the straight rows of knee-high corn, corn that had been irrigated every day for the last month. I'm fine, I said to myself. I would think about the deep well, the aquifer below, the elements that would nourish the corn. I would imagine the green fronds of corn being as high as an elephant's eye. Howard and I hadn't spoken very much in the last few days. Together we had told Emma and Claire about Lizzy. For as much as ten minutes they asked us about her whereabouts, and did it hurt, and why didn't she try to swim out? They couldn't grasp the fact that we would never see her again, but they tried, for a moment, chewing on their fingers, looking up at the ceiling. "Will it ever happen to us?" they wondered. "No," we assured them. "Not until you're very old." Lizzy, for them, was suddenly a different sort of creature, not like them in any way. Before she died she had been invulnerable, just as they were. Something had changed, something had turned her into this—other. When they understood that they were all right, that they could not be harmed, they went merrily on their way.

Howard and I had moved around each other with exaggerated care, unsure of what lay beyond politeness. He went out in the morning, and that's when I put my head in my pillow and stared into the blank white cotton. In the last two days, when he had come in from chores, he had found me sputtering apologies. He had told me to please be quiet more than once. There was no arguing, no shouting in indignation, because he'd told me to stop talking. He knew what was proper: It was stupid to invoke the spirit of the dead lamb, Buster we had called him, which Nellie had served for dinner in the form of chops. It was cowardly to suggest that we dry up the cows and go somewhere for a few weeks, until the worst was over. "Please, Alice," he had said, "let's just keep quiet and get through this."

I hadn't realized at first, in line, that Howard's lower lip was trembling, that he was fighting to compose himself. As he turned away from me I understood that none of the last week had been real for him until now. He wiped his nose on his new sleeve. I felt as if I could see through his suit, to his hairless chest that despite his supernatural strength, had always reminded me, not of hard manly strength but of china, smooth white china that would shatter if you weren't careful. I remembered how at the hospital Howard had said that he felt we were outside of time and circumstance, and then after it was over, back at home, he had had his blissful routine, hours in which work was rest. He had done the chores alone, thankful, I'm sure, for the numbing tasks. His rusted irrigation rig was leaking and the cow had prolapsed. He hadn't wanted to call the vet and spend at least a hundred dollars just to see him show up, so he had pushed the uterus back in, and sewed her with a shoelace and a darning needle, and given her a shot of penicillin. It was probably unheard of for a dairy farmer to take that kind of risk with such an expensive animal. If she died from infection he would be so sorry he meddled, and if she got through it he would be a champion farmer.

The last few days for Howard had been made up of action. It stood to reason then that for him the church service was the time to feel. Maybe he was remembering how we had seen Lizzy in the hospital nursery when she was four hours old. There was one photo album and the video of the second birthday party. Her face was covered with white frosting, a balloon popped, and she cried. Dan and Theresa had probably spent their time since her death talking together, about what a fine baby she had been, how she crawled and stood and walked, irrepressible she was, all in the same month. They would shake their heads and wonder at how extraordinary she'd been. They'd go over and over their little stockpile of stories until there was no point in repeating them. They swore they would keep her memory alive, swore it, and swore it. But she slipped away even as they spoke. Maybe they'd have other children and move to a different state. When Audrey was a teenager she would occasionally remember that there'd been a sister who had drowned in the neighbor's pond, the baby who was frozen in the photograph in the den.

I remember feeling as if I was at quite a distance from the gathering, that I was much more composed than I should have been. Theresa, who knew from her practice as a family therapist, had told me once that feelings are never wrong. Emotions in varying degrees exist, of course, and have to be acknowledged, but they, in and of themselves, she said, do not have moral weight and should never be judged. That was more latitude than I could ever give myself, and I knew full well that my composure, the unreasonable calm, was wrong.

I stood in line calculating how I was going to pay the formal respects. It would have been far preferable to be downstairs in the church basement cutting the cake in preparation for the "lunch," or standing guard over the formidable coffee urn. I had offered, that is, Howard had offered for me. He had dialed and redialed numerous times until he finally got through to the Collins's house. Theresa had told him that there were plenty of people to cover the bases.

"To cover the bases?" I had said, and Howard, because Nellie was standing in the doorway, did not reply. He rolled his eyes up and blinked, and then he left the room.

There was nothing more to say to Lizzy's relatives. Theresa and Dan's life would be forever changed. I couldn't do effective CPR, hadn't been organized enough to know where I put my swimming suit, couldn't take care, was a heathen who barely knew how to pray. "I'm sorry," wouldn't really suffice.

My damp shirt was sticking to my stomach, and my wrists still smelled of the new Calvin Klein perfume, "Escape," that I had found at Hutchin's in the magazine. Howard's mother had ironed the flowered skirt, and I had shaved my underarms as well as my legs with great care, with the fear that one unsightly black nub would be taken as a sign of disrespect. I was tall and fought, without much success, the habit of slouching. In line I stood erect. I reached up and pulled my hair out of its rubber band and smoothed it through the circle of my fingers, and refastened the band. It was then that I saw Mrs. Mackessy, several yards behind us. I had seen her at the hospital, in the waiting room. I had waited in the lounge for three days, doing nothing. Waiting. It seemed that from now on everywhere I went there were going to be surprising people who would remind me of unpleasant things.

In the line at church she was respectable, as always. She was wearing a full white skirt and a pink shell, and her hair was held back by a gold banana clip. She was blowing air up into her face, her bottom lip pushed out like a pout.

"Look alive," Howard whispered, prodding me.

I nodded. Right. Look alive. He had never used that expression before. I didn't like Mrs. Mackessy, and her boy lurking behind her skirt; I didn't like them being in line and on top of it she was acting as if the service was an obligation, an inconvenience. They didn't belong—they weren't really friends. I knew that Mrs. Mackessy and her husband had gone to Theresa for marriage counseling. I remember thinking that they weren't our kind, that they were the sort who would take their welfare checks and go bet on dogs down at the racetrack.

"Alice, move along," Howard said, with the exacting tone of a school master. I walked the three yards to his side. I tried again to think what I was going to do when I got to the receiving line. Should I clasp each relative's hand, or kiss a cheek and pass wordlessly on? What about Theresa's older brother, the one who looked like a thug? He might be waiting for me with a knife up his sleeve.

What do I do? I asked my dusty feet. If Howard knew how I felt he would guide me through the line. I'd rest my weary head on his shoulder and weep quietly, inconsolably, and he'd whisper to me, all the way through. I hoped I would cry the right amount. I guessed I should hug Dan whether or not he welcomed it. He would feel me quivering and perhaps understand my fear. What to say? What to say? I hated that Howard had told me to be quiet. In church I would try my best to cry enough to make an impression, but not so much that I couldn't stop. Because the service was not much more than a show, like a wedding, a clean and public accounting of the horror and mess that had gone before.

I took a deep breath and licked my lips as I rounded the bend into the vestibule. The casket was before us, the white casket with gold trim around the edges, as if it had come with a little girl's vanity and canopy bed set. It was the size of the box Emma's coaster wagon had come in. A person couldn't take it in at once but had to adjust, by degrees, to what amounted to a terrible glare. Lizzy had been laid inside, propped up by the white satin pillows. Her dress had puffed pink sleeves with bows on the seams and a yoke with bows across the chest, and a pinafore with lace stripes sewn to the eyelet. They had shut the lower half of the casket. She had been so swollen in the hospital and they probably hadn't been able to get shoes on her feet, or tights. She looked larger than she had in life and yet there was something almost two-dimensional about her form. The outfit, the silver headband in her hair with five pink roses in a row along the top—all of it made her look like a wedding cake. She would never have stood for it! She would have screamed and thrashed, yanked at the bows, thrown off the headband. I pulled at Howard's sleeve trying to find his hand so we could run and run. We had to get away, couldn't stand the heat and the pressure from the crowd to move forward.

"Howard," I screamed under my breath. He was staring at the body. The tears running down his cheeks were soaking into his stiff white collar.

"My Lord, Theresa looked awful yesterday when I saw her. I made her sit down and tell me all about it." The voice from behind us had a high buzzing quality, like a dentist's drill. I couldn't keep from turning, to see back around the corner. She was a monstrous old bag with innumerable moles on her face, underneath the powder and the deep pink rouge, a color not found in nature. She had come from a meeting, some happy gathering which required a "Hello! My name is ____" sticker. It was beginning to peel and curl along the edges. She was, according to her tag, Mrs. M. L. Glevitch, and she had as good as seized me: I could not take my eyes off of her. The makeup stopped abruptly at her neck. She was wearing a blue polyester long-sleeved dress that probably had all the comfort of a garbage bag, and thick, dark brown stockings and heavy oxblood red shoes—brogans, I thought must be the word for shoes of such weight. She took her large, dark blue handbag and mashed a bug on her arm with it. She and her friend must have cut in line, because they hadn't been there before. "You will not believe this." Mrs. Glevitch lowered her voice. "Theresa insisted that the undertakers put a diaper on Lizzy." She looked at her friend next to her, tucking a corner of her bottom lip into her mouth, widening her eyes, and nodding her head just once. "Theresa got hysterical when the Swanson brothers requested underpants. That sweet girl screamed. I was there to pick up Lois Wright's death certificate for Otis. I heard Theresa with my own ears. I heard her scream"—she lowered her voice still further to a forced whisper—" 'Lizzy's not even toilet trained.' "

The friend shook her head and clicked her tongue against her teeth.

"And then Chas Swanson, he took Theresa by the elbow and led her into his office, put his arm around her, said anything she wanted would be fine—"

"There she is," the friend said, pushing against me to see around the corner to the bier.

"Chas Swanson," Mrs. Glevitch went on, ignoring her friend, "sees death two–three times a week at least, and he was crying himself. I saw him wiping his eyes with his handkerchief after Theresa left."

I turned to look at Lizzy again. Her short brown hair was dull and kempt. On her chest, her strange flat hands molded around it, was her bear. It had been pink when she was born, but it was gray now and the nose had been bitten off. In a circle around the bier were her things: the Sesame Street pop-up toy, the jack-in-the-box, four rag dolls, a Cabbage Patch preemie named Spencer, a cobbler's bench with one of the pegs missing, and a Fisher-Price barn with the fence, the silo, and the animals set up at their troughs.

I groped for Howard's arm, his wrist, his suit coat, anything to grab hold of, and at the same moment something from behind that felt like a large vinyl purse poked me.

"No," I said to Howard, "don't force me." I began to cry as I said again, "Don't force me." I turned around, tripping over the brogans, stepped flat on someone's sandals, and then pushed my way past the sweating people in the doorway. Once I was in the parking lot I lit out. I ran without seeing, past the cars, down into the ravine, across the highway, and into the Jacksons' cornfield. I was sure I could hear her, Mrs. M. L. Glevitch, telling everybody, announcing through her megaphone, that the pathologically sick girl was running from the funeral. What a story she could make of it, having seen it with her own eyes! Not to mention the fact that her own steel-toed shoes had been stepped on by the girl herself! There had been no doubt in her mind right off that the tall blond one was the culprit; you could tell by the eyes shifting, not daring to look at you straight.

I ran until I got to a grove of trees, a narrow, wooded corridor that rose steeply above the field. I climbed and stumbled, grabbing at thin, tender saplings, breaking them while great clods of dirt rolled down the incline. I kicked a rotting trunk so hard I fell down and sat. My pumps were covered with dirt and dust. I pulled them off, threw them aside. "Come back," I whispered. "Come back." The crumbling earth was rough and uneven and cool. It felt good to lie down. Even up on high the ground was quaking from the traffic out on the highway. I remember hearing a truck with muffler problems, roaring in the distance. I remember thinking that there wasn't anyone who could help me, no one who could comfort me, no place to go for forgiveness. I had the notion that maybe, just maybe, the roar was the Giant Earth-Moving Machine, the Gem of Egypt, coming to pick me up in its massive claw and rock me back and forth, back and forth, until I was fast asleep.

Chapter Five

———

NELLIE STOOD BY THE stove frying bacon the morning after the funeral. She was telling me how her world had collapsed when her second son was stillborn. She was carefully turning the sizzling meat with a fork, saying that she had labored twenty hours, and before she could speak her mind they knocked her out. "When I woke up no one said anything. I asked where my baby was and the nurses just went about their business, Ho hum. The doctor came in around ten and told me. Walt was away on business and couldn't get home because of snow."

I knew she was making a valiant attempt to help me come out of myself, to make me aware of the fact that other people had also suffered. I stared at the table thinking only that Nellie and I were nothing alike. Mother Nature, with her own irrefutable logic, was to blame for the son's attenuated beginning and premature end. There was no reason for Lizzy's death, no cause except carelessness.

"His birthday comes and I still feel the loss," Nellie was saying.

"Huh," I said, stirring my cereal. I had long since been the age to inflict damage, and yet I hadn't gotten used to the fact that my own generation had inherited the earth for the time being. The boy I had shared a post-office box with in college was the head architect for a forty-million-dollar museum in Fort Worth. It seemed improbable that a thirty-two-year-old knew enough to keep such a large structure from caving in. There was fear and danger in everything, and it was a wonder we weren't all paralyzed by the possibility of death, the threat of disaster in the routine pleasures of cars, toasters, the air, tuna fish, our friends. Nellie might have done something that seemed to her reasonable, such as scrubbing the bathtub with a powerful cleaning agent, only to find that it had leached through to her skin and into her blood and killed her child.

Despite my rational mind that had always kept me from faith; in spite of the fact that I had always suffered from what I had, in the 1980s, been able to identify as low self-esteem, I couldn't help feeling that I was more wretched than nearly anyone who had ever lived. As Nellie prattled on, it occurred to me that Howard was no doubt heaving and sweating in a far field, working, and at the same time keeping his own pain at bay, by putting it into a historical perspective. And so I tried, for a minute, to make myself feel smaller and happier than others before me who had been accused. I raced through all of the history I could think of, past the ancient Romans who had certainly sullied their hands with their relations' blood, past the Rosenbergs, the Nixons, John Hinckley, Jr.'s parents, past the nameless multitudes serving time for momentary lapses and crimes of desperation. It was no comfort knowing that others had gone before me. It was despicable, I knew, that where there should have been ordinary grief in my heart, there was, in its place, shame and dread. My remorse, my inability to make amends, was undiluted, stronger, I was sure, than those of any of the guilty characters I could conjure or name.

"I tried to go back and think of all the things I did during the nine months that might have caused the trouble." Nellie was still talking, laying out the bacon on a paper towel. "Even though there wasn't the awareness there is today, I had been careful, and I certainly didn't smoke or drink."

It was eight o'clock in the morning and Emma and Claire were in the living room in front of the television, within its electromagnetic field, watching cartoon characters beat each other over the head with bananas. I'm going to march in there, I thought, and smash the set. Why had we ever allowed the children to watch cartoons? I had always said that letting them sit before the tube was as bad as feeding them a diet of Hostess Ding Dongs, and yet I also was often too tired to think of alternatives. All the harsh words, the spanking, the swearing, being weak when I should have been firm—the panorama, the complete history of what I had done wrong appeared before me in living color, and the garbled profanities thundered in my ears. I pushed my chair back while Nellie was still talking, went straight to the television, and punched at the large black buttons. The image sputtered and then vanished.

"Turn that back on!" Emma shouted. Claire chanted, "On. On."

When I shook my head, snapping it back and forth, Emma said, "I hate you, Mom. I HATE YOU."

"Emma, lamb," Nellie said, coming into the living room with a dish towel in one hand and a plate in the other, "don't talk to your mother like that."

"But I want the TV on," Claire whined.

Emma crossed her arms and turned her head, giving her grand-mother the view of her exquisite dirty neck, and the Goodwin Cro-Magnon jaw. It was perhaps hard for a five-year-old to respect an older woman who was fixated on her granddaughters' bowel patterns, who referred to the effort as "doing your duty." Emma's gaze fell on the Barbie with the long black tresses and she grabbed it, waving it in Claire's face, tormenting her by the evident fact of possession. "That's mine!" Claire cried on cue. "Emmie has mine!"

I turned right around and went back into the kitchen. Nellie had told me I should eat something. I sat at my place, in front of a bowl of Grape-Nuts, small pieces of gravel that would aid my digestion. Nellie had somehow turned the clock back one hundred years; she was the farmwife, the unsung heroine, up at the first glimmer, making a cake for noon dinner. She lived by the creed that there was no wound or woe an angel-food cake couldn't heal or conquer. The twenty-five-pound sack of flour was bursting from the cupboard, and all the new, clean, glinting Jell-O molds were stacked against each other on the drain board with the sym-metry of a chorus line. There was a leg of lamb thawing on the counter, and the green onions, miraculously salvaged from the dead garden, drying on a napkin. There was food everywhere I looked. There seemed to be enough time to pickle and preserve and nourish. I was dimly aware of Nellie, luring the girls to literature in the living room. Their voices were far off, as if they were ghosts of little farm girls from long ago.

The day before, I had lain in the thicket for quite a while, until I realized that the light was fading, that once it was dark I might not be able to find my way out. I was walking along the road, halfway home, when Howard drove by. I hadn't realized at first that he had passed me. He slowed down and pulled over to the shoulder. He sat looking at the dashboard while I crossed in front of him, shuffled around to the passenger side, and opened the door. I felt as if I'd been called to the principal. My heart was throbbing in my throat and I wanted to bury my face in my hands, to tell him, through my fingers and my sobs, that I hadn't meant to, that it was a mistake. He waited for the click of my seat belt before he signaled. He drove leaning forward, his nose nearly against the windshield, as if he was worried he might run over an ant. I scratched and scratched at my ear, although it didn't itch.

He parked next to Nellie's Oldsmobile Achieva in the driveway. He took the key from the ignition and remained seated, staring at our beautiful white barn with the gleaming blue silo nestled into its side. "There were four grown men carrying Lizzy's casket down the aisle," he murmured, "when one would have done. When my father died it was sad, but nothing like this naked grief—"

I had blocked my ears, said I didn't want to hear another word.

"That's fine, Alice," he said, turning to me, "but if you're going to be dramatic you're going to have to pay the—"

"Don't you think I know what that old bitch, Mrs. Glevitch, is talking about right this minute?" I had shouted. "She's telling everyone, 'Alice Goodwin, the girl who—who drowned the baby—stepped on my brogans as she ran from the funeral. Alice Goodwin didn't have the moral fiber to pay her final respects.' Don't you think I know?" I had screamed. I didn't ordinarily raise my voice, but there was a thrill to the misery when it came at such a pitch.

"Okay, Alice," Howard had said. "Calm down. Forget it now. Let's go get into bed and forget it."

I had looked at him, at his eyes that were too close together, as if they were snaps to hold his nose to his face. "Right," I had said. "Forget it. Is that what I'm supposed to do, Howard?"

He had been ducking his head to get out of the car and hadn't heard me. "What are brogans anyway? Alice, why do you let total strangers drive you batty? They don't know you."

But I knew better. What Mrs. Glevitch thought she knew was as potent as truth, and pretty soon would become truth. Word was out about me, and she would take the bits of information and dress them up with her distinctive brand of poetry. I was quite sure that Mrs. Glevitch would wave her wand, and behold, Alice Goodwin, rising out of Lizzy's ashes, refashioned to fit the crime.

After we got home from the funeral I had run upstairs, to get away before Nellie appeared from around the corner. I waited in the hall as the guest-room door opened and her capable stride sounded through the living room into the kitchen.

"How was it?" Nellie had asked, after she fussed over the suit, praising its splendor: the colors, the textures, the weight, the classic cut, the fact that it could be worn in every season. Such a suit would never go out of style.

"The service, it was"—I could hear Howard letting his shoe drop from his hands to the kitchen floor—"a nightmare."

"Oh, my land."

There was a muffled silence. Howard was probably telling Nellie about my sudden departure from the receiving line.

"At the beginning," I heard him say then, "the pianist played 'The Requiem for a Dead Princess'. That did everybody in. Reverend Nabor stood at the pulpit trying to compose himself. Finally he said something like, 'These are the times that try our faith.' He said that he usually could find a few positive things to say in a funeral oration, but on this occasion it had been difficult to find the thread of goodness."

"Dear God."

"He spent the next twenty minutes trying to prove himself wrong. The glories of heaven, the mysterious ways of the Lord, the lessons Elizabeth was sent to teach. In the end he said he hoped God had spent some time with a two-year-old before. The congregation tried to laugh."

There was a pause before Nellie said, "Gracious. I think that church needs a new minister. Where's Alice? Is she all right?"

I had closed my eyes and leaned against the dresser. Howard's other shoe dropped to the floor. I kept hearing the thunk, reverberating, growing louder and louder, until I had to clap my hands over my ears.

I stood at the kitchen window, watching Nellie coax the children into the yard with marshmallows. They weren't going to give up the television without exacting a price, pound for pound. Nellie was having to increase the bribe. I went upstairs and lay on the bed. It was eight o'clock in the morning and the sun was shining right on my face and it hurt again, to breathe. It hurt to stand and it hurt to lie down, and it hurt to open my eyes to the light and it hurt to shut them and see. There was nothing to do but lie absolutely still and remember music, remember the steps. Howard banged the door and came in the kitchen to find, not the good wife sitting eating a bowl of cereal to insure regularity, but Nellie cooking eggs and another round of grocery-store bacon from pigs that had been fed antibiotics and stressed in cramped quarters.

"That smells good, Mom," I heard him say. "Where's Alice?"

Nellie was trying to be unobtrusive, trying so hard to be no more noticeable than the sensitive waiter who whisks away the plates and brings on the next course while the young people conduct their romance. There were indications of her presence everywhere. She had dug out shirts that had been stained for years and they were all soaking in mysterious solutions in the bathtub. She was making Howard's favorite foods to fatten him up, including the fabulous Jell-O recipes which brought together the exotic and the ordinary. She had never thought to teach him to cook and without a mother or wife he would have been in danger of starvation. Nellie meant only to sustain, to clean, to help in my absence, but through the ceiling I could see her look, her shrug, eyes rolled heavenward in answer to the question, "Where's Alice?" I heard Howard start up the stairs and then Nellie say, "Let her alone for a little while, Howie." Howie. He was thirty-six years old. "Give her some time."

Bless her heart, I thought, working up the energy to roll over and stretch my arms across the entire width of the bed. She hadn't liked me at the start, and I hadn't grown on her at all over the years. "Bless your heart," I said, out loud.

I slept until late afternoon and while I slept I made it a point to dream of my old life, years before. Nellie took the children to the park, the library, and the custard stand in Blackwell. She brought them home and prepared dinner while they sat two inches from the television, farther and farther from Dickens and Shakespeare as the minutes pressed on. Although Nellie had been married to a businessman, she was clearly born to be a farmwife. Dairy farmers need wives who like to cook bacon and make stupendous lunches with at least two starches: warm homemade bread and corn muffins; three vegetables: beans and stewed tomatoes and acorn squash; and slices of hickory-smoked ham glazed with brown sugar and pineapples; and cherry pie with whipped cream for dessert, and chocolates passed at the very end. Peanut butter and jelly were not enough for a man who was feeding the nation. Nellie wore a white lace apron she had brought from home that hung like strings of beads around her neck. Her gray hair was held in a bun by clear plastic hairpins. She was wearing support hose and white cushioned shoes that had been fashioned by a podiatrist. She could tend the dairy farmer, fix him his cocoa on the winter mornings when he came in from chores, kiss his forehead, and sit him down in the La-Z-Boy so he could listen to the weather radio. They could put me up in the attic where I could grow old in peace, shrieking only at night, like Rochester's mad wife.

At suppertime I came downstairs. Howard was still out with, as we fondly spoke of the herd, "his ladies." I should have been helping him. The women and children sat and ate and mopped up the sweat rolling down our faces. I took a warm white roll from a basket lined with a red-and-blue-checked cloth. The house was going to rise on a waft of hot air. Nellie would open the oven door just one more time and the blast of heat would dislodge the house from its foundation, and we would sail over Wisconsin and drift south to Kansas. I sank my teeth into the soft doughy roll and it collapsed like a pricked balloon. It was impossible to chew what felt like thick dry cotton in my mouth.

"Excuse me," I whispered.

"Where are you going?" Emma called. She followed me into the bathroom, watching me spit into my paper napkin.

"I'm sorry, Nellie," I said, when I'd returned. "I think I'm sick."

Claire wrinkled her nose and said, "Why did you turn off the television?"

I should say something of comfort: I will stop feeling so sorry for myself tomorrow, I promise; Lizzy prefers heaven to earth; your father's obsessive devotion to his herd and his crops is nothing compared to his love for you. But I sat at the table without saying a word.

Howard put them to bed. I heard him in Emma's room, playing his clarinet. He played, "Ain't Misbehavin'," while the girls danced around him in their white slips. "Play, 'Don't You Touch My Mojo,'" Emma shouted. Instead he played the beginning of "Rhapsody in Blue." The clarinet sounded like a siren from way down at the firehouse, sending out the call for help.

The second morning after the funeral Howard slapped his coveralls on the entry floor. He took the stairs by twos up to the bedroom, the thundering of his boots inspiring fear and trembling just as if he were shouting Fee Fi Fo Fum over the racket of his ascent.

"Alice," he said, sitting down beside my head, "it's time to get up." He didn't sound angry. He wasn't shouting. He was never one to pick a fight; if someone asked him, I'm sure he would say we had never had a cross word in our life together. He was looking at me dispassionately, I thought, the way he might watch a middle-aged bank clerk count his deposit. Although I had most often felt that our marriage was safe I, and surely he as well, had grievances, complaints, Theresa assured me, which were normal in any relationship. I had married Howard knowing that nothing made him happier than the sight of milk surging through the pipes to the bulk tank. I suspected, later, that when he had first looked into my eyes, so long and so intently I blushed and felt faint, he was actually thinking of milk price supports. The milk barn was his war. He was the general and the cows were his soldiers. He ran them through their maneuvers twice a day, seven days a week, fifty-two weeks a year. Although I had known the dairy life was his dream when we were married, I did not fully understand the demands of the day-to-day routine. I usually had enough presence of mind to remember how satisfying it was, juggling my jobs, helping to keep Howard's dream afloat, his idea of the good life that was far better than any I could have imagined for myself. But I confess that on occasion, in moments of fatigue or worry about money, I lay in bed, plotting his punishment. The children and I would cut him out of our lives, leave him to the cows, if that's what he wanted. I would cash in our one IRA and go to Greece, walk naked along the white beaches, and not only drink goat's milk for lunch, but like it, love it! We would be revolted by the sight of the cow for all of our days to come. We would turn brown and dance like Zorba.

"Is there someone you could call, that you could talk to about this, some old friend who could help?" he was asking me. It was such a sensible question, so like Howard to think of the obvious path.

I slunk down under the sheet. My Aunt Kate would have come, if she were alive, and she would have had us cutting up quilt squares on the kitchen table. She would have the sewing machine going at eighty miles an hour while a fragrant concoction with a ham hock simmered on the stove. So that I wouldn't cry I blurted, "The crazy dentist! I could call the crazy dentist from our folk-dancing days. He had hair like Bozo, honest to God, red tufts that stuck out on each side of his head, and he always wore these horribly greasy checked pants, and the zipper was perpetually half mast, and he never opened his—"

"Alice," Howard said, "we have to get on with things."

Things? I wasn't the least bit interested in things. It's you I want to talk to, Howard, I might have said, if I hadn't been so weary, so dispirited. I had disgraced myself so thoroughly that there was not much chance of redemption. Couldn't he see that I was alone, utterly solitary in that disgrace, as singular as the first village leper? I had been in error for half my life, wrecking whatever came my way. I wasn't patient and wise with my own children, or the children at school. Our house was sinking into the ground, and I stood watching it crumble around us, without the energy to take caulk and scraper and paintbrush in hand.

"Theresa called a while ago," Howard said.

That news startled me and I sat up. I couldn't imagine going to Theresa's, you-hooing and putting the copper kettle on, sitting down at the oiled butcher-block table, and waiting for her to come down the stairs with her only daughter trailing after her. In all the years we'd lived in

Prairie Center I'd managed to make only one real friend. I didn't have any reserves for lean times. How would we be neighbors now? I wondered if we'd avoid each other in the grocery aisles, going the long way home so we wouldn't pass on the road.

"Mom is leaving for Rumania next week," Howard said, in the soothing tone he used with a cow when it's having trouble delivering. "It's time to get up."

"I can't," I said into the pillow, wittingly using the short sentence that had been forbidden in Howard's formative years.

I spent the next two days sleeping. I told myself that I was resting from the rage of parenting, that I had been shattered by my squabbling children. I had been exhausted without realizing, and now I couldn't move another inch. At night, wide awake, I prowled the house. The plangent strains of the clarinet drifted up from the front porch, where Howard was playing. I stood by Emma's bed, wiping the sweat off her forehead and gently pulling the thumb out of her mouth, hoping to spare us the cost of the orthodontist. I adjusted the fan so it blew to the place she had moved. In Claire's room I kneeled and looked through the slot of her bed rail, so that I could get a better look at her puffy face. Claire was going to be the beauty. Her lips were parted and a fine thread of drool seeped from the corner of her mouth. Her eyes weren't shut all the way and I could see the white luster between her lids. I stuck my hand through the bar and felt her dimpled fingers.

When they were grown, our children would freely offer their objections about their upbringing. They would sit me down and tell me what I had done wrong, itemizing my character flaws. The time would come when they would outdistance me in every way; they would be far smarter than I, wiser, better adjusted, generous, all the good things from their father. They would know how to navigate through the world. I would have to listen and admit that they were right. They would never forget the time I had tried to beat the milk of human kindness into Emma, shouting, "Be nice to your sister," as I spanked her bare bottom. I wondered if they would forgive me my inadequacies.

After I checked the girls I drew on pants and a sweatshirt against the mosquitoes that bred in the dew. I walked through the hay field. If a person squinted, the lights up in the subdivision looked like the Dipper, Cassiopeia, the Swan. "You used to live there," I said to Lizzy. "Lizzy Collins of Prairie Center, Wisconsin. At Christmas your house has the star on the roof—that's how you'll know it. Your neighborhood association has strict rules and they only allow white lights, and they can't twinkle on or off. So your star will stand out both from the heavens and from the rest of the town's garish displays."

I saw the life that might have been Lizzy's moving along the dark horizon. She was round and rosy, and her mother always did her best to dress her up. She might well have been in the pack of girls who in kindergarten start out with clapping games and jump-rope stunts and end up years later as cheerleaders and student-council members. She might have been just as we all dreamed to be. I could see her at sixteen in the tall grass behind the baseball diamond, willing the boy to kiss her, it being worth the jigger bites.

Maybe Dan and Theresa knew what they had learned from Lizzy, but I couldn't think what lesson there was that might even begin to compensate for her loss. I stood watching the bedroom lights going out, one by one, until there was nothing but the halos from the yard lights, meant to frame the burglars as they tiptoed away with the VCRs. Surely there was a formula: If I do ———, Lizzy will come back. The act of contrition was just beyond my grasp. If I stared at the pond, at the haze of insects fluttering over the surface, it might come to me. I will close my eyes, I thought, and wish hard. I will hear a noise, like a fish jumping, and when I look I'll see Lizzy, coming to the surface, shaking off her pink scales, finding her new arms to do the breaststroke to shore.

Four days after the funeral Nellie announced over the lasagne she had made, Howie's favorite, that tomorrow she would have to go. "I'm not sure I should leave you," she said as she walked around the table, putting a hunk of garlic bread on each of our plates.

"We'll be fine, Mom," Howard said.

"I could call tonight and tell them—"

"We'll miss you, but we'll get along. They're counting on you."

At the end of the meal Emma was inching her hand toward Claire's place mat, and Claire, uncharacteristically, let out a gorgeous and savage scream.

"Girls!" Nellie breathed.

Howard reached for his J.I. Case cap on the counter and said in his usual terse way, "You two. We're going for a ride."

When the car started, the muffler sounding its call, Nellie cleared her throat and adjusted herself in her chair. She and Howard had planned this time for our little talk. I knew it, could see the pleasure of conspiracy in her big sincere face. "Alice, dear," she said, wiping her mouth with a napkin, "I can't help worrying about you. You're going to hurt yourself, sweetheart. You've just got to be more positive. You've got to stop thinking such black thoughts." I knew what she was going to say next. The words were going to barge out of her mouth: In a time like this, Alice dear, a woman still needs a mother, and if there's anything you want to talk—

"I had my Aunt Kate," I said, before she could speak. "She wasn't mother but I adored her." I pulled on my sandals, huaraches they were called, with soles made in Mexico from old tires. They looked like something a dog had gnawed and buried and dug up and gnawed again. "She bought me these sandals at a folk fair and they're still good after fifteen years."

It wasn't nice to say to poor Nellie. She loved everyone to look their best, to be brushed and clean and polished and polite. I was curse to her, I knew, disheveled, beaten down, nothing that a good attitude couldn't improve if only I would try.

"I'm going out," I said, putting my hands on her shoulders, wishing one gesture could make amends.

At the water's edge the mosquitoes bit my forehead and flew up my nose. I closed my eyes and listened for the slightest ripple, for the break of water. We would someday swim in the pond again, but it was hard to imagine how we'd have the nerve to break the taboo for the first time—it was horrifying to think of putting our mouths to that particular water, letting it touch us. Theresa, I thought, probably wouldn't ever be able to walk down the lane or maybe she wouldn't want to come to the farm at all. When the gnats became intolerable I made my way around the pond and into the woods. It was an old growth forest, the burr oaks, hickory, walnut, and red oaks towering to the sky, and underfoot the May apples, Dutchmen's britches, wild ginger, poison ivy, shooting stars, and trillium. The canopy overhead protected the wildflowers from the sun, and the wavering golden light that came through was laced with swarming insects. I thought of the other deaths I'd lived through: There had been my mother, my father, my Aunt Kate, and a woman I'd known slightly in college. Grieving for those people had entailed also a general wonder and fear of death, for one's own death, for the inevitable end as dust. Lizzy's death, a child's death, I considered, should be at remove from oneself, the grief more pure. I wished I could forget her for just a minute so that I could take a walk or be with the girls, or cook a meal, or wash my face, without feeling the weight bearing down on my shoulders, the leaden yoke around my neck, so heavy I felt I must stoop.

I came to the stand of sumac in what used to be a clearing. Beyond lay the orchard that had not been pruned or cared for in fifteen years. Howard had thought each spring that finally he would have time in the coming season to trim and spray and pick the existing apples, as well as plant new varieties. He was forever optimistic, forever deluded. The twenty trees seemed to lean toward me, their gnarled, bent forms like old men gathered together in the village square, whispering. They were judging me, I was sure they were. They frightened me, until I looked straight at them, at the flaking bark, at the denuded spots where deer had nibbled. There had been no discipline, no guiding hand in the trees' rampant growth, each bough greedy for light and space, suckers spearing through to the heights, all a tangle, a glut of regeneration. I didn't ever want to go back to the house, to Nellie and Howard. Better to stay in the orchard and be judged by the old trees who thought themselves stern but were ineffectual, temperamental as brats. I pulled myself up into the crotch of what I thought was a McIntosh, and then I climbed to a higher limb. I tried for the thousandth time to think where I could go to get better, where there might be someone or something to receive me if I ran away. I could at least sleep in a sling, hang it from a branch like an outlaw, and wait until the morning, when Nellie would be gone. There was a wood thrush in the distance, singing its love of beetles and berries, summer and twilight, and there came the faintest breeze in my face. The apple tree felt hospitable, and for just a bit I didn't feel quite so sick. I didn't hear anything but the bird and the rustle of the wind, and there was peace because it was hours before I'd have to go home again. I didn't hear the twigs breaking, didn't hear the tread of feet over dry grass. The noise of the cry struck and rang out in whorls through the night. No word, but terror was in the center of it, and even as it rippled away the sense hung in the air. I slipped, caught myself for a second, before I saw Theresa, and when she came clear I actually fell, spreading my arms out and sliding, scraping my back to the ground.

She was about ten feet away in the next row. Her open mouth was twisted, but she had made her noise and the quiet was like the silence after a car accident, when there's nothing but smoke coming from the wreck.

She'd scared the bejesus out of me with her scream but I wasn't going to let on. I stood up, absently dusting myself off, my mind racing, trying to think what to say, something about running from the funeral, about Mrs. Glevitch, something about how I was always thinking of Theresa, always thinking of Lizzy. That was what I was doing, always thinking of them. "I—" I began.

"You scared me," she said with tears in her voice. She was walking around in circles, patting her chest, breathing so heavily I thought she might hyperventilate. "I'm not up to a fright like that."

"I'm sorry," I said meekly.

She dug in her shorts' pocket and produced a pack of Camel Lights and a folder of matches. That Theresa carried cigarettes around was as unlikely as Reverend Nabor having cocaine on hand for his visits to the elderly. I couldn't help jerking my head back, out of surprise.

"I know, I know," she said, "just a few now and then, when I'm alone. It's a habit from my bad girl days at St. Ben's, sneaking a pull in the john. It's helpful right now, like an old friend." She put the cigarette to the corner of her sagging bottom lip, struck a match against a cardboard match paper, and managed, when the flame was almost to her thumb, to get it started. She leaned against the tree in the next row. I didn't know what else to do but edge my raw back to a resting position against the

McIntosh. It was an odd thing, to be stuck with someone, as if we were in the confines of a stalled elevator, when we had four hundred acres, plenty of cover, any number of good hiding places.

"It's hard for me to see you right now," she said quietly. "It hurts so much. I sometimes come down to sit near the pond, but I mean not to disturb you. I called the other day and when the phone was ringing I realized that I couldn't talk to you at all. It's something I'm struggling with, along with everything else, this business of how to take up life, how to start out again. I'm praying half the day."

I wanted to apologize, not only for Lizzy's death, but for the disturbance at the funeral, and for scaring her just then, making her think there were ghosts in the orchard. "I'm sorry—"

She was exhaling and waving her hand back and forth. "There's nothing to say—that's one of the terrible things for both of us. I know you're sorry, and like the good girl I was raised to be I'm even sorry you're sorry. I haven't been able to think too much about you, Alice, but I know I will, that the time will come when I'll probably feel your pain too. Father Albert talked with me about you; he made me take note. I do know your pain is there, that it must be fierce. I hurt so much I can't even think."

"I know," I whispered. I started to sidestep away because there was clearly nothing to be done. I had thought that I'd been as good as dismissed, that our unexpected meeting was over, that there would be no more visits for a long time. But I was held there, not only by her very real presence but also by the idea of her. I thought that we had sometimes seen ourselves in the other, that we were more alike than we acknowledged, that we started from much the same lump and might have turned into something quite like the other if we'd been switched at birth. I had been brought up to be off-balance and was; and she had been raised to hold all things in perfect equilibrium, something that was so unusual it too was beyond the norm. I yearned to keep myself straight and in order, but of course never could, and she longed, without any success whatsoever, to let herself go, to let everything occasionally fall to pieces. We were leagues apart on the outside and I think we were amused by the differences, the variation that had been wrought perhaps most of all by circumstance. We had understood one another, felt a sympathy, an affection, as well as been critical of the other's idiosyncrasies. We were friends in a deep way, in a way that involved obligation and trust, a solid faith in the other's love. I had never had a friend like her and I felt her life moving alongside of mine in much the same way I felt my husband's days and passages to be a complement to my own. Only with the prospect of her letting me go had I begun to realize how important she was.

She took another pull and choked. "Damn," she said, between her hacks. "I've forgotten how."

"You'll remember," I said, the first words of comfort I had offered her since Lizzy's death. "You'll remember," I said again, coming out from the trunk.

She began to talk, apparently not realizing that I was trying to take my leave, that she had said I should go. "It's awful," she said, "losing my daughter, and feeling that I've lost you too. I don't feel that you're gone exactly, but that you're—misplaced. I've never felt so alone. I keep thinking, I've got to tell Alice—and then I realize that I can't call you, that there is this pain in my chest, like my breast is being cut clean through." She put her head down to her knees and let out one thin wail that sounded like the far off call of a loon. "Isn't it terrific," she said, righting herself, "how much a person can cry?" She looked out at the woods, the tears running down her face. "Isn't it phenomenal how long it goes, and then there's this period of the strangest calm, grace, it must be, and then it comes on again, all that, sorrow, and you feel as if you're not a big enough —vessel—to contain it?"

I nodded. There were hundreds of tiny, malformed apples in the McIntosh, each the size of a thimble. I didn't know about grace, but I had nearly been swept under numerous times.

"I walk down to the pond every night because I think of her there. I sit looking at the water and I sense her, I really do. If I can only keep her in focus, hold her there, I'll be all right, I'll be all right." She took a long drag. She was talking out to the orchard, as if the trees had come to stand in straight rows for the purpose of listening to her; I felt sure that even if I hadn't been present she would still have been talking, to the grass, the birds, the possible spirits. I slunk back into the unyielding trunk of the tree. "I drove to Neenah today, to talk to Albert Satinga," she went on. "Everyone says I have to get on with my life and keep busy, take a vacation, get a puppy, plant a garden. I smile and agree—God, I was so well brought up it makes me ill. Inside I'm screaming at the advice. My sister signed me up for volleyball on Wednesday nights, and a counted cross-stitch class at the Sewing Center! She's only trying to be kind, but I just wish they'd all leave me alone. Dan has been getting up at four o'clock and going to the Dairy Shrine—"

I could picture him in his basement office, his ceramic cow knick-knacks facing him on the desk. I wondered if he could work, if sometime months from now he might unveil an exhibit, a surprise to the community, a brilliant installation about the invention of the threshing machine. It was also conceivable that he might sit down at his office for a year and have nothing to show for himself. I had been afraid of Dan at first; after the days in the hospital I had not feared him less but I began to be frightened for him as well. He may have tried to look unflinchingly at the possibility of the endless dark hole, the hereafter, not so much for himself, but for his little girl. Most of the family would probably have hoped to find solace in the conventional images of heaven. Although I hadn't yet visited Lizzy's grave, it certainly would have had all the crudeness of the earth, of planting a seed or burying a hamster. Theresa had talk and inborn strength on her side: There she was, talking at me in spite of the knife slicing through her breast, and the fact that theoretically we had nothing to say to each other. I didn't know if Dan could look into the abyss without falling in himself.

She was alternately wiping her face with her hands and dealing with the cigarette, which seemed conspicuous and awkward to her, something ill-fitting and new that requires an adjustment, like walking for the first time in high heels. I started to ask if someone was planning activities for Dan, but she didn't hear. "Yesterday," she said, "I just had to see Albert. It's crazy, I know, but I had to. I left Audrey with my sister. I made an excuse about how I had to go settle with the insurance company and finish out a staffing at the office since I'm not going to work anymore this summer. I couldn't wait to get up there, to see Albert."

I was looking in on a private moment. It was not for me, Theresa resting against the tree, smoking and talking. I felt I shouldn't look at her. It was logical that she should go see her old friend, Albert Satinga. He had been a priest at the parish church, as well as Theresa's English teacher at St. Benedict's High School. He had been in his middle twenties at the time, stocky, she'd said, solid, with black eyes and what still looked like peach fuzz growing over his ruddy cheeks. At sixteen Theresa thought he was the most intense person she had ever known, that no one in Prairie Junction could hold a candle to the beauty, the faith, the poetry, of Father Albert. As sponsor of the school yearbook he had students on the roof, hanging upside down to photograph the gargoyles. Theresa, I knew, had worshipped him then, and she had merely loved him seven years later, when he was defrocked for several reasons, not least for passing out subversive literature to students, *The Catcher in the Rye,* for example, and no doubt most of all because he had been smitten by a confessor, sight unseen. He was fascinated by the nameless, faceless woman's stories of life with a brute. For weeks he scanned the nave from the pulpit during the 6 A.M. mass. Her voice was low, an excellent thing, he knew, in a woman. He couldn't have asked for more one Monday morning, when a creature with unnatural blond hair, stiff as bristles, thrust her fragile, gloved hand into his already-in-motion priestly handshake and murmured, "Father Albert." Four months later Albert left the church in disgrace and a year later his marriage, which had hardly begun, was over. Theresa tended him up to the brink of a nervous breakdown. Afterward, when he was out of the hospital, he went off to Red Wing, Minnesota, to learn how to repair band instruments. Now he was living in Neenah, Wisconsin, working at a music shop repairing valves and worn pads on clarinets and French horns, flutes and tubas.

"I just didn't have the time or privacy to call him between the hospital and the funeral," she was saying. "I don't know how I got through the work of arranging the details, the coffin, my God, the dress, the shoes— my mother was hysterical for all of us, I think. I still feel as if I'm moving, that it will take a long time to come to a complete stop. That's why I need to visit the pond, to get a grip. Every now and then I'd feel a moment of calm, hovering above the lunacy, as if I was somewhere between Earth and Lizzy. It was so strange, shopping for her, what color would she like, what fabric, as if she was going away to college."

Imagine Lizzy going to college—for a split second I considered it a possibility in the far-off future, that she might return to go to Vassar or Smith, because a girl, no matter what was hindering her, couldn't pass up that experience. I needed to leave the orchard and go home to Nellie and

Howard. Their censure and good intentions would be easy to suffer compared with this conversation that wasn't meant for my ears and to which I could offer nothing. She bent down to put her stub in the dirt. "I had to go up there, out the main drag of Neenah to the instrument repair shop." She lit another and threw the match into the bleached grass. "Alice," she said, turning and looking at me for the first time, "sometimes I get the queerest feeling. It always lasts for just a minute. It's—it's that we are all as expendable as kittens. Do you ever get that?"

I was surprised and then appreciative that she'd directed a question to me and I nodded vigorously.

"God," she said, shaking her fists, "I really hate that feeling." She pulled a handkerchief from the pocket that seemed to contain no end of interesting things, and demurely blew her nose. She wasn't exactly facing me, but she had changed position, her side, instead of her back, to the tree, so that an observer would have had the impression that we were having an interchange. "I went to the repair place, and I stood by the window looking in on Albert in the workroom lumbering around, pawing through the drawers filled with gaskets, you know, parts. He stuck his oily hand into a drawer and pulled out some sort of greasy pipe, turned it over and over, like coons do in the garbage. I kept thinking he was some kind of animal—I couldn't help it. His red shirt had a white, 'Albert,' sewn in cursive on the pocket, like gas-station attendants have. Can you believe it?"

She didn't wait for me to answer. She had become as extroverted and manic as I had become introverted and slow. She was not all right; she was like an animal herself, something that's got a foot stuck in a trap and is going so wild it can't figure out what limb is hurting. I wondered if she would tell the story to anybody she saw on the street, or sit down at Del's, the diner in town, talking at everyone who came in for coffee, whether or not they wanted to hear.

"I looked at the sheet music until the woman in the shop was busy with someone else, and then I charged through the door, to the back. I put my head down on that greasy counter and I couldn't stop, I just sobbed; I sobbed, 'Father, forgive me, for I have sinned.' "

"You did?" I said, unable to suppress my astonishment.

She shook her head back and forth, exhaling a tremendous blast, her bottom lip jutting out so that the smoke went up into her face. "Old habits die hard," she said, "especially old Catholic habits. I'll bet he hadn't heard anyone call him 'Father' in ten years."

"What did he do?"

"I could tell he didn't know about Lizzy. I thought someone might have called him. He was sort of in shock, I guess, seeing me in the middle of his workplace. I was crying my head off, bawling him out, screaming like a madwoman, telling him the repair shop had no business hiring someone as inept as he was, that he should"—she hiccuped—"be corrupting youth with good books and leading young girls to the Holy Spirit."

She doubled over and coughed into both hands, and I thought, although she was several feet from me, that I should go thump her on the back. When she stood up she walked toward me holding on to a branch as if it was a guard rail. "I could never tell Dan about it, or my sisters. They thought he was lecherous. You're the only person who really knows about Albert."

It was folly to take the compliment to heart, but I couldn't help feeling pleasure for a minute, in the secret, in her trust.

"I swear," she said, "that even among the instruments, under his bright 'Albert' shirt and his strained pants—he's huge, I mean he's absolutely enormous—I swear that in the midst of all the grease and glue his holiness shines through. He's fat, he needs a haircut, but you can't help knowing you are in the presence of the Holy Spirit."

The light was growing dim and she was beginning to look like a specter herself. I was grateful she was talking to me instead of to the trees. "We went to the coffee shop down the road, and we sat across from each other with cherry sodas, the way we used to do in high school, on the sly. It could have been fifteen years ago; it was as if no time had passed. He made me do something I'd been afraid to do for myself. He insisted I tell him the story of Lizzy's life, from the start to the finish. At first I panicked, thinking, I'm not going to be able to draw hers as a full life. I was terrified I'd find out—that her story would come up so very short, or I'd make her sound like a little saint when she is flesh in the best sense of the word. But I started, from nearly after conception . . . God, I can't believe it—I could remember everything, back to nearly every doctor's visit, and hearing her heartbeat on that stethoscope thing. I went through the birth—I spared him no details, including delivering the placenta. The nurse wanted to save it so she could bring it to a Lamaze class that night. I said absolutely not, I wasn't going to have my placenta in a bucket for a group of scared parents to look at. Albert sat on the edge of the booth, like he couldn't wait to hear about her first tooth, for the sleepless night to be over, for the I.V. to be put in—remember the time she got dehydrated? Last year?"

It seemed years ago, decades ago, and now Theresa was going to talk at high speeds through the seasons, through the rain and sleet and snow, until she was briny and then moss covered.

"He made me write down the words she knew—there are fifty-six. That's pretty good for a two-year-old, isn't it? It took me hours to tell her story. Albert took the longest coffee break in the history of the Industrial Society and he'll probably get fired for it. But it struck me, it hit me that Lizzy had a full life, compressed to be sure, but, but in its own way it was full of everything that we all experience, if we live to be one hundred. I realized that I could spend the rest of my days screaming because she won't get to grow up, but Albert made me look at what was, at how mysterious and extraordinary she was, at what a gift we were given in Lizzy. He blessed me for the long work of grief we have ahead of us. He blessed me, Alice. He gave that to me, do you see? Don't you see?"

I looked up from the job I was doing, picking at the bark. I wasn't quite sure I saw. From the outside it looked as if Lizzy had missed almost everything. She would never fall in love at sixteen, or read *The Secret Garden,* or smell violets again, or eat cotton candy, or fly for the first time on a bike.

"When I was done Albert said, and there were tears streaking down his face, he said, 'I'm going to miss that girl.' He never met her! He moved over next to me and we rocked together, back and forth, just hard enough so that one edge of the booth came up like a swing set will, you know, that isn't grounded in cement?"

What I could see of her in the dusk, in the glow of her cigarette butt, startled me so much I choked on thin air. She was smiling at the sky, her mouth wide open in a fanatical grin, as if she were trying to beam all of her faith up to the dark, dry, invisible ether. She began to whisper, and I had to move closer to hear. "It was so strange, when I left him. I was driving way too fast. I knew that it was night, of course it was, but it was as if the highway, was—radiant. That's the only word I know to describe it. It was radiant."

For her sake I tried to picture a glowing highway, a ribbon of light all the way from Neenah to Prairie Center. "No one would believe me," she said out loud. "I won't ever tell anybody. I can't tell Dan why I'm afraid to go on vacation. I'm afraid to leave, for fear she'll come back and we won't be home. What will she do if she finds we aren't home?" She came closer yet, bringing her forearm across her cheek and mouth. "I just have to remember," her voice trembling, "I have to remember the Holy Spirit. The anger, the regret, the fear—floats off like mist when I remember the presence, when I feel the warmth and the glow of the Holy Sp—"

"Where are you going?" I said. I had just realized that she'd mentioned something about leaving.

"Where are we going?" she repeated. "Ah, we thought Cape Cod at first, but then we decided it would be better to take the train out to Glacier and climb. Climb. Alpine meadows and marmots and snow-capped mountains."

The gnats had found us, were flying at our faces, thick as snow. Theresa went into a frenzy, slapping her nose, her legs, her arms, her chest. "This is horrendous!" she shouted. "I'm going, these things are terrible. Audrey is doing the best of any of us. She skips all over the park shouting, 'My sister's in heaven, my sister's in heaven!' I bet she imagines heaven is like Disney World, with water slides and Coke and people dressed up as Big Bird and Minnie Mouse."

She was running away from me, slapping at herself. It was almost like old times: Theresa rushing off home and talking halfway down the walk. She called, "Don't ever tell Dan I smoked, okay?" And then she retraced her steps and came toward me, oblivious to the swarm around her. "Maybe heaven is whatever you want it to be," she said. "For me it's mothering, even the bad parts. I'm very clear about that now. For Lizzy it should be just about the whole nine yards except baths, and Mrs. Klinke's German Shepherd. She's gung ho about—about life. I keep telling her, 'Hang in there, Lizzy. I'll still be your mom when I'm eighty. I'll remember everything, absolutely everything about you, and when I get there we'll pick up where we left off.' "

Chapter Six

———

SHE LEFT ME REELING in the orchard. She was quickly out of sight, on her way home to her quiet husband, or to the pond where, perhaps for her, the angels would sing. Maybe they were always there, but Theresa would hear them, and see them as they made themselves visible to her, one by one, across the water. Theresa had been remarkably fluent. Despite her crushing blow she had been coherent. I envied her her Holy Spirit even as I told myself that God didn't go lighting up highways. I didn't know if I was now allowed to visit Vermont Acres and carry on, or if we were finished with our business, nothing left for us but the exchange of awkward pleasantries in public places. I tried to think again if our bond was strong enough after all, to carry us over the disaster. We had more than once admitted to each other, with the ardor of schoolgirls—and with hope that the feeling was returned and with fear that it wasn't—that we were each other's best friend. I tried to think how I would cope if Emma or Claire met with disaster up at Theresa's, if they got stuck in one of her modern conveniences and died. I wouldn't forgive her the needless contraption or her negligence; I could never meet her without placing blame. Despite Father Albert's advice to consider my pain, despite Theresa's generous heart, it was impossible to imagine that she could forgive me enough to at least resume some kind of superficial patter. And I didn't know if the forgiveness itself was light, glittery stuff that showered down and absolved a person and set them free, or if, instead, it was heavy, cumbersome, a new debt, a currency that was continuously renewed no matter how much was paid out.

I didn't want to bump into her again, and since I didn't have any idea where she was going I wandered, as slowly as I could, in and out of the trees. Was Theresa, despite her ability to construct whole sentences, well? It was so tempting to indulge in the idea that all the dead people were up in the sky, impervious to the effects of gravity and the orbiting shuttle litter, waiting for us to take our turns and come to them. Lizzy, my Aunt Kate, my mother. I didn't notice the gnats after a while, as I thought of heaven, of Aunt Kate miles above smelling of tobacco and lavender soap, stooping to receive Lizzy. I had hurt a great deal and for so long through my childhood that I had years before made heaven into a stock routine: My mother was yonder, her apron tied around her trim waist, waiting and waiting with her hands folded at the table, with the cookies overlapping slightly in a circle on the china plate, and cold milk in tall glasses.

As I had grown up, the fantasies were seductive only temporarily, before the logistical problems of heaven reared their ugly heads. Did young people stay forever young, did old people revert back to their prime, were unpleasant characters, people who would have been likable if they hadn't had lousy childhoods—were they given personality make-overs? What if my mother really didn't want to sit with my father at the same craft table during the celestial craft hour? What if she'd taken up with someone who loved her for herself, who could meet her needs?

Any loss I suffered always took me back to that first loss. My mother died when I was eight, of lung cancer. She had majored in home economics in college, in preparation for her life as my father's spouse. Her death taught me that there wasn't any such thing as logic or mercy. She had had a native distrust of fatty acids long before it was fashionable, and in the face of her family's scorn she served up margarine and replaced the Sunday pot roast with fowl. She had no vice other than excessive glee when she beat my father at bridge. On those rare victorious occasions, the otherwise perfect 1950s housewife stood up from the table and executed several entrechats in her flat black pumps. My father, who has remained a mystery to me long after his death, drank moderately, expressed himself infrequently, and only if my behavior was rude and unseemly. He sat all day in the fog of his own cigarette smoke in his office where he designed pulley systems. And yet he woke each morning without a cough, each foot gliding into his proper slipper under the nightstand.

When the neighbor, Mr. McCrady, kindly explained the biology of cancer to me, how cells went haywire, I imagined my mother's lungs crusted with fat slimy coils, like snails without shells. It was no wonder she had trouble breathing and had to be under a doctor's supervision. Because I knew that my mother had had me in a hospital, and because, like all children, I was not rational, I had the idea that the two events, the birth and the cancer, were linked, and that I was responsible. I'm not sure I've ever really forgiven myself for her death. My father and I ate chicken potpies in silence, night after night for the nearly eight months it took her to die. I went to school, and after, climbed the stairs by twos up to my room and shut the door. I read, and worked on my map of the world. I felt well hidden in our cavernous five-bedroom Victorian house with three stories and four-and-a-half baths.

On the afternoon of the death my father came home and went into the study, and before he shut the door I slipped in and stood by his desk. I had made up my mind to find out why there was a flood of food coming in from the neighbors at the back entrance. My father, I later learned, had discouraged them during my mother's illness, but now, with the official word, they could restrain themselves no longer. Something had changed. I was slightly more frightened of the change than I was of asking him for an explanation, so I took a deep breath and tried to frame the question.

Before I could get the words out he looked up and said, "Mother's gone." He took a flat square box out of his drawer and handed it to me, as if I had come in expressly to fetch my present. There was a tape reel inside. The doorbell rang then and he came past me. I made for the yellow case in the hall closet that held the tape recorder. It was heavy, and I had to stoop to pick it up with both hands. I managed the stairs to my room, closed the door, and then barricaded it with my dresser. It was no easy task to push the white bureau from one end of the room to the other. I threaded the tape, and then lay down right next to the small silver holes around the middle of the box. When I reached over the top of the machine and turned the lever to the ON position, a voice I'd always known said, "Hello, Alice. I'm going to read you some of this book that I love, and that you love too. *Little House in the Big Woods,* by Laura Ingalls Wilder. 'Once upon a time, sixty years ago, a little girl lived in the Big Woods of Wisconsin, in a little gray house. . . .' " Her voice was coming off a shiny ribbon. I understood, all of a sudden, what my father had meant. My mother wasn't just gone to the hospital. She was dead. With my face down on the rug the voice came right into my ear. It was as if there was a rough hand grabbing me by the scruff of the neck and carrying me to a new place. There was nothing to do but lie perfectly still, no way to fend off the gripping hand. I closed my eyes and saw under my lids the yellow daylight going dimmer and dimmer. The voice went on, one tangled word after the next, until the end of the second chapter, when my dead mother said, "Good night, Alice. You make me so proud. I love you. Good night." I lifted my head. It was midafternoon. Why hadn't she recorded the rest of the book?

When the tape finished it went around and around, the end unmoored and flapping. It flapped while I got up and stood in the center of the room, waiting for something, anything, to happen. It flapped while the neighbor woman, Mrs. McCrady, banged at my door and demanded I come downstairs. By the time she managed to push through I was out my window, up on the roof. As a last resort she left a dish of canned peaches with Miracle Whip on top, on the window ledge, and I remember laughing a little at her, to think I was like a mouse who will come in to sniff, and then eat, the poison.

At the funeral I sat in the front row next to my father, fiddling with the frayed end of my black plastic belt. He prodded me when it was time to stand and sing. "Sleep, my love and peace attend thee, All through the night." Everyone around me was blubbering as they tried to sing,

> *Angels ever round thee,*
> *All through the night.*
> *They should of all fear disarm thee,*
> *no forebodings should alarm thee,*
> *They will let no peril harm thee*
> *All through the night.*

I stared at the blurred words in the hymnal, hating the angels for taking my mother, and I thought then that I wouldn't possibly survive to be an adult, that I couldn't carry the thing in my heart that weighed so much and hurt, that I couldn't possibly carry the load through all the years ahead of me.

At first I listened to the tape quite a bit. The flat black box on my dresser called to me. "It's mother. I'm here." I had to slide off my bed, had to pull the recorder to the outlet, and thread the brown ribbon through its slots. I knew that if I could look into the closet fast enough she would be behind the dresses, kneeling in the clutter of old shoes, with her arms outstretched. I flung open the door. Nothing. Nothing but the small thin words coming like worms out of the box in the corner of the room. The voice was out of breath, reading with forced expression. My mother hadn't really been interested in the book after all. She had been in a wheelchair with a headband holding back what was left of her hair. The last time I'd seen her she had stretched out her veiny, trembling hand and then let it fall to her side, too tired, too tired to want me. It had been a trial to her to read the two chapters, each word an aggravation. I put the tape recorder in its yellow case at the back of the closet and shut the door. I sat on the bed and stared down the wall across the room. My mother was curled up like a cat inside the tape recorder, clawing at the holes, waiting for me to open the lid.

Aunt Kate, whom I had met briefly when I was four, was suddenly and improbably in our kitchen, cooking and quilting, making paper, doing our wash, working terrible jigsaw puzzles that were reproductions of Surrealist paintings. She wasn't really my aunt, but a childhood friend of my mother's. Years later I found out that she'd been living in Sweden and that she had not been told about my mother's illness. She had no idea when she received an envelope in Stockholm that it was going to contain my mother's last will and testament. She was fifty-one and half my size, with gray hair cut in a bob. The angels themselves could not have come up with a better replacement. She had been married once, very young, without success. Aunt Kate packed up her life in Stockholm, moved into the attic room in our house, and lived with us until she died of a heart attack, the summer before I went to college. It was an unlikely arrangement but my mother must have known that it would work. My father retreated into his gears and gadgets, into his study, where the liquor cabinet was kept. He was like a reclusive border, taking his meals on a tray in front of the news, ducking out in the morning to the office, coming home late. Aunt Kate treated me, not exactly like the daughter she'd never had, but like an old friend she'd traveled a great distance to find.

My freshman year in college I used to take the tape my mother had made for me to the music listening room. There the music students all sat in a row listening to Copland, Monteverdi, Handel, and Schubert, following their scores and chewing gum. I had been so lonesome and I wanted to hear from someone I knew. My mother's voice came from the machine into my earphones. Her words, at full volume and in stereo, ran down my throat like water. I closed my eyes against college. I shut out everything in the present, waiting to be filled. All I needed was her voice to guide me through the darkness.

Chapter Seven

———

THE MORNING AFTER I'D met Theresa in the orchard Nellie got up at five o'clock, kissed Howard good-bye, and left for Minneapolis. She was admirable and courageous, going off to Rumania to tend sick babies for two months with a team of doctors and teachers. I had skulked around the back door the night before until she was out of the kitchen, and when the coast was clear I'd made a beeline for our bed. I'd gone straight to sleep without apologizing or thanking her. And I hadn't gotten up early to send her off either. I had been rude and ungrateful. While I was dozing in broad daylight, hours after she'd gone, I dreamed that I might write to tell her that I was going to try to follow her good advice and look on the bright side. Emma came whimpering into the room because the figurine that had come in her Happy Meal had been stepped on and was mutilated. She buried her head in my arm and said, "I wish you could get up. It's hot. I want to swim today. Why can't we swim?" Before I could think what to say she pulled away, knowing I wouldn't respond, and went to find Claire.

I got up that morning only because Howard told me I must. He came into the bedroom after his chores. "Emma is hungry," he declared. "Claire's diaper is soaked. Either you feed them or I feed them." As always, he spoke in clipped sentences which went right to the heart of the matter. He was so good at fixing and managing, tending to details. The barn was as beautiful and clean a barn as could be found in all of Christendom. He pulled back the sheet, sat down, and put his hand over mine. "Why isn't Claire toilet-trained? I'm having trouble with the irrigation rig again." He pulled me up and held me with his arm around my shoulders. "Alice," he said, "I need your help."

I had forgotten that I was going to be naked. I looked at my feet first, and then at my breasts and my stomach and thighs and knees. I was a ghostly color, gray, as if I'd been stored in formaldehyde. I thought of the leg of lamb that we'd eaten a few days earlier. Nellie had put on my soiled canvas apron and gouged the bone from the meat, made gashes all over and stuffed them with slivered garlic, and then put the bleeding slab over hot coals. Sheep were animals who knew weariness and rest, hunger and thirst, the pleasure of a rotten melon. They had the instinct to care for their young, an instinct which looked exactly like love. And then I thought for an instant of Lizzy in her coffin in the ground. How strange to put someone in the ground! I couldn't put Emma or Claire in a box and bury either one without losing my mind. I would still think of that body as the person, as the child who would be terrified and alone and smothered under all that dirt. I saw out the window Lizzy's bones lying under her party dress, her short toe bones inside the patent leather shoes. No, I said to myself. Not that. I had to quickly shake my head as if I might possibly work like an Etch A Sketch, the contents of my mind forever erased with one or two jerks.

"Did I tell you?" Howard said, leaning over to find a clean undershirt in his drawer, "that a traveling salesman appeared out of nowhere after the funeral, trying to sell coffin insurance to Dan and Theresa?"

"Coffin insurance?" I said. "Well, you never know. You can't be too careful."

"What?" Howard asked.

"Nothing."

"What did you say?"

"What?" I asked. I sat down. I was naked except for my socks. I had forgotten the order of things. I was a mother, and mothers were supposed to rise to the occasion because they had children to care for; they were to cook the stew in a crisis because there was no alternative to nourishment other than death. We were not to die until the youngest child graduated from college. Howard, how can I cook the stew when I don't know what clothes to put on next? I wanted to ask. Maybe it was better if the children died first, because then a person could relax, stop worrying, and just take up grief.

"What are you doing, Alice?"

He occasionally said my name as if he were a viper, drawing out the *S* sound. There was a plastic tub on the dresser, underneath one of Howard's dirty shirts. I had nothing on but my socks. That was butter, now soft and rancid, in the tub. I hadn't remembered coming in the bedroom on the day Lizzy drowned, but I must have.

"Your children need you, Alice." He hissed under his breath, right into my face, "Alicccce." I could see that he was trying to bully me back to health. I might have done the same if he lay dying. Emma was watching television and calling for us, and Claire was banging a cereal bowl on the kitchen table.

I took a breath. I was going to open my mouth and bellow across the mountains, "I DON'T KNOW WHAT TO DO." The echo would come back, Knowwhattodo, whattodo, whattodoooo. Instead a noise came up from my throat, as if a rope had been made tight around my neck. I didn't have the strength to dress and go down to the kitchen, and the bed looked so beautiful, stripped of the top sheet, like a clean white raft. I sank back down wanting to chart a course, to have it take me someplace.

"Shit," Howard whispered. He rarely swore and therefore his curses always carried a punch. "What's going on? Bear up, Alice. Go get breakfast. Keep in motion, for the sake of Emma and Claire. Keep in motion. Say that to yourself."

He forced open our sticky drawers and pulled out my underwear, a brassiere, a gray T-shirt, and a pair of shorts. Then he yanked me up and began dressing me. He lifted my feet and put them through the underpants holes. It was important, I considered, to wake Emma and Claire every morning and feed them, and make them rest in the afternoon, so that they could grow up and have children, and make them get up and feed them, and tell them to rest, so that they could grow up and have children. That was called motion, and it was good. I drew the underpants from my ankles to my waist. I remembered long ago lying with my head on my hands on mercifully hot cement, watching the women and Aunt Kate swimming laps at rest time at the public pool. The women all looked the same in their tight bathing caps that mashed their foreheads into their eyes. The back of their legs were mottled like cottage cheese. They swam languorously, their dimpled arms coming over their heads in the crawl. When they got to the other end they turned on their backs and came kicking home. I had eaten my breakfast and gone to bed, perhaps had a brief teenage moment of absolute beauty, and woken up into one of the middle-age swimmers.

"I have a floral bathing suit with a skirt and padded cups," I said.

"I'm not going to let you do this." He was talking to me calmly while he put the shirt over my head. "No one blames you. You understand that." He took hold of my hands and stuck them through the armholes. "You're making yourself feel responsible for an accident that could have happened to anyone. Did you call Theresa? You do the shorts. I'll get Claire. Emma needs you. She doesn't know what is going on. She needs you, Alice."

He was speaking just the way my father would have if he'd ever really talked to me.

"And brush your hair. Please," he called from down the hall. "Dave and Phil are coming out this morning."

I puzzled over that information. Dave and Phil. When he reappeared with Claire in his arms I was still trying to think.

"What, Alice?"

Just as he was asking in his kind, kind voice I remembered Dave, the soil scientist from the University of Wisconsin, and Phil, his graduate student. They were monitoring our farm for foxglove and earthworms, phosphorous and nitrogen.

"I did talk to Theresa," I said.

"Great. That's great."

She had said at first that she couldn't pass the time of day with me, and then she had spilled over with news as if she hadn't talked with anyone for weeks. If I'd been Theresa I would have turned the love she felt for me into hate; I would have quite easily and naturally fed the festering thing. Is it possible, I would have liked to ask Howard, if I'd had the courage—do you think it's possible that she'll forgive me?

I went through the motions of breakfast. Milk on the table, spoons at each place mat, Life, Grape-Nuts, Cheerios, and cornflakes in a line, to suit everyone's fancy. After we ate I held Claire in my lap, Emma at my side, and we read from our illustrated book of fairy tales. Next I sat on the floor and dressed and undressed the baby dolls. Their miniature white plastic shoes said on the bottom: "Made in China." Wrinkled, bent Chinese women were sitting in an airless factory in Hong Kong stitching up dolls' shoes so our Wisconsin girl children could role play. I closed my eyes, longing for some place like the primeval forest, a smell of bees and honey and first growth, a place where animals live together serenely because they are afraid of their own strength. When Emma and Claire started to tug at the same doll dress and shout at each other, I put my hands to my ears, my head to my knees, and splatted out a car-horn noise.

"When I was your mom," Claire said, coming to me and putting a clammy hand on my arm, "and you were a baby, I beed sweet and nice."

"That's wonderful," I said, reaching out to touch her shiny dark little cap of hair.

"I was never mad when I was your mom."

Maybe Claire knew best. Maybe she was the reincarnation of my mother, Barbara Gardner, who had died so early in life of lung cancer. Maybe my mother died willingly because she knew full well that she was going to return to earth as my second child. My mother had decided that it was better to be an infant again than to be married to my father, and finally, then, she planted herself in my womb.

Emma piped, "When you were a baby we put a pacifier in your mouth to keep you quiet."

Maybe Lizzy was already planning her return, sitting in a waiting room with magazines and soft music and potted lemon trees growing up to the ceiling. I thought of Theresa and Father Albert walking out into the empty parking lot after drinking their cherry sodas, the two of them embracing under the three-pronged fluorescent light, Theresa feeling the blaze within her at once, what seemed to her to be the love of God.

At lunch, "dinner," Howard called it without much affectation, he and the children and I sat at the table and ate. Most of us had whole-wheat bread with Cheddar cheese, warmed in the microwave, and milk, and slices of store-bought honeydew melon and a few limp leaves of lettuce from the garden. Bad Emma had white bread and butter, no cheese at all, and no melon either, because once, two years before, she'd been served a piece with a beetle crawling along the rind. Claire ate everything as is. We were the last dairy family eating Dinner, Prairie Center, Circa 1990. Although Howard hadn't told me, I knew that the cow with the prolapsed uterus had died because I'd seen her trussed up with chains behind the tractor. They would come and get her, take her away to a plant for glue. He was glowering at me for something I must have said. I was staring out of the window thinking about how I had never planned to live this long, how in my child's mind I was sure I was never going to reach the age of eighteen.

After lunch the team from the university came. There were several of them, bright, responsible people wearing their co-op grocery-store T-shirts, bringing along snacks that had been purchased in bulk. The women looked like I would have if I'd stayed in Ann Arbor. They wore their hairy legs and underarms as a badge signifying their higher power of reasoning and their disinterest in conventional standards of beauty. The women of Prairie Center, as a demographic entity, shaved or waxed all the way up to their bikini line. It was later that afternoon when Emma and Claire and I were standing out by the mailbox at the roadside that we saw the Collinses go past. Dan was driving, Theresa was in front next to him, and Audrey was in the back seat. They were going to climb and climb, trying to find awe within themselves. Theresa had said she was afraid to go and that she couldn't tell Dan about her fears, but Dan was probably struggling too, over the same appalling thought: She isn't dead, because she can't be, and she'll come home to a deserted house. I lifted my hand to wave. He saw me and drove on. Theresa was bent over her map. Audrey pressed her nose to the glass and opened and shut her fist.

I left the girls playing in the sandbox in the yard, and went upstairs to lie down by the fan for just a minute. Next I knew Howard was shaking me, saying, "Wake up. Go downstairs and make supper. Please."

We each had our own clocks on either side of the bed. They were old wind-up clocks from our Ann Arbor days. His was a Big Ben and mine a Little Ben. Naturally the Big Ben's ticking was lower than mine, and louder, the father of the clock family. Mine was staccato, shrill, as if it was panicked by the passage of time. They didn't tick in sync, and Howard's was always set fast. I remember waking up and thinking the clocks were sparring, that they would battle over their precious minutes and the way to tick until they exhausted themselves and wound down and just quit.

I went to bed at 7:40 his time, 7:30 my time, listening to "Lucy in the Sky with Diamonds," on the clarinet in the next room. Emma and Claire were floating down the hall in their summer nighties. Howard was proving his mettle as a father, make no mistake. He was so much better at handling their spats, and wrestling, and telling stories. It probably made sense for me to plow and cultivate and plant and repair, and for him to manage the children. I closed my eyes until it was the next day, and he was shaking me again, putting my own clothes in my hands, guiding me with unending patience, telling me what arm to put in which hole.

"I know you, Alice," he said, setting my tennis shoes next to the bed. "Someday you'll turn this into a story. You'll tell a group of dinner guests about the time you were so depressed I had to talk you through dressing. You'll say something about how I had to dust your feet off to put your socks on."

I squinted at him, trying to think what he was saying about this time turning into a joke at a later date. If I'd felt slightly better I might have punched him in the mouth. The only dinner guests we ever had were Dan and Theresa. There was yellow lint stuck between every single one of my toes. I lay down again and closed my eyes.

"Alice—Alice." He hunched down, and I imagined that he was going to beg and plead, use Russian diminutives to lure me out of bed, sing to me, offer money, a vacation, a diamond. "Alice," he said, "we can't change what happened." He was leaning over me, brushing the hair out of my face.

I was just about to rise up a little, hold him around the waist, press my cheek against his stomach, tell him that everyone seemed monstrous to me, ready to devour me in one bite. Howard, I'm trembling—can't you feel it?

"I don't know exactly how people get through this kind of thing," he was saying, "but I know we have to carry on. It might be a good idea to see someone, a professional. I don't know much about what's available for help. You can't get out of bed, you haven't talked to anyone. Aren't you supposed to go to the school board meeting tonight? Weren't they going to discuss your contract? If you could see yourself you'd realize how frustrating it—" He turned and called into the hall. "What, Emma?"

"They'll lynch me in the inner sanctum," I murmured.

"What?" Howard said.

"Could you please come here for one short minute?" Emma shouted.

"What did you say, Alice?"

"No," I said, "nothing." When he was out of the room I eased back down on the bed.

That night I put on a light blue skirt and one of Howard's new white T-shirts that had yet to go yellow in the wash, and a small straw hat that was unraveling. I drove with great caution along the back roads to the grade-school cafeteria in Blackwell. I didn't want to exceed twenty miles per hour because my feet seemed to be unattached to the rest of my body. The principal had sent me a letter a few weeks before explaining that there were parents who wanted to volunteer in various capacities in the following school year. The administration and the PTA had noted that there were seasons when my office was a bottleneck and that it might be helpful to have a parent dispensing over the counter medication. Blackwell Elementary was a titanic K-through-Eight school, the last in the state, with nearly seven hundred students. It was true that my office was sometimes chaotic. They had told me that it was important to be present at the meeting so that the board could discuss those prospects and also go through my contract.

The five board members were all men in the prime of their lives. One was a sod farmer with fingers like rolls of quarters, one a dentist, one did something obscure with imports, one designed watering systems for lab animals, and the last sold security systems. They looked strong. They could very well hoist me up to the street light, tie me there and leave me hanging until morning.

Maybe Howard was right, and therapy would help me. Maybe I could get some medication that would make me sing Tra-la-la from morning to evening. The board members were shuffling through their papers and whispering to one another as I took my seat in the cafeteria. There were other teachers in the next aisle, including Luther Tritz, the band director. Perhaps something had come up in his contract too; perhaps there were parents who wanted to conduct or teach the youngsters tonette fingering. Luke was a short, stocky, orange-haired man who looked as if he bathed compulsively in carrot juice. I had not gotten around to telling Theresa about my recent enthusiasm for old Luther Tritz. As far as I knew he was not capable of laughter. Once, at a staff appreciation dinner, I had seen a ripple appear on his orange forehead when the assistant principal made a tasteless joke. I used to walk slowly past the music room in the morning so that I could watch him taking the red music folders from his uncluttered metal cabinet, and then put two at each stand. I had not yet explained to Theresa that the fascination I had with Mr. Luther Tritz, all the way down to his pure Episcopalian heart, was nothing more than an intellectual exercise. It posed the problem of the upstanding community leader with a wife, five children, and a recreational vehicle feeling something only natural for the blond-haired grade-school nurse. There was something so fetching about him when he played the tuba in the marching band and conducted simultaneously. And a man who had a job that started at 8:30 in the morning and ended promptly at 3:15 couldn't help but be irresistible.

Catherine Trumper, from the local newspaper, was sitting next to him. She had supposedly had an affair with the high-school football coach during a season when she filled in for the sportswriter. She had flowered in her extreme youth and then gotten fat, apparently without realizing. She had on black high heels and a tight blue and purple striped dress made from oil by-products. Her partially exposed freckled bosom, confined in its push-up bra, was barking and whining to get out. Surely he had sense enough not to be attracted to someone as blatantly lascivious as Catherine Trumper. There was so much of her she was lapping over into Luke himself. He looked straight ahead, as if she could press against him all day, all night, and he wouldn't notice and wouldn't care.

The august board members were discussing asbestos removal. The schools in the district were riddled with asbestos and the water had sulfur in it and smelled like rotten eggs. Luther Tritz was watching me; I could feel his washed-out blue eyes on my face. When I turned to meet him straight on, presto he swung around to look behind himself at absolutely nothing. He knew why they had summoned me—he was in on it, too! Catherine Trumper didn't even have to lean over to talk into his orange ear; she was telling him that I had meant to drown Lizzy, that she had heard from a reliable source, a woman with heavy shoes and crusted pancake makeup, that I had locked Lizzy out of the house, that I had screamed at her to go to the pond, that I had tied a brick to her ankle and then pushed her in. I looked like I was doing artificial respiration at the side of the pond, but I was really untying the brick, trying to undo the knot in the string, trying to cover it up.

Luther Tritz was nodding his head. He guessed he knew right along that I was unbalanced because I used to stand in the doorway and gawk at the boys screwing their woodwinds together.

"Mr. Chairman," Catherine Trumper called out, "can you dollarize that asbestos removal for me? I didn't catch those figures you were quoting."

"Well, Cathy," Mr. Chairman began. They would dollarize indefinitely while I undressed Luke from top to bottom. I wondered if he was fuzzy from head to foot. I could see him so clearly in the shower, his orange hair slicked down with water. "Oh Luke," I would say to him. "Luke, Luke, Luke, you dear sweet wet Luke. Can you smile for me, Luke?" It would be a lifetime job, trying to get one little grin out of the band director.

David Henskin, the principal, was eyeing me, trying to gauge if the rumors he'd heard were true. He was at the end of his career, and yet he was still a formidable man, with steel-colored hair; the small black-framed glasses that were known, when I was small, as "retard glasses"; and the fresh, smooth, smelly skin of a man who has to shave more than once a day. He looked in my direction and then he snapped to attention because they were moving down the agenda to the issue of the boiler. He was in his element when it came to the boiler. It was old. He loved the apparatus, but the new models were also beautiful as well as efficient. Everyone on the board was knowledgeable about heating and cooling systems. The men were warming up on the ruined and dangerous mechanicals so that when the time came to deal with the school nurse who couldn't do CPR they would be prepared. If Luke could just give me a sign, a small flicker of recognition; then I would know he didn't think I had meant to drown Lizzy.

He was looking right over the top of my head at the chalkboard. I remember how sick that made me feel, as if I was in a boxcar that suddenly lurched to a stop. I covered my face with my hands to try to steady myself. I couldn't bear the smell of school lunches, years and years of school lunches, and floor wax, new basal readers, workbooks, gym classes, bad boys, obedient girls. This was the world that, with a great deal of luck, my children would inherit. They were aching to grow up. They would think, as they got older, that their adulthood was going to be filled with an embarrassment of riches: ice cream after every meal; sexual intercourse, mystical in nature, morning and evening; happy hour with wine coolers, all with no repercussions. In fact, the grown-up world was sitting at school-board meetings while the men ordered the boiler of their dreams, and Catherine Trumper wrote down everything they said. The adult world was fabricating lust for the likes of Luther Tritz, who was probably extravagant only in his organizational skills. Emma and Claire would no doubt live in a society where it was no longer possible to turn away from the daunting problems many of us had ignored and insisted were none of our business. The garbage and disease would come crashing into my girls' yard like waves coming to shore, along with the lost and broken and heartless people, shouldering their semiautomatic weapons. Instead of guiding our children in their interests, instead of sharing with them the fascination of history and music, we should prepare them for the cruelties, for coping with famine and menacing gangs.

I looked up then, out the far window, and there, just within sight, the sun was going down across the river. It was dull red, no longer shining over the land, its rays brought home to roost, contained within its sphere. The sky was streaked with lavender, a pulsing pale blue, purple and smudged pink and orange melding into one another all the way to the horizon. How I longed to rush away from that cafeteria, into the cool of the dusk, into the color, the color—after weeks and weeks of blasting heat and sunlight that had bleached the landscape to a lusterless gold.

Luther Tritz was staring blankly at nothing, when he could have been enjoying the scene out the window. He had probably become deaf after his years listening to junior-high students channeling their pent-up energy into the slender mouthpiece of a brass instrument. He probably didn't laugh anymore because he couldn't hear what was being said. There was not much pleasure left for him because his senses were shot. I used to imagine that he looked at me across the parking lot in the mornings with a gleam in his orange-lidded eyes. Now he believed that I had been about to take Audrey to the pond to give her the same treatment, but that Mrs. Glevitch came to the door and within minutes had her Mary Kay samples spread out at our kitchen table. Mrs. Glevitch—and it wasn't the first time —had saved the life of an innocent victim. He believed the postmortem had revealed bruises all over Lizzy's body, that I had taken a large stick and—NO! I wasn't going to lose my grip, I wasn't! I wasn't! I would leave the people in the cafeteria, Luke, Catherine, David Henskin, leave them, never think of them again, leave them to their distasteful thoughts about me, their thoughts about their cars, their games, their lawns, their vacations. I wasn't going to think about awful, ugly things, was going to dive nose first into something exquisite! —Thirst after beauty, seek it out while everything crass and rude and demeaning and dark falls dead like flies in beauty's wake. I was going to think of Lizzy as the lovely child who babbled and fluttered, made of flesh instead of rotting away—

Look at the sunset! I heard myself cry out.

The board members, the administration, the honest and responsible teachers and citizens in the audience, and the members of the press, continued to listen to a consultant talk about how difficult it was going to be to remove the oil tank that was buried under the school yard. They hadn't heard me. I was having that same problem I'd had at the hospital, speaking under a curse so that no one heard me. I didn't know if I had shouted or not. I wanted so much to tell them to look out the window, at the sunset. We had all forgotten color. Violet. Pink. Purple. They were displayed in front of us now, like a primer, to teach us what we had forgotten. I pushed my chair from the table and headed past the front row, in front of the table where the Powers sat, the board and administration, in front of the man who was trying to continue his presentation. I had both hands over my nose and mouth as if I might be going to vomit. Everyone was staring at me with their jaws unhinged. To leave in the middle of a discussion about the boiler was unthinkable. It was suddenly

so funny, the boiler, the oil tank, Luke and Catherine, the seriousness of
the evening and the splendor of the sky. I clutched my rib cage and went
laughing out the door, and laughing down the hall, and into the girl's
room, and against the bathroom stall door, and laughing sitting on the
toilet, and laughing into the sink, and laughing until I felt as if I'd been
socked. Stars bloomed over my head like fireworks.

When I came out of the bathroom I nearly walked into the woman who
was standing right outside, by the drinking fountain. I shied back into the
door.

"Mrs. Goodwin," she said. After the four years that I'd been working
in a school I hadn't gotten used to the fact that grown people addressed
each other as Mrs. and Mr. For me, Mrs. Goodwin would always mean
Nellie. "I'm Detective Grogan from the Investigation Unit in Racine, and
this," she said, turning to the policeman who was just coming from the
boy's room, "is Officer Melby."

I think I nodded, sizing them up, and started to walk away. It didn't
seem to mean anything at the moment, that two police officers were
speaking to me, or that an introduction implied a beginning. I was sick
and tired, had had enough. She was dressed in street clothes, in beige
slacks and a white sleeveless shirt. He, in his black pants, the billy club,
the badge, was hard at first to see for himself. As a child I had felt that
nuns and policemen did not inhabit their uniforms, that the outfit stood as
if on its own power. But Melby was a handsome man inside his suit, big,
brown-eyed, very white clear skin, fine front teeth. The woman followed
me, falling into step and saying, "We'd like to talk to you for a minute, if
you don't mind."

"Me?" I said, stopping, leaning against a locker.

"Just for a minute." She smiled. She was shorter than I was, with
curly blond hair, some of it falling into ringlets. She had blue eyes and
freckles across her nose and the continuous smile of someone who wants
to please. I needed to go home because my head was pounding and
everything looked so awfully clear that even the dim hall light was killing
me. She kept smiling, winningly, as if she felt we might be friends. "We're
trying to get some information about Robbie Mackessy," she said.

I remember going limp, almost falling down. They weren't going to ask me about Lizzy because I hadn't meant to let her out the door. They knew she had run down the lane while I was upstairs for hardly any time to speak of. Robbie Mackessy was in trouble, that was all. "Uhhh," I said, gently banging my head against the locker.

"Not pleasant memories, I take it?" she said.

"I've tried to forget," I said sarcastically, as if it was funny.

"You had difficulties with him?"

I looked up at the ceiling tiles that were decorated with straight rows of black dots. I'd known him too long already. I used to crawl home from school after a hard morning to the dream world of the farm, to the back-breaking work that seemed to me as old as time itself. I'd pull up carrots and it could have been someone's hair I was yanking on. There was comfort in knowing absolutely what needed to be done.

"Difficulties," I said. "You could say that." She was so pretty and petite, and she had a locket around her neck. And my head hurt and the dark was coming on and I wanted to go home more than anything and go to sleep and sleep off days and days and sleep off life.

"How long have you known him?"

I had to think. He had been in the county pre-kindergarten program when he was five, and in kindergarten when he was six. "It must be two years," I said.

"Uh huh." She nodded into her pad of paper. The other officers down at headquarters probably called her Grogan with a measured amount of tenderness, and she probably liked that, made her feel at once like one of the men and at the same time like the only girl in the family. They couldn't abuse her because she was delicate, yes, but strong enough to demand careful handling. "You probably developed quite a relationship with him then?"

I laughed, at the idea of a relationship.

"No?" She put her long red fingernail into her mouth and tilted her head from left to right.

I was about to say that he was afraid of me, but that wasn't true. Robbie Mackessy had never seemed to be afraid of anyone. I couldn't very well say that we had never gotten along, that he was a disturbed boy, cruel, hard, who enraged me every time I saw him. Officer Grogan had a Pre-Raphaelite beauty but I conceded that if she was going to be a cop then the name Grogan suited her. "I guess kids are usually afraid of the school nurse," I said.

"Afraid?"

"I'm a tall person with the reputation for having a needle in hand. The youngest ones are nervous because they believe I'm going to give them a shot, even though of course I don't do that at school. Some of them know me because I'm one of the shot ladies at the free clinic."

"That's quite a label to live with."

I wanted to go to sleep against the locker. The officers would never know the half of it. Robbie had the unbounded energy of someone who is chronically angry. He used to come in my office, stand at my desk, and stare at me. Maybe there doesn't seem much harm in being stared at, but I could have told the officer about how I never knew what he was thinking, or what would come next. It unnerved me so much I often had to leave the room and dance, a few tight little steps, outside of the office. It was what he wanted, for me to come undone. If I asked him what was troubling him he'd stare at me. If I asked him to let me take a look at his throat or his ears he'd stare, and if I said, "Well then, go back to your room," he would stand and stare. If I ignored him and went about my duties he might still stand and stare, derision in the affected blankness of his face, and then he often made an inaudible but clearly derogatory comment about my movements or clothing or style. If I suggested that we take the short walk down to the principal's office so that Mr. Henskin could examine him he'd shrug and start off, as if he were the one who was taking me for punishment.

I didn't want to think about him, wouldn't think about him because I had other sad affairs with which to occupy my mind, as well as the setting of the sun and my trip down the highway to get home. "I have to go," I said to the officers. "My husband has chores and I—"

"Just a few more questions, please, Mrs. Goodwin. The more we know about Robbie the better we can assist him."

"What sort of trouble is it?" I thought to ask.

"We aren't at liberty to comment, I'm afraid," she said. "We were hoping you could tell us if you noticed any signs at the end of the year, if he seemed anxious, if there were any behavior changes you noted."

I tried to remember. I shut my eyes, falling into a gray sleep. "No more than usual," I whispered. I didn't care if they couldn't hear. They'd have to come so close they'd have to hold me to listen. "The parents send him day after day to school sick," I maundered. "He's a baby, really, at five, even at six. The parents are legally entitled to school and the school is obligated to care for him. Robbie went to the Latch Key program too. He was in that building twelve hours a day sometimes, from six to six. It must have felt like a cage to him, a dumping ground, a kitty carrier. I don't think they let you dream in those places." I opened my eyes and looked at the two of them, and again I felt like laughing, because they were listening so intently to my aimless thoughts.

"What kind of sickness did he have?" Grogan asked.

"Sore throats, ear infections, the common cold, allergies, bee stings, influenza, chicken pox, skinned knees. He had strep throat about five times last year. I had the feeling that his mother was, well, sloppy about medication." I was being only too kind. "Strep throat can be quite serious," I said, frowning like a concerned health-care worker.

I had once gone to the guidance counselor about him because I could never get him to take his Suprax. He spit it up in my face or on the floor and I know for a fact that one bottle of about six ounces costs fifty dollars. Mrs. Watson, her dyed beet-red hair pulled severely into a bun, was a broad, square woman with all the softness and curves of a Sherman tank. She was supposed to be a resource person, but she was always thundering at the children and the staff alike, as if what you'd come for and what she had to give away was something bitter, for your own good. She said to me, "Go back to your office and make him take it. It's medicine, he needs it, you are responsible for making sure he gets it down." David Henskin was an older, remote person who also gave the message that we were to take care of our own problems. I used to have nightmares that Robbie missed his medication and died standing by my desk.

"Robbie destroyed my idea that I could help, or make a difference," I said, apparently out loud.

"How do you mean?" Grogan asked.

If she knew Robbie at all she would know what I meant. It was obvious the way he spat at you, called you names, busted you to pieces. It occurred to me only then that maybe they knew what I had done. Of course! They had come to question me because I had slapped him once, last year. I had nearly convinced myself that it hadn't happened but Grogan saw—she knew. She was shrewd behind her Tupperware Party face. Stay calm, be calm, I ordered. It hadn't been too hard, that slap. I had hit him and that actually was the truer reason I hadn't gone to the principal, for fear Robbie would tell. I had been composed since that day months before, when I had struck him across the cheek. I had been sure that I would be fired, that I was finished, that my license would be revoked. I had waited, day after day, week after week, month after month. He had stared at me with such scorn, stared until I walked over to him and slapped him back and forth. He had stood with his arms at his side, continuing to stare, as if I hadn't gotten anywhere near him. I hadn't told anyone about it, not even Howard.

"No," I said, "I have to go now." I couldn't abide the dark hallway, or the men on the school board, or Robbie and his mother, or Mrs. Watson and Luther Tritz and pretty Grogan and handsome, dumb Melby. *Bless me, Grogan, for I have sinned.*

"Are you okay?" Grogan asked. "You didn't look too good at that meeting."

I hadn't noticed them in the cafeteria, but they must have been watching. They had been spying, because they wanted to get me. I'd slapped Robbie and been so careless Lizzy had drowned. "I'm not well," I said. I felt woozy and I had to touch the wall with both hands to stop it from whirling.

"I'm sorry to keep you standing," she said. "Why don't we sit on the bench at the end of the hall there. This really won't take too much longer."

"I can't stay!" I shouted. "I'm sick, don't you understand?"

"We just have a few more things—"

"I'm having a complete nervous breakdown! Do you want to know the truth? I'm having a complete nervous breakdown and no one will let me do it in peace and quiet." I couldn't hold back the tears any longer. "Oh God," I cried, as the floodgates burst.

"What's the matter with you?" Grogan asked sternly.

"I hurt everybody!" I sobbed. I was thinking of Nellie just then, thinking what an ungrateful wretch I was. I started to run away backwards, and then I turned and hurtled through the door. When I got to the car I jammed the keys in the ignition and screeched away. The sound, the howling coming from my mouth, was such a strange, loony noise, I had to stop making it to listen, to know that I was calling for Howard.

Chapter Eight

————

WHEN I GOT HOME the sky was not yet dark, but a luminous blue, the color and quality of neither day nor night. A few stars, a planet, were shining. I went upstairs to our room, undressed, and got into bed. Over the burr of the fan I could hear my heart beating its muffled private thumps. I had had a run in with Mrs. Mackessy once, before I'd smacked Robbie. I could talk myself into thinking I hadn't really hurt him, make small adjustments to the picture to alter the angle of my hand and the force of the stroke. I had also convinced myself that the scene with Mrs. Mackessy didn't amount to anything fearsome. She had come to pick up Robbie at noon, to take him away early. He had been sick to his stomach all morning and naturally no one had been home or within reach. I was sure that he'd been ill earlier, before he got to school. I had sat with him for three hours, swabbing his hot forehead, holding him while he vomited. He was too miserable to struggle, too worn out for mischief, and for once he seemed to know that he needed me. He didn't have the strength to lie down after he'd sit up to retch, and I'd have to set him back in place, on the cot.

My rage at Robbie Mackessy's mother had smoldered as I tended her boy. I can truthfully say that I felt for the child, who had seemed to me, on so many occasions, to already be ruined and well beyond rehabilitation. Mrs. Mackessy had sent him to school sick because she didn't care much about him, because she assumed he was the school's problem and not hers. At noon, from my office, I saw her slowly getting out of her car, smoothing her dress, tossing her head so that her golden mane fell down her back. I watched her walk down the hall in an intricate gait like a horse that has spent its life learning dressage. She picked up her little feet and set them carefully down starting at the toe and working through to the instep and heel, all the while turning her head from side to side, her hair flicking back and forth over her shoulders. She was fifteen minutes late to pick him up so she could take him and dump him elsewhere. She was the manager of a steak house in Blackwell, no doubt a complex job involving hiring and ordering food, arranging schedules, as well as hostessing. That day she was wearing a conservative boxy blue dress with thick red piping around the collar and cuffs and hem. She had gold sandals with straps that crisscrossed, Jesus sandals in gold lamé.

"What's he got?" she demanded.

"The same thing that was wrong with him when you sent him to school," I said.

She pressed her lips together, and narrowed her eyes to look at me.

"When you have children," I went on, trying to sound professional and dispassionate, "occasionally you have to think of them first, before yourself."

She stepped toward me and said into my face, "You mind your own goddamn business."

I smiled as hard as I could. "It's your negligence that keeps me employed," I said. "I suppose I should thank you, Mrs. Mackessy." It was pointless to fight with her, I knew, but I had waited too long, itching for battle. Robbie had finally fallen asleep and she breezed past me, into the cubicle to get him.

"He's dehydrating," I called into the inner room. "If you are interested in the life of your child you'd better get him to a doctor." I went closer in and I said then what I never should have. I said, "If he keeps coming to school sick I'll report you to— It's not right, that he's always so run down. I'll do that, Mrs. Mackessy. I'll report you."

"I'll report *you*," she snarled, coming past me with Robbie slung over her shoulder. She turned, almost cracking her son's head in the molding of the door. "I'll get you put away if anything is the matter with him."

It had been October, and I'd gone home at noon to help Howard harvest the corn. I remember how he scolded me for driving the tractor dangerously fast, and how cross I had been for several days, waiting for something to happen in the aftermath of Mrs. Mackessy's threat. I hadn't done anything wrong in my job except for disliking them so much. There was more than enough bad feeling between both of us to make me feel uneasy.

A wind was coming up again, and the branches from our maple tree were scraping against the house. I put the pillow over my head, wanting to sleep without seeing and hearing Mrs. Mackessy. I had hit Robbie Mackessy in December because he had stared and stared at me in such a hateful way. He had absorbed the blow. It was as if the sting had gone right to a spot inside where he stored his wounds. He had stood by my desk and for the first time he looked like a lovable child. He had been perfectly still as I struck. When I stepped back his cheeks were dewy, pink, and he smiled. Later on last summer I remembered that smile again, and it seemed that he must have known how much that single blow was going to hurt me. He smiled on and on as if the slap had been a kiss. He smiled as if he was going to take it home to his mother and then watch: She would prance down the hall, doing a high step, lifting her skirts, foaming at the mouth, fully confident in her ability to win the prize.

I was thinking the wrong kind of thoughts again. I should try to get well and be positive; I should think of the ravenous green worm who all of a sudden finds himself making a cocoon, drops off to sleep, and wakes a butterfly. Perhaps that was death, nothing more alarming than complete transformation. *Keep in motion. Think of beauty!* "Keep in motion," I whispered. "Keep in motion. Keep in motion."

I was almost asleep when Howard appeared in the doorway. I was dimly aware of him coming toward the bed, sitting down, and then putting his hand on my thigh. I rolled toward him, wondering how to explain the little debacle down at the school-board meeting.

"You got back early," he said. He stretched out next to me, with his boots on, moving his hands down my spine and over my rump. "How'd it go?"

I bit down hard on the foam pillow and said through my teeth, "Disaster."

He began kissing the nape of my neck, and he said so fondly, between the kisses, "How many times have I told you to chew with your mouth closed?"

He smelled of motor oil and he was literally breathing down my neck. I wasn't going to cry. I was going to ask him to stop trying to make me get well. I was not going to cry, and I was going to tell him about Grogan and Robbie, about Mrs. Mackessy, about Theresa down in the orchard. He might have thought I was waiting for him, the way I used to in the old days, waiting in bed in my black negligee, with my sultry, standoffish look that meant only one thing. I was wearing a white tank top and I was face down so that he could not see my expression. He was lifting my shirt in the back, routing out my breasts from underneath me when I turned and pushed him over with my pillow.

"Come on, Alice," he said, popping up and laughing. "You don't have to beat me to make me want you. I miss you. We need to play." I made a mental note to tell Theresa about him someday if we spoke again: Howard and I could be mortal enemies, but in the interest of sex we could frolic for half an hour and then resume guarding our fortresses. It was like the Germans and the Russians playing soccer on the battlefield on Christmas Day. I lay back thinking I was going to start crying after all, not ordinary tears, but a new brand, each the size of a small fresh water lake with vacation bungalows neck to neck. He was kissing my eyelids and my cheeks. I found my mouth moving against his in what I suppose was a kiss. I needed to tell him about Grogan, about how I wasn't sure why I was shivering even now, but that there was a specific reason which would undoubtedly be evident sooner or later. I put my hands in his thick, coarse black hair that was like some ancient medicinal holy stuff that could staunch blood and cause other general healing wonders. Maybe when he slept I could pull out a clump and wear it in a locket around my neck. It might make me well overnight. I felt as if the weight of Howard's heavy head was on my mouth. He had me now, as he kissed me, the weeks of sorrow and weariness and the dull ache after comfort, all of that pressure was on his lips, moving against my mouth. I remember the feeling coming over me, slowly, slowly, that this was how it went, the way down under the water, sinking and sinking, past the murky seaweed, looking up to the surface, looking up into the paddling feet of a turtle. I relaxed and I saw the moon come through the water and glare at me. My hair was floating in front of my face, just beyond the kiss, and my outstretched hands pawing the water were like someone else's, gesturing me to come closer. If we could stay that way forever; if we could stay filled to the brim and floating toward the darkness, never suffocating or dying . . .

It was in his fervor, when he started clutching at me, that I suddenly couldn't bear it, not any of it. He was coming down and down on me, over and over, crushing me as he thrust. I had to get out, couldn't stand the heat, couldn't endure his damp body, and still I hardly knew that I was heaving up, gasping for breath, knocking him over, leaping from the bed. I stood at the dresser, panting.

In the dark I could see him thrashing like he'd been shot and then curling up into himself. "Why are you doing this?" he said quietly.

I used to get pleasure from being the parents, making love with the door closed, getting up afterward and making sure the girls hadn't woken during the naughty interlude. Howard swabbed his stomach with a T-shirt, and then gathered his coveralls and his underwear and left the room with the things in his hands. He had never taken his boots off. I was still trying to breathe, having an idea finally what it might have felt like for Lizzy when the world overhead wavered and was gone.

The next morning Howard didn't come into the house until nine o'clock. I watched him walk across the lawn, and then stand outside the kitchen door as if he was uncertain about who lived at his address. His coveralls were flecked with hay. He looked as if he had taken the skin off of his face and not put it back on properly. I had no idea where he had slept. He was trying to get something from his pocket and after a moment he produced a washer, a screwdriver, and a piece of plastic tubing.

I went out onto the porch and crouched on the orange and red rag rug that he, in his color-blind pride, had bought for me at a church bazaar. The night before had been peculiar, certainly for many reasons, but not least because somehow in my mind Lizzy, Howard, Mrs. Mac-kessy, and Robbie had become joined, as tenuously but surely as a short string of paper people holding hands.

"In case you haven't noticed," Howard said, coming around the cor-ner, "we need food. The list is on the table."

I could feel my eyes going wider and wider, staring like a heifer will. "And congratulations," he added, "for getting up." The bad heifers never got over being skittish. I was tilting my head back and licking my lips.

"I can't stop to talk now and you can't either—" He nodded in the direction of Claire, through the door. She had taken a paring knife off the counter in the kitchen and was starting to spear a peach.

"Alice, will you look at Claire? I'm going now. Keep in motion, do you hear?" He moved to me, reaching for my shoulders, to shake me. I shuddered and backed off into the screen.

"What do you expect me to do?" It was a reasonable question. There was disease in the barn. The fence in the back pasture had come down, and the cows had been heading up to Vermont Acres. Lottie, the rebel cow, had stumbled into the backyard of a Mrs. Klinke, who had been hanging up her wash. Mrs. Klinke had responded as if it was King Kong who had peeked his face over her dish towels. The university team was coming again soon to do their research in spite of the fact that all of the crops were withering. I flew past Howard in a way that he would surely find dramatic and went up the stairs, back to our room, a place that I had always thought of as safe. He had suggested I use the words, "Keep in motion," as a sort of mantra. He was so very capable when it came to motion. He could smother me with his pillow and then make love to me somewhat against my will, drag me to a therapist, shove grocery lists in my hand, but he had no hold over my inner life. He couldn't stop me from standing on the vinyl tabletop at the school cafeteria and command-ing everyone to applaud Mother Nature. I had tried to follow his direc-tions because I trusted his instincts. I should have explained to him that I felt as if I had fallen from space into a well and that it would take more than a proffered human hand to get me out. The tub of melted, rancid butter had spilled on the dresser, onto the filthy runner. Emma was pummeling Claire in the living room. Howard shouted over the racket, "I'm leaving."

From the bedroom window I watched him walk past the barn to the machine shed where the tractor was parked. He stopped and looked up to the subdivision. He was listening for the neighborhood boys on their all-terrain vehicles. They rode back and forth over his alfalfa, mashing it down. When he caught them they denied that they owned bikes, although they were stashed in plain view in the woods. Howard stood cocking his head, listening for the bikes. His posture was terrible. His chest was sunk in; he was nothing like a rooster claiming his dusty yard.

Claire was shrieking now. I walked downstairs, and I walked through the pantry and the kitchen and the mud room and into the bathroom. I slammed the door as hard as I could and then I pounded at it, and then kicked it open, and slammed it again, so that the paint chips went flying off like sparks, and the spice rack hanging above the stove fell off its hooks. The bottles tumbled down the cold air return. When I was done slamming I stormed into the living room, grabbed Emma in front by the cloth of her sleeveless shirt, and shook her. When both girls were wailing I matched their noise—"I'M GOING TO THE GODDAMN STORE, DO YOU HEAR?"

I kicked the toys on the walkway, opened the car door, sat myself in the driver's seat, and started the engine. Music, at top volume, came from the tape deck, as if Howard's cassette had been poised to narrate my situation: *"Oh, hang down your head, Tom Dooley, Oh, hang down your head and cry. You killed poor Laura Foster—"* I pushed at button after button on the console until I hit Eject. It was almost funny, coming upon that particular song, under the circumstances. There were a dozen songs on Side A including "Charlie Is My Darling," "Loch Lomand," and "The Ash Grove," and yet "Tom Dooley" was the one, the words filling the car as if to taunt me. *"You killed poor Laura Foster, And now you are bound to die."*

I draped myself over the steering wheel, to rest. If only I could survive until the girls were through high school. It was Claire who would save me, who would take me by the hand and lead me through the difficult years ahead. She was beautiful and easygoing, diplomatic and tolerant. She would be crowned Homecoming Queen and for the first time the people of Prairie Center would turn to us, her parents, and wonder how it was we had produced such a graceful, congenial, amazing child. Having her by our sides would grant us free admission into the very life of Prairie Center, chairs set out for us every morning at Del's for breakfast, and a standing invitation to Dr. Larson's annual Memorial Day picnic. "Oh, hang down your head, Tom Dooley," rang on in my ears. "Oh, hang down your head and cry."

Emma came tripping out of the house, her bony knees knocking against each other. Claire was waddling behind, short and plump and dark. Emma's bangs had grown halfway down her nose and her shirt was slipping off one shoulder. She looked so forlorn I had to turn away. I would get everything Howard wanted. We had Nellie's carefully labeled casseroles, but no paper products or bananas or mayonnaise. I stared at the tattered list while the girls climbed into their seats. We were going off to the store, just as we should. If we could go to the Piggly Wiggly today, then there was no telling what might happen tomorrow. It might be that everything would fall into place and we would keep in motion so continuously, like the planet itself, that we wouldn't even feel our effort, working to put one foot in front of the next.

My children were sitting in the back seat, each studying a picture book on her lap from the car book bag. They were waiting for me to take them to the store. They didn't seem scarred, didn't act like bumpkins. They were wearing name-brand clothes and had somehow managed to come through looking very like their thoroughly modern Prairie Center sisters. I was considering whether or not I should remind them of my bad behavior by apologizing, when the squad car turned up the drive.

Howard came from the milk house and went to the officer. I was already out and to the gate, to the stretch of grass by the garden. I lay down on the parched ground and looked as hard as I could at the blue sky. I wanted to feel the sheerness of space, to somehow reach what was empty and quiet, to hold what was right beyond my grasp.

Howard

Chapter Nine

———

LAST SUMMER WE USED to strike out and drive up and down country roads. Even with the sun blazing away I wasn't sure which way was east, which was west. The girls would gradually close their eyes and slump over. Or else the corn rows, passing by with machinelike precision, would hypnotize them. They'd sit in a stupor. I tried to brace myself against thought. There was no good in thinking. I concentrated on the asphalt straight in front of the car. We were in a capsule, the girls and I. We were suspended in time and space, while the folk music drifted from the tape deck like smoke. *"So be easy and free, when you're drinkin' with me. I'm a man you don't meet every day."* The slightest thing would jolt me back to our present life. A fence, a gate, a cow, wash on the line, the moon in the sky. For weeks just about everything brought me back to Alice. After last summer Emma and Claire also stopped looking at a thing for what it is. They also began to ask, in their own way, What's here that doesn't meet the eye? They don't look at a river without wondering if it's dirty and if the fish are sick.

On an ordinary morning in the hottest, driest summer on record, two officers got out of their car and went around the house to find my wife lying on her back in the dead grass. She was holding her arms straight up, flexing her fingers. She kneeled while the hefty one handcuffed her and recited her rights in a stream. It is a familiar-enough scene, but startling in one's own yard. The cop sounded like a kid who's saying grace, mumbling the whole paragraph as if it was one long, meaningless word. I am as guilty as the next person, thinking that hardship comes to others. Last summer on that Tuesday morning I would have been less surprised, and also filled with reverence, if a space alien had landed in the wheat field and dragged Alice to Mercury for an examination.

When I questioned the policemen they made no answer. When I insisted I was coming along, Alice turned and said, "Stay here, I'll call you." The short officer with glasses smacked a piece of paper in my hand. "What is this?" I demanded. I didn't have time to sit and read. I was walking sideways, together, apart, together, apart, asking Alice to explain the problem. Under no circumstances, I said, was I going to sit at home while she was driven off by two men who were younger than both of us.

The cop said, "Do you want anything from the house, Ma'am?"

They weren't listening.

To the officer Alice said, "Can I bring some books? What am I allowed?"

"Books are okay. Extra socks, white only, that's about it."

She stopped on the sidewalk. She said so calmly, as if she had expected to be hauled away, "I'm in trouble, Howard. Read the piece of paper. Robbie Mackessy says I—awful things. I don't know how this could have happened but I have to go along. What you need to do is take care of the girls."

Alice gave me a painting for my thirtieth birthday, from the Go Back in Time Company. An artist in Pittsburgh produced an oil portrait of myself as a Napoleonic soldier. Alice went and hung it in the bathroom over the toilet. The painting was a good likeness. I couldn't take a piss without feeling disoriented. Last summer on that Tuesday morning at nine-thirty she stood handcuffed on the sidewalk looking at me. It was only the first of many occasions during those months that seemed to take place out of time, or in a historical moment I had yet to identify. "It's no use coming after me," she said. She turned then and went into the house.

They must have realized she was harmless because they undid her handcuffs while she filled a grocery bag with books, paper, envelopes.

They had let her go, I thought, because they knew she was innocent. But if they had shackled her in the first place it wasn't right to spring her loose. I wondered how good they were, if they allowed their captives to rummage around for their Lugers. "No," she shook her head mournfully, "I don't have plain white socks. Let me look at this warrant thing," she said, taking the paper from my grip with her free hand.

"Alice—"

"Here," she said, holding out her wrists to the policeman. "I'll call you when I sort this out, Howard. I'll need a lawyer—maybe you could get a hold of Rafferty."

The girls were hiding in the Ford, springing up and peeking every few minutes and then ducking down. When Alice came from the house she went to the car and in a flash she grasped Emma's head through the open window. She did so with her hands in manacles. She held Emma's face. She moved to the front window and did the same with Claire. She had cast some kind of spell on them and they knew they shouldn't say a word. They opened and closed their mouths. "I'll call you," she said to me, just before the officer shut the door after her. As they pulled away, Emma and Claire emerged from the back seat and came to my side. We stood in the dust of the driveway. When the car rounded the bend and disappeared we continued to wait. I guess—and why not?—we thought the road might straighten out to reveal her destination.

After a minute we blinked, shook ourselves. I said we'd go inside and make some Marshmallow Fluff sandwiches. Claire started to whimper. Emma kept it up longest, looking down the road. She probably would have felt about the same if she'd woken to find that a tornado had touched down while she'd slept, a whirlwind that had taken the one thing she valued most. Claire began climbing all over me, suddenly feverish with anxiety. I told her that Alice would be back soon, probably before we were finished with our sandwiches. Inside I turned on the TV to the "Today" show. I left it going, without sound. The girls crouched at the window, expecting Alice to be delivered at our doorstep at every next instant. "She'll be the next car," Emma kept saying. "I know this next one will be hers."

I slathered the Fluff like Spackle over the bread and put a piece at each girls' place. Without stopping to consider I went to the phone to call

Dan and Theresa's lawyer friend, Paul Rafferty. "No, I'm sorry, sir," the secretary said, "he won't be in until Thursday."

"I—I think it's an emergency," I said.

"Well, let's just transfer you to Mr. Finn for the moment. He'll be out of his meeting within the hour. Where are you calling from, may I ask?" She had the saccharine voice and labored patience of a preschool teacher. "Let me see if I have it right," she said, repeating our number.

"This will be her car!" Emma shouted, as I hung up. I half-believed her and I went to the window to look. My god has always been a laissez-faire deity, giving you the initial goods and sending you on to make your way. When Ayatollah Khomeni died I watched the hundreds of thousands of identical black-scarfed women grieving on television. I had never seen anything like it. It was their belief that was shocking. They carried it without thinking, like ants hauling bread. I didn't know what else to do on that Tuesday morning except walk out and check the irrigation rig. The girls ate as they ran. As I lifted Claire into the spray and while she squealed I was pretty sure that what had happened only moments before was some kind of prank. There was no reason to worry. I had the idea that we would check the rig and then we would go and get Alice. I had wanted to topdress the west hayfield but I'd have to put it off until tomorrow. There had been a mistake, which she would explain at first with restraint. Over the summer, with subsequent tellings, the story would become more amusing. I guessed her tendency to exaggerate would be her right in a case like this one. The rig was so old and rusted it was practically useless. We weren't to the barn when Alan, our driver who picks up the milk, hobbled down from his truck. He came forward grinning as usual. He thought I was going to listen to his jokes and schemes. That Tuesday morning I waved once and then walked as fast as I could with the girls back to the house.

We were slapping some more Marshmallow Fluff on the heels of the stale white loaf, to take with us in the car, when the phone rang. "This is my one call," she said.

"What?" I went around the corner into the bathroom, as far as the cord would allow.

"This should teach me, Howard. Did you read the warrant? Robbie Mackessy says that I did unspeakable things to him. I said to the deputies in the car, I said, 'Aren't you sick of this kind of thing? Doesn't it bore you to tears? Is it that we're saturated with the notion of abuse, we can't see anything else anymore? We are all nothing to each other but potential abusers— Is that it?' They looked straight ahead and didn't say a word. Remember that cable channel we got at your mother's, that dial-a-fetish program? Maybe that's what everybody else in the whole world is watching and thinking is normal. Remember there was that guy with the shoe, and the woman who—"

"Alice—" I broke in.

"I'm trying to keep my mouth shut, I am Howard, really. But in a way it's so—typical. I have the urge to shake these people, to tell them to come off it. Last year a third-grader in Walworth was charged with fourth-degree abuse for pulling another boy's pants down on the playground. He had to go to court, swear to ten years of therapy. I think about the time John Croger cornered me in the alley and felt my breasts—well, I was in sixth grade, that was the dark ages, nothing to be done about it. As horrible as it was I knew that it was just dumb boy stuff."

"Alice!" I had to shout to make her stop. "Will you tell me what—"

"The town of Prairie Center is set against me, that's what I know." She lowered her voice. "Do you remember in the winter when I invited Sally Hunter over? Don't you remember that she and Emma went upstairs and took off their clothes and played operating room, and then they went screaming down the hall and jumped on the old mattress stark naked? I didn't really think anything of it. I thought, How nice, they're getting along so well. Sally went home and told her mother she had her butt sewed up by Doctor Emma and that when she's at our place she is not required to wear clothes. Darla Hunter called in a fury: 'What is it about your sexed house?' That was a good one, our *sexed house*. I tried to keep a straight face, tried to tell Darla that we belong to the missionary-position club and have a once-a-month average and that furthermore I thought it was normal for children to play— Oh Christ, Howard, I don't have all day here. God knows I didn't have a very ordinary childhood, but at least I got to play dirty doctor under the Meyers's porch."

"Alice—"

"They booked me, Howard. I was in the bullpen."

"What?"

"Only for a few minutes, and alone. It smelled. I had to stand hand-cuffed to the counter, while they got my name and address. They took my fingerprints and a mug shot that goes right into the computer. In a minute they'll give me my Day-Glo orange jail suit that says RACINE COUNTY JAIL in black-stenciled letters on the back. I'm not kidding, it's the whole works. When I'm arraigned I'll have to shuffle into court with my feet in shackles."

I said her name again. I thought to say, "Why? Why you?"

"Did you get Rafferty?" she asked instead.

"He's on vacation. He won't be in until Thursday. Finn is supposed to call back any minute. Alice, why—"

"I want Rafferty. Theresa says Finn is lecherous and drinks too much and tells off-color jokes. I couldn't have someone defending me who is a judge for the Miss Dairyland contest. I don't want anyone but Rafferty. They've got me on probable cause, some kind of lawyer deal where they're pretty sure you did it, sure enough to put you in the slammer. Listen to me! I'll come out of here speaking a new language and all with the timbre of a truck driver. Robbie was checked out by a child protection worker and they've had a couple of investigating officers on this case for weeks. For all I know they talked to Darla Hunter and she told them about our *sexed house*. While I've been lying in bed crying my eyes out over Lizzy, they've learned that I'm an unbalanced, vicious woman who runs from funerals and tortures young children with rectal thermometers and tongue depressors. They drag you off in a squad car you almost start thinking you're crazy or guilty."

Alice was born exaggerating. She probably sputtered and howled much longer than the trauma of birth requires. I was used to taking a lot of what she said with a grain of salt. I didn't know her well, when we were married. I knew her enough to think there wasn't much point in having the years pass if she wasn't along for the ride. She is an intemperate person, one minute shut up in herself and the next dancing a jig, telling an implausible story about a mouse running up her leg at the doctor's office.

"I'm coming right away," I said. "We'll get Finn for today. I'll be there in thirty min—"

"No," she said. "There's nothing you can do. Just call the office and have them tell Rafferty it's critical, to call you the instant he's back. I'll talk to one of the public defenders here in the meantime. Can you imagine what Rafferty does on vacation? Something eccentric, stamp collector's camp in Reno, or—or Morris dancing with the bells and handkerchiefs. I trust him even though he's peculiar, don't you?"

"I need to come," I said.

"No! Listen. You couldn't even see me now. They're taking me up in two minutes." When I realized she was indisposed, I began talking at her as forcefully as I could in low tones. The justice system was corrupt, I knew, but they couldn't slap her in jail without adequate proof. Finn would get her out within the hour, when his meeting was over.

"Howard," she said, her voice wavering. "You don't realize about this. I'm in here now and it's going to take more than the truth to get me out." Before I could answer she said, "There's one thing. One thing." She had regained her composure and sounded again as if being at the jail was part of some plan that only I hadn't known about. "You have to promise that under no circumstances will you bring Emma and Claire here to visit me. Don't come if you can't find a sitter. The visiting time for my group is two-fifteen on Sunday."

"Sunday?"

"You're supposed to get here beforehand to register. I couldn't stand for Emma and Claire to see this place. I couldn't stand to have them go away again after fifteen minutes. You have to say you'll promise."

I was not planning on her stay lasting for more than another few hours.

"Howard," she said, "are you listening? You have to promise."

"Yes, I'm listening—"

"All right then. Call Rafferty."

"Alice—"

"My time is up. Call Rafferty. Please."

"What was that about?" Emma asked, from around the corner.

I was raised, along with millions of other boys, to strive, to compete, to work hard to get to a crucial destination. It was unspecified but all important. The cost of the trip was the accumulated sum of our school, church, and scout labors. We went to Sunday school and were told about God, but we also knew that His power was not much compared to Hard

Work and the salvation of Free Enterprise. We were told that we could do anything if we put our minds to it, and wanted it badly enough. Mental strength then, and desire, were for us what constituted bravery. I thought, in my younger years, that there was some sort of design that I would unerringly become a part of in adulthood. I thought there was one singular pattern that was for me, and was mine alone. I would work and work and then I would be rewarded by receiving a plot of land and a dairy barn, a sign at the end of the driveway that said, The Howard Goodwin Family Farm. Registered Guernseys. Milk Producer of America.

I hung up the phone knowing that there had been a mistake, that I would get a hold of someone in Rafferty's office, and with persistence—that's what it would take—persistence, the whole thing would be cleared up in an hour or so.

"Mom had to go to Racine for a while, but she'll be back," I said to Emma.

"She didn't really say good-bye to us," she choked, looking out the window.

I sat down at the kitchen table and with one hand drew Emma to me and held her. With the other I stroked along the grain of the wood. We would drive in and demand to have her back. When Finn called he would understand the vagaries of the law and see where we could inch in and get our way.

"When will she be home?" Emma asked.

I kept smoothing my hand over the table. The farmer we bought the place from told us that the table was the one on which his great-grandmother served corn bread to the Indians up in Winston, a half hour or so from Prairie Center. I bet I've told that story to the girls twenty times. I make the table come alive and I tell the whole thing from its point of view. The year is 1836. It watches the Indians barge in with their scalp belts slung around their waists. They want to see the coffee grinder and the white baby. Our girls have gotten in the habit of begging me to tell them what's happening today in the life of Emma and Claire Goodwin, from the view of the table. It has an uncommonly deep voice and it usually gives them good advice or a moral. I can't put my elbows on the slab of oak without thinking of it taking us in, its clear eye watching me.

"It's awful when you make supper," Emma said. "You always mix everything together and I can't undo it into piles."

I had not given Emma any real answer or put her fears to rest about my cooking when Finn called. I uncoiled the long phone cord as I walked into the bathroom, closing the door behind me. I didn't have much information. I had difficulty describing the problem. "My wife has been arrested, I think for s-s-sexual abuse." I hadn't stuttered in years, not since I was a kid. For a second I was as surprised by the sound of my own voice as I was by the strange story I was trying to tell. "They handcuffed her," I said.

"Yes, well, they always do when the charge is a felony."

"A felony," I repeated. "She hasn't done anything."

"If the police acted lawfully," he said, "then the arrest is valid. That's the question to grapple with right now." I remembered then, that night years before when Alice and I went to the county fair. Everything on the grounds was caked with grit. There was no escape from the intoxicating smell of corn dogs and horse manure and axle grease. We had laughed at the sight of Mr. Finn, "Judge Finn," Alice had called him. We laughed watching him hand up the envelope at the end of the Miss Dairyland Contest.

"Was there a warrant?" he asked.

"Ah, yes," I said. "I saw it for just a second."

"I suspect what happened here is the police felt they had reasonably trustworthy information, sufficient, as the law reads, to make 'a reasonable man' think it more likely than not that the proposed arrest is justified. We call that 'probable cause.' In arrests with a warrant, the determination of probable cause is made by a judge up at the courthouse."

"Alice knows Rafferty personally. She would really like him on this."

"I'm sure you know, Mr. Goodwin, that it is essential she have counsel immediately. They'll set bail sometime today. Mr. Rafferty isn't in until Thursday—"

"I understand," I said.

"There are two things you can do right now. You can retain a lawyer, which I strongly advise you to do without delay, and you can pay the bond when it's posted."

Although he had clearly given me specific instructions, I was still waiting for him to tell me simply how we could get her out. I understood the workings of the court system well enough, but it is fair to say that I was stupefied at the beginning. I guess the process seemed obscure because we were in the middle of it. A person doesn't ever think much about being in that kind of trouble, or plan for it. I thought that Alice would be exempt from the rules because her arrest was a blatant mistake.

"If you'd like me to represent her until Thursday—"

"Thank you, thanks for the information. I appreciate—"

"Look," he said, "Mr. Rafferty isn't in until Thursday. She should have someone, a public defender, anyone until then. Does she understand that she should remain silent until—"

"Thank you," I blared. "We'll do that. Thank you very much. I'll be in t-touch."

Alice has sometimes told people, I guess in a way I find objectionable, as if I'm a show animal, that one of my strong points is my ability to stay calm. She had been excessively calm on the telephone, all things considered. I already felt the need to make up somehow for what she had lacked. I careened from the paper-towel dispenser to the refrigerator to the cupboard. I went around the room a couple of times trying to make something other than Marshmallow Fluff sandwiches for my daughters. All the drawers were wide open and I kept bumping them. I called the jail and was told that they did not give out information about inmates over the telephone. I got through to the public defender's office only to learn that the person handling Alice's case was in court. When the secretary put me on hold it occurred to me for the first time that I might be powerless to get Alice out before morning. I needed to tell her not to breathe a word, not to open her mouth. I gripped the sink, queasy for a minute, afraid that she was going to blurt to anyone who'd listen, that business about the "sexed house." I pulled out the clutter of pans and appliances and pots that we always threw down below in the cupboards. We hadn't had time or energy or the talent for organization. The cupboards were proof of our deficiencies. The slippery bread pans had been stacked and stored without being washed. The ice-cube trays were filled with spider webs and insect skeletons. There were three large plastic bags stuffed with lids and no jars anywhere in sight. Ordinarily such a mess wouldn't have mattered to me. Emma and Claire examined the things with enthusiasm until they realized that the black specks on the contact paper were mouse droppings.

That morning I had been going to fix the water tank in the upper yard, cut the rest of the lousy first crop of hay, and topdress the west field. I needed to worm the sheep, pay some bills, cultivate the soybeans. The hay was worrisome. There wasn't going to be enough to last the year. And already there wasn't good pasture for the cows because of the drought. Alice often complained that there wasn't time to do anything well. I suppose she was right. She had once said something in anger that cut me to the quick. She had said that farming was only really about staying in the exact same place, that there was no moving beyond milk, beyond manure, beyond soybeans, that it was the same year after year. Nothing is farther from the truth. There are seasonal variations, medical challenges, new technologies to consider and balance against the proven ways. Each year there is new life. That morning last summer I had the sensation of standing still in a way I had never experienced before. It is not pleasant to feel still, forcibly still, stuck. I didn't think that stillness was the variety that had worried Alice.

Later that afternoon I got between Emma and Claire on the sofa. I tried to read *Hansel and Gretel* to them. The air as well as the uncertainty had a suffocating effect. They couldn't listen. When Hansel was making his trail the second time with bread crumbs Claire asked, "Can't we take a bath?" They both sprang up to get towels and run the water. If Alice had seen me dusting, pulling out towels and cleaning supplies in the bathroom to wipe the shelves, she would immediately have realized the degree of my anxiety. There was already a distinction which would be with us for the rest of the summer. There was out there, beyond our front door. It was a shapeless and hot landmass with Alice on it, somewhere, picking her way home. The only other point of reference was inside our house. The rooms of our house were the things we owned and knew.

That afternoon I kept reaching for the receiver to put a call through to the American Embassy in Bucharest. After a minute I'd hang up. I wasn't sure what message to leave for my mother. She used to ask after the crops and the animals, out of politeness. She didn't know specifically what to ask because she didn't have a working vocabulary for the farm. I always explained what I was doing, and why I thought it was interesting or necessary. If I called her over in Rumania she would have to ask detailed questions in order to get as much as a vague answer. When the phone rang at three o'clock I pounced on it.

"Howard—" Alice began.

"Are you out?"

There was a television on in the background there and I could hardly hear her. "The public defender just took the bar a month ago," she said. "He was more nervous than I was."

"Where are you?"

"Upstairs," she said. I had to think if she could mean above me, in our bedroom. "Fourth floor, pay phone. I can call all I want now that I'm booked. Listen, they say there are other children coming forward with charges. The judge talked about how a public health worker is a person of trust and how angry communities are when that trust has been violated. That's why the bail is unusually high. The lawyer thought I should have been given a chance at release on property or signature bonds, but I wasn't. The judge set a cash bond."

"How much?"

"Too much."

"How much?"

"It's wild, Howard—it's, it's one hundred thousand."

One hundred thousand what? Horse chestnuts? Hickory nuts? We had five hundred dollars in a savings account which we had started when Emma was born, for college. We had weeks before not only refinanced the farm but borrowed ten thousand dollars from the bank for a hay bine, a baler, and a rack. The hay bine was a dream, conditioning the hay, cutting the drying time in half. With the pop-up baler I could make six hundred bales all by myself in an afternoon. If Alice and Dan helped I could do twice that. It was possible that I might be able to get several thousand dollars from my mother, but one hundred thousand—it might as well have been two million. "I'm going to write you a letter," she said quietly. "I'm all right." She said something then which almost made me laugh. "Don't worry, Howard."

"Don't worry," I echoed.

"They have nothing to go on."

"Alice—" I said, waiting for her to interrupt.

"The women in here are young enough to be my daughters," she said after she'd waited for my response. "I'm worried about you three," she whispered. "I'll be all right. This is only an indication of things to come, for the next life. I'll be in hell, and you'll be in heaven with the girls. We'll have to consider ourselves lucky if there's even such a thing as Sunday visitation."

When I didn't respond she said weakly, "I'm kidding, Howard. It was a joke."

After the call we got in the car. It was the first of many such excursions. We'd edge toward Racine and then veer north or south. I'd think in a hallucinatory moment that I could go straight to the jail and wrangle her out. That first trip we opened the windows and cranked up the radio. The girls put their heads in the breeze and closed their eyes. I followed the arrows for the winding roads, assuring myself that she would be home by morning. It wasn't possible for her to be held any longer than one brief night.

Over the next few days several problems arose. I shouldn't have been surprised on Wednesday when I pulled the *Blackwell Dispatch* from our mailbox, the dark headline proclaiming, "Prairie Center Nurse Charged with Sex Abuse." Below, in smaller print, it said, "Principal sets meeting for concerned parents." I stood on the driveway, hoping to look away and then back again at a different lead story. I hadn't taken off my clothes the night before. I hadn't slept much, or at all, sitting in the living-room chair. The sunlight stung my eyes. Claire crawled up my leg, screeching at me to feed her while I stood and read.

Alice Goodwin, age 32, was arrested early Tuesday morning at her home, 22394 Walnut Lane, for seven felony charges, including two counts of reckless endangerment, child abuse, and three counts of second-degree sexual abuse. Mrs. Goodwin, a LPN, is employed by the Blackwell School District and holds the part-time job of school nurse. She had been under investigation for several weeks prior to the arrest. If Goodwin is convicted of these charges the combined maximum penalties would be over $100,000 and fifty years in prison. Racine County Circuit Court

Judge Rhone also ruled that additional counts of felony charges to be filed in an amended criminal complaint will include reckless endangerment and sexual abuse.

In addition, Goodwin is under investigation in the drowning of Elizabeth Collins, two years old, of Prairie Center. The suspect was baby-sitting when the child allegedly ran from the house and drowned in the pond on the Goodwin farm. The principal of Blackwell Elementary, Mr. David Henskin, said today that he was shocked by the arrest and that he will assist the investigation in any way he can. A meeting for concerned parents has been set for Friday, June 16, at 7 P.M.

I suppose it was then, stuck on the driveway with Claire, that I began to understand the nature of the problem. We weren't going to be able so easily to remedy what to us was a mysterious error. Even with Rafferty's help Alice wasn't going to be able to slip from jail without notice. By the end of the morning, after the phone calls started coming in, I knew full well that her trouble was like mercury, spilling and slipping, running into unexpected corners. I was dazed by the equation that overnight made Alice's private trouble equal to everyone's trouble. I had waited in the chair until dawn. I was waiting, and also standing guard against something outside I couldn't name. I hadn't known that it was already spreading, that it was at large.

I carried Claire inside and put the whole box of Cheerios into her outstretched arms. Emma started in about not having her very own box of cereal when the phone rang. "Shut up," I said to her. I had never used those words to my children before, or in front of them. "Shut up," I said again, handing her the box of cornflakes.

"Mr. Goodwin?"

"Speaking."

"This is Sylvia Romero, from the *Racine Journal Times*. I'm sorry to bother you this morning—"

"I *hate* cornflakes," Emma squalled.

"—I know this must be a very difficult time for you. I'm sure your wife's arrest—"

"Must have come as a sh-shock," I finished for her. I covered the receiver with my hand and stamped my boot at Emma.

"I'm sure it was! These unfortunate types of situations seem to gather force on their own. I'm sure you know that since this story broke yesterday there is already a lot of talk in your part of the county about your wife. We are very concerned that you too have an opportunity to tell us what you know about the charge. It is only fair that you—"

I hung up. I hung up and poured milk into the girls' cups, and sat down, rubbed my eyes, took off my T-shirt. When the phone rang again I considered, for three or four rings, not answering.

"Hello?" I said finally.

"I want to tell you what she did." It was a gravelly woman's voice, not someone I recognized. "My daughter says your wife used to come up to the locker room when they were taking showers after gym class. She says she ran her hand down her friend's back, up and down her back. She says she stood and stared at the girls while they were naked in the shower. She kept running her hands up and down the girl's back until the girl got away. Your wife also told a neighbor, twelve years old, that she could 'get it on,' I believe those are the words she used, with a tampon."

I wiped my left underarm with my wadded up T-shirt, and then I said, "Who are you trying to reach? This is K&L Rental Cars."

"Let's drive," I said to the girls. "Let's go driving."

"We're not done eating," Emma cried, "and you don't even have a shirt on."

I snatched the keys from the pegboard and started out the door. Ken Hegeman, the editor of the *Blackwell Dispatch,* was just pulling into our yard. He had done an article on the farm two years before, when "Sustainable Agriculture," an old concept, was the brand-new buzz word. I'd done a lot of experimenting with compost preparations, which I used in place of pesticides. I'd been getting reasonable yields all along. Because of stray voltage near the barn and the amount of pasture land we had I also was a strong advocate for rotational grazing. The somatic cell count in our cows was about as low as it goes. I would have liked to have used horses instead of tractors, but it wasn't practical for the acreage. I latched the screen door and started for the back stairs, whispering, "Come on, come on, come on." I pulled Claire along with me as I ran. The girls sat straight on the bed in our room. They were breathing heavily and straining to hear more than their own breath. We waited while Ken rang the bell and knocked at the window at regular intervals. Later, after he'd given up and driven off, a crew from the Channel Four news team parked their van across the road. They filmed the house. I locked the doors and we went upstairs again. That time we waited in the windowless hall. There's an old mahogany dresser by the bathroom filled with junk. Again, for something to do, we began clearing out the drawers. We threw out sheaves of paper, old shoes, dried-up rolls of masking tape, various odd baby toy pieces, and incomplete decks of cards. It was a game for the girls, like a hunt for treasure. All of the stuff was useless.

After the van was gone we sat in front of the fan in the bedroom. Claire fell asleep while I taught Emma to play War. What if the Channel Four news team found more secrets in our house than I would care to believe? I shuddered to think how an unpainted, clapboard farmhouse would speak to them when they reviewed their footage. For the first time I saw the place as an outsider. It would look to their experienced eyes as if it should be condemned.

When I had clear thoughts, they were of one thing: how I could lay my hands on one hundred thousand dollars. If we sold the car, the old combine, and the new baler we might get seventeen thousand. If I sold the farm equipment or the cows I would be without income, without the means to pay Rafferty. If my mother had eighty-five and I could come up with fourteen or fifteen we could get Alice out. When I was not thinking clearly, I wasn't sure what I was trying to get her out *of*. I'd start through the process, trying to link Robbie Mackessy to a faceless investigator, and to Alice, and to a stark cell in the jail in downtown Racine. Again and again, after I'd made the impossible connections, I knew that I would have had less disbelief if she had just gone and died.

Occasionally a sudden bolt of reason would come to me and I'd understand certain facts. Everything that I could think of to sell would in some way cripple us, or cripple the cause. There were very few places we could go any longer. It was going to prove difficult, if not impossible, to find someone to watch the girls while I was away trying to get Alice out. We had always been satisfied with our circumscribed life. We had been proud, I think, to know that we could get by with so little. As for child care, the few people I might have ordinarily called upon for help were in distant parts. Dan and Theresa were out of the question, besides still being in Montana, and the girls' regular school-year sitter was at her summer cabin in Boulder Junction. My mother was doing her good deed in Rumania.

I had finally called the embassy and left the message for Nellie that no one was hurt, but that she should phone her son as soon as possible. "Is something the matter?" she asked when she got through. There was a lag and an echo, so that I heard my hello coming back to me as she asked, "Are you all right?"

"Ah—"

"What is it? What is it, Howie?"

I was loathe to tell my mother that Alice had been arrested for hurting a small boy or that she'd been running her hands up and down the backs of junior-high girls in the locker room.

"What is it? Do you need me, sweetheart?"

"I'm going to have to have some money to get Alice out of jail," I shouted, hoping that sheer volume would make her understand the particulars.

Because of the echo we were talking over each other. "I can't hear you, sweet. This is a terrible connection." She asked again, "Are you all right?"

"Alice has been mistaken for someone else and is in jail." That was the story. That was what had happened.

"Oh, for goodness sakes. How long will it take them to clear it up?"

"I'm not sure," I said. "They set the bail at—"

"With all due respect, honey, I really think Alice brings troubles down on her own shoulders. I love her dearly, you understand, but she sometimes has such a bad attitude. What did you say they think she did?"

"Sh—she." I could tell my mother that it was fraud or embezzlement, that the school was missing a few hundred dollars from the petty-cash drawer. "We'll get through it," I said. "We'll be fine." I would tell her everything after the preliminary hearing, after I heard the charges for myself. I couldn't very well tell her what I myself didn't understand.

"You need me to come home! I can hear it in your voice."

"No, that's not it. If we can just get her out I'm sure it will blow over."

"What about the girls? Who are they mistaking Alice for? The world is so chaotic! The mess here is unbelievable. The hospital conditions are primitive, there are so many AIDS babies, not enough medication, not enough food. We're doing what we can—"

"That's great, Mom."

"—But my goodness, the children just break your heart."

"Do you think you could loan us some money? A few th-th-thou—"

"You'd think with computers they'd be able to straighten out those kinds of mistakes right away."

I thought that maybe it would hit her, after she'd hung up, that Alice was locked away, and she'd call back wanting, the second time, to listen. She didn't have much left to give—that much she had recently made clear to me. But it was possible she had an emergency stash she could bust into. I would ask her for the full amount tomorrow, after I'd had some sleep. "Could you call back on Thursday?" I said. "I'll know more by then."

"Surely they'll have the mistake cleared up."

"You're probably right, Mom."

I can't say I had any better luck with Rafferty, when he called the following morning. When I explained the spurious charge he made a noise like a belch. "—Don't believe it," he said. He began to tell me much the same thing Finn had said about how probable cause is established. Alice trusted him implicitly and thought he would save her. She trusted him, not because the charge was false, but because she thought him irresistibly decent. We had met him at a barbecue. Within minutes Alice and Rafferty were dancing around on the Collinses' patio. He knew a dance she'd learned when she was in high school. She was basing her trust on the fact that they both knew the same Hungarian polka. He had the kind of nasal voice that makes you want to somehow clear his throat for him.

"This can't be pleasant for you," he said.

"No," I agreed.

"Of course not. It's very upsetting. I just got into town but I'm going to run over to the public defender's office, check in at the jail, and talk to

Alice." His voice was all nasal passage. It was hard to believe he wasn't holding his nose and talking at me for the amusement of his secretary. "Can you come in tomorrow, around ten? I'll have a better feel after I've talked to her. The bail is outrageous for someone like Alice and first thing we'll petition the court, get the bond in a reasonable range. You must be sure not to discuss any aspect of the case on the telephone, either from your home or in the visiting room. That's critical."

He did not continue until I acknowledged his command.

"About tomorrow," he went on, "—by the way, I know how dreadful this is for you, believe me."

"I'm not sure," I said, doubting his knowledge of my state of mind.

"Would another day be better?" he asked.

"Another day?"

"You said you weren't sure—"

"No," I said. "I'll be there."

I hung up, slammed a pot down on our oak table, as if that could stop the table from watching. I had to have a plan now, a plan, a good plan. All of my knowledge of the law I had learned years ago in the flickering shadow of "Perry Mason." Still, I knew enough to know that Rafferty, Finn—none of them, had genuine understanding. I told myself that a person didn't live with someone for nearly seven years without having a pretty good sense of their limits. Lawyers, people in the system, politicians, were so crippled by bureaucracy and jargon they no longer had common sense. As a nation we were losing our collective minds. There were any number of issues to point that up. Any number. Look at anything, any institution, any organization, any system for dealing with problems. Take the AIDS epidemic, for starters. I'd been reading the articles buried in the paper for enough years to figure out that AZT might be killing people instead of the AIDS virus. My old friend Lloyd was sick in New York City. You could follow the whole thing, see the illness becoming so politicized that no one dared to speak about the jarring facts. The dishes were going to break if I threw them much harder into the cupboard. I had to have a plan right now, a sound plan, a way to fight. First of all, I had to find someone who would watch the girls, for my meeting with Rafferty, and for the visiting hour on Sunday. I had to talk to Alice, really talk to her, to know why this had happened. It wouldn't take me long to go and come back for the fifteen-minute visit. There had to be someone we knew who would care for Emma and Claire. Someone who would watch over them for a little over an hour on a Sunday afternoon. I could hear the *boyng, boyng* of a jew's harp. It took me a hell of a long time to figure out that it was coming from me. It must have been my nerves. I was thinking I could hear the damn things.

Cathy Johnson came to mind after I'd put all the clean pots away. She was a nurse who worked with Alice at the immunization clinic. She had told me a while back that she worried occasionally, in the middle of the night. She worried that an infant might be brain damaged from a measles shot.

"Cathy," I said, when she answered. "This is Howard Goodwin."

"What is it?" Her voice was not full of concern, the way I remembered.

"I was wondering—ah, you—you've probably heard about Alice." I waited for her to speak. I waited to the steady rhythm of the *boyng, boyng.* I waited and then I said, "I was wondering if Emma and Claire could—if you would be able to watch them tomorrow or Sunday afternoon, for an hour or so. I'm in a slight bind and I—"

"I don't think so," she said. "Those aren't good times for me. If you'll excuse me, I was just on my way out the door."

"Oh well, thanks anyway," I said.

The girls were outside running through the sprinkler. I had let Emma hook the hose up to the pump even though we might later regret squandering water. I could see them from the window running back and forth in their matching pink-and-green-striped swimming suits. The phone was still in my hand. I was also hearing the drone of the severed connection. The girls were quietly holding their fingers over the rusty holes of the sprinkler. Each time when they let go and the water came shooting up at them, they screamed and ran. They were playing as if they did not have a care in the world. They were smart girls, and pretty. They were caring, good girls and their neighbors were set against them. They were running, spreading their arms and flapping.

I made the next call to Suzannah Brooks, a neighbor of the Collinses up in the subdivision. Suzannah home-schools her three children. Every year she brought them down in the evening for a field trip to see the dairy operation. I had let them feed the calves, squirt milk from a cow's tit, pet the kittens, slide down the hay chute. "Hello, Suzannah?" I said.

"Yes, this is she."

"Howard Goodwin."

"I've been praying for you. I feel for you, I really do, and I pray for that poor child. I honestly can't think what the world is coming to. I think of the Scripture: 'A worthless person, a wicked man, goes about with crooked speech, winks with his eyes, scrapes with his feet, points with his finger, with perverted heart devises evil, continually sowing discord; therefore calamity will come upon him suddenly; in a moment he will be broken beyond healing.' I pray that your wife is not beyond healing. I don't know how you're going to live with her if she ever gets out, how she'll live with herself. Jesus will save you in the end if you give over your trouble to him."

"Oh," I said, and hung up.

On Friday morning, I brought the girls along with me to Rafferty's office. There are several rejuvenated Victorian houses along the way to the courthouse in Racine. If Alice had been allowed an open window we would have been able to shout at her from Rafferty's office. His is the green house with yellow and purple trim, right next to the phone company. Downstairs, in Finn's quarters, there is swirling wallpaper that makes a person dizzy. In the bathroom there are stenciled balances one after the next at waist level. Finn's wife does the decorating for the downstairs, according to Theresa. Apparently when Dolores Finn appears with her pattern books Rafferty stands guard on the stairs. He tells her she can go no farther with her paintbrushes and dried flower arrangements.

Outside of Rafferty's office there were stacks of boxes to the ceiling. They obscured whatever decorative motif lay behind. The place didn't feel like a rich man's lair or a sanctuary where a learned person plots the triumph of justice. The built-in bookshelves along the far wall were filled with novels, do-it-yourself manuals, Peterson's guides to the flowers, trees, birds, and shrubs, as well as the thick, drab books of law. I moved the Sears tool catalog off the sofa in the hall and settled the girls there. They each had her own bag of Starbursts. A whole bag, each, sixteen ounces of individually wrapped candies. They also had new crayons and pads of paper. I had bought the things on the way, at the Target in Racine.

Rafferty is tall and thin, with large protruding eyes behind his thick lenses. He has slightly buck teeth, a graying goatee, and the sallow skin of a prisoner. He made small talk, hunting and fishing talk, while I made sure the girls would stay. He looked as if he had never seen the light of day. I wasn't certain he had ever had blind rage, or if he had always tolerated, with what to me was a kind of grotesque calmness, the system and those of us who had run amuck. As he shook my hand he said, "Your wife is all right. She wanted me to let you know that she's going to hold up." He left the door ajar and motioned for me to sit. "Let me outline my fees first," he said, "get that out of the way." Without knowing exactly, or even vaguely, where it was going to come from, I told him I'd have the initial payment for him by September at the latest. "No problem," he said, writing something down on what looked like the back of a grocery receipt. I was thinking of my mother again, thinking that if she were home by September she could help us. The one hundred thousand that fell from the sky for bail money would be ours eventually, at trial time, and could be used to pay the legal fees. Rafferty reminded me to say nothing to the press, that there had been more than enough damaging publicity already. "I'm sure you know that there's going to be a meeting at the school tonight? Meetings like those breed germs. It's best for us, just at the moment, to stay put, to quietly begin to build our case. We'll see what the other side has to say in a few weeks, at the hearing. I've seen it happen before: The temperature goes skyrocketing for a while, but if there's not really anything there, people get tired of fanning the flame." He got up and walked to the window. He stood looking out to the street. I wondered if he was thinking about the other kinds of cases, those that start with nothing and then take on a life of their own. There had been plenty of incidents, when in the interest of some lofty virtue the public was more than willing to do away with constitutional rights.

"You don't know anything about apple trees, do you?" he asked. "I planted a whole line of them along the driveway outside here and they haven't done a thing in five years." He turned to look at me. "Dolores Finn tells me it's all the pollution from the street—" He may have noticed my expression. He may have realized that it was inappropriate to talk about an apple tree when my wife was sitting in jail down the block for no good reason.

"Dolores is probably right," he said, clearing his throat and walking back to his desk. "I spoke with Alice yesterday, as you know. Your wife is unique, an individual, Mr. Goodwin, as I'm sure you are aware. She is made of very strong fabric." He pulled up a large vinyl appointment book and studied it, going forward and backwards through the pages as he spoke. "There's an uproar about this situation, and it's going to be complicated if other people come forward, and if Lizzy gets dragged into the mess. I talked with Alice for quite a while. I'm going to be very interested in the preliminary hearing, to see the personalities on the other side, to see what they have to say. Usually these cases are the other way around, the respectable people with roots in the community accusing the barmaids. It's a lot harder in those cases, to represent the barmaids. Now, at the pre-lim—"

"Could they let her off?" I asked.

He looked up at me from his book. "No, no, let me explain. Preliminary hearings are held for three purposes: first of all, to ascertain whether there is probable cause to support the charge against the accused. Let me warn you that charges are very rarely dismissed. There was a warrant for this arrest, which means the judge has already evaluated the complaint for probable cause. The second reason we have a prelim is for discovery, if you will, for the defense to get information from the prosecution. And last, at the hearing, the judge decides whether or not to bind a person over for trial. The only way you can get her out at this point, right now, is to pay the bond." He was still looking through his worn date book. If there was anything to like him for it was the fact that he wasn't surrounded by leather, oriental rugs, brass, and marble. It was hard to be scornful of a man who stores his papers in orange Golden Guernsey milk crates.

"Usually in a case like this, when the accused is an upstanding community-minded person, the bond is between three and ten thousand. Somewhere in that range. I'll argue with the judge, make a motion to reduce the bail or change it to a property bond. The farm is your greatest asset in terms of bargaining for the bail. A chunk of property like that indicates that you are here to stay. But I can tell you right now: It's going to be a fight. How many students are enrolled at Blackwell Elementary—did she say seven hundred? You have fourteen hundred parents in a feeding frenzy, my bets are the judge isn't going to make out like a softie."

Rafferty closed his book and rose, hiking his pants up at his waist and then tucking his shirt in all the way around. He worked at this with the fervor of a small animal digging a hole. "We'll see what they come up with at the hearing in a few weeks," he said.

It was clear that for him the meeting was over. I wasn't anywhere near ready to leave. He hadn't enlightened me. I still wanted to know why he thought Alice had been singled out. I guess I had the hope that Rafferty could declare the whole thing a gross injustice and that would be the end of it. He thrust his hand at my chest as I rose. I looked at it, wondering what to do. I had to think, left from right, hand from foot, to find the correct limb to meet his shake.

"Try to get some rest," he said then, bumping my arm with his knobby fist in what I suppose was a gesture of camaraderie. "We'll get through this, you'll see. It isn't the first time this has happened, and I'm afraid it won't be the last. We'll stand firm and plow over 'em." He went to the door and opened it wide. "I'll be calling as I frame specific questions." The girls were on the sofa, their mouths full of candy that stunk of artificial banana, strawberry, blueberry. I knelt down to pack up their things. "I'll see her today," he was saying, "I'll tell her that we talked, that they"—he nodded at the girls—"look fine."

At the front door Claire said, "Look, Daddy, we're like Hansel!" Behind us was a trail of Starburst wrappers all the way down the stairs. They were hot colors, bright bits of paper. She laughed. "We'll be able to find our way back from the forest!"

Chapter Ten

——

ON SATURDAY NIGHT I called Miss Bowman, our egg lady. We used to get our own eggs, before the neighbor dogs killed all of our chickens. I had thought the hen house was dog-proof but the black Labradors managed to squeeze in through the swinging door. I had shot at them and missed. They each had the audacity, Alice said, of a fox. The only dealings we'd had with Miss Bowman was the weekly exchange of a dollar fifty for two cartons of eggs. She was a scrawny, gray-haired woman who raised chickens and terriers. She was strange for many reasons. Without saying a word, she used to hand me Jehovah's Witness tracts. There was also something wrong with her right eye. She didn't seem to be in pain. It was the bystander who suffered, looking at the half-closed lid and the displaced half-iris.

"Miss Bowman," I said.

"Who is it?" Her voice creaked from what I assume was disuse.

"Miss Bowman, this is Howard Goodwin, your egg customer from down the road."

"Uh."

If it had been Salem in witch-hunting times she would have been the first to go. She would have been suspect because she talked to her animals, because she was a single-woman property owner, and because she was disfigured. She was about as out of touch with the world as someone like me could hope to find.

I said, "My girls were wondering if they could come down and help you with your chores. You don't know them very well, but they've always liked visiting you when we make an egg run." It was true that Emma and Claire argued over who would pet the Scottish terrier that was chained to a post in the yard.

Miss Bowman was quiet on the other end of the line.

"Their mother and I happen to have kind of an important meeting tomorrow afternoon, in fact, and I was wondering if the girls could come over for an hour or so. I'd be glad to pay you. I'd pay you."

She may have been struck dumb that anyone would talk to her about something other than the price of eggs. I waited a while for her to respond. She was breathing heavily, the "ah, ah, ah," of each breath coming right into my ear. She finally spoke. "They mouth off?"

"They're good girls," I said. "They are very good girls. Would around one thirty be all right?"

"Who was that?" Emma called from the landing.

"Miss Bowman," I said. "Tomorrow you—"

"I'm NOT going to her house." She came into full view. "I'm not! She only has half an eye!"

There were moments, and that was one of them, when my knees almost folded up, when despair passed over me like a waft. It had been enough to call Miss Bowman and ask her to do something she wasn't suited for. Claire was sitting right in front of the television, just about in the screen. I squatted down and whispered in Emma's ear. "Tomorrow," I said, "if you do not go to Miss Bowman's for one short hour, I will not be able to visit Mother." I had never called Alice "Mother." "I won't be able to find out how we can help her. I won't be able to find out when she is coming home. If you sit here and make an awful stink, I will stay and watch you. Mom will sit and wait and wonder."

"I want to come too," she protested, her voice weakening as she spoke.

"Ch-children aren't allowed."

"Why can't I come? Miss Bowman looks like a bird, like one of those naked birds that fell out of the nest." In fact that was exactly what she did look like. I forced myself to whisper, to speak mildly. My new and gross instinct was to shout. I had never laid a hand on the girls. I could now imagine shaking them hard. Rafferty had called that morning to tell me about the parents' meeting at Blackwell Elementary. They had brought in a speaker, a social worker who directs the Sexual Assault Unit at a Milwaukee hospital. She had urged the parents to watch their children carefully for nightmares, biting, bed wetting, masturbation, spitting, or any unusual behavioral changes. She suggested making an appointment with a physician who would be able to determine if physical injury had taken place. She wrote down alarming statistics on the blackboard about the prevalence of abuse. "We can all stay here and we won't know any-thing about Mom," I said to Emma. "And she won't know anything about us."

Emma covered her face and wept without much sound. I sent her into the living room to sit with Claire. Because they fought over the seating arrangement, I packed them off to bed without a story. I could hear Emma crying in her room for a short time before she fell asleep. Rafferty had tried to make the parents' meeting sound benign, even casual, not much to worry about. I'm sure the social worker didn't tell the parents that many of the behaviors she described were normal for young children. I knew, and Rafferty also knew, that those parents might as well have poured gasoline in a circle around our house and thrown a few matches in the grass.

In the end, on Sunday afternoon, I left the girls in Miss Bowman's living room. I left them standing in front of her whatnot. They were holding their own hands, trying to keep themselves from reaching out to touch the china pitchers and the glass-blown figurines. They stood, mute and wide-eyed, in spite of themselves, at the rare view of Miss Bowman's life. She had plastic slipcovers on her sofa and the chairs. They had a stiff new look to them. I wondered if she'd put them on to protect her uphol-stery from the girls. There was an upright piano in the corner, boxes of canning jars and lids on the coffee table, a bowl of orange velvet apples on a metal tea cart. There were egg cartons stacked halfway up the wall. The house smelled of cats and the gas stove, of mildew and overripe fruit. Miss Bowman stood paralyzed in the middle of her kitchen. Her territory had never been besieged by midgets before. She was clutching a potholder with two hands at chest level. "Don't touch," she squawked.

"I'll be back soon," I said.

Emma shot me an anguished look, calculated, I suppose, to make me feel worse than I already did. I had talked myself into believing that Miss Bowman's house was a safe and wholesome place for children. "Demented" appropriately described our neighbor. It would upset Alice, when she'd found that I'd given the girls over to the egg lady. I got in the car and left them. I drove past the covered bridge to Vermont Acres. By now everyone up in the subdivision would have discussed the trouble. I went past the single new home in the middle of what used to be Clarence Holland's horse pasture. It's a formidable Southern-type plantation house with pillars and shutters, a verandah, and no shade trees. I guess the homestead is supposed to be imposing out there by itself, all dressed up and no place to go. Alice imagined that the owners, the doctor and his wife, spoke in Southern accents, that the wife wore a corset and a hoop skirt, that their servants cooked grits over an open fire. Dr. Miller might have already examined some of the schoolchildren, to see if they'd been hurt. I turned on Highway P, the road to the city center. Past the old Sinclair Station that had been the library since the Super America Station opened out by the racetrack three years before. The librarian, Mr. Benchler, was a retired history teacher with a hook for a hand. Alice said she couldn't help thinking he was wicked, like Captain Hook, not only because of his infirmity, but because he was cranky and unhelpful. I'd found out some interesting things from him about burial mounds in the area and never even noticed his hand.

On that windy Sunday afternoon, the dust from the wide street was blowing up at the library and next door, at Del's. The diner was the backbone of the community. I used to think that when I reached middle age I'd go down to Del's for my breakfast, or for coffee. In twenty years or so I'd become an honorary old guy. They served you coffee in large white pots that you got to keep at your table. It was pretty weak and usually not very hot. Alice liked the idea of sitting long enough to drink a whole pot. Del himself, a large man, literally took up three stools at the counter while he read his paper all morning. Every now and then we used to stop in for cherry pie. The girls had cocoa for their beverage. I waited for the day Lavelle would ask me if we were having the usual.

I went on past the fire station, the town hall, the Dog 'N Suds, the mini-storage units, and the branch bank that had recently been held up. Alice had been so relieved to find that every branch bank was vulnerable to raids, that a scheming thief had not pored over county maps to discover the single assailable town in southeastern Wisconsin. She used to say that when archeologists dug up our civilization they would find nothing but branch banks and master bathrooms and mini-storage units. I heard Alice at every turn through the cluttered countryside. She wasn't going to survive in jail. She had been fragile, the last few weeks. I knew enough about what happened in prisons, knew enough not to dare to consider the possibilities. She might be lying on the floor as I drove, beaten or sick. Everything about that summer, even as it happened, was like a dream that is hardly remembered, a fragment a person is afraid to recall: the drought, Lizzy, Alice's sickness, the policemen, Suzannah Brooks and her Scripture, Miss Bowman.

I passed under the interstate, into the new land of car dealerships, the outlet rug stores, the adobe Mexican restaurant, the Wisconsin Cheese Palace. I'd always had affection for Racine, a manufacturing town that got shoved out of the limelight in the 1800s by Chicago and Milwaukee. By the turn of the century it had come into its own because of a few solid entrepreneurs. One of my boyhood heroes was J. I. Case, the man who made threshing machines and farm implements. When I was in eighth grade in Minneapolis, I did a report on Racine with the nonsensical title, "J. I. Case: the Man and the City." I had written to the Case company for information and they had sent me a cap with their logo sewn like a Boy Scout's badge on the front. It was a picture of the globe with an eagle perched on the North Pole, its strong talons keeping it always on top of the world. When I became a farmer I wore nothing but J. I. Case caps through the summer, until it was too cold to forgo a stocking hat.

So I knew that the port city had always been a factory town, a durable goods place, inhabited primarily by hardworking Scandinavians, Germans, and Eastern Europeans. It's a modest town, a little run down, a city where people don't seem to feel any need to put on airs. There's a high school named after William Horlick, the guy who invented powdered milk. They have a good library, a zoo, a couple of fine hospitals, a Frank Lloyd Wright creation called the Golden Rondell that looks like an unidentified flying object. They have Johnson Wax, fresh Kringle, and Lake Michigan. I think it's supposed to be a secret, as if it's a mint, that the Western Publishing Company makes baseball cards. If I know it's so, everybody else probably does too. Along a stretch of Spring Street in Racine, before the time of Christ, the Woodland Indians had garden plots for their corn. Alice and I had taken a walk there, a few years before. It was a pilgrimage for me, I guess. She could tell the seedy houses and the litter were getting me down. "I'm sorry, Howard," she had said. "There might be a molecule of air, or something, left from that long ago." She kept breathing in, picking up glass and pieces of dirt, in an effort to make me feel better.

When you round the bend on Highway 20 you see before you a five-block stretch of municipal and county buildings, the phone company, several churches, and law offices, one after the next. Five square blocks devoted to God and the law, all connected by Ma Bell. The few Victorian houses wedged between the churches have been given new paint, brass fixtures, hanging plants, understated signs: Akgulian, Akgulian & Larson. Keep driving east and you'll come to the courthouse. It's there before you expect it, a monolithic gray slab with inscriptions on the front about justice. Alice said later in the year that it was inevitable, the building, surprising and inevitable, with no charm or grace, just like a Porta Potti in the middle of the forest preserve. That is the sense you have when you come upon it.

The Law Enforcement Center went up across the street from the courthouse about ten years ago. Nobody realized that 146 beds would soon prove inadequate. Now there are close to 500 inmates in the jail at any time. It's a simple brick square, built for utility, with narrow gold windows that shine in the daylight. That first time I visited I got out of the car and stood staring at the place. An older woman stopped in front of me. She spoke as if we'd been in the middle of a conversation. "You know," she said, "Racine has the highest crime rate in all of Wisconsin."

"What?" I said. "Is that right?"

"There ain't no room in there." She pointed up at the jail. "They're going to have to start pushing the criminals into the lake. If you ask me, that's the place for them anyhow."

"A lot of them haven't had trials yet," I said.

She smirked and came closer. "Well, you know they done it."

I walked on, into the small entry teeming with people who were either trying to make their way out or waiting to sign in. If we were visiting we were to remove our watches, our jewelry, our pens, our keys, and deposit them in the lockers. At the appointed time we were pushed through a series of doors into the visiting area, the long corridor with carrels, the Plexiglas windows, the telephones. Those places are well-known to all of us who have sat drugged before the Monday night movie. Dan would say that they are therefore a part of our national landscape, as significant and noteworthy as attractions like the Grand Canyon. He maintained, and he's undoubtedly right, that courts of law are interesting to the public because they are the last vestige of power and mystery in our crumbling civilization.

I sat down on a round stool in cubicle three, as I'd been told. I waited. It was probably power and mystery that made my nerves play, all of them, ringing in my ears like a brass band. The glass was smeared with hand prints, the palm marks of the children who have tried to melt themselves through the wall into their mother's or father's laps. She was going to come through the door on the other side. Perhaps she'd be too sick to speak. The man sitting in the next cubicle smelled of garlic and had such greasy skin and hair he sparkled. We avoided eye contact, staring straight ahead. We were ashamed, as if we were waiting for a peep show.

I remembered the time Alice and I went swimming the day we moved to Prairie Junction. We'd gone and had tuna sandwiches and pie at Del's. When it got dark we went for a swim in our own pond, on our own farm. I had thought it would be fun to strip and swim together. I wanted to celebrate the occasion. After a few strokes she swam under until she was in the middle of the pond. She stayed there treading water. Her head was thrown back and she was barely moving. She acted as if she was alone. I climbed up onto the dock and dried off. I waited for her to come out of her trance. Finally she did the breaststroke in my direction. In the shallows she walked through the water dabbing at the surface. She was obviously having some private joke or thought. She never said what it was.

I sat waiting for her in the visiting area at the jail and I wondered if she would again be as far away as a person can go while they are still with you. She was going to be beyond reach. There would be nothing I could do to help her. It was like death, to be beyond reach. But of course it wasn't death, this visit from someone as untouchable as a ghost. Her group came through in single file. She was third in line, wearing the orange shirt and pants that looked like they were made of burlap. The man next to me began shouting at his daughter for getting herself into trouble again. Alice was standing very straight, looking ahead like a soldier. The receiver was slippery in my hands. When she turned into the cubicle I said, "Visit means both to bless and afflict."

Howard. I could see her lips moving as she reached for the phone, and then I heard her. "Howard. Two things. I know Nellie is in Yugoslavia. Would you please keep this to yourself? I don't want you running to her this time, do you hear me?"

"She's in Rumania," I said.

"I know, I know. I couldn't ever face her, or you, for that matter, if she had to pinch and save or pawn her jewels, sell her house, just to bail me out. I don't know how to say it any more clearly. I couldn't stand it. This is my deal and I'm not going to have her throwing her precious last dollars at it."

The phone fell out of my hand. When I got it back to my ear she was saying, "I know it sounds ungrateful, but I don't mean it to. It's only that I couldn't stand it. Number two, don't do anything foolish like sell off parcels. You have to swear that you won't do something rash like try to get zoning changes and sell off the old orchard. I know I've complained about the farm over the years, but I didn't mean it, not really. I love that place. I've been having nightmares about your going to great lengths to get money so I can get out of here. I had this dream that you were like a kid with a lemonade stand out in the front yard, only you were selling off whole cows. I know you, Howard. I know you! I just don't want you to do something we'll both regret later."

I had not seriously considered selling any part of the farm, I suppose because Rafferty had told me it was our greatest asset. It also was not something a person could dump onto the market expecting to make a quick fortune. "I want to have you out." I had to yell to hear myself. The father was on one side of me, fuming and swearing. On the other side there was a teenage boy whose jeans were slashed up and down his legs. He was so excited he had to stand to talk.

"Look it," she said. "They have to give me a trial in three months. They can't keep me in here longer than ninety days. Well, okay, they could if Rafferty needs more time and makes a motion to delay. Still, three months, four months—I'm telling you I'm all right."

"Alice," I said slowly, "Rafferty said we shouldn't discuss the case over the phone. We have to be careful. But can you help me understand? Suzannah Brooks is praying for us, no one will speak to me—"

"We don't have time to explain. It's happening. I've seen Rafferty. He's so strange he makes me laugh, with that voice of his, thick with adenoidal drippings. He should probably have them removed, don't you think so? Aside from his goatee and the way he's always rubbing it, he's smart, he's decent—"

"I saw him too." And again I said, "I can't understand this." But we were talking at the same time. We might as well have been on different continents, satellites beaming our voices back and forth over the long distance.

"You have to realize," she was saying, "that Mrs. Mackessy has had it in for me for a long time. I've been thinking these few days how Prairie Junction, Prairie Center, whatever the hell our town is called, has been changing so fast, all the houses going up, the racetrack, the strip along the highway. It's gone through so much change we don't even know what it's called anymore—"

"We shouldn't be talking about—"

"Those Hmong people have moved in down by the mill. Hmong people in Prairie Center! The old-timers probably think they're done for. Sometimes people get so confused by how fast everything's moving they have to throw somebody out, to make them feel better. It could have been anyone, really. The neighborhood associations in the new subdivisions have had so many disputes about how high the fences should be, what kind of annuals you can plant, the Christmas decorations they'll allow. This ought to unify them."

"Jesus, Alice," I said under my breath. I didn't know how she could see it in such an impersonal way. I had thought she was going to be frail and withdrawn. I had thought I might have to coax her to speak.

"Don't look at me as if I'm cracked, Howard. I'm not saying I deserve this. I was feeling pretty sorry for myself last night and I thought that I should pray, that I should ask Christ or God, whoever, to save me from prison. And then I realized that there's no point in believing now, just to be saved. That's a fair-weather friend. If I had believed before I was in trouble that would be one thing, but to believe now—"

I was trying to understand what she was saying. And I had to keep her in line so she didn't mention anything in a way that could be misconstrued. Also I needed to pinpoint what was different about her. As she jabbered on about whether it would be right to go to the daily Bible class, I realized that I hadn't talked with her since before Lizzy drowned. She hadn't spoken in weeks. She was chattering the way she often used to before Lizzy died. She was the one who usually held up more than her end of the conversation. She had the same lulling and companionable effect of the radio in the barn, something I tuned in and out of. She was coming close to the glass, peering at me. "Are you okay, Howard? You look sort of awful."

We had so little time and I didn't yet know how this had happened to her. That was what I had set out to learn, above and beyond seeing that she was in one piece. "Alice," I said, "there have been some calls. I need to figure—"

"What? What are people saying?"

"We shouldn't be discussing it here—"

"That's ridiculous! I have a right to know what people are saying so I can defend myself. I have a feeling each story is going to be more and more outrageous. Tell me! Tell me what's being said."

"One woman, a stranger, said that you told her daughter—"

"What?"

"That you could g-get it on with a tampon."

She shut her eyes and wrinkled her nose, as if she was trying to think back to a smell. After a minute she threw up her right arm. Her eyes, her mouth, both of them popped wide open. She stared at me before she began her explanation. "How do we live in this world, Howard?" She waited a beat, perhaps expecting an answer. "How do we do it? You try to be a decent person, try to rise above the savage and ugly things, but not so far above that everything seems distasteful. Maybe it's just not possible. Most of the kids at school are good and sweet, but the ones who aren't, the minority, ruin it for everybody. Last fall, last year, I walked into the girl's bathroom because I heard hooting. I told you this. Josie Marone was standing at the sink, Josie Marone, a very smart, very developed sixth-grade girl, the one who wore the off-the-shoulder prom dress for the chorus concert. It turned out—I'm sure I told you about this. I must have. It turned out the girl in the stall was having her first period and Josie was trying to talk her through using a tampon. I told Josie a tampon wasn't appropriate under the circumstances and I bought a sanitary pad from the dispenser. The poor girl was mortified. As I was leaving, Josie said to me, 'So, when you use a tampon, do you get it on?' Sixth grade. What do I say to that? She was sniggering, thinking she was going to get a rise out of me. 'Josie,' I said, 'sexuality is about intimacy, about closeness, about giving and receiving,' you know, that line. Sometimes I just don't want to live in this world. Maybe the sex in advertising and the movies is triggering children's neurons and they're going through puberty earlier than ever before. Couldn't that happen? We should go to Ireland, to some poor country where there's no birth control, no plastic toys, where people drink a lot of beer and grow vegetables."

She leaned back on her stool to check the wall clock. "Oh, not yet, not yet," she moaned. "Our time is nearly up. Okay, okay, so Rafferty says it should be simple, that what I told him makes it relatively easy to sink his teeth in and fight the good fight. I'm supposed to have a hearing ten days from my preliminary arraignment, by law, but Rafferty's delaying so he can study up. His first order of business is to try to get the bail reduced. The state is pushing him to get going and he's trying to string them along. There's this whole pecking order with the phone in our pod, and the second time I got to it you were out. And then someone jammed it and they say they're not going to fix it. I'm not sure I could handle talking to the girls anyway. I'm so far away from them— Are they okay? Where are they this afternoon?"

There was a beep, our warning signal.

"And another thing, tell them the truth, as much as you can. Tell them that once in a rare while people blame the wrong person for their own troubles. Tell them I hope I'll be home in ninety days, that I'll be out by September. And Howard," she said. She came close to the glass again. She was like a dolphin brushing by in an aquarium. We looked at each other. She didn't say anything more. I think we were both remembering the night before she was arrested. The last time we'd touched one another, and exchanged a few words, had been that night. I hadn't understood what was going through her mind, why she had struggled and crashed up, making the floorboards shake, the dresser tip. The next morning I hadn't known how we would mend the rift. It almost seemed for a moment, as we watched each other, that her imprisonment was the result of that night. The implications had been serious, terrible. The phones went dead. She was waving at me, backing away with a crooked smile on her face. Her hideous togs hung on her. They had been made for a tall, fat person. They were orange, like reflectors, something you can see in the night when you shine a light at it.

I stood in the entry of the jail for a while, thinking, I guess, that something might happen. That the older deputy who was sitting at his computer terminal behind the glass might get up, might ask me if I was Howard Goodwin. He might glance back at his screen and tell me that something had flashed across to indicate that I could take Alice home. I had gotten out of the habit, on the farm, of thinking of most of us as wretched. Everyone hanging around looked as if their lives were filled with nothing but hatred and stupidity and hard knocks. Of course. What did I expect? And still I stood staring like a foreigner at the sullen, pimply woman who looked all of twenty, baring her rotten teeth in frustration as she tried to pour the Dr. Pepper from a can into her baby's bottle.

On the way home I pulled over by the Washington Park Golf Course to watch the men in pastels buzzing around in their carts. My father had been an avid golfer and I sometimes watch the game, I guess for him. There used to be three effigy mound groups in that park along the Root

River, from about A.D. 1000. One was in the shape of a panther that measured eighty feet in length. The mounded earth was landfilled years ago to make way for the golf course. It had been a disappointment to my father, that I hadn't taken to golf. He hadn't been able to believe that I'd played with a friend without keeping score, that we'd gone to the course because I liked to walk around outside.

When I turned into Miss Bowman's drive the girls were sitting on the railroad ties at the foot of her crudely terraced garden. They weren't fighting or talking or scratching in the dirt. Miss Bowman came out of her kitchen door. She watched us with her one good eye as I helped the girls into the car. "Thanks," I called. "I really appreciate it." She stood on her porch with her hands in her apron pockets. She was inert. I picked up a small sharp stone and I realized, just in time, that I was thinking of throwing it at her. I wanted to see if it would make her move or speak. A week before I would never have had the reflex to throw anything at anyone. "We'll be by for eggs one of these days," I said. "Thanks again." I waved. "So long." At the last minute I remembered that I was supposed to pay her. I got out of the car and ran up the stairs to the side entrance. She was stirring onions in a frying pan at the stove. When I opened the kitchen door she yapped and whipped around in alarm. "Here," I said, setting the five dollars on the table. "Thanks so much."

I gunned the old Ford and screeched out of the driveway. The Scottish terrier was going berserk at his post. "Well," I said, once we'd turned the bend and the barking noise had died down, "What did you do?"

Emma was sitting in the back with her arms folded across her chest. "Nothing. She followed us everywhere! She's stupid."

"She's stupid," Claire mimicked. "She sings to herself."

"You said you would bring Mom home." Emma's voice was husky. Now that I had actually seen Alice I knew I was accountable to the girls in a way that I hadn't been before. We sat in the car in our driveway and I told them that their mother was in the county jail because sometimes people blame the wrong person for their own troubles. I'm not sure I sounded convincing. Emma blurted out that that wasn't fair. Claire was still chronicling the oddities of Miss Bowman: She stored her potholders in the oven, the dogs drank out of the toilet bowl, she couldn't even open one of her eyes.

"Shut up," Emma said to Claire. "But how is she going to get out? How will she ever get out of jail?"

"She was eating crackers right in front of us!" Claire shouted.

Emma whooped her sister over the head with a book. "I said shut up, you idiot! *How* is she going to get out?"

I parked the car by the house and gathered up Claire. She was in shambles. We went inside where I tried to put her back together. It was a temporary fix. I then delivered a short lecture on the criminal justice system in our state. I explained that they couldn't keep Alice for more than ninety days, three months, until the end of September. Emma, with either her innate understanding of manmade systems, or else her American instinct to throw money at a problem said, "Couldn't we pay to get her out?"

"It will take a lot of money," I said.

"Grammie will pay."

"Yes, well, maybe she can help us."

"What if she can't? I'm not ever going to Miss Bowman's again. Never. Who will take care of us?"

Emma was probably thinking in practical terms, such as who would spend hour after hour amusing them, day after day until September. I was thinking not only of those hours, but also of the details. I had never washed the girls' hair, never cleaned out their ears or cut their toenails. I wasn't in the habit of cooking. I might not have thought of any of the rituals if Alice hadn't outlined a timetable for them in a letter of instruction. The letter, the only one I'd received from her, had arrived a few days earlier. Once a week, she said, she clipped fingernails, scrubbed behind ears, washed the hairbrushes in the sink, and set them face down on a towel to dry. She told me I should sort the laundry by color, as if it was important. "Don't put cotton in the dryer," she warned. She reminded me not to be hard on Emma about eating things she hated, not now, especially.

What is this? I had said to myself after I read the letter. I didn't know how Alice could be so matter-of-fact. I didn't know how she had the serenity to think of such inconsequential things. I thought back to how calm she had been when they took her, and then about how animated she'd been during our visit. I wasn't sure if she was ill, or if in fact she was getting better. I was as mystified by her behavior as I was by the charge. Even the drought, and the sick lamb who had lost control of its limbs, even I suppose, the death of Lizzy—all of that hard luck and tragedy was something a person could expect as they grew older. There was nothing in our experience, nothing that had prepared us for being taken from our life.

And although I probably sound like a simpleton, not knowing that you clean a child's ears or wash underwear in hot water, I had been absolved of those tasks for years. Alice and I had divided up the duties from the start. She had once said that that was one of the beauties of having a farm, that she didn't see herself stuck with the drudge because all of the jobs were tedious. We were in the whole mess together. We had laughed over the picture of ourselves toiling as if we were part of a chain gang. Thoreau thought it was a misfortune to inherit a farm or even, I suppose, willingly own a farm. Farmers are poor brutes, he said, slaves to the soil. They spend so much time working, their aching fingers trembling with fatigue, their backs giving way, that they don't have time or energy for the finer fruits. I have always thought that work is as common and fine as air, something that we become a part of. I am drawn to the out of doors, to the ordinary pleasures of everyday work. Alice used to say that if I was a bird I'd be the first one to sing, the wayward robin who's cranking it up before a ray of light gives anyone allowance.

I have thought a fair amount about our farm, about our house that was built in 1852. It was still a good house, even though it didn't look like much. There are thousands of those houses across the Midwest. White clapboard houses with old windmills in their yards, many of them standing empty now on the prairies of Kansas and Nebraska. They are a series of squares, built according to need. Ours are deceptively strong houses, stronger than the winds of a twister, determined against insects and drought and long winters, determined against time, against all of the generations that have passed through them. I have tried to imagine the men and women who have broken their bread in our kitchen, and tilled the soil and fallen asleep at night, too tired to take their boots off, as I sometimes was. The farmer who built our house, Thomas Clausen, kissed his wife good-bye and walked off to fight in the Civil War. An old guy down at Del's told me about him. When Clausen came back from the war he turned the other way and went to California to pan for gold. I don't know if his wife and children begrudged him his absences.

Alice once told me that pioneer women suffered from anorexia, that there was evidence that proved it was so. I couldn't imagine Thomas Clausen walking up the lane from California only to find his wife skin and bones. I was used to thinking of that first family as long-suffering but philosophical, wise and robust. I found a picture up in the attic of a later family, standing out in front of the house, all of them, even the baby, looking grim as hell. I actually don't have too much rapture about time past, although Alice has accused me of being hopelessly sentimental. There has never been a time of simple light. Still, I try to imagine the land for the taking, and what it must have meant to have space for as far as the eye can see. The Wisconsin Indians in 10,000 B.C., perhaps sleeping right where our yard was, hunted mastodon. *Mastodon.* They ate bison, giant beavers, caribou, and elk. It is unthinkable now that anyone could ever have drunk out of our rivers and lakes. I don't have the power to imagine what it must have been like. I can't even visualize the endless prairie, the vast tracks of woodland. I can't hold it in my mind long enough to know absolutely what we've lost. And so the loss is magnified, knowing, as I do, that my powers are poor, and that our world has become diminished beyond all measure.

I have thought about the boy who lived on our farm, Gurdon Huck, who in 1908 fell off a hay wagon and broke his neck. I found his father's log of weather and planting and harvesting, on the floor of our closet. It was under a hatbox like a piece of trash. His last entry says, "June 9, 1908. Yesterday our boy fell off the wagon. Broke his neck. Dead." I showed the notebook to Dan, but I wasn't willing to give it up to the Dairy Shrine. It belongs to the house. In the attic, in an old trunk, we found books on agriculture and etiquette and religion, a fountain pen, a bag of lace, a cracked platter, a pie tin filled with black-and-gray stones. We had no idea who gathered the stones or where. We brought them downstairs and set them in the middle of our kitchen table. They were smooth as could be. As the weeks went on they gathered dust and crumbs and jelly spots. They came to look less and less like relics from the ages and more and more like us. I cleaned them up and put them back in the attic.

The people who lived in our house probably considered, as most of us do, that our moment is what is real. It wasn't too long after we moved to the farm that for me time began to run together. That way of seeing probably comes with age. The past seemed to flow into the present, in some instances taking over the here and now. It was all the traces that made me feel the quickness of passing time, of passing generations. Alice wondered what we should do with the old things, the laces, the stones, the pens, the books. For her it was a matter of deciding between Goodwill and the monthly trash pickup. "They'll stay in the attic," I said. I tried to tell her that that pile of stuff served as a reminder that we are passersby, nothing more. Yet I also believed that those few things in the chest, all of the associations long gone, the layers of wallpaper in our bedroom, the journal in the closet—all of that experience matters. Alice reiterated that I was an incurable romantic. I could only say again that the past, the details of the past, in some terrible and impossible way, matters. I say impossible because what seems important today is probably not tomorrow, and in any case most everything is lost and forgotten, or else destroyed. I stubbornly believed, in the six years we lived on the farm, that the people before us in our house left their history to us, knowing that we would safeguard it.

It took those six years we lived in Prairie Center to really know the place. Even Claire, young as she was, knew the haunts and the hunts. In May, when the grass was so green it hurt to look at it, the air so overpoweringly sweet you had to go in and turn on the television just to dull your senses—that's when Claire knew it was time to look for the asparagus in the pastures. If it rained she wondered if she should check our secret places for morels. In June, when the strawberries ripened, we made hay and the girls rode on top of the wagon. I was ever mindful of the boy who had fallen off and broken his neck. In July, the pink raspberries, all in brambles in the woods and growing up our front porch, turned black and tart. In August, the sour apples were the coming thing. In September, there were the crippled-up pears in the old orchard. In October, we picked the pumpkins and popcorn. And all winter, when there was snow, we lived for the wild trip down the slopes on the toboggan.

Maybe I dreamed this. I'm not sure anymore. I remember, that first April, when we found the crocuses coming up all over the hillside in the back beyond the pond. Alice went to the slope and knelt. She turned to me, her face flushed with pleasure. She said, "Do you think the farmwife who planted these tried to imagine us as she dug the holes? Do you think she made a prayer for the farm? 'Here's hoping for another hundred years! Here's hoping for Howard Goodwin!' "

Chapter Eleven

———

IT IS A RULE of nature that taking a day off on a farm sets a person back at least a week. I had been keeping up with morning and evening chores and letting everything else slide. In the early hours, on Monday before the girls woke, I mustered the energy to kill the lamb that was half-dead. With five years experience I still considered myself new enough at killing. I was clumsy. I stunned the lamb with a blow to its head and then quickly slit its throat. I had killed the lambs and the chickens for food, and occasionally I had to kill something as a kindness. I knew that each time I slaughtered an animal I thought less about it, and that if I let it, the process might become pretty well mechanical. I struggled between wanting to numbly get on with the job, and the need to pause, to offer thanks to the breathing animal, to wonder at its essence before I knocked the life out of it.

I knew without looking past the front porch in those first weeks that each day something more was lost in the drought. It didn't seem to matter much. Our life without Alice was wrong. After Rafferty failed to get the bail reduced, he told me that there was nothing to do but wait. His refrain was that one word: Wait. I don't think he had any idea how cruel his pronouncements were. Nothing to do but wait. And just how does a person wait, I wanted to ask. I remember sitting in the chair in the living room, too tired to close the windows and doors against the continuous blast of scorched air as I skimmed over the library books I'd gotten on the legal system. The girls lay on the carpet, panting. It was strange, how in the heat and quiet they lost their childishness. Occasionally they'd rise up and put a Lego block on top of another. Snapping one block into the next used all their strength. They were like inner tubes with slow leaks as they sank back down to rest. They lay without pillows, with their heads turned sidewise, flat on the floor.

There was the reckless and false accusation to consider, and there was the simple fact of missing Alice, of needing her. I held on to that fact. It would have been easy to be distracted by the anger that had been unleashed against us. I had to remind myself over and over that the real reason we were listing and badly off course had nothing to do with the community uproar. It had everything to do with the absence of our navigator. She managed us. She managed our bodies and even our minds, our spirits. She put her foot down when we stank from the barn, and she informed me when I needed a haircut. She made me talk, something that has not been my strong point. She wanted to know about things like the Black Hawk War. Although she'd forget the major points between the tellings, she always seemed to be interested. She was ignorant about history, and in particular about her own times. "Who was Barry Goldwater again?" she'd ask. "What was it that happened at that convention in 1968, the one in Chicago?"

Without her, without the family, I might have worked night and day. Before supper she went out on the porch and rang the old dinner bell. I came, thirsty and hungry, back to our time and place. I remembered this: the food steaming on the table and Alice playing a Mozart sonata she loved. It was the only thing she ever played on the tinny piano that had come with the house. She sang to the girls in her hoarse voice, what she called her "loony voice." She read to them for hours and she let them paint her face all over with clown makeup. Alice once told me that when her mother died it was as if the lights had been snuffed out, as if the volume had been turned down so low you couldn't hear anything. If Emma and Claire had been able to put words to their feelings they might have said the same.

Not that she and I hadn't had unpleasant weeks or even months in our marriage. Not that there weren't times she'd bitch unmercifully. I'd dig my fists in my pockets and get busy. There were whole seasons when she was harried, when everything irritated her. You'd want to stay out of her way. Ours was not an easy life and carrying her nursing jobs, as well as the household and the chores, was a strain. Still, I refused to believe that she wasn't made of strong stuff, that she would buckle under what was our chosen path. The two or so times we actually fought she smashed a plate and stormed out into the night. I have always disliked an argument. When I tried to be the voice of reason, when I pointed out that it might be wiser to continue what I mildly referred to as, "the discussion," she flew off the handle again. Later, in jest, she accused me of being more even and mature than any reasonable person could tolerate.

I met her in Ann Arbor, when I was growing vegetables down by the old railroad tracks. I used to take my goods to the market once a week and set up two sawhorses and a board. I'd put out my broccoli, pea pods, carrots, tomatoes, cucumbers. Anyone would have admired the enormous purple cabbages that I'd picked at dawn, with dew on the outer leaves. I had always wanted to be a farmer, although my father was determined I be a businessman. I studied History at first, and after he died I took up Dairy Science. I was an undergraduate for an embarrassing number of years. Alice walked by my table one morning when I was in my last semester. I remember how she stood staring at the eggplants. They were beautiful, as shiny as patent leather. Her blond hair was in a braid, coiled and pinned to the back of her head. She was carrying a basket filled with leeks over her arm. She was the most statuesque person I'd ever seen. She was wearing a strange thing, a quilt, a bed cover that had been cut up and made into a wrap. I wasn't in the habit of making remarks to women I didn't know. All the same I heard myself saying, "You must be hungry after the long trip on the *Mayflower*."

She continued to study the eggplants, and when she'd had enough she looked directly at me. "I am," she said, without blinking.

I was distracted then by the Oriental men surrounding my produce. I didn't have time to watch her back away. "How much? How much?" They were all asking at once, holding up their vegetable of choice. I was tossing bags at them, telling them to help themselves, racing between the scale and the change drawer. I bumped into her because she was somehow right next to me, in her bedclothes, trying to read the price sign upside down on the other side, on the customer side of the table. She was on my side now. She was frowning, counting on her fingers, trying to work out the sum of two-and-a-half pounds of broccoli at forty cents a pound. She had gone over the holy invisible line between vendor and buyer. She'd walked straight over to my side and without instruction began to determine weight and count out change.

I had been with enough other women through the years who were appealing at first because they were so eager to please. I used to fall for the long-brown-haired girls with big white teeth who tried so hard to be interested in the world and life. I finally figured out that they were only after the drama of romance. There was a particular way they'd sit at my feet and turn their bright faces to look up at me. They'd switch their political allegiance if I said so, want the same breed of dog, become vegetarian. I guess I understood that adoration is short-lived, and that really what they were giving me was the temporary power to crush them. I'd have to tell them that I was unwilling to commit myself as yet, that it was nothing personal. I didn't like how they'd cling to me, begging for the right to remain.

That day I first met Alice I asked her if she could come back the next week, to help. She said she didn't know. When I mentioned that it was busy as early as 6 A.M., that I had to unload and sell simultaneously, she said, "I'm not up that early."

I thought of thanking her for her help and leaving it at that. She had a basket filled with leeks. I didn't think that single people bought leeks. A person bought leeks to make soup for a household. I knew that if I let her go I might not see her again. I got her to sit on the back of my pickup truck. "You'll get your farm," she declared, after I'd quickly outlined my idea for the rest of my life. It wasn't that she was clairvoyant. She said that of course she didn't really know what was going to happen, but that if a person was quiet and observant the way she'd been for twenty-odd years, you got a feel for the patterns and the personalities. She said that all she'd done through her long school career was sit at her desk with her arms folded across her chest and watch the teachers, the students, and the administrators. She dreamed about their lives, and imagined them in various predicaments, to save herself from dying of boredom. She advocated public schools and the rigors of monotony, in fact, because she said it forced a person to cultivate an inner life.

Some Saturdays, over the course of that autumn, she came to help, and others she didn't. I lost sleep when she didn't come. I thought about her all the time when I was awake. Once I knew her address I worried that she would move without telling me. I worried that she'd change her phone number or that she'd walk by my table hand in hand with someone else.

The first time she took a shower in my apartment she came out of the bathroom with a towel wrapped around her head in a turban. She was wearing my tartan bathrobe, a flannel thing my mother had given me and I had never worn. She stooped to put on her shoes. There was one blond strand of hair down her back, that hadn't been caught up in the towel. She'd come with her clean knapsack and taken from it things which intrigued me. They turned out to be everyday products in exotic packaging. She'd brought a toothbrush made from boar's bristles and toothpaste in a black tube, a birth-control device and accompanying gel, and a wooden soap box which she said was impractical. I was still young enough to hope that having, living with, the right hard-headed woman, was the key to happiness. She was self-contained, I thought, didn't need anyone to show her the way. As she stooped in her turban, it seemed to me that if every man had a woman who looked like Alice in my bathrobe the world would be an untroubled place.

At Christmas, when I took her to visit my mother, Emma was conceived. My father had always threatened to disinherit me if I got a girl pregnant outside of wedlock. Even in high school I had been scrupulous. They say that some women know when conception has occurred, that their sixth sense tells them. My mother had shown us to our separate bedrooms. When I thought she was asleep I crept down the hall like a teenager to Alice's bed. At the moment of penetration Nellie crashed into the bathroom. She began brushing her teeth and then tapping her toothbrush on the porcelain sink. I clapped my hand over Alice's mouth. I wasn't sure my mother was ever going to get the water out of the bristles. It was a persistent, demanding sound, like the racket people make on champagne glasses with their forks at a wedding. I remember thinking that that is probably the noise sperm and egg make as they collide and burst into one.

Everything fell into place. Three weeks later Alice discovered that she was pregnant. A month later she turned twenty-five and came into the substantial sum her Aunt Kate had provided for her. My father was dead and could not disown us. We got married by the justice of the peace in Ann Arbor. With some help from my mother, along with Alice's contribution and my meager savings, we bought the farm at Prairie Junction. Alice felt sure that my father, dead two short years, would overlook our one glaring indiscretion. She said that he would see that it had led us to the straight and narrow.

At first Alice wrote us several times a week. She wondered about common things, things which surprised me. She wondered if the church ladies were bringing casseroles and cakes and nut breads. I assumed she was joking. We were not churchgoers and yet I knew if ours had been different circumstances the ladies would have come to our aid. They would have brought the kind of food my mother can turn out with factory precision for the needy.

I guess it was both on the telephone with Nellie and in my letters to Alice, that I began to learn the fine art of dissembling. I labored over the words as I wrote. Without telling her the truthful details that were frightening, I wanted to provoke Alice to fight for herself. Each day I woke freshly shocked at what had seemed, in the few minutes I had seen her, like the strangest acceptance on her part of a flagrant obstruction of justice. She was remote from her own tragedy. It hadn't seemed to affect her much more than an oil spill off the coast of Guam would have. If only she'd beat her wings inside her iron cage, I thought, she might have a chance of getting away. Sometimes I wanted to have her in my hands, to shake her. I wanted her to understand that everyone had turned us out. It had been impossible to talk with the vet about the white muscle disease running through the sheep flock. He had put me on hold and never come back. Because I meant to be kind and because I wanted to arouse her indignation, I never said much of anything in my letters.

When my mother finally got through again on that first Sunday, I did not answer a single question honestly. "Howie," she said, "I've had such trouble getting a hold of you. How are you? Are the girls all right?"

"We're okay, Mom."

"Did they clear up the problem?"

It was a fine question. My mother seemed to know not to ask about specifics. The "they" could stand for our collection of friends and enemies. "The problem" was so beautifully general either a yes or a no would suffice. Rafferty himself had said he'd found a simple way into the case. "It's coming along," I said. "I'm going to need some money for the lawyer's fee. What I really need right now is bail money—to get Alice out. To pay her bond."

"I don't see why you should have to pay when it was a mistake. I'm very short on reserves right now, Howard." She called me Howard whenever we talked about finances. "What do you need?"

I tried to come right out with it. *One hundred thousand.* "Ninety," I said. "Ninety thousand."

"How many thousands? Good land, did you say nineteen?" She sighed. I could hear that sigh across two continents and an ocean. She sighed again. It is remarkable that a sigh is substantive enough to get picked up by a receiver, beamed up as an electronic impulse to a satellite, and transmitted back down to earth. "Howard," she said, "you know I'd do anything for you. I was perfectly happy to lend you money toward your farm. Not that that way of life doesn't worry me. It's not stable, doesn't bring in enough to provide the things you ought to have. Your father and I worked hard all our lives and we saved a fair amount. I lent you a good portion of our nest egg. Maybe you don't understand, honey, that—"

"I've got the girls in the tub, Mom. I need to check them, so I'll sign off. We're over the hump on this, so you don't need to worry."

It was eleven o'clock at night. The girls were asleep. If I stayed on the line my mother would continue on with the speech I knew from memory. She'd catalog the things she'd done for us. Alice had once made the harsh comment that Nellie was a testament to the fact that insipid people could do a great deal of good in this world. I had resented her saying what was so obvious on the surface. My mother had in the past acted like a pampered housewife. In reality, however, she had always done thankless community service jobs as a nurse. She had been a volunteer for the Red Cross for several years, flying off to places where there was not basic sanitation much less four-star hotels. I know it is true that my mother, as mothers do, wanted what was best for us. Alice would debate that, saying that the evidence spoke for itself. Nellie, she maintained, was a passive-aggressive busybody who had never liked her daughter-in-law. Nellie, she said, tried, wittingly or unwittingly, to botch up our lives just to prove that I had made the wrong choice. Despite the old saw, it's been my experience that good intentions can actually get a person a fair distance. I would never bet my life on anything, but if I did, if I had to, it would be on my mother. I would bet my life that she had always had the best of intentions and that we had benefited from them.

I didn't mention to Alice that I'd talked with Nellie. I didn't tell her that two days after she was taken we went to the grocery store in Blackwell. The waters parted for us as we came down the aisle. The few women in the dairy section peeled away, staring. At the end of the junk-food aisle an older gentleman with stubble and a sweat-stained green T-shirt tight across his chest and belly stood in wait. He spat on the linoleum at my feet. He breathed heavily and scowled in my face. We left our groceries in the cart by the magazine stand and walked quickly out of the store. Emma and Claire did not contain their distress. We drove twenty miles after that, to buy a loaf of bread and a gallon of milk.

I also didn't tell Alice that the night before the preliminary hearing Rafferty stopped out for about forty-five minutes. We talked in the kitchen after the girls were in bed. He explained that he made it his business to leave no stone unturned in his cases. He'd had dinner at the restaurant Carol Mackessy managed, he'd said. Shrimp in pesto sauce. Not half-bad. We would talk in greater detail after the preliminary hearing, but he said that even now at this early date he liked to feel that he had stepped into the players' skins. His eyes were too big for his sockets, which gave him an intensity he may or may not have had. Not into my skin, I said to myself. He sat at our kitchen table, drawing straight lines across his legal pad. There were occasions when I wondered if he was a charlatan. I wondered if he'd actually gone to law school, if he popped up to prey on helpless people. I'd have to remind myself that he came highly recommended, that he was a good friend of Dan and Theresa's.

He seemed surprised when I told him I didn't know much about Alice's family history. What I'd been told about her upbringing I can say in two simple sentences. She is an only child who was raised by her mother's best friend. Her father died of kidney failure when she was twenty-two.

"That's all?" he asked, opening his eyes wider. Alice said once that she always worried about making astonishing remarks in front of Rafferty because she feared his eyes might pop out.

It occurred to me that what little I had said made her sound like a psychopath, like a woman who couldn't confide in her own husband. I think he sensed my discomfort. He began asking logical questions about the farming operation. I found myself explaining in great detail about how to get a good seed bed for alfalfa. I told him my calf losses were about three percent, a statistic I was proud of. I'd made plywood four-by-four hutches for the newborns and then I'd feed them whole milk diluted with hot water, from nipple pails. Pretty early on they'd get a mix of corn, brewers' pellets, oats, and minerals. I didn't tell Rafferty that Alice would go on binges, talking about the problem of chin hairs for a full hour, chronicling the different electrolysists she'd been to in her life. I used to laugh until my side hurt at her impersonations of the hairless ladies rooting out her follicles. There were times though, when I could hardly get her to notice I was standing in her way. She imagined that Claire had lived before, that she'd been a princess in ancient Egypt, that she had previously learned how to charm animals and men.

When Rafferty asked me about Lizzy's death I told him, as best I could, the sequence of events. There were several things I omitted, however. When Alice shouted, "Don't force me," in the church vestibule at the funeral, everyone froze. Lizzy's relations, all in a line, pulled away from their embraces, their handshakes, their words of comfort. They looked at my wife tramping out the door. I stood still and stared at the floor, trusting that time would pass. It did. Finally the woman behind me huffed, "Well." That served as a signal for noise and motion to resume. Theresa was the only one in line who was kind enough to ask after Alice.

I don't remember exactly what I said to explain or excuse her before I went into the sanctuary. I put my head down for the opening prayer. Right away I realized I was cursing Alice instead of turning my thoughts to Lizzy.

Even as I was telling Rafferty about the percentage of butterfat in my Guernseys' milk, I had the feeling that I'd lost part of my memory, or experience. Something was happening to my brain. I used to be certain about plenty of things. That certainty was slipping away as I rested between my sentences. I didn't tell him that my wife had been sleeping twenty hours a day. I didn't say that she hadn't been able to speak or dress herself. I told myself afterward that omission isn't much of a sin. It's a safety valve, nothing more or less, for those of us who have been brought up to be honest at all costs. I didn't mention the night before her arrest, when I'd come into our room and seen her on the bed. She used to do that, go to bed while it was still light, because she was waiting. It used to be a sign. I had come in that night and found her lying on the bed with her clothes on. She was shivering, in the heat. All that was in keeping with our common language. I knew that she had finally come back into herself because she raised her head and turned toward me. I was sure then that she'd been waiting.

I couldn't have explained what had taken place that night, to Rafferty, or to anyone else. I hadn't given it much consideration myself. She had knocked me over. She had kneed me in the jaw as she flew up. Rafferty was saying he didn't know how people got over the death of a child. He stared at me from across the table. I felt my jaw with both hands, like the hurt was fresh. I said they'd probably never recover. He asked me if there was anything else I should tell him. That night before they came to get Alice I had misunderstood the signs, the private language, the rituals—things I had taken for granted for years. Rafferty kept his eyes on me, as if I was the culprit. I said again that I didn't know how you'd continue after a loss like that. I wondered if I had ever understood Alice. I wondered, how, after years of our life together, there was only a handful of sentences that I would admit to a stranger about my wife.

Chapter Twelve

———

THERESA APPEARED AT OUR door the night after the preliminary hearing. I wasn't expecting to see her. It was mid-July and they'd been gone almost a month. I had been trying to clean a cherry stain off the new white T-shirt my mother had given Emma earlier in the summer. Emma had realized, too late, that wiping her dirty hands on the shirt would spoil it. She was trying to be calm and hold steady while I scrubbed hard against her ribs. Claire was in the living room, glassy-eyed, watching a musical-variety show. If my mother had been with us she would have rushed to the shirt and held cold compresses to the stain. Out of the corner of my eye I noticed a shadow in the yellow light of the evening. I thought a cloud had passed over the sun. Theresa came right up to the screen and pressed her hands against it, around her face. "Is anyone home?" she asked. Her voice was so small I wondered if she hoped we were gone.

The stain had gotten smeared and was worse than it had been at the start. In the weeks that Alice had been gone I had done my best to keep up appearances. If we let ourselves fall apart the neighbors, or the police, might descend upon us and pick our bones clean. Even though I had vacuumed and disposed of old tuna cans for the sake of normalcy, there were certain tasks I didn't do well. For one thing, I was not in harmony with the soiled shirt, the way my mother would have been. For another, I couldn't work up sympathy for extraneous items such as throw rugs. Why wash the table, sweep the floor, settle the rugs, swab the counter after every meal, when we're coming back within four hours to disrupt what I've labored over to make right? I ask the question only half-jokingly. Alice always said I had a high threshold for filth and squalor. When we first knew each other in Ann Arbor she had me pegged as a nose picker in the car, the kind of person who wipes his hand under the seat if there isn't a Kleenex. I said, "What's the alternative?" She looked over her sunglasses at me as if the answer was obvious. She used to occasionally get on the bandwagon after she'd been with Theresa for an evening. She'd rail on, something about how my household dysfunction was a habit my mother had nurtured in me from infancy. There'd been clear female boundaries in my birthplace, she said, across which males did not venture. I assume she meant the chain-link fence around the broom closet and the dishwasher. So I was cultivated to be an unremorseful slob. Dairying has only reinforced my natural tendencies. I'm outside all day long, in dirt and dung and chaff. It's unwieldy in nature, no cap on dust, or broken machines that must come to rest somewhere. There's no end to bailing twine, rusty nails, old fencing materials a person might someday want to use again. Beyond a certain point I've given up trying to bring about order.

"We're in here," I said to Theresa as I opened the door. I wondered if she knew about Alice's arrest. I wondered if she was going to quote some Scripture or put my eye out. She looked around herself as she set foot in the door. She saw, I guess in one penetrating glance, that I'd been doing the best I could. She saw that my best effort wasn't worth much.

"I've been trying to get a cherry stain out of Emma's white T-shirt," I said, to explain why everything else had gone by the wayside.

"Let me," she said, reaching for the dish towel in my hand. "Hold still, Em." I relaxed some then, figuring that if she was going to worry over a spot, she might not know. She kneeled, massaging the shirt for a minute. "This isn't going to work," she said. "Boil water, Howard. For a fruit stain you pour hot water from above. You hold it way up—there's something about pouring from a distance that makes a difference. It's all in the heat and distance."

"Heat and distance," I repeated. "Better take off the shirt, Emma." I filled the kettle at the sink and then walked across the room to the stove. "Here," I said on my way, pulling out a stool for Theresa. After I fiddled with the temperamental knob on the one working burner I went to the table and stood across from her, trying to casually lean on a chair with my elbows.

We watched Emma taking off her shirt, trying to work her way around the wet spots so they wouldn't touch her face. I couldn't remember ever having been alone with Theresa before, without other adults. I can't say I actually knew her outside of the context, the strictures, of other people's associations with her. She was my wife's good friend. She was my neighbor's wife. She was the mother of our children's playfellow. If our families had dinner together, Dan and I would often stand outside before the meal was ready. We'd talk about whether I should buy the new high-tensile wire fences or stick with what I had, about the Potawatomi Indians, about storm systems, local history, town politics, national politics, the Brewers, the achievements of our daughters. At dinner, around the table, Alice might get off and running about doing something commonplace. She could make a transaction at the walk-up window at First Federated in downtown Prairie Center sound as elemental as a Greek tragedy. She'd fling her arms around, raving. Her hair would come out of its band. Sometimes I'd rein her in. She tended to see the world in black and white, and if I'd make a remark about how the bank manager wasn't actually evil, that he was forced to be conservative because of federal banking regulations, she'd lower her eyes and pinch up her lips, butter a piece of bread. Theresa would urge Alice to go on, to continue the story. It was always Theresa who would say something lighthearted and probably true. "Don't pay any attention to that man," she'd say, laughing at me. "Men, they know too many details for their own good." With modest prodding Alice would continue, looking to the right of me. She meant to tell her story only for the benefit of our neighbors.

Emma had removed her shirt. The three of us stood watching the coil under the teapot turn orange, as if the electric stove had the mesmerizing power of a campfire.

"What is this about, Howard?" Theresa had a naturally soft voice. When she spoke, a person had to watch her mouth to understand what she was saying.

"What?" I asked.

"How are you?"

How was I? I needed to get Alice out of the county jail. I needed to work. I was spending the day walking in circles, getting close to nothing done. I needed to care for Emma and Claire, and protect them. I made them take naps in the afternoon so I could rest from their noise. They were then wide awake half the night. We had run out of food and I didn't know if I had the energy to drive far enough away to buy groceries. It seemed that the world beyond the farm was itself floating farther and farther from us. I wasn't sure I was going to meet the month's payment, let alone come anywhere near the bond or Rafferty's fee. I wasn't at all sure that our cows were going to have anything to eat in the coming winter, or for the rest of the summer, for that matter. I was hungry myself. "I'm fine," I think I said.

"I'm so upset about this," she whispered across the table. She was taking quick, short breaths so she wouldn't cry. She rolled her eyes and pushed her glasses up. "We only got home this afternoon. We took longer than we planned. I hate this country. I walked in the door—I nearly tripped over the stack of papers in the hall. I'm standing reading, saying out loud, 'What? *What?*' And who should come along but Suzannah Brooks, of course, the model Christian, making sure I've heard the dirt. When she said 'Robbie Mackessy' I just shut my mouth and closed the door."

I put my hand to my lips, to make her stop talking. I didn't want her to say anymore in front of Emma.

"If I'd been here I could have prevented this, I just know it. I would have insisted on interviewing Robbie. I would have talked to the police. I know the Mackessys—I've had them in therapy. Give me four, five hours, and I could tell you their troubles. Carol's parents, both of them, were profoundly deaf. I mean, they'd never heard a thing. They had about six kids and every single one of them ran wild. Carol never said exactly, but I've a feeling that her two older sisters are—"

"Let's talk later—" I began.

She was skipping from thing to thing, literally rattling on. She was shaking both hands, spitting as she spoke. "Robbie is an accomplished liar! I've seen children like him who will do anything to manipulate his family. His mother has given him plenty of opportunities to build his con-man skills. When I told Dan that Alice had been arrested, that she was in jail, he said, 'Don't worry about it.' *Don't worry about it!* Can you believe it? That man is practically unconscious. When I told him I was coming down here he said, 'That's probably not a good idea, Theresa. You know how people talk.' Do you see what I mean? He's lost his senses! I put it to him: I said, 'They're in trouble, so they're not our friends anymore?' The worst of it is, I don't have a clue how to help him. It's my business to tend people who are suffering. If he was a patient, a stranger, I would say the right words. Oh God, I don't know. I've seen this kind of thing before, Howard. Someone makes an accusation and the judge can't dismiss it because it's so loaded. The press, the parents, the civic leaders get all sanctimonious about believing the children. The school nurse! It would kill the poor judge's career if he let Alice walk the streets." She quit talking and bared her teeth. She squeezed her eyes shut and let off some steam with a guttural, *"Gaaahhhh."*

"Emma, go upstairs and get a clean shirt on," I said. She stood at the head of the table, fixed on Theresa.

"And Myra Flint, the child protection worker—they put Myra Flint on Robbie? This whole thing is like a bad joke, like a caricature of the system. I mean Myra, if you haven't been abused in this life she'll sniff it out in past lives or future lives. Robbie has a lot of symptoms of a character-disturbed child, and you know what? Myra Flint isn't going to see that! Robbie is going to wrap that woman around his little finger, I'll bet you. I'll bet you money on that one. And Mrs. Mackessy will do the same. I get so frustrated trying to treat people like the Mackessys because they don't want help. Some people actually work to make changes, once in a rare while. But Carol had no interest in figuring herself out. None. She wanted what she wanted. She'd go off on weekends to—"

"I don't want to talk about this right now," I said, moving Emma into the living room. Theresa was laughing, saying, "And anyway, I just can't believe that anyone could possibly think that Robbie would make a reliable witness. I'm not sure he hasn't been abused, judging from the family, but to think that he's going to testify and be coherent. I can just see it, Howard! I can see Robbie telling his mother that something dreadful has happened and Carol, all of a sudden, and finally, tuning into that kid. What do you expect? Robbie has at last figured out that he has to get hurt, really hurt—not just fall off his bike and skin his knee—for his mother to give him the time of day, for his mother to be outraged. What did the paper say about three more boys filing charges?"

"Please," I said, "I don't like talking about it—" I cocked my head toward Emma in about as exaggerated a way as I could.

"Oh God," she cried, "I'm out of my mind, Howard. I really am. I'm so sorry. What can I be thinking?" She had Emma's offending shirt in her hand and she twisted it around and around and then thwacked the wall with it.

"What are you doing to my shirt?" Emma whimpered.

"What, honey?" Theresa asked.

"What are you doing to my shirt?"

"Oh, Emma, oh for goodness sakes. I'm just so darn mad, I don't know what I'm doing. We'll get this stain out, you'll see. Howard, I'll go, I'll—"

"Why don't you run upstairs and get your pajamas on, Emma?" I said. "By the time you're back down the water will be boiling. We'll watch Theresa do her heat-and-distance trick." I was moving toward the porch, hoping that Emma would do as she was told.

"When's the preliminary hearing?" Theresa whispered at my back as I led the way. "They usually put the hearings off forever."

"It's been," I said, sitting down on a bench I'd made from a slab of walnut. "Monday. Yesterday. Rafferty made an effort not to have it continued indefinitely."

Emma came to the door and stood watching us. "Please, Emma," I pleaded. "I need to talk to Theresa and when we're done we'll get us some—" We didn't have anything good to eat. "When we're done we'll do the shirt." She turned slowly and disappeared around the corner.

"What happened? Tell me." Theresa was sitting on the edge of her chair across from me. She must have sat right there any number of times, asking with the same urgency. She and Alice often had some big secret. They were always cackling in disbelief.

The dark was moving in and the few crickets were striking a note here and there. I peered through the door and I could just make out Claire, curled up in front of the television. She had fallen asleep while women with chops and synthetic cleavages belted out their distress. I went and shooed Emma from behind the wood stove in the kitchen. She dragged along to the stairs, her head hanging down, her arms limp at her side.

Alice would have been able to make a good story from the hearing in spite of the fact that it was supposed to be a low-key affair. Rafferty had told me that the preliminary hearing was not the place to draw out the details. He said that if he brought into focus the slatternly mother, the ill-mannered boy, months later at the trial the D.A. would have had the time to create Mrs. Mackessy as Mother Theresa and Robbie as the all-American choirboy on a PBS special. He had told me that the defense holds everything close to the chest, that it is the prosecutor who must play the hand. At the hearing the judge might be sympathetic to the poor single mom doing her best to raise up her child. At the trial Rafferty would introduce the real Mrs. Mackessy, as well as sing, and dance, if necessary, Alice's praises: the fine caring professional nurse who is being blamed for Carol's neglect and Robbie's failures.

For all my background in history, I had been thinking lately that stories were pretty useless. The first scientists, way back, in pre-Socratic time, figured out that if they were going to understand anything they would have to discard narrative in favor of empirical methods. The Creation myths explained, after a fashion, who and why, but science would tell how and what. I had tried not to see the hearing as a story but as a series of facts which explored these questions: How did this happen? What is Alice? It was an absurd question, I realize, What is Alice? And yet I found myself asking, and not knowing how to answer. I had gone over and over the hearing in my mind and with each passing hour I was more and more bewildered. That night Theresa came over I thought, for about five minutes, that the splintered facts might make sense. I thought I might be able to lay out the pieces for her. With her experience she would amplify and connect where I could not.

"I think a lot about Alice," I said.

"Oh Howard," she blew, "if you only knew how I think about her.

My sister asked how I could still be friends with her and I said, 'If the same thing had happened in your built-in pool, do you think I'd stop speaking to you?' I feel as if I've lost two people, that's what no one, least of all my husband, understands."

I couldn't, of course, ask her what had been nagging at me since the day before. *What is my wife, Theresa?* I mumbled something about how we have air-conditioned squad cars instead of wooden carts but that nothing else had changed much since the Inquisition.

"And you can pay your fines with American Express," she added. "You're right! The changes are insignificant."

On that Monday I had left the girls off at a day-care center in a shopping mall on the outskirts of Racine. It had been the only place I could find that would take them on a drop-in basis. The morning had gone badly at the beginning. The gallon jar of milk had fallen out of the refrigerator and shattered on the floor. The car keys had gotten lost. A cow in her prime was sick with diarrhea for no good reason. When we got to the day-care place, Happy Haven, Emma and Claire screamed about it. I had to shake them off of me and leave them sobbing in the hands of two high-school students. They had badges on their red aprons that said, "Trainee." Out in the parking lot I could still hear my daughters crying. When I was trying to drive away the engine flooded. I had to sit for fifteen minutes before the car would run. I wasn't sure by the end if I was hearing their appeals or imagining the worst. The noise continued as I drove. I could still hear them after I was a mile down the road.

There were jackhammers going in front of the courthouse. I was very hot in my suit. There's an inscription on the north side of the entrance, a quote from Goethe. "In the government of men," it says, "a great deal may be done by severity. More by love. But most of all by clear discernment and impartial justice. Which pays no respect to persons." Those jackhammers were going in my ears and the sun was bearing down through my suit coat, my white shirt, my T-shirt. I read the quote several times. There was so much sweat dripping into my eyes and stinging that I couldn't read very well. The trouble with Goethe, I thought then, is that when it's you on trial you want to be particular, an individual. You don't want to be one of the indiscriminate masses.

Even though it's only a dowdy provincial courthouse it's enough of a hulking edifice to remind the passerby that inside some men are ruined while others make their fortunes. Around the entrance there are crude bas-reliefs of the common man plowing and forging chains, trying to stand up straight under their burdens. "You know that thing Goethe said about justice that's carved on the courthouse wall?" I asked Theresa.

"Oh God," she said, grimacing. "Justice! That place could stand to have a few window boxes, some happy-face decals on the revolving doors."

I was aware that I was shaking as I made my way to Branch Six. As I said, I had always thought that Racine was a good place, where farm implements are made, where the folks at Johnson Wax decide how best to make the world clean. I'd always imagined Racine at the top of the globe, along with that eagle on my J. I. Case cap. Even in the stairwell, up the six flights, I could hear the clamor. When I reached the sixth floor I stood on the cement landing. I could see through the small window out to the hall. I could see a swarm of mothers, their big heads bubbling up and down as they called to one another.

"They're not going to let us in!"

"They can't keep us out!"

"The judge can lock the door if he wants too!"

Suburban rebels, storming the citadel. They were armed with their long, sharp earrings, their heavy necklaces and bracelets, their clean, white canine teeth, their steel-colored helmet hair. I wasn't sure about Goethe. "In the government of men a great deal may be done by severity. More by love." So far so good. "But most of all by clear discernment and impartial justice." Fine. "Which pays no respect to persons." I wasn't aware of anything in heaven or earth that more simply determined the outcome of any conflict than the force of personality. Gorbachev dismantled Russia on the strength of his personality. It didn't hurt him, having the glamorous Risa in tow, a woman who carried a credit card in her pocketbook. Take the personality away from Mrs. Thatcher and you'd have nothing but a woman with a hairdo who went to the shops to buy her husband his dinner. In Branch Six, if Mrs. Mackessy looked like a sleazy broad to the judge, he wasn't supposed to hold it against her. If Alice came in, gray and battered in her orange suit, he couldn't allow himself to feel sympathy. If she told her most amusing story he would not laugh. If he asked her what had become of her life she could quote Shakespeare. She would say the line she used when she was looking for something: "I feel it gone but know not how it went." An elected official, he wasn't supposed to be moved by the battalions that were presently laying siege at the threshold of Branch Six.

I studied history in college to pay respect to persons. I had always been drawn to generals and their battle plans. I was interested to know what motivated the likes of Bonaparte, Patton, Hannibal, Pickett, Lee, Grant, and Custer. In high school I had learned only dates and battles and treaties. I had a vague idea what the notable characters left in their wakes. I'd known by the age of five that some of us wield power, that the likes of Rickie Kroeger could wheedle cookies out of my mother where Nick O'Brien could not. My mother had informed me that in God's plan some were weak and others strong.

On that Monday morning in Racine I opened the door and stood facing the backs of the perfumed women. People were jostling into the crowd from the elevator, much as if they were getting on a crowded train. No one registered my presence right away. It was as the shudder of recognition began to move through the crowd, as a hush began to descend, that the door to Branch Six opened. I'm still not sure how Rafferty managed to hook me in, to reach me from the door and pull me through to the inside. "You can't do that!" The women were shouting. "Stop him! Get to the door. This is against the law."

The judge in his black robes stood before the rabble, his arms up. From behind he was a dark mass filling the entry. Each person out in the hall was found wanting and could not come farther. He told them they'd need an injunction if they wanted to be present. He shut the double doors and locked them. Inside there were the usual trappings: the blond veneer panels, the half-moon lamps along the wall, the green leather-bound volumes in shelves built into the judge's bench. I guess the furnishings were to make us feel that we are in the hands of men who have had the time and silence to become wise. I moved along the back, toward the windows. "You'll want to sit closer," Rafferty called from his table. "You won't be able to hear."

"Being in court feels like going to church to me," Theresa murmured that night on the porch. "Everyone's getting ready—lighting candles, pouring coffee—what's the difference? There's that same quiet, an almost fearful silence. I'm still sometimes afraid in church, and I'm always afraid in court. As a kid I thought if I didn't genuflect the right way I'd go straight to hell. There's all that drama and ritual in both, and the mystique of the priest or the judge. I think court has become like church for a lot of people, don't you think so? Of course there's all that infernal waiting. In church at least the priests are on time for mass."

I don't know how long I waited. Rafferty had gone out one of the side doors. Judge Peterson went behind his screen, holding his insulated coffeepot. The court reporter and the bailiff were whispering, trying to laugh without making noise. I sat, thinking about Goethe. I hoped that Horace Peterson, over the course of his career, had become an expert judge of character. A connoisseur. I hoped that he had gone beyond Goethe and was so knowledgeable about persons that therein lay the clear discernment. He looked like a tired fifty-five. I held out the hope that he would not need to see Alice more than once to understand the error. She was a beautiful woman with a braid down her back. She carried herself well. She was educated. Yes, she was temperamental; she herself said so. But she was definitely upstanding, of course she was, and principled. At the same time, for good measure, I also held out the hope that he had gone soft over the years, that a beautiful woman could sway him. It didn't matter to me how she got away.

There must have been a cue because all at once Judge Peterson came back to his bench, coffeepot in hand. The bailiff opened the door to the holding room and Alice shuffled in, just as she said she would, the manacles around her feet clattering as she moved. She didn't search me out. She looked straight to the windows, to the white sky. Her orange clothes hung on her. The pants puddled down around her ankles. The crotch came to her knees. Rafferty was holding a file and talking to her. It was midsummer and he was wearing a heavy suit coat. Susan Dirks, the prosecutor, and Mrs. Mackessy and Robbie, appeared from behind the screen and came to their table.

"How did Alice seem in court?" Theresa asked. "How was she?"

I heard myself say, "They made her look like a mental patient."

"How could they do that, Howard?" she asked softly. "What do you mean?"

"Like someone who shouldn't be allowed to dress herself. Because she'll put on something too big."

Theresa crossed the room and came to my side. She put her arm around my shoulders and turned her head to look up at me.

"She says she's fine," I muttered, trying to move out from under her little hand.

"Rafferty once told me something funny," Theresa said, without moving. "When he can't stand the prosecution he says he imagines the attorneys and the witnesses floating down a tranquil river. They float on down without knowing about the unexpected drop off, with its protruding sharp rocks. He says he sees them—in his mind's eye—getting dashed to pieces at the bottom of the falls. He's able to stay calm that way."

"That's helpful," I said. I managed to get up, on the pretense of needing to pull my handkerchief out of my pocket. I blew my nose away from the direction of her sympathetic gaze. I hadn't had much of a chance to talk with Rafferty about Susan Dirks, the assistant D.A. She was a slim woman, elegant. She had the kind of hair I think of as endemic to Wisconsin, Minnesota, Michigan, and Iowa. Maybe Indiana, for that matter. It's ruffled hair, like corrugated metal, with short stuff in the front that looks as if it's been blasted out of an aerosol can. She was wearing a glittery black jacket and a short, black skirt. By choice she had a lot of cumbersome gold jewelry around her arms and neck. When everyone was assembled, Alice, in contrast, in her oversized orange pants, looked all the more like she'd been the stupid one, to come to the party wearing the wrong clothes.

As I sat back down next to Theresa, telling her that neither one of the lawyers gave much in the way of opening statements, she said, "What was that about the admission, the 'I hurt everybody' line? Suzannah Brooks kept saying that in my face, just about gloating."

I winked a few times, involuntarily, thinking I hadn't heard her. The admission had cost me a night's sleep. I hadn't been planning on mentioning it to Theresa. I guess I still didn't know if I was primarily worried, or baffled, or angry. To get anywhere, I knew I had to choose from the three possibilities. I had tossed for hours trying not to give way to anxiety. The investigating officer had testified at the end of the hearing. Under oath he stated that Alice had shouted at him, shouted, "I hurt everybody." I had wanted Theresa to tell me what Alice was without my having to supply some of the crucial information. I hadn't known how I would tell her some of the more damning assertions. Without repeating the incriminating evidence, I wanted to ask, Did she do it? Theresa would say no. She'd say no a second time. Her look would change then. She'd show a side I had never seen before. She'd frown, disbelieving at first. And then somehow contempt would mar her pretty face.

She didn't give me a chance to wonder how Suzannah Brooks had heard something that was said behind locked doors. She turned and put her hands on my arm again. "I can imagine why Alice would say that, can't you? I mean, with what happened to Lizzy, it makes sense to me that she'd feel generally culpable. I know I would. Rafferty will make sure the confession is excluded from the trial. He'll find a loophole, you know how lawyers operate. Probably she hadn't had Miranda read to her yet, so anything she said will be inadmissible. That was Alice expressing what was a feeling, not a fact. If you know her the way we do, it makes sense. She doesn't very often let down her guard, but it's obvious she's got a lot to work through. I don't think she's resolved half of her family issues. That's one of the reasons she can seem so funny, because she's really so raw. She's turned a lot of her pain into humor, but we all know that deep down it's just plain hurt."

I couldn't help turning to look at her, at her unwavering gaze. I saw that she was certain she was right. She wasn't making up something to soothe me. I suppose the qualities she described were what had drawn me to Alice in the first place: She could alternately seem self-possessed with her hair in a bun, and then she'd untwist her braid and dance with abandon. I was grateful to Theresa, grateful she could account for Alice's remark. For about three seconds I'd say I felt practically euphoric.

"That's what I love about Alice, don't you?" Theresa went on. "She blurts out these things that are refreshing, these searing one-liners, only sometimes she doesn't have brakes working, and you wish you could gag her."

If a person could gag her. If only a person could gag her! She should not have said those things! It was wrong of her to have aired her dirty laundry to a police officer. It had been impolitic. It had been idiotic. Why would anyone say to a police officer, "I hurt everybody"? Theresa shook my arm gently. I suppose she could just about see me thinking. If Alice had been in the room I would have had to leave so as not to show my temper. "So what happened?" she said. "Tell me about it. Did Robbie testify? Please, tell me."

Alice would say that I'm not usually sensitive to people's clothing, but it was clear that clothing was itself central to the hearing. Robbie was dressed in a beige three-piece suit, as if the proceeding was a display for future lawyers of America. We were supposed to pay no respect to persons. Mrs. Mackessy was the image of ideal suburban motherhood, up in the witness box with her boy on her lap. She was wearing one of those denim dresses that look like a feed bag. We were supposed to picture her tooling around in her paneled station wagon to the vet, the scout meetings, the parish bake sale. In fact, she drives a 1979 Impala. You can tell she's babied the thing because the body's in pretty good shape. Her long ratty hair was pulled back with a pink ribbon. Alice said later that that's what unhinged her, the pink satin ribbon.

When Susan Dirks directed Mrs. Mackessy into the witness box, Rafferty jumped up from his chair and walked quickly to the judge's bench to object. There was no reason, he said, for the boy to sit on his mother's lap. Alice remarked that there was something in the quality of Rafferty's voice, and his composure, that made his requests and his conclusions sound reasonable and true. She probably had a point. He was quiet and forceful at the same time. He suggested to the judge that the D.A. knew she had a shaky witness and a weak case and that she was bolstering it in any way she could.

The judge overruled, on the grounds that the hearing was stressful, that Robbie had the right to feel secure, and that a child could testify more reliably if he was not frightened.

The bailiff told Robbie to hold up his hand and promise to tell the truth, and nothing but the truth.

"Okay," he answered. He leaned back into his mother. When he grabbed the armrests he was surprised and pleased to find that the chair swiveled.

"How you doin', Robbie?" Susan Dirks asked. "You comfy?"

"Yeah."

The building was air conditioned, well regulated. We were all comfy.

"This won't take too long," she told Robbie. "I'm going to ask you some questions, and then the gentleman, Mr. Rafferty, over there," she pointed, "in the—plaid suit, will ask you a few things, and then you can get back home."

Robbie nodded. Alice used to say he looked as if he might evaporate if it wasn't for his big mouth. He had pale eyes. He had pale hair. Everything about him, even his suit, was pale. She had said, months before the summer, that he had the most impassive face she had ever seen in anyone, young or old, that he had a habit of staring, that it unnerved her. At the hearing he sat on his mother's lap looking at the floor by Mrs. Dirk's feet.

"How old are you, Robbie?" Susan asked.

"Six." As far as I could tell the kid hadn't blinked yet.

"That's wonderful, Robbie. I'm sure you're old enough to know the difference between telling the truth and telling a lie."

"Yes, Ma'am," he said.

Alice bent her head then. She kept it bowed, as if she was praying.

"If I told you that your jacket is purple is that the truth or a lie?"

"That's a lie."

"What's a lie, Robbie?"

"It's bad," he said, looking again at Mrs. Dirks's shoes. "It's when you make it up."

"Yes, that's right. It's a lie when you make something up. What does it mean to tell the truth?"

"It's important to. When it—it's when something really happened, like you don't make it up or nothin'."

"Exactly. And in this court it is a law that we all must tell the truth. We are under oath to tell the truth. That means we have promised. You just promised to be truthful when you answered Mr. Malone's questions a few minutes ago. It is your job to tell us what you know is true. Do you understand?"

At that point the judge allowed Rafferty the opportunity to ask Robbie questions only on the subject of his ability to understand the oath and answer the questions truthfully. Rafferty leaned against his desk and briefly fired away at the boy. I think even a six-year-old child would have sensed Rafferty's need to display his superior intelligence. Rafferty spoke coolly, in no way attempting to soften his revulsion.

When Susan Dirks resumed her questioning she stood a few feet from the Mackessys. Her arms were folded over her flat chest. She had one foot out in front of her, her toe pointing up, her spike heel dug into the short nap of the carpet. "Can you tell us some of the things that you like to do best, your favorite things?"

"Nintendo. I ride my bike. My dad got me a G.I. Joe." He listed his pleasures flatly, as if they didn't really matter to him.

"Do you pretend with your G.I. Joe, Robbie?"

He sank down into Carol Mackessy for a minute. She held him around his middle and rested her chin on top of his head. "Yeah," he said.

"Does your G.I. Joe, say, fight battles?"

He sat up straight all of a sudden, under his mother's chin, making her head snap back. "I pretend that he's fighting bad guys, like niggers and them and—" He was coming alive, looking past Mrs. Dirks for the first time. He pointed his finger and began moving it in an arc, spraying the benches, emptying his full magazine. *"Ba bam, ba bam, ba bam,* he wipes 'em out, blows up buildings—guts splatter, ugh, he got me—"

To the court reporter Rafferty said, "For the record, the witness is holding his hands in front of him, pointing his finger as if it were a gun, and moving it from his left to the right."

Both Mrs. Dirks and Mrs. Mackessy had not been prepared for Robbie's display. Mrs. Dirks had unfolded her arms and was holding her hands out in front of her like a choral director. Rafferty objected that the D.A. was signaling the witness. In any case it was not a gesture that Robbie understood. Mrs. Mackessy was trying to cope with her unexpected whiplash. She had had to quell her flash of anger. With her forearm and a balled fist she had pulled him hard into her belly.

"I see," Susan said to Robbie. "You imagine all of that."

"Yeah, but it ain't real, no way. It ain't even real on TV. It's like they made up these pictures at a TV station and beam 'em into your house. It's just pictures somebody drew."

"When people get shot on television are they really dead, Robbie?"

"It's people on there falling over. They get rich to do it."

"So you pretend sometimes, and you watch TV, and then there are real-life times—"

"It's real when you're alive."

"Did you ever tell a lie, a little lie to your mom or dad?"

"I try not to," he said.

She must have smiled at him. You could hear a warmth in her response. "We all try not to tell lies. It's hard sometimes though, isn't it?"

"Uh huh," he said, without moving his eyes from her feet.

"How do you feel if you tell your mom a little lie?"

"I took some candy once and she found out."

"Did you lie at first about the candy?"

His nod was like an old man's, an almost imperceptible downward movement of his jaw.

"How did you feel when you told the lie?"

"Real bad. After she—afterward I said I was sorry."

"How do you know that you're not to lie, Robbie? Who teaches you that sort of thing?"

"My mom. You can tell when someone's telling you a true story and when it's a lie. I learned that."

"How can you tell?"

"A lie is real strange, like you can't believe it, like you'd say, 'Yeah, right.'"

It was hard to imagine Emma, in another year, being so forthcoming. Alice made the comment at one of our visits that Robbie was clearly a remarkable child, someone who understood, even at six, that being in the public eye made his life a story, that there was value in the story.

"What happens to you when you lie, Robbie?"

He moved his eyes from her foot to the floor of the witness box. "She gets mad."

"People who lie get punished, don't they?"

"Yes, Ma'am."

"You understand that people who lie in court get punished too?"

"I know."

"Of course you do. You are a smart six-year-old. I need you to concentrate very hard now, to do your best to remember, and always to tell the truth."

"Okay," he said.

"Do you know the lady in the orange outfit, sitting at the table there?"

Outfit was a generous term to describe Alice's garment. One of the strange things about Robbie was his gaze, and the fact that throughout the proceedings he didn't alter his position more than two or three inches. He turned his head away from Alice, and then looked at her out of the corner of his eye. "Yeah," he said.

"How do you know her, Robbie?"

He resumed looking at the floor by his own feet. "She's the nurse."

"Where is she the nurse?"

"At my school."

"What was your teacher's name last year, Robbie, in kindergarten at Blackwell Elementary?"

"Mrs. Ritter."

"Mrs. Ritter. Did you like going to kindergarten?"

Rafferty was tipping back in his chair. His hands were stretched out in front of him, folded on his clear desk top. He seemed preternaturally calm sitting like that next to Alice. She had not once raised her head since Robbie had first answered Mrs. Dirks with a "Yes, Ma'am." I wished she would lift herself up and watch. It didn't look good. The judge wouldn't think well of her, unable to face her accuser.

"Why was Mrs. Ritter your friend?" Susan asked.

"She was nice to me. She said I didn't have to finish my work sheet sometimes."

"I see. And was there any other reason you thought she was nice?"

"She gave me snacks."

"She gave you snacks, or everyone in the class snacks?"

"Everyday we had cookies and popcorn and crackers. You had to go in the hall to get the milk."

"So Mrs. Ritter was a friendly, pleasant person to be around?"

"She had a gerbil in a cage. You could take it home on weekends."

"At your school, Robbie, you remember that you get to the nurse's office by walking down the corridor, past the second-grade classrooms."

"Uh huh."

"Then there's another narrow little hallway."

"Yeah."

"There's a set of rooms in that area, isn't there, for the principal and the secretary and the guidance counselor and the nurse?"

"I think so."

"The nurse's office is the first one."

"Yeah, the first one."

"You visited the nurse's office many times last year."

Although Robbie was looking at the floor he lowered his eyes still further. It was an eerie change. It was like something coming down, a curtain coming down and hiding him. "She was bad to me," he said.

"Who was bad to you?"

"She was. The nurse."

"How was she bad to you?"

"She hollered at me."

"Where did she holler?"

"In the nurse's office."

"Why did she shout at you? Do you know why she would need to holler?"

As I said, I had had plenty of experience watching Perry Mason as a youth. It seemed to me that Rafferty should have been objecting to some of Mrs. Dirks's questions.

"To get me to do stuff that I didn't want to."

"What did she want you to do, Robbie?"

Mechanically, as if he'd been told to do this, he stuck his fist into his own stomach. "It hurts," he said dully, "like *uuuuuugh.*" His mother kissed his ear and then wiped her eyes with her palm.

Rafferty moved right to the judge's bench. He pointed to Mrs. Mackessy as he spoke. He rarely shouted, but there was a thickness in his voice when he meant to object strenuously. "Objection, Your Honor. Dirks is bolstering the case by having Mom up in the box. Is the court paying for her tissues? I'd like my client's friends and relations to be allowed up in the box at trial time for her moral support after she's been in jail for months."

"Simmer down," the judge snapped. "I'll ask you to please remember the age of the witness."

"I know it hurts," Mrs. Dirks said to Robbie after Rafferty was seated. "I'm sorry, sweetheart." Her term of endearment sounded as if it had been generated by a computer for the phone company. "But your being here will help us find out the truth so that it won't hurt again, so that other children won't be hurt."

There was disgust in Rafferty's tone when he objected. The judge overruled. Dirks walked briskly to her table and removed a doll from her shopping bag. They are now called anatomically detailed dolls, instead of anatomically correct dolls. She held it to her chest as if she were protecting it. "You've seen this before Robbie, in Miss Flint's office, haven't you?"

"Yeah."

"Would you rather use the doll to show us what happened in the nurse's office? Would that be easier than telling us in words?"

His nod was imperceptible.

"All right then, sweetheart."

Robbie accepted the doll, awkwardly holding it at first with his shoulders hunched up. He held it as if it were fragile, like a real infant. It was dressed in blue shorts and a red-and-blue-striped T-shirt. It had brown yarn for hair. Robbie turned the doll to face him. He seemed to melt, to finally have an expression. He was squinting at it. His thin mouth trembled and turned down at the corners. I'm sure I will never forget how he looked at that doll. He was shrinking back, in its stead. He whimpered, studying its face. He was squeaking. It was then that Alice sat up. She turned around to see if I was there, I suppose because she knew how I would look. I felt her eyes on me and it was with reluctance that I jerked away from the boy, to acknowledge her. I thought, even as she stirred in her seat, that she was trying to scramble the message. Robbie was going to have to do something hateful to the doll. She was distracting me. He didn't want to go ahead; he didn't want to recall what had been done to him.

Mrs. Dirks was providing a tray of tools a nurse might have in her office. She was offering him a stethoscope, cotton balls, tongue depressors, tweezers, scissors, Band-Aids, and a roll of surgical gauze. She was holding the tray as if it was a platter of hors d'oeuvres. Alice had caught me. She had looked expressly to see if I was uncertain. She had seen something in me that I would have preferred to keep to myself. I was not going to watch the boy give cruel and unusual punishment to the doll. I wasn't going to be part of the bizarre play. "It's a lie when it's strange," Robbie had said. It followed by his logic, that that room, the building, the un-fathomable story, everything there was a lie.

"Do you know what that is for?" Mrs. Dirks asked, when Robbie selected a tongue depressor.

"You say *Ahhhh,*" Robbie said.

It had gotten dark on our porch as I tried to tell Theresa the salient details of Robbie's testimony. I explained that he seemed to understand the difference between the truth and a lie, that he knew it was wrong to lie. At the very least, I said, his visits to Alice had apparently upset him. I got up to light an old kerosene lamp that had come with the house. Except for small exclamations along the way, Theresa had been quiet. I was thankful for her presence, and even her sympathy, but I was tired now. I couldn't go any further. I looked around the corner to see if Emma was hiding again, and listening. She was in the living room, lying next to Claire in front of the television. "You know the Woodland Indians, who lived here about 500 B.C.?" I said, shaking the match out. "The fathers taught their sons, at puberty, to experience the dream life. They believed, they knew, in fact, that there were divine spirits in the forest and in the prairie. By fasting and through dreams they made intense contact with the spirits. And they believed, when they died, that a god guided their soul to paradise, to a large village where there was peace, perfection. You'd play lacrosse forever. I remember reading in college about the fathers passing down this dream life to their sons. Nothing like that is given to us. I don't think there's anything that can be compared to it in our life. Sometimes I feel an association with the people who used to live here in this house. Not ghosts or spirits. It's only a tie to the past, a kinship of ideas, maybe."

"Oh, Howard," Theresa said in alarm, "this is so awful for you."

I looked across at her. I hadn't actually realized that I was speaking out loud. I didn't often talk to anyone about the Indian's dream life, or my own dream life for that matter. I sat back down on my walnut bench. I mumbled that it was a lot worse for Alice than it was for me. We didn't say anything for a while.

At the hearing I had waited with my head down while Robbie poked his doll. While he displayed his adult knowledge of sexual matters. I couldn't concern myself with the impression I was making on the judge. A child couldn't look the way Robbie had unless someone had taken advantage of him. You couldn't act traumatized at age six. He'd looked scared at first, and pained at the remembrance, and then when it came to him perhaps more vividly his eyes had widened, as if he couldn't pull away from the scene. "Four score and seven years ago," I had said to myself, my head between my knees, "our fathers brought forth upon this continent a new nation, conceived in liberty and dedicated to the proposition that all men are created equal. Now we are engaged in a great civil war, testing whether that nation, or any nation so conceived, can long endure." Was it worth killing forty thousand men at Gettysburg for that one flawless speech? Sometimes it almost seemed that it was. I used to say the Address to myself when I was doing chores. It felt like a mantra from my short TM days, only fuller, something that was in my veins as well as my head. "The world will little note nor long remember what we say here, but it can never forget what they did here." With my head down I wondered what good would come out of the summer. I wondered what hope we could possibly take home that would endure beyond the present horror of sitting quietly in Branch Six while Robbie Mackessy tortured his doll.

"What did he do?" Theresa was asking in her gentle, insistent way. "What did he do to the doll, Howard?"

I hadn't looked up during the rest of Mrs. Dirks's questions. I had said the Gettysburg Address over and over to myself. I also remembered how it was that I'd wanted to farm since I was a boy. I'd wanted to farm ever since the time I planted a wheat field with my Uncle Erwin, sitting on his lap, on the tractor. Later in the summer I visited his farm again, in Zombrota, Minnesota. I got to see the wheat, the sea of green wheat we'd planted. I never forgot how beautiful that field was, the wheat moving in the wind like waves. Years later, in college, I read that in one hundred years there was going to be no topsoil left, that we have been going through topsoil faster than we are squandering any other natural resource. That was as much information as I needed, to follow the path Uncle Erwin had begun for me.

"I don't know exactly what Robbie did to the doll," I said to Theresa.

"He didn't perform?" she asked, in all seriousness.

I hadn't sat up until Mrs. Dirks was saying, "Okay, Robbie. Thank you. You are a real trooper. You are a very brave six-year-old and we thank you." I had hoped that Alice would turn her head to look again. She would see that I was unaffected. She would see that nothing Robbie had done had made an impression.

With the kind of acumen that even Alice does not have, Theresa said, "I wouldn't have been able to watch the whole thing, if I'd been you, Howard. With Alice sitting right there, I would have just shut my eyes and blocked my ears."

She made my head swim. I had to put my hands to my jaw before I could speak. "Rafferty got up for the cross-examination then," I said hoarsely. "He was wearing a battered plaid suit coat that made me think of a great old cheap store in Chicago. Goldblatt's. My Aunt Penny used to send me toys that lasted for about ten minutes from Goldblatt's. To work there you had to wear suit coats that matched the sofas in the furniture department."

We both knew I hadn't answered the question. "God," she heaved. "And he earns more than a decent salary. He could afford to go to Saks, or Brooks Brothers."

Rafferty had leaned against the railing which fenced off the empty jury box. "Hi, Robbie," he said, as if they had never previously met. "My name is Paul, by the way. There's not many people, even Judge Peterson here, who calls me Mr. Rafferty." I had thought at first that Rafferty was trying to put the boy at ease, out of decency. He had told me that the judge would not throw out the case, that the burden of proof in a preliminary hearing is low. I had known from the start, seeing the cumbersome machinery of the court, the gears creaking and turning slowly, that even if Robbie fell apart, it was going to take a lot of time and money to wipe Alice's slate clean. I didn't understand until later that Rafferty's every calculated gesture and word was designed to make Robbie disrespectful and sour.

"Say, Your Honor," Rafferty said, "may I advance to the witness box?" The judge nodded his head. Rafferty carried a wooden chair from his desk and went right close to Robbie. He hiked one foot on the seat of the chair and then leaned his elbow on his knee. "Let me explain something to you, pal, before we begin." Pal. He'd pounced on the word, said it sarcastically. He passed his hand lightly over the top of his head. Alice said that his well-greased, wavy hair always looked as if it had come out of a mold. "When I ask you a question, if you know the answer, you can tell me Yes. If you don't know, you may tell me No, or I don't know, or I forget. As Mrs. Dirks said, the important thing is to tell the truth. I want you to understand that it's fine to tell me that you don't remember, if in fact you don't remember. All right?"

Robbie was staring down and to his right, about as far from Rafferty as he could look. He made no indication that he'd heard Rafferty.

"Who was the first person you told about Mrs. Goodwin?"

"My mom."

"Your mom. You knew she would understand because she does that sort of thing you described with her boyfriends, right?"

Susan Dirks of course blasted up from her seat. "That is hearsay, Your Honor, it is irrelevant and it is beyond the scope of direct."

"Question withdrawn," Rafferty said calmly.

Mrs. Mackessy had tightened her hold around her boy. She was trying, without much success, to bury her face in his short hair.

"Did your mom hug you when you told her?"

Robbie hesitated. He was still. "Yeah," he said finally.

"Would you say she gives you a hug once a day?"

"Objection, Your Honor," Susan Dirks said, with marked restraint. "This line of questioning has no bearing on—"

"Sustained," the judge muttered.

"Sometimes they can't stand my questions," Rafferty explained to Robbie, "and then I get into trouble. You ever get into trouble?"

"Sort of," Robbie said.

"Sort of. So you told your mom and then she called the police and they got you an appointment with Miss Flint. I'd like you to try to remember that first time you saw Miss Flint. Think for a minute, what it was like that day you visited her at the office."

Mrs. Mackessy shifted her weight and Robbie went up and down with her, as if he was on a mechanical horse.

"Did you tell Miss Flint about Mrs. Goodwin right away?"

"She has games and stuff."

"Did you play with her for a while?"

"Yeah."

"Did she ask you about Mrs. Goodwin?"

He didn't answer.

"Did you tell her about the things that you thought happened at school?"

He shrugged.

"This woman," Rafferty said, pointing his pen at the court reporter, "is taking down everything we say. So you have to give me an answer."

Robbie didn't blink or make the slightest movement.

"Who tells you that Mrs. Goodwin is bad?"

He remained motionless. His eyes were cast down. He was pale and his face didn't seem to have any contour.

"I know what happened took place a while ago," Rafferty said, "so if you don't remember that's fine. Did Miss Flint tell you Mrs. Goodwin was a bad person, Robbie?"

"No."

"Did Susan Dirks tell you to say Mrs. Goodwin was bad?"

"She said to tell the truth."

"Who told you that Mrs. Goodwin did those things?"

"Miss Flint."

"Miss Flint told you that—"

"I showed her—"

"Did Miss Flint show you first?"

Robbie looked up at Rafferty. "I showed *her,*" he said, scoffing, as if the question insulted his intelligence.

"Exactly what did Miss Flint ask you first?"

"Did the nurse touch you?"

"Miss Flint asked, 'Did the nurse touch you?' "

"Yeah."

"What did you say?"

"I showed her on the doll."

"Did you ever see your mom doing some of those things with her—"

"Your Honor," Mrs. Dirks cried, "we all know what Mr. Rafferty's tack is here. He violates the dignity of this court, as well as the witness. Mr. Rafferty is asking questions which are based on hearsay, which are argumentative—"

"Mr. Rafferty," the judge said slowly, "you will remember the age of the witness. I am warning you, do you understand?"

"Yes, Your Honor." Rafferty removed his foot from the chair and stood straight, with his hands clasped behind his back.

"What color pants were you wearing when that happened in the nurse's office?"

He shrugged.

"You don't remember?"

"I forget."

"Did you wear a belt?"

"My dad gave me suspenders with Batman."

"Did you wear your suspenders to the nurse's office?"

"No."

"Did you wear a belt?"

"I don't got a belt."

"Did your pants have a snap on them at the top?" Rafferty opened his jacket and pointed to his own waist. "Right about here?"

"Maybe."

"Who unbuttoned your pants in the nurse's office?"

"She always pushed me down."

"Who unbuttoned your pants?"

"She did."

"Who is she?"

"The nurse."

"Did she unzip the pants first?"

"Yeah."

"So she unzipped the pants first, and then she unbuttoned the pants."

Most children would have said yes, I'm sure, to be done with it. Robbie appeared to think. "She unbuttoned the pants first," he said.

"Where was the principal?"

"I don't know."

Rafferty asked where the guidance counselor was, where the secretary sat. For several minutes he asked Robbie to again describe his pants, if there were pockets, how the nurse got them down to his ankles, if she took them off, where she put them. For a good many of the answers Robbie said he didn't know.

"On May eighteenth you had a beesting, Robbie, and your arm got puffy. You went to see Mrs. Goodwin at her office because of the sting. Do you remember that day?"

"I think so."

"Do you remember what she put on your arm to make the sting feel better?"

"She hollered at me," he said in a monotone.

"What did she holler?"

"She called me bad names."

"Bad names?"

"She said she was going to tie me to a chair."

"Did she tie you to a chair?"

"She always pushed me down."

"Did she treat you for the beesting that May eighteenth, when you got stung on the playground?"

He shrugged, his shoulders jerking up and down just once.

"Did she treat you for that beesting?"

"I don't know."

"You don't know? You don't remember?"

"I SAID, 'I don't know'!" Robbie glared at Rafferty for an instant before lowering his eyes back to the carpet.

"So you did, so you did. Why did Mrs. Ritter have to send you down to the principal's office so often, Robbie?"

"Objection," Mrs. Dirks called.

"Mr. Rafferty," Judge Peterson said, "your line of questioning is argumentative. I am not going to tolerate badgering. Let's get on with this hearing in a dignified manner."

"Yes, sir," Rafferty said, nodding his head and clasping his hands at his navel, altar-boy style. "Did you ever start fights, Robbie?"

No answer.

"Did you ever use words you weren't supposed to use?"

"I don't know."

"Did Mrs. Goodwin ever give you medicine?"

"Yeah."

"So sometimes you weren't feeling well, and she gave you medicine so you'd get better?"

"Yeah, right," Robbie said, looking up again. "She gave me medicine so I'd get sick."

Rafferty moved forward quickly. "Do you talk back to your teachers, to the principal, the way you're talking back to me, young man?"

Mrs. Dirks called for a side bar. There was a short inaudible conference up front with the judge. When they were finished Rafferty went and stood the proper distance from the boy and his mother.

"Wasn't Mrs. Goodwin trying to help you by giving you medicine when you were sick?"

"She pushed me down."

"What did you do when you went to her office to get your medicine?"

"She push—"

"You'd walk in the door of her office, right?"

"She was always pushing me down."

"When you got in the door?"

"Afterward."

"After what?"

"After she made me go in the box."

"What box?"

"In the dark room."

"What dark room?"

"That place the sick people go."

"Does your father live with you, Robbie?"

"No."

"Does your mom bring her boyfriends around the house?"

"Objection," Mrs. Dirks said. "Irrelevant."

Rafferty spoke as he walked to the bench. "Your Honor," he said, "I'd like to establish whether or not the witness has ever been exposed to adult sexuality at home."

"I'll overrule this time, Mr. Rafferty," Judge Peterson said. "Be mindful that I'm prejudiced against you this morning."

"Thank you, Your Honor. Ever any boyfriends around?" Rafferty asked again.

"I don't know."

"Does your mom have the same boyfriend all the time?"

Mrs. Mackessy now had that impassive look, identical to her son's.

She was staring out into the empty courtroom. "Does your mom have the same boyfriend all the time?"

"Sometimes they're the same."

"Do you like some of them?"

Robbie's occasional glower had been hostile all along. It was more and more poisonous as the questioning progressed. "They're okay."

"Are there some of them you don't like?"

"I SAID, they're okay."

"Do your mom's boyfriends play with you, Robbie? Maybe take you to the ball game, or the pool, or the park?"

"I got my own friends," he snapped.

"You have friends? What do you do when your mom goes somewhere without you, and you stay at home?"

"Play." He said this with a sneer, as if he was trying to match the sarcasm of "Pal."

"Watch TV?" Rafferty asked.

Robbie did that quick up-and-down shrug. It was like a puppet's motion, an invisible handler working the shoulder strings.

"Did you watch TV this morning?"

"Yeah."

"What did you see?"

"I don't know."

"Can you think of one program you saw this morning?"

"I said I forget."

"You forget what you saw two hours ago?"

"I turn the channels back and forth."

"Oh, so you don't sit and watch one show for long?"

"My mom got us sixty-four channels."

"So you can see a lot of different programs, I bet?"

"I just said, we have sixty-four channels."

"What are your favorite shows?"

"I don't know."

"Do you watch cartoons, shows like 'Goof Troop,' 'Ninja Turtles,' ah, 'Tiny Toons'—what's it called, 'Loony Tunes'?"

"Yeah."

"Now that you're six do you stay up late sometimes?"

"Yeah."

"And you watch TV at night, flipping through those cable channels?"

"Yeah."

Each time Robbie said "yeah" he had more disdain in his voice.

"Does your mom get videos from the video store?"

"Yeah."

"So sometimes at night you might see a video she brought home?"

"Yeah."

"Did you ever see naked people on TV, Robbie?"

Susan Dirks shook her bangled fists, calling out again that Rafferty was asking irrelevant questions, tiring the boy, getting nowhere. "We're not having a trial here, judge," she yapped. "All I have to do is prove that the charge is reasonable."

The judge seemed to have contracted a stiff neck. He turned his head with evident pain from Mrs. Dirks to Rafferty. "Your objection is overruled, Mrs. Dirks. Bring this to a close, Mr. Rafferty, before I lose my patience."

"Did you ever see naked people on TV, Robbie?" Rafferty asked in the same even tone he'd used the first time.

"No."

"The people you see on TV all through those sixty-four channels you're flipping through always have every bit of their clothing on?"

"Yeah."

"Do your mother's boyfriends stay overnight—"

At the same time Susan screeched, "Objection," Robbie stood up from his mother's lap and shouted, "No!"

"Question withdrawn," Rafferty said. "When you're at school did you see the nurse about once a week?"

"I TOLD you I'm allergic," Robbie said. "I get rashes and fevers sometimes."

"When did you tell me you were allergic?"

"At the beginning."

"Did you tell me what you're allergic to?"

"I said, I'm allergic."

"All right then, you're allergic. When your allergies flared up did you go see the nurse?"

"Duh."

"Isn't Mrs. Goodwin's office right next to the principal's office?"

"I don't know."

"Isn't it also next to the secretary's desk?"

"Yeah."

"And the counselor's office? Mrs. Dirks just told you they were, if you didn't know before. Did you ever think of going to the principal's office right next door for help?"

"He would holler at me."

"He also hollered at you?"

"She was always pushing me down."

"There isn't a door for the nurse's office, Robbie. Wouldn't the principal have seen what was going on in Mrs. Goodwin's office?"

"He don't see everything!" He was pouting. For the first time he looked like a child.

"Why did Mr. Henskin holler at you?"

"He has to make sure everyone is good."

"Weren't you good?"

"I don't know."

"Mrs. Goodwin's job is like that too. Her job is to help children get well, if they're sick. Did Mrs. Goodwin check your ears or your throat because you were sick?"

"She was always pushin' me down, tying me—"

"Right out in the open, where the principal could see if he walked by?"

He lowered his eyes again. I thought then that if I'd had one hundred thousand dollars I would have paid it right there. I would have paid the money if I could have seen what Robbie saw, if I could have known what was true.

"It was dark in there. It's like a cave."

"Why didn't the principal hear you?"

"I couldn't make no noise."

"Why not?"

"She said she'd cut me up."

"Where did the nurse push you down?"

"On her bed."

"Was she trying to give you medicine?"

"She wanted to look at me. She said she'd bite me."

"Did she bite you?"

"She said she would if I moved. She said all my blood would come out of there."

"Isn't a nurse supposed to help you if you're sick?"

"She hollered at me. She was always—"

"When you needed medicine did you cooperate with her?"

Robbie looked at Rafferty again. "Yeah."

"If she had to check your throat did you help her out by sitting still?"

"I told you," he said, whining now, "I tried to help but she was always pushing me down. She told me not to tell; she told me she'd come after me if I tattled."

"You were so sick once Mrs. Goodwin had to sit with you all morning. She had to hold you while you threw up. She sat by your side until your mother came to get you—"

"She always pushed me down," he cried.

"She put cool cloths on your forehead and tried to get you to eat little pieces of ice cube. You were that sick."

He had turned into his mother and was sobbing. "She pushed me down. She always pushed me down."

During the hearing I thought that nothing could shake me more than Robbie's expression already had. But when he was finished the investigating officer testified. He quoted Alice. She had shouted at the police. She had said, "I hurt everybody." I thought I must not have heard him. It was one thing to have the boy look hurt, and another to have my wife saying she'd done wrong. I continued to assume that I had not heard properly. For almost a full hour Rafferty grilled Officer Melby about technicalities, about why he hadn't read Alice Miranda, under what circumstances he read Miranda, what other questions he had asked Alice, how long he'd been observing her in the lunchroom. I couldn't think of any reason or excuse, no matter how ill a person was, to say to an officer, "I hurt everybody."

Rafferty sat at his table for the short closing statement. He had taken his suit coat off. It dangled behind him from his index finger as he spoke. He argued that the state hadn't made out its case on all the charges. He stressed that Robbie didn't have a very clear memory about the abuse, that he could come up with almost no specifics other than the anatomical details, which of course had been provided by Miss Flint. He concluded by asking the court reporter to please type up a transcript for him.

Mrs. Dirks, for her part, spoke about how a public health official is a person of trust in any community. Alice had violated that trust. Every school personnel was now going to be suspect, and parents would no longer feel safe sending their children off to learn their letters. Alice had spoken for herself to the police, and Robbie had merely corroborated her admission.

The work with the doll could not be undone. The judge mumbled about the serious nature of the charge. As if the angry women were present he urged parents who had complaints about Mrs. Goodwin to either formalize their charges or stop the rumor mills. He set the date for the formal arraignment and the court was dismissed. Alice got up right away. She stood on her toes, trying to see out the high windows. Then she turned to look at me. I don't know what she expected to see. I wanted to cut over the pews and grab hold of her. She smiled, that pitying crooked smile, before the guard motioned her to go. I leaned forward, resting my chin and mouth against my sleeve. I must have chewed my lip all the way through. Later, when I took the shirt off, there were bloodstains along both of my cuffs.

I sat for a while. I was unsure how I was going to make my way through the ranks outside. Rafferty slid in beside me after everyone else had gone behind the screen and out the back hall.

"It went well," he said. "Better than I thought it would, actually. Mrs. Dirks doesn't usually lose her cool." He chuckled at that.

"Why'd she do it this time?"

"It's important to go after the boy in the prelim, to be vicious, if you will, so that he'll turn against me at trial time. He'll remember what a creep I was, and hold it against me. In front of the jury, you see. Jurors, especially older jurors, don't warm to disrespectful children."

He stank of aftershave.

"I think we accomplished that," he continued. "I don't have any doubts that Robbie will be belligerent, smug, and foul. I will be all sweetness at that point, trying hard to empathize, to understand."

He waited for me to say something.

"Mrs. Dirks knows the ploy, of course," he went on. "She tried at first to keep her objections to a minimum. She didn't want to give Robbie the idea that I'm as bad as she thinks I am. But when she started caterwauling, in spite of herself, she only reinforced the idea that I am the ogre."

"I see," I said.

"I've got a hunch about the boyfriends. I went sniffing around all weekend, as I said. I wouldn't be surprised if they dropped charges. They might try to settle out of court, which I will not allow. Dirks knows me. She knows their only real choice is to drop charges." His aftershave was a slow-moving, noxious odor which only now had reached my nostrils in full. "Don't look so shaken up," he said. "They know now that the boy can't make it in court, and if they have any brains at all they'll realize that the mother has less of a chance than he does."

"What about the admission?" I asked.

"Well, naturally they'll walk that one around the block and make it piss on every tree. We'll get it excluded. We knew it was coming, so it wasn't a surprise."

"We knew it was coming?" I asked.

"Alice told me that she'd been—what were her words?—'babbling incoherently' to the investigating officers."

I thanked him and got out, down the six flights of stairs, away from him. I went as quickly as I could. The band of women in the hall had gone off, presumably to feed their anger elsewhere. I stood on Wisconsin Avenue on the hot pavement across the street from the jail. I stood looking at the narrow mirrored windows on the fourth floor, where Alice's pod was. She had always spoken about Robbie in such disparaging tones. There wasn't much substance to him. I had thought he'd be a tough kid, brawny, someone you'd want to wrestle. How could she have hurt a boy without the principal and the secretary and the guidance counselor knowing about it? She had once squirted me all over with whipped cream and come running behind sticking out her long tongue. The topsoil of the entire county could have blown into Lake Michigan right then. I wouldn't have noticed or much cared. "I didn't see anything," I said under my breath. The metal plates over the jail windows were blinding in the noonday sun. "I didn't see Robbie looking at that doll."

When I'd finished telling Theresa about the hearing she put her head down in her lap. Just as both Alice and I had done at some point during that long and surreal morning. Theresa was frozen, glued to her chair. I wasn't sure if she was praying or somehow crying in that pose. I had told her some of it, as best I could. I'd thought at the start that I'd see something in the telling. I'd thought there might be answers among my sentences, something obvious and inevitable.

"So what," Theresa said, without looking up, without moving, "did Robbie say Alice did to him? I'm not clear on that."

I had come up to the scene so many times. I couldn't get to it. I knew Alice had always admired me for the fact that I was "solid"—that's the word she often used to describe me. In fact, I was like a mouse skittering back to its hole in the face of a shadow. I had not watched Robbie abuse his doll but I'd gathered what private acts he thought Alice had done to him.

I started to get up from the chair, hoping that Theresa would leave, now that she'd heard most of the story. "I need to check Emma—" I started to say.

"What does Rafferty think?" She was trying to hold me. There was a thin stream of light coming through the door from the upstairs hall light and the flicker of the television. The rest of the house was dark. "He thinks the way into the case is through the mother, a boyfriend or two."

"Is he any good, Howard?"

Now there was a question which took me by surprise, I must admit. Dan had been friends with Rafferty for years. Rafferty was one of the few Dairy Shrine Angels, having contributed over a thousand dollars to the museum. Dan had told me that Rafferty could have worked in any major city, in any firm he liked, but that he chose to stay in Racine.

"How do you dispute the injury to a doll?" I said. The words came out the side of my mouth. I thought that if my fists came uncurled my hands might knock something over.

"I'm sorry, Howard," she said, stretching her arms toward me. "I'm sure Rafferty is the best, I really am. It's just that I'm so concerned about Alice. These things are capricious. I love Paul, I do. He's such a character —but sometimes he gets caught up in the drama of the trial. I've been on the receiving end, hearing amazing stories over the dinner table. He's a nut, you know? Every now and then he does lose a case. I've been to the jail and—"

"She says she'll be all right," I said. "Three months, four months."

"But it will be so much more than that. They always make motions. Trials are always delayed. That place is crowded. They've got four hundred fifty people in there, on average, at a time. Half of them are going cold turkey from crack, or even cigarettes—there's no smoking anymore. It's noisy all night long, it smells, it's never dark to go to sleep." She covered her eyes with her hands. "God, Howard, I really can't bear to think of her in a cell." She put her head down again and started to cry. I thought that if she made one more irritating comment it might be difficult to resist striking the back of her neck.

"I'm sorry, I'm so sorry," she sniveled. "Do you know what? I'll take the girls tomorrow. I'll take them until this thing is over. I've got all summer off. You need to work and Audrey will love to have company now that—"

Now that what? In the hour that I'd been talking to Theresa I'd forgotten that Lizzy was gone.

"Would you let me do that, Howard? Take care of the girls?"

The kettle was clattering on the stove top. I hadn't heard it until now. Most of the water had probably boiled away. My children were sleeping on the dirty floor in the glare of the one station we could get. It probably came out in a fairly gruff way when I said, "That'd be fine."

Chapter Thirteen

—

THE NIGHT AFTER THERESA first came down we started a routine that went smoothly for a few weeks. I got out early and did the chores, before the girls were up. They were to ring the old dinner bell if they needed me. That had always been the rule, when Alice and I used to milk together. It had never been put to the test and I wasn't sure I'd be able to hear the call over the whir of the compressor. Usually they were just beginning to blink and stretch when I came back to the house for breakfast. Theresa showed up around eight to take them away to Vermont Acres. They were only too happy to go. They waited at the screen door, watching for her to come along the cornfield. She always went into the house to pick out the things she knew they needed. She found suitable clothes for whatever activity she had planned.

A few days following the preliminary hearing a social worker from the Child Welfare Office called to set up an interview for Emma and Claire. It was a factual conversation, about times and dates. She didn't say why a government agency thought it necessary to talk to my children in the downtown office. My first impulse was to slam down the phone. I cordially told the woman that I'd like the opportunity to speak with my attorney first. "Your attorney has nothing to do with this procedure," she said.

"I understand," I replied, in ignorance. But I knew enough about the so-called procedure to envision my children swept out from under my feet in the name of protection.

Rafferty spoke faster than usual when I called him to ask for his expert opinion. "They'll never let me be present," he said, "but I'm going to demand that they videotape the sessions. I've seen cases where they conduct the interview, mislay the notes, and then remove the children from the home. Don't worry, don't worry, we won't let that happen. This problem is another thorn, nothing larger than a thorn. Another hassle we'll have to deal with. We can't say no to them because they'll take the kids off in a second. Standing in their way implies guilt, and implicates you."

I remember weakening, seeing the kitchen go fluid and red. The place spread, the trembling walls streaming beyond their own boundaries. I was at first hot, and then suddenly cold, hard. How Alice could have done this to us, I didn't know.

"We need to be calm, as best we can," Rafferty said, "and cooperative. It's an unusual situation, because the children themselves have not come forward. Typically, the kids report and then the whole process kicks in. There's only a suspicion here. The social workers can't ask leading questions; they can't order foster care unless the girls say something very explicit. Your children are going to have to be specific, come up with details, I mean details, in order for this thing to get to court. You know they don't have that kind of vocabulary."

Theresa was far more comforting, and also far more enraged. When I told her I had had to make the appointment for the girls she came at me with her talons spread and stopped just short of my chest. After she'd turned away and gone at the wall she said, "Theresa, get a hold of yourself." She shut her eyes and put her praying hands to her mouth. She began to apologize without changing her stance and without punctuating her sentences. "I'm sorry, Howard, forgive me, this whole thing makes me very angry, extremely angry." She appeared to be asleep. "But I think," she said, slowing down, "I think you will be all right. Most of the people I know over there in the department err against children, actually.

Myra is one of the more extreme case workers. A child has to be pretty mangled to be removed from their home. There has to be bruises—real wounds, and you have to say in plain English what's been done to your privates. Claire and Emma will have nothing to tell them. Nothing." She looked up at me and said, "I marvel at how coolheaded you are. I feel murderous, I honestly do. It's so good for the girls, that you can be level. They'll be fine because of your tranquility."

Just like an old rock, Alice might have said. Solid, hard, dark all the way through. Had the latest thorn been my only worry it would have been aggrieving in an all-consuming way. It was a sorer kind of aggravation than the others: The girls were innocent and should have had nothing to do with the trials of their parents. Removal would permanently damage them. Because the thought of them being taken from me was incomprehensible and untenable, I by and large refused to acknowledge the process. I went out and worked. I worked as if my life depended upon it. I worked as hard as I could, without conserving my motions, so that sleep would come at night.

I moved, always moving, forcing my hands and feet to their accustomed tasks. There is an old saying most people probably know: Live as if you're going to die tomorrow and farm as if you're going to live forever. I guess through the good and the bad times I tried to follow that saying. Take deep breaths, savor the moment, appreciate what you have. Build up the soil, mend your fences, put your money into good breeding stock. I spent my time during those weeks mulching potatoes and the garden, pulling thistles, and clearing a field of its stones. In one flowering thistle there are twenty thousand seeds. With my leather gloves on my hands and a heavy shirt on my back I walked the farm, pulling up the thorny plants by their roots, tossing them into piles, and putting the flowers in my bag. At night I burned the blossoms. All across the farm there were the piles I'd made of uprooted thistle plants. They turned white in the sun. The weeds were enemies and even in death they did not look completely vanquished. I must have pulled thousands of thistles in those weeks. I must have picked up thousands of stones. I had already lost the spring wheat, and the stunted corn was nearly dead. It was reasonable to clear the lowest field on the farm. There might be some moisture left in the subsoil, and if it did rain the field might hold the water. It might be a good place to try for some winter wheat. I could think of enough reasons to spend the day clearing the field. The truth is I didn't know what else to do except pull thistles or walk along the furrows I'd made, picking up stones.

There is never an end to stones in a field. You can clear the five acres one summer and come spring there will be a new crop. With each freeze and thaw stones are pushed up through to the light of day, as if they have the sense of a seed. And if a field is plowed, there the stones are, sitting like old potatoes, brought to the surface by one's own hand. So I walked and stooped and carried stones, some the size of my fist, others the size of a melon, to piles I'd made, or I'd heap them on the hay wagon. I wore nothing but my drawers underneath a pair of filthy denim coveralls. I'm sure I smelled. There was plenty to worry about and I sometimes had to stop to organize the fears. There didn't seem much point in trying to understand why such a thing had happened to Alice. I tried not to think about the reason. I attempted, as I moved, not to worry about the girls. I couldn't consider their looming appointment without feeling as if my chest was going to cave in. In retrospect I'm not sure I had one clear thought as I worked. It was hot and I kept going. I also wondered how I was going to feed the cows for the winter. The girls were safe up with Theresa, that was the thing to remember. I carried stones trying to keep my focus. Think, I told myself, about how to set Alice free. Think how to hold the family together, to keep it from scattering like the thistle seeds I was keeping in my sack, tight in the blossom. There were afternoons when setting the jail on fire seemed an adequate solution. Think how to keep the girls protected from the system that would pull them in, hold them, change them. Once I set myself the assignment, I pictured a faceless child welfare worker and Susan Dirks and Rafferty, all of them floating down the river toward a steep drop off. They looked around in discomfiture when they found themselves going over the falls, toward the sharp rocks. *Susan, Paul, are you comfy?* Alice came unbidden behind them, flailing and screeching as she fell.

While I walked I also did my level best not to think about Robbie. I tried to imagine the doll stripped of its power. There had to be something a person could do to change the doll so that it wouldn't cause Robbie to look so injured. I had been brought up to think step by step, from A to B and so on. My father believed that outside of the IRS the world was a logical place. For three days I made a stone wall along the slope of the driveway. I concentrated on keeping the bolt of fear at bay, the fear that the girls would be taken away. I guess in addition I spent a fair amount of time in the no man's land that comes with wanting. I wanted in a savage way, as a child wants. I wanted in spite of reason, and without hope. What I wanted at times seemed simple enough. I wanted to open my eyes to the first light of May. I wanted to find that the summer had not yet begun.

The first few days Theresa brought my lunch in a sack when she picked up the girls in the morning. She'd just leave it on the table. It wasn't too long before she said I should come to the house and eat with them. She said it was oppressive, that it wasn't healthy to be working in the heat without taking a real break. I said I couldn't, that she'd already done enough. She lowered her eyes while she spoke. "I don't want to stand still, Howard. I don't want to stand still to think. But I don't want to have to go out and be social either. I've gone to lunch with my co-workers, and my sisters, and some old friends, and my mother, and we talk about redecorating our kitchens, and we laugh, as if choosing wallpaper is very, very hilarious. You need the same thing I do, to move and not think, and you need the silence and the talk that is not circling the pain. Please, just come up for twenty minutes, get something to eat, tell me about your morning, about the crops, and I'll talk to you about the girls."

Her recognition of my need was not unnerving. I found her perceptiveness consoling. She might just as well have put cool compresses to my forehead. I said that I'd stop over, that I'd like to. I did miss Emma and Claire during the day. I missed their noise. It was always a relief to lay eyes on them at lunchtime, to see that they were playing happily. I needed to have that check, to see for myself that they were still with me. During the day I'd get to feel as if there wasn't much that was alive, that everything was drying up and dying. I used to praise the cats for their cunning, and now they seemed vile. They tossed the young rabbits, and the chipmunks, into the air, swatting and pummeling long after the animals were crippled. Every morning another few sheep were cast, the muscles in their bodies useless. I was killing one or two each day. Theresa said it wasn't right to be alone so much, to have time to brood.

At noon I climbed along the dusty cornfield. I'd go through Mrs. Klinke's backyard, down the treeless street, Rhode Island Court. I'd walk right up to the front door of the Collinses' house. I always knocked. We didn't speak about risk—the threat of neighbor's talk. Dan was always at work and we rarely mentioned him. I was aware that my every action had to be beyond reproach, and also sure that I no longer had much of anything to lose, that I was pretty well damned. The one time I started to wonder if it was worth my putting Theresa in danger she turned on me with a ferocity I had never seen in her. She asked me not to bring it up again. I think we both understood that for a certain grace period she was exempt from community censure. She was safe because of Lizzy.

The girls always came rushing from a far corner. They climbed all over me for just a minute and then they scattered as quickly as they had come. There were good smells coming from the kitchen. Theresa had thick hunks of warm homemade brown bread already buttered in a basket, and watermelon and cantaloupe cut in slices in platters. There'd be a spread of cold cuts, tomatoes, lettuce, radishes, fresh pea pods, a glass pitcher of icy lemonade. She made chilled soup with strawberries, or cucumbers. Although I have always stuck up for old houses with history and bad plumbing, every day I looked forward to stepping inside that 1982 ranch house with a garbage compactor and central air. I often had the urge, in those weeks, to stretch out on the chaise lounge in my dirty rock-gathering clothes, to sleep in a place where you needed a blanket.

I had not let it out of my mind since that first night we spoke that Lizzy was dead. Theresa always came to the door and let me in. I was careful to look at her for a minute, with the knowledge uppermost in my mind, that Lizzy was gone. Theresa had a particular way of smiling. She seemed to be winded. She was always striving to find a bright side. She opened the door and I guess we stood there maybe two beats longer than necessary. I think we were gauging each other's sadness, or maybe acknowledging each of our distinct and common troubles. We looked, and then she opened the door wider, and I stepped into the hall.

We sat down to lunch, the three girls, Theresa, and I. They gave me a review of their morning. They had painted, or made a maze for the hamster. They had dressed up and conquered the world with the old-fashioned female weapons of high heels and strings of pearls. Emma occasionally wanted to know what I had done. "What, again?" she'd say, when I told her I was gathering rocks. She was not impressed by the fact that ice had once come down from the Pole in tremendous solid sheets, a mile thick. So what if all the large and small animals had had to run from the cold as it came pressing upon them. She squirmed in her chair when I tried to explain that piles of stones were dumped right where the glacier melted. "Tell me some other time," was her refrain as she slid from her chair and ran down the basement stairs with Audrey.

Theresa and I often talked quietly at the kitchen table. Before the children's interview she worried out loud for me. Who was assigned to the case? Should we tell Alice about the session? What did Rafferty think? Could Theresa herself legitimately call over to the office and talk to Rose Ann Lexin? She'd never met the woman. It was touchy, to put in a word to an unknown quantity. She'd eventually come back to the fact that there was nothing the girls would say to incriminate anyone. On the subject of Alice, Rafferty had said over the phone that there wasn't any reason to tell her, that she'd feel helpless and panicked in her isolation. To Theresa I said, "I would want to know."

"You'd want to know," she answered. "You think you'd want to know. But imagine being in that place and having that kind of worry. You can't even go outside and run around. You can't scream, without having a dozen people jump on you. I agree with Rafferty. There's no point in telling her. I think knowing would drive me close to insanity, Howard, I really do."

"And afterward?"

"Afterward is afterward. You can tell her when she's out, play it down. Rafferty's probably right, that it isn't anything more than a thorn."

"Nothing more than a thorn," I said.

She was kind enough to ask for my permission to talk with the girls about the session. She said that of course she would never bring it up, but if they mentioned it she would reassure them, providing it was all right with me. When we spoke about Emma and Claire, I sometimes had the fleeting sense that we, she and I, were a team with a yoke around our heads, blindly pulling the load behind us. I most often felt that the burden was mine alone, and then at lunch, every day, there was the slightest easing. I'd forget that it was going to lighten until I knocked at her door.

"They seem fine, don't they?" she often said. "They seem fine to me."

I always said I thought they were fine. When we had exhausted that subject she told me stories about her large family and her Catholic up-bringing. Sometimes we sat in an easy silence. The kitchen was cool and clean. I've thought since, how effortless life seemed in that house. After lunch I went out to the glassed-in porch that was also air conditioned. I sat on the wicker chair, at the wicker table, to write my daily letter to Alice. Theresa did the dishes and as she worked she sang. She had a light, sweet voice. It was cool in that house, as I said. It was hard to feel terrible there. I was tired and comfortable and full. I had nothing to say. Once or twice I fell asleep with my head on the table.

If I had the energy I'd read Dan's *Wall Street Journal*. When there had been the slightest possibility of drought, way back in March, corn prices were already skyrocketing. A month later, when the corn was just being planted, when there was rain in the five-day forecast, corn prices fell. Now, because half of the Midwest's corn was failing, corn futures were better than gold. It isn't enough to walk through a field, day after scorch-ing day picking up rocks so that you can plant a few seeds, and then cultivate it, week after week, with nothing more than hope and the advice of your local extension agent, and then through the wet fall wait for a bright, dry stretch so that you can work night and day harvesting. It isn't enough to watch your work come apart in a hailstorm, a windstorm, a freeze. All that isn't enough to get a fair price for corn.

When I started to complain about the stock market Theresa said, "You talk as if you're an old fart. Like you grew up in these parts and aspired to be an old fart."

"That's awfully nice of you to say," I said.

She laughed. "I meant it as a compliment, I really did!"

The girls were on the deck spitting watermelon seeds at each other. Theresa rested her cheek in her cupped hand and watched them out the sliding door for a long time. She closed her eyes tight for a minute every once in a while. I gathered that she was wincing at what for her was still unthinkable. I tried not to look on. I wondered what to say that could be of help. At the same time I knew there was nothing anyone could say. She couldn't see the other girls without wanting Lizzy. She couldn't believe in her death, and yet after their vacation out West she had gone down to

Police Headquarters to talk to the officers about the drowning. She insisted, apparently, that nothing of a criminal nature had taken place at the
pond. It was Rafferty, not Theresa, who informed me of the meeting.
Sometimes, over lunch, I couldn't keep from watching her as she struggled with her thoughts. I'd wonder about her while she was right across
the table. Hers was a strength that was admirable.

On the twenty-third of July I took Emma and Claire from Vermont
Acres after lunch and drove them to Racine for their interview. I had
tried to be as casual as I could. They stood still with their faces upturned
while Theresa cleaned their mouths with a wet dishcloth. The people
were nice, she explained. No need to worry. The room was stocked with
toys and games, stuffed animals and dolls. She put some spit on her finger
and slicked down Emma's cowlick. The girls knew enough to be afraid.
Nothing we said allayed their anxiety. In the car Emma asked if she
would be taken away. "No," I said, again feeling the heat rising in me,
seeing the road and sky in front of the car blaze and pitch.

Rafferty was waiting in the airy brick entrance at the Law Enforcement Center, where the Police Investigation Unit is housed. Emma and
Claire did not know that their mother was in the next wing, four flights
away. They took turns getting a drink from the bubbler while Rafferty
whispered at me. "This place is up for grabs," he said. "They're not sure
what to do. They don't know if they have to honor my requests or if they
can tell me to go to hell. Lexin said she'd put it on tape, the other one,
Anderson, said they are under no obligation to do so. She made a ruckus
about how taping children makes them uncomfortable. I smiled very
prettily at her. I said that your girls had spent their formative years in
front of a camcorder, correct? And that we would be glad, egregiously
glad to pay for any expenses incurred. Then, goddamn it, if anything
comes up, we've got it all right there. They have to haul the tape into
court and it's clear as dog shit, pardon me." He turned to the girls. "How
are we today?"

They looked out at him from under their bent heads. Emma whick-
ered, "Go-o-o–d."

Two young women came from a long hall, conferring as they walked
toward us. They ignored Rafferty as he made the introductions. The
attractive one knelt to look at Claire's stuffed animal. Her natural speak-

ing voice seemed to be at the pitch of a whine. "What have you got there?" Claire turned her face into my leg. "It's okay, honey," the woman said, clutching my daughter's hand. "Your dad will be right here, waiting for you. There's a rabbit down the hall that wants to meet your bunny." Claire hesitated, trying to think if it was worth leaving me. "There's a kitty, too, and a frog. Do you think your bunny would like a frog?" Claire went slowly without looking back.

"I'm Mrs. Lexin," the blond woman said to Emma. "Let's you and I talk for a minute while Miss Anderson is playing with your sister."

Theresa had mentioned an anger on my behalf strong enough to make her want to smash her recyclable glass against her garage door. As I sat listening to the noise of Rafferty's talk, I did not so much want to break anything specific. I felt I might have shouted with a force unusual to me, those flights up to Alice's pod. *Look! Look at your daughters!*

Although the time went slowly Claire was out in about ten minutes, and Emma shortly after. Claire had been crying, judging from her feverish look and her matted lashes. Mrs. Lexin, a good ten years my junior, called me into her office. She had short hair and glasses that took up half her face. She was studying her folder. "The girls are quite upset about their mother, about her having been taken away."

"Yes, I'm aware of that."

"We'd like to see them again, tomorrow, if you don't mind." When I didn't answer she glanced at me. "Would that work out?"

I nodded.

"It is clear that your girls are experiencing a good deal of trauma about their mother being gone and I would recommend to you, Mr. Goodwin, strongly recommend, that they see someone to help them through this time. We have a listing here, of therapists and human service agencies in the county. You are not legally bound to seek out help, but it would be most beneficial, under the circumstances."

I would have liked to say that they'd been fine before they came for the interview. "Thank you," I said from between my clenched teeth.

"They were brought up to try, try again, if at first they don't succeed," Rafferty said as we went out the doors, back into the furnace of the July day. Claire was whining into my shoulder and Emma was silent, keeping close at my side. "Most of us are raised to toe the line, conform, follow the rules. Rules sure make the world go around, but I've got a bit of the anarchist in me. How beautiful it would be to buck the system. To get away with thumbing your nose at a few key people in high places. The trouble is the stakes are always too high. Too high." He came down on my free shoulder. "Tomorrow, then. More of same. Same old crap, same conclusion. Onward. Upward. Back to work." He tweaked Claire's chin. "You make sure your father watches his manners, girls." He ruffled Emma's hair and then he darted between the cars to get across the street.

The second interview went much the same as the first. Claire hugged her rabbit and cried. Emma too did not want to play. She remained dry eyed. I was proud of her. She was polite, tight-lipped. She wanted to go back to her dad, she told Mrs. Lexin. When she was asked if anything bad happened at home, Emma spoke about the cat that had jumped up into the engine and gotten ground to bits. It had been I who had started the car. I was again given the recommendation that the girls get immediate help from a local therapist. As we left Rafferty looked at me and said, "We have one thorn out of our big, soft pads." To Emma he said, "Isn't that right, kiddo?"

Emma yanked on my shirt after he was gone. She wanted me to squat, to get to her level so she could whisper in my ear. "I don't like him," she said.

As the weeks wore on I stayed beyond the lunch hour at Theresa's. Each day I stayed longer. Finally I put yesterday's paper on the chaise lounge as protection against my dirty clothes and sat on it. I read *Time* magazine and *Country Home*. Theresa went about her chores. It was hard to catch the words to the songs she sang. I read, feeling her movements in the next room. "Aren't you ever going back to work?" she said once. I jumped to attention. "No, no, no, Howard," she said as she laughed. "Get back down. I'm teasing you."

In the long, hot afternoons I dragged the irrigation rig to ever drier ground. The rig wasn't working up to speed and still I worried that the well was going to run dry. The marsh that I had at first used as a water source was nothing now but a slick of mud. Normally there might be three or four feet of water. The pond was considerably lower than usual and I found several trout belly up, like old shoes, floating near the bank. I cultivated the soybeans and the orchard cornfield, the two crops I meant to save. The mullein and burdock had grown well without a drop of rain, crafty, strong, leeching from the soil what was not rightfully theirs. When I couldn't stand the heat I went in and sat by the fan. I'd sift through the stack of books I had in the living room that were to make me reasonable and informed. Rafferty had given me a newsletter for Victims of Child Abuse Laws. VOCAL, it was called. He thought I might want to pursue a support network. I didn't feel I had anything in common with the grand-parents accused by their grandchildren, or the fathers charged by their daughters. Nothing in the literature explained how Robbie Mackessy could have looked at his doll with so much distress.

I called Rafferty nearly every day around four o'clock. I wanted to be sure he remembered that Alice was still in her cage, that I was still waiting out in the sun. "Any word?" I always asked. He had failed to get Alice's bond reduced in a hearing at the beginning of July. In August he spent a good deal of time working toward a motion to suppress her admission at the trial. He was confident he would win the day because her rights hadn't been read to her when she babbled on. That motion also failed. At the end of August he asked for an extension, which pushed the trial back another six weeks from the October 12 date. Later there was yet another extension.

I hadn't talked with Dan much, since the drowning. At the funeral we had clasped hands without saying anything. I had gone up to Vermont Acres a couple of times in the days afterward. We had stood around kicking a stone in the driveway. We tried to talk as if his work at the Dairy Shrine was still interesting and useful. He didn't come down to help me milk anymore, the way he had for nearly six years. In fact, I hadn't seen him since he'd returned from his vacation. Theresa said he went to the office before dawn and didn't come home until late. I wasn't sure he knew my children were virtually living at his house.

I started the evening chores around five, as usual. I have always loved the steady rhythm of the milking machines, the milk surging into the pipes and along into the bulk tank. For what it's worth, I could go through the routine on that farm, still, with my eyes closed. I moved slowly in the dripping heat. I knew that eventually I would have to go into the kitchen and find myself something to eat. Like clockwork Theresa brought the girls down at seven-thirty. She usually stayed long enough to explain that she had just thrown a few leftovers together, that it was nothing. There was always a brand-new brown lunch bag on the kitchen table. Inside there might be a roast beef or ham sandwich. There was liable also to be quite a few other things: an apple, a piece of pie, a plastic container of fruit salad, and a brownie. I was always startled, relieved, thankful, simultaneously. I tripped over myself, thanking her. She always ran away backwards, waving. I suppose a person likes being appreciated, but too much praise makes your ears ring. I probably should have felt like a schoolboy. Maybe I should have taken offense at her motherly attention. I didn't. I was tired and hungry and her lunches were good.

After she'd gone, the girls and I halfheartedly whacked a baseball around. Sometimes they drew a picture for their mother, or had me read the day's letter which she always wrote them. In her letters she asked them to remember the dramatic or funny or frightening times that were already a part of our family history. "Remember," she wrote, "when we came upon the dog in the woods wrapped around the tree by its own leash? Remember how Dad helped us climb a tree before he moved in, closer and close to that dog, and how when he cut the leash, the poor thing stood there for a minute, barking and barking, before it took off? Remember how we felt like monkeys up in that tree?"

After a quick bath I read to them, a short book. They rarely asked for more, or complained. I didn't play my clarinet and they didn't dance. They lay on Emma's bed, waiting for me to go away before they shut their eyes. They had been sleeping together since Alice had gone. They wanted me to leave the room so that they could forget. They were smart to know that sleep would take them to another time.

My primary goal was to preserve our family, to make our home secure for the girls. Had it been possible I would have changed places with Alice. What made it tolerable for us to go along, week after week, was the fact that she was managing there. That fact continued to surprise me. She was usually cheerful and philosophical during our Sunday visits. Her skin had turned the color of old asphalt early on, but otherwise she seemed healthy. What took its toll, more than anything else, it seemed, was her need to say the right things, to make the visit go along happily.

"I'm alive," she said at one meeting, several weeks into the ordeal. "Please don't look at me as if you're trying to figure out if I'm breathing." She covered her nose and her mouth with her hands and then let them slip to her chin. She pulled her lower lip down so that I could see her pale gums and her crooked bottom teeth. "Are the girls all right?"

I had debated whether or not to tell her about the interviews once they were successfully concluded. I had thought I might write her. I didn't know how to explain the episode simply on paper. It was afterward, I guess in relief, that I often considered asking Theresa if I could borrow her garage door for the purpose of smashing my old milk bottles. I couldn't speak to Alice about the interviews in person with the time constraints and the continent of glass between us.

"They like going up to Theresa's," I said. "They—"

"There's my cell mate," she whispered, turning to look behind her. A large blond-haired girl with sores on her face passed behind Alice. "I keep hearing all these voices, sort of like your life flashing before you, only it's on audio. What's that sonnet—'They that have the power to hurt and will do none—' "

"What?" I said.

"It's about how great you are if you don't give in to the temptation to be cruel, how noble it is to be strong and at the same time gentle. You know, the perfect human being. I have this terrific urge to read poetry to my fellow inmates, but they'd probably sit on me and stuff up my mouth with wrapped vending-machine candy. I opened my eyes this morning, Howard, and looked, and it was exactly like the first day at Camp Everglade. I remember when I was nine, waking in the musty cabin and saying to myself, 'I didn't ask to be sent here.' I said that out loud this morning. This is real, you know that? This makes everything else seem like some vaporous thing, some heavenly vision. But then I hear some of the sad stories and I feel like Virtue itself. All these crazy sayings keep going through my head, phrases like, 'There but for the grace of God go I.' I have never thought those words in my life. Theresa always used to say that. I wonder if she does anymore. How is she? Does she mind taking the girls? Is she feeding you?"

When I didn't answer instantly she said, "You don't have to look so sheepish. What, does she bring you down lunch boxes with a chilled can of soda in an insulated pouch, and salt in a little cardboard shaker for your hard-boiled egg? I can almost taste her fruit salad with kiwis and strawberries and a half-dozen other things that are out of season." She had closed her eyes with the imagining, and when she opened them and looked at me she said, "She does! She brings you fruit salad! I can see it in your face! I bet you don't ask her how much she's spent on groceries either."

"She makes me lunch on occasion," I said.

"I'm glad! I'm very glad. I've been worrying that you're going to starve. At least I can rest assured that you're getting the major food groups now and then."

I remember again feeling as if I'd been caught at something. Alice had wanted the girls to play with Audrey. I had thought all along that I was only doing her bidding. I must have known, as she talked about a recipe that Theresa had made with fifteen dollars worth of capers, that my afternoons in Vermont Acres had become increasingly important to me. If Alice had changed her mind, if she had said that the girls shouldn't play there anymore, I would have stopped the routine with reluctance.

"I brought you these books on the legal system," I said. "There's one here about testifying in court. I think you should glance through them and see if there's—"

"I want novels," she said. "Rafferty will look after the rest."

"You have confidence in him," I stated.

"He's great, isn't he? How are we going to pay him? I have about two hundred dollars in my savings account. Don't we have an IRA? No, we cashed that for the baler, didn't we? What will Nellie say when you tell her that we have the best criminal lawyer in the universe? You're only supposed to have the top dog if you're guilty. What will Nellie say?" She started to make her voice go higher, " 'That Alice, always seeing the dark—' "

"I want to have you out," I said, trying to be calm and honorable and sentimental, as always.

Her stretched, mocking face, the huge, open eyes, the elongated, pursed lips abruptly collapsed. She pinched the phone between her neck and her shoulder and hid behind her hands. "Howard," she said, between her fingers, "I'm sorry I just said that about Nellie. I didn't mean it. And

I'm the one who insisted on Rafferty; I'm the one who said the stupid things to the nice investigating officers who I thought were Mrs. and Mr. Deputy Friendly." She held the phone away from her and shook her head. She adjusted herself and sat straight. "You have every right to be furious, don't you, and you're just as steady as can be. I put so much stock in these visits, you can't imagine." If she'd been a different sort of person she might have begun to weep. "I'm living in my head, that's all. You can't guess what's swirling around in here—a million things I never thought before. Seeing you is like being allowed to look up through a skylight to see the polestar. So I know where I am. I see you, and everything that's charging through my brain falls like dust to the ground and settles, and I think, North, South, East, West. Howard. Howard." When I didn't say anything she took a deep breath and went on. "So, you're getting fed. I just want these fifteen minutes to be the perfect visit. It's like some date I've been looking forward to for weeks." She smiled ruefully.

I always drove home from the jail shaken, not because my wife was in an awful stink of a hellhole where sunlight never penetrated, but because she was in a stink of a hellhole and surviving so admirably. I wasn't sure what to do about that. She was spending her time reading Stendhal, Tolstoy, and Chekhov, Emily Dickinson, Laura Ingalls Wilder, Damon Runyon, P. D. James, J. D. Salinger, and who knows what else. I guess I had expected that she would continue on her downward spiral that had begun after Lizzy's death. I wouldn't have been surprised if she'd fallen apart, although I couldn't have said exactly what that would entail. It had taken me a long time to understand that she needed help. It had finally registered one morning when I was trying to get her to notice Claire with a sharp knife in her hand. She hadn't cared about the danger. She had turned around and gone upstairs to the bedroom. She'd kicked me in the jaw the night before, in bed, flown up from the sheets as if she'd been stung. I had known then that Alice needed professional help. That she was bearing the county jail now threw me for a loop. My wife had gone to jail and was as stoic as Mary, Queen of Scots. I was at home, wandering around picking up rocks from fields, unable to fix myself a sandwich or a bowl of cornflakes.

Periodically, during the long afternoons, I'd have to sit in the shade and try to think out a few things. At thirty-six I was coming to understand some fundamental truths. I finally knew that all of our meanings are put upon us from the outside. There's nothing much inside that belongs to us at the start, or even along the way. We are shaped, time and time again, by luck, the prevailing winds. I had been formed and re-formed a dozen times, according to the personalities of my housemates. In high school I went to a friend's cabin and did nothing but sit and fish under the hot sun. I kept looking in the mirror during those months, seeing not only my shaggy hair, my unshaven face, but also the clean-cut, good, smart, strong young man my father insisted was his son. Alice thought I had powers which probably all along I knew I actually did not have. She seemed to trust my capabilities. She would certainly not have believed me if she'd known how willing I had been to go to Vietnam. I had stood in line to get my physical after I'd been drafted. I was eighteen. I had been in ROTC in high school and I figured there wasn't any chance of getting Conscientious Objector status. My father and I had talked about what it meant to fight for my country. We had talked about the burden of democracy. I would go to Vietnam and kill enough people and then hopefully I'd come home. I worked hard at accepting the duty. My friends and I argued about the war all summer. I talked myself into thinking there was justification for the conflict and that I was heroic to go. I probably sounded like a self-righteous ass. When I went for my physical I was excused because of a heart murmur. Not good enough for fodder. My hair grew long. I marched quietly in Ann Arbor and once in Washington, hoping my face wouldn't show up on the evening news in Minneapolis. That wasn't the last time I have felt one way and then right away felt another. When I told that story to Alice, she heard only the parts she wanted to hear. It was a happy ending, my being rejected. But to me, over the years, the story became emblematic of a flaw. My gravestone will say, "He never stayed any course. He was never sure."

The weeks passed. I had lain in bed on the night of the Fourth and listened to the firecrackers going off in the subdivisions. Our Independence didn't seem like much of a victory. There was a storm one morning at the end of July. I went out on the porch and watched the rain come down. According to the gauge there was six-tenths of an inch. Around noon the sun came out. The steam rose from the damp earth and by evening the soil was dry. The soybeans grew fairly well with my attention and the irrigation. All the sheep were dead. The cows lay under the oaks in their pasture in the heat of the day and chewed their cuds. Theresa used to say that the animals were blessed because they did not have the capacity to know or plan or remember. They didn't seem blissful as they chewed. They endured endless passing hours. They endured the daylight and the dark of night. Their blessing was probably wasted on them, as I suppose so many of our blessings are wasted on us.

The last night Theresa came down wasn't much different from any of the other nights that had come before, except that we had the previous accumulated nights and days behind us. Although she seemed unflagging, she must have been worn out after those three weeks. She had told me earlier, at lunch, that Dan was in Chicago for the weekend, at a convention of museum directors. We had laughed at the image of him at a black-tie banquet in the main hall of the Field Museum, having cocktails with the presidents of the Smithsonian and the American Museum of Natural History. We said we were sure that he too was laughing at himself honorably representing the Dairy Shrine. I had said again at lunch that I hadn't seen Dan in well over a month. "He's working all the time. Spinning his wheels," Theresa had said under her breath.

I was in the kitchen that evening when she brought the girls home. Emma came running to the porch. She shouted from outside, "Can Audrey stay over?" Theresa opened the door and set the bag lunch down on the kitchen table. Before Theresa could say no, I said, "That's fine with me." I'm not sure what I was thinking, or if I had even heard the request. The girls wrung each other's hands. Audrey alternately clasped Theresa around the waist and jumped to her shoulders, beseeching her to say yes. I realized, too late, that Theresa could not allow her only daughter to stay in our house. The idea was absurd. We both spoke at once. "I would miss you too much, Audrey," Theresa said. I was saying that it probably wasn't a good night for it after all. She and I turned to each other as we were talking. I think we understood what had gone through the other's mind.

"Wait," Theresa said. "Settle down." She put her hands on Audrey's shoulders and made her keep still. "You girls get ready for bed and play in Emma's room while Howard has his dinner. Then we'll go home. Audrey can stay some other time. We'll plan it—no, no complaining. You've got your chance to stay for a while."

Everyone seemed to think, with very little protesting, that it was a tolerable compromise. We went upstairs. Emma first, and then Audrey and Theresa. Claire and I brought up the rear. There were baskets of laundry in the bedroom. I was afraid she might offer to take the dirty clothes home. She passed by and looked in without saying anything. As they got ready there was chipping and chattering. They made the house sound like a menagerie. There was peace in the commotion. I helped Claire into her pajamas and brushed her teeth. I put my clarinet together and stood in the doorway of Emma's room with the reed in my mouth, watching my neighbor brush my daughter's hair.

"How do you get a comb through your curls?" Emma asked Theresa.

"Well," Theresa said, "I shampoo every morning. When it's wet I quick brush it. All I have to do is let it dry and it comes out like this. If I brush it or comb it when it's dry it gets frizzy. It sticks out—it's big and awful." She bit her lip as she smiled at me, over the top of Emma's head.

"Really?" Emma turned to me to check if what Theresa had said could be true. My daughter's hair and simple body were made of straight lines. I'd never given much consideration to our friend's thick loopy curls, but I could see how they might be interesting to someone who had been bald for her first two years of life.

"Do a song for us, Daddy," Claire shouted.

"I think I've forgotten," I said. I hadn't practiced in several weeks. I was going to sound rusty. While I put the reed in place I thought through my repertoire.

"I didn't know you played," Theresa said.

"I don't really," I said. "I just, ah—"

" 'Sing Me a Happy Song'!" Claire cried. "That's my favorite."

" 'We Can Work It Out'!" Emma demanded. "Or, 'Morning Has Broken'! My dad," she said to Audrey, "he knows all the songs."

I played badly. Theresa continued to brush Emma's hair. The three girls sat politely and listened. When I was done Theresa tucked them in the same bed. "Goodnight," they called. We paused at the door. "Goodnight," we said.

We went downstairs, the two of us. We could hear them plotting their riot. Theresa said she didn't think they'd last long, that they were tired. I looked through the bare cupboards trying to find something to offer her. There was milk in the refrigerator. "I'm fine," she said. "You eat." She fed her family skim milk, not our whole milk with the cream sitting in a lump on the top. She always insisted it was milk to bathe in, not to drink.

"Go ahead," she said, gesturing for me to sit at my own table, in front of the sack she had brought. She opened the cupboard, reached up for a glass, went to the sink, and poured herself some water. I looked in the bag. There were two bacon and lettuce and tomato sandwiches. The toasted wheat bread was saturated with what was undoubtedly low-fat mayonnaise. There was a bunch of grapes, carrot sticks, cold cooked beans in a baggy, and three chocolate chip cookies. I didn't know what to call Theresa anymore. What should I say to her, this person who didn't fit in any category I knew of. Friend, I suppose she was, although I'd never had a friend before who had gone to such lengths. I should say thank you. That hardly seemed enough. *I don't know what I'd do without you,* while true, was going too far. *You are good to me,* was corny. It was awkward, all of a sudden. In the amount of time it took me to look in the bag I no longer knew what to say. I should say something. Here I was so hungry, eating her food, food that she'd made expressly for me. She had drunk some of her water and was looking slantwise at an ant slugging along the linoleum with a crumb.

"That was nice for Emma and Claire. Upstairs, putting them to bed." I cleared my throat. "This is awfully good."

She nodded, keeping her eyes on the ant. She kept watching it while I bolted her sandwiches. I couldn't think what we had talked about over so many lunches. I half wanted to get away.

"Thank you for making this," I choked.

It was with some difficulty that she tore herself from the ant and turned her gaze on me. There was a whole wad of bread in my mouth, bulging in my cheek. I stopped chewing. I don't know how it happens that two people can find themselves lost in an ordinary kitchen. The old clock, the hum of the refrigerator, the fan going in the living room—nothing was making noise anymore. The table, the cluttered counter top, the full compost bucket by the sink, the chatter from upstairs—everything fell away. We were caught in an empty place. It was just the two of us, shining at each other.

It wasn't until she shook her curls, put her hands to her face, that we looked away. She was breathless and flushed, as if she'd run a long distance right to our table. I stared up, chewing. "It's just a mess," she wheezed. "Alice felt responsible for Lizzy. My friend Albert talked to me about—what did he call it?—'the quality of mercy.' The quality of mercy. He talked about how mercy blesses the giver and the receiver. The way he said it was beautiful. I've tried hard to think how Alice must feel. I wouldn't want to trade places with her, not for a minute. She'll always feel responsible, won't she, nothing we can say will make her think she shouldn't have done something different. I say that to myself, 'the quality of mercy,' when I'm despairing. I say those words as if I'm doing the rosary and I know, Howard, I know that embracing your family will bless me."

She was trying to catch her breath and talk all at once. "What am I saying? Of course I'd change places if it meant Lizzy would be alive. But do you see what I mean? It would be so convenient to use Alice as a great big depository: The 'Alice did it' dump. That's tempting—very tempting. My sisters have fallen into the trap but I'm not going to, Howard. I'm not going to. They say that Alice deserves to be locked up. If I disagree, they give each other knowing looks—a 'We know Theresa's sick in the head' look. I made the mistake of telling one of them that I feel responsible for Alice. I think they were about ready to commit me. But I do feel responsible for her, because I could have prevented the charge, because Lizzy's—death gave Carol Mackessy the spark she needed. You feel beholden to me for the food and the baby-sitting. I can't stand it! Could we please stop seeing it in these terms? We belong together, that's how I think of it. Your girls are helping Audrey, they're helping me get through the day. Sure, sure, it would be nice if Dan could wake up, if he could step out of himself long enough to realize that Alice is actually in jail because the community is going through a purging ritual. I just feel—well, mute half the time. Dan will drop over dead working before he figures out that the way through grief is grief itself. He's fighting it with all his strength because he thinks it will kill him."

I was eating as fast as I could, tearing the grapes off their stems. I should tell her that she was more than adequately helping me get through hour after hour. Going up to her house was on a par with climbing out of the pit of hell. The time in her kitchen was what I looked forward to every day. I sat on the chaise up there just so I could hear her sing. And I looked forward to her coming down at night too, seeing her for just a minute when she brought the girls home. The need was both startling and obvious. It was something I guess I should have known. The need I had, for her, for Theresa Collins, was so clear I couldn't see straight.

"They're quiet up there," she said. "They played so hard today I guess I'm not surprised. Let me go make sure they're okay." She moved across the room to the stairs. I had forgotten what it was like, to be drawn to a person. I didn't know how I could have stood in the doorway day after day looking at Theresa without actually seeing her as I was now. I'd forgotten how your blood flows toward a person when they move, so that all at once you know what the pull of gravity feels like. And you know that this is something strong and important, something that you need for life, this woman moving through the room.

When she came back down I was at the sink, waiting.

"I don't want to leave her," she murmured. She stood across the table from me. "You know that."

"Stay a little longer," I said. "I'll carry her up the hill. I'll carry her home in a minute." I mentioned that it was cooler out on the porch and that there was a moon.

"I don't care about the moon," she said.

"Come out on the porch." I could feel her behind me as I went, feel my blood drawn to my back.

"I need to go home," she whispered.

We stood in the middle of the dark porch, on the rag rug that Alice has always especially liked. "Sometimes," Theresa said, "I'm certain about the goodness of God. Sometimes I'm sure that Lizzy is in safe keeping. But tonight, I'm really scared, Howard. Tonight, everything feels as if it's tipping. Tonight," she said, coming closer, "it's so confusing. Everything feels dangerous because of you, and at the same time everything feels dangerous except right where you are."

She flew into my outstretched arms, hit hard, and stayed there. That is how I remember it. I meant to draw her in and she was already against me. "They put her in the ground," she cried into my chest. "It was hot, that yellow windy night she was buried. It was blowing, blowing. I couldn't stop them from burying her. I couldn't stop it." We held each other, swaying back and forth. She was so heavy, too heavy to hold up. We sank to the hard porch floor, nothing between us and the stone but the thin rug woven from old jeans and shirts. We held each other against each fresh racking sob as it came.

Chapter Fourteen

———

I LEARNED EARLY ENOUGH, when I was six, that the world is a sorrow-ful place. Our neighbor, Peter Nicols, was messing around on the tracks a few blocks from home. He got electrocuted by the third rail. With the windows open that summer I occasionally heard his mother. She made an exhausting noise. I thought she was singing up and down the scale even though I knew what she was doing had no relation to music. It scared me for years after, that the boy had been alive one minute and was dead the next. It was unacceptable. How was it that he couldn't take back a one-second mistake? After all this time it still seems impossible that a person can be killed instantly, without knowing. I tried to say to Theresa the night she came down that I had not yet been able to get beyond the shock of Lizzy's death. I didn't know that she was gone unless I thought hard about it. "I don't understand," was what I managed to say.

We lay on the rug for a good part of the night. We held on to each other. We had to thrash, with the sadness. It was inside us, beating inside us. We couldn't hold still. When we thought we were at last done we'd slowly work up to begin again. It was a cycle that didn't seem to have an end. At one point Theresa cried, "I don't think we're ever going to finish, that we'll ever get to the bottom of this great, fathomless reservoir." I couldn't see past the moment either. I didn't know how we'd be able to stand up, dust ourselves off, go home.

Every now and then in a sudden calm she lifted her head and spoke. Early on she said, "When I account for my children, like a mother duck, I think, Audrey is in the den, Lizzy is in the ground. How many times do I have to say Lizzy is dead, before I'll know it? How many times? When people ask me how many children I have I need to say two. Because I still have two, don't I? I always sound flustered and the people get mixed up and embarrassed. Oh, but one is dead, they'll finally figure. But I still have two children. Lizzy is still my child." She lay back against me and it continued, the rolling and thrashing and sobbing. "It feels like we're only the husk for some wild thing tearing around inside us," she wailed.

In another lull she said, "Wouldn't it be handy if you could take your eyeballs out, let them get on with the long tiresome work of crying?" We had laughed a little before our losses brought us down. "What am I going to do, Howard?" She kept asking that same question again and again.

I said I didn't know. I can't say how long we wept and then how long we lay quietly. I knew that time was passing only because the moon kept rising. We lay on the floor sniffling. She was awfully heavy in the crook of my arm. I could feel her eyelashes on my neck and her breath through my shirt. I was afraid to move, afraid the slightest change might make her go away. When the moon passed over the windmill she hoisted herself up and looked into my face. Where her glasses had gone I can't say. "Sometimes I just want to die," she said in that soft way under her breath. "I just want to die so I can go where Lizzy is. Sometimes it seems a punishment, as if I'm trapped on earth."

I pulled her back down and kissed her dark hair. "No," I said. "It's all right here." I hated to think that she wanted to die. Everything about Theresa radiated goodness. A person could understand her uncomplicated sorrows. I could feel her relaxing again into my chest. We would get up in a minute. I would turn on the glaring porch light and we'd resume our life. We were tired, and finally insensible. I could hardly lift my head. We must have both slept for a while. Perhaps she also thought she'd break away in the next minute, and the next, and like counting sheep, the exercise put her to sleep. It felt good, to sleep. For the first time in what felt like months I slept soundly. Her skin smelled so fine as I drifted off. I don't think I dreamed about anything but her strange, foreign smell.

In my memory, when I go back to that night, the clock does not tick. The only thing that moves is the night sky. On the porch that means nothing to us. We were leaden, spellbound, like Shakespearean lovers who have drunk a potion. When she woke, sitting up in alarm, I turned and pulled her back to me. That action surprised me as much as anything. I knew her movements in my sleep. That I was lying on the floor in the middle of the night with my wife's friend, my neighbor's wife, my children's playfellow's mother, did not seem to matter. "I need to go home, Howard," she said into my shirt.

"Stay."

"I can't," she whispered. She hovered over me, stroking my cheek with her knuckles. I didn't want to wake up. I unfolded her hand and brought it to my lips. She let me. She smiled, as if it was an indulgence, allowing me to kiss each finger, one by one. I made a point to smell her skin as I kissed. It came to me that hers was the fragrance of an early spring morning. It wasn't the efforts of a genius soap manufacturer. It seemed to me that it was her own scent, that smell of fresh loamy earth and light. "You smell nice," I uttered. "You smell like spring dirt."

She laughed out loud and then quickly put her small hand to her mouth. "Coming from you I take that as a compliment." She shook her head. "Dirt." She leaned down. I thought she was going to kiss my forehead. "Dirt," she said again. "I love that."

We may both have thought of Alice. Theresa may have considered for an instant that she would have to tell Alice what I had said, that it bore repeating. I thought how Alice often accused me of calculating milk price supports when I was making love to her. She was far away and seemed inconsequential. I dismissed her.

"Please don't tell me what I smell like," I said.

"Rain," she murmured. "How about that? You smell like rain."

"Ah, rain."

She traced over my eyebrows and eyelids, down along my jaw, brushing slowly over my mouth. I watched her. She outlined my lips with one finger before she came away. The night seemed as if it would go on indefinitely if only she would again rest against my chest. We would talk of dirt and rain. It was she who held the charm, who could make not only the clock but also the moon stop. I don't know if she was weighing the importance of the night against real life. I wanted her to touch me, to keep stroking my face. I shut my eyes and I could still feel her next to me. Her smell was more intense without sight. "Howard," she said finally. I knew there wasn't much time left. I pulled up slowly. I put her loopy curls behind her ears. "How do you get a comb through this hair?" I asked. She laughed with abandon, without stifling her pleasure.

I held her face and she smiled in that hopelessly breathless way. I guess I knew there would only be that one instant to kiss her. I hesitated, seeing the night in the distance, already a memory. The desire I felt for her could only always be seen as good. She was beautiful and wise, her voice and song, her face and laugh, a salve. "Theresa," I breathed into that kiss. I held on as long as I could, moving inside her mouth, all brightness, tongue to tongue. Her eyelashes fluttered like a small animal's heartbeat, against my cheek.

When she pulled away I followed her mouth. "That's all," she whispered, gently pushing me off. We bent our heads together, knowing full well the reason for stopping. I helped her to her feet and then she let go. She nodded. That was the signal. I went to get Audrey. I walked up each stair, one by one. The night vanished quickly behind me. I considered as I moved, going down, returning to the porch, to see if that pocket of time and space was still there. The girls were sprawled all over each other, arms and legs in a tangle. They were damp, heavy. None of them woke as I moved them around. Audrey chewed and groaned. She had curly hair like her mother's. She was warm in my arms. I couldn't help looking at her, also seeing her in a way I hadn't before. I held her carefully, this child, Theresa's child. I made my way slowly down the hall, telling her that I was taking her home.

Theresa was already outside on the lawn, shifting from left to right foot, back and forth, the way a person does in winter. She was holding herself around the waist. She'd found her glasses. The nearly full moon, waning now beyond the chicken shed, made the world seem cool. She ran between the rows of dead corn, and I followed, unable to keep up with her. When we got to the edge of the property I handed Audrey over. She didn't need to tell me not to come farther. I watched her trudge with her load along Mrs. Klinke's hedgerow. When a dog barked up the street I went down on all fours, expecting the lights to come on in the houses. The people would stream into their backyards, looking for the trouble.

When I opened my eyes the next morning I was in my own bed. Alice's clock said 3:30. The sun was shining on the ceiling in long, pale rectangles. It took me a minute to realize that the clock must have run down long before. I imagined Alice looking through the walls of the jail, through the metal windows, across the waking city, over the fields, to our bed, to me. I imagined her wistful smile, and her voice, her sarcastic, "What are you going to have for lunch today? I *know* you like that fruit salad!"

I could tell by the slant of the sun that I was already an hour late for milking and still I lay looking at the ceiling. I remembered the night before with absolute calm, what both Alice and Theresa had remarked was my strength. Theresa and I had wept until we were finished. I had held her, wondering if it was true that a sorrow like hers, like ours, could eventually fade. I think I hoped that it wouldn't. I hoped that we would always be able to walk onto the porch, just the two of us, when everyone else was conveniently absent. I hoped that we would always be able to dip into that current of sadness.

I suspect I knew then, lying in bed, that we could no longer wait, according to Rafferty's instructions. It is difficult to pinpoint exactly when our lives began to unravel. In a snap I can trace the wrongdoing straight back to Alice. Like Theresa, I resist that temptation. I know it is not honest or fair to place all of the blame on my wife. That morning I did not get right up. I lay thinking that years from now if someone came across a chronicle of Alice's life, the summer of Lizzy's death would be the one period of time that stood out. She would be the great-great-grandmother who spent several months in jail. The ancestor who abused the boy. Future generations could blame their bad traits on her. It seemed cruel, that her afterlife was already determined. If I was noted it would be only in relation to Alice. Her husband. Perhaps being the faceless name next to the fleshed-out ignominious great-great-grandmother is an even crueler fate. I lay under the sheet, watching the morning pass. I knew how much energy it was going to take to catch up with the work. It was then that I first said to myself, I can't do it.

I wasn't surprised when Theresa didn't come down on Saturday. It was late by the time I started chores. I was swabbing Maggie, an older cow who picked fights if she felt put upon, when Emma appeared in the aisle. The girls rarely came out in the morning and she startled me. "What do you want?" I said. I must have been speaking in accusing tones because Maggie turned to look at me.

"I didn't do anything," Emma whined. "Why aren't you done yet, anyway?"

I stood slowly. My insides burned and ached as I inched to an upright posture. "Guess I'm tired," I said.

"Where's Theresa?" Claire called from the doorway.

"When is Mama coming home?" Emma said, tugging at my shirt. "I forget when you said she was coming back." My daughters were still wearing their pajamas. Emma's were so worn the print of the material was gone. You could see through to her skin. Alice might get convicted and spend years serving time. With all the skill Rafferty could muster he might not be able to fight the boy in his three-piece suit and the abused doll that had had to endure atrocity, real and imagined, in court case after court case. I had abstractly considered the possibility that Alice might not get out of prison for years. I had not yet thought about what we would actually do if she was to be held captive for the better part of our lives. I was confused so early in the morning by what had happened in the night. It came to me as I stared at Emma's shabby pajamas, that I thought I knew Theresa and that my knowledge was based on a feeling, not anything more reliable than a blind man indelicately pressing on a face with both hands to get a sense of its form. I had thought at one time that I knew Alice, but that knowledge also had proved to amount to nothing. She probably knew me more than I wanted to be known. I felt very tired. I didn't know if I had ever loved anything. I guess I couldn't have said what it meant to love someone. We had a life together. Alice was my wife. Those things suggested an illusion and implied love. I have since wondered if a person can know how deep a thing goes without getting outside of it, without taking it apart, without, in fact, ruining it. I could have one night with Theresa, more tender than any Alice and I might have together, and still Alice would exert herself. My wife would slip away, I would lose her, but she would still have a hold. The certainty of those things made me feel sick. I leaned over, thinking I might vomit into the gutter.

I made my way down the aisle, going laboriously from cow to cow, the four milking units working at the same time. If Alice was convicted we might live our lives on parallel tracks. She on the inside, the girls and I on the outside. We would visit at regular intervals. She might get to come to Emma's eighth-grade graduation. She'd shuffle along in her manacles for the first outing of her prison life. The evening news would cover the touching story. I wondered then if Alice's present imperturbable state might not last her for the rest of her days. She might insist upon my release, calmly laying out for me our divorce, the name of my future wife, the training necessary for my new occupation. She might think I could leave her to be counted at the wake-up call day after day until she died of a prison epidemic. She might spend a good part of her time writing Emma and Claire, reminding them of that dog caught on its leash, wound around the tree. The dog was the one thing I managed to save.

"Daddy," Emma grumbled, "I said, 'When is Mom coming home?' You aren't even listening to me."

"September," I said. "October."

"How many minutes?"

I did a quick calculation. If she got out in six weeks, in the middle of September, which certainly wasn't going to happen, but if she did, it was somewhere in the neighborhood of forty-three thousand minutes. That sounded manageable. "Forty-three thousand," I said.

"Oh." She was satisfied. She stooped down to pet a kitten she'd tamed. "Do you think cats know how they look?" she asked. The scruffy white one in her hands had a black nose, one black eye and a black circle on its back.

"No," I said.

"I wouldn't want her to know she's ugly."

If I'd been in the mood it would have been time for an allegory. I kept moving down the aisle. My father used to tell me the story of my great-grandfather, solely as a scare tactic. I was the only child and worse yet, a son. My father had to tell me what could go wrong in life so that I stood a better chance of avoiding the pitfalls. There was no reason for me to repeat anyone else's mistakes. He was determined I make something of myself. The great-grandfather seems to have had a nervous breakdown after his third wife discovered she was pregnant with his ninth child. The two other wives had both died during or shortly after pregnancy. The grandfather took sick, is how the lesson came down to me. My great-grandmother supported the family by taking in laundry. Months later, long after the baby was safely delivered, the old boy came to his senses. When he fully understood what he had done to his family, how he had humiliated them and abandoned them, he died on the spot. So the story goes. I think my father needed to tell me about him not because it was family history, but because it taught the horror of Shame, the goodness of Duty.

I interrupted my rhythm of washing the udders and slipping on the milking units to watch the girls climbing barefoot on the hay bales in the corner. I didn't know how they could stand the sharp tufts on their feet. The cows swished their tails and stamped. There's a Bible verse my mother always used to say: "In the day of prosperity there is a forgetful-ness of affliction: and in the day of affliction there is no more remem-brance of prosperity." She used to say things like that when I was going about my ordinary business. Memory does not serve a person well, is what I got out of that one. Not twelve hours had passed and my memory of the night before was changing. It was dispiriting, to think that something that had seemed good was going to go through several revolutions in my mind. The girls, already dirty so soon in the morning, had come to the barn to remind me that nothing is ever simple. I could insist to myself that the evening was one thing—two people responding to sadness. That's how I aim to remember it. I also imagine that Theresa and I are each other's best secret. Both of us probably think back to that night when we are in need of consolation and the idea of love. On the porch with the moon climbing ever higher I had thought that I loved her and that there couldn't be anything wrong with loving her. In the morning light I knew that it was treachery to think so.

We spent that Saturday at the pond. I sat in the shade with a hat pulled over my eyes while the girls paddled around in their life jackets. We had not gone down the lane since Lizzy's death. It was hot, always hot, and everywhere we sat or stood felt like a blistering sidewalk. "Can't we at least swim?" Emma had pleaded. Swimming or not swimming wasn't going to bring Lizzy back, I said to myself. The girls had stood on the bank looking out to the water, remembering, I think, that the pond was dangerous. Gradually they let the small waves lure them to the edge. It wasn't long before they forgot Lizzy had been taken there.

I didn't recall until the next day that there would be no one to leave the girls with for my Sunday visit to the jail. I had promised Alice I would never bring them along with me. I thought for less than a second of calling Miss Bowman. I stood by the phone in the kitchen for quite some time, putting my hand down on the phone, taking it off again. It seemed reasonable to call Theresa until I was touching the receiver. Just pick it up, I said to myself. No, I responded. I can't. I paced back and forth across the kitchen. I had promised Alice I would never bring the children to visit. But first, I argued, there was no one who would take the girls. I would tell Alice that Theresa was regrettably busy, or away. I would tell her that they had stayed with Miss Bowman in June and then she would understand my difficulties. Second, it was true that after well over a month on my own I knew our situation better even than Alice. Emma and Claire needed to see her, to know that she was still herself. She always asked so urgently about them. She had a hunger for them, strong enough, it seemed, to propel her through the Plexiglas. She needed to see them too. I didn't come near to admitting to myself that the girls would serve a purpose, that they would deflect attention. They would shield me from Alice's keen eyes. That Sunday morning I convinced myself that what she wanted all along was to see Emma and Claire through the filthy window. It would perk her up to hear their voices through the static of the phone line.

Over one of the many bowls of cold cereal we ate in Alice's absence I said, "Let's take a drive this afternoon. Let's take baths and put on clean clothes and go cheer Mom up."

Emma was about to take a bite but she lowered her spoon, set it back into her bowl. "You mean we can visit her?"

"We can visit her," I answered.

"You mean we're allowed?"

"It's not a nice place, Emma," I said. "I think you already know that. You remember we won't be able to be in the same room with her. There's glass in between. But I think it would make Mom h-happy, to see you."

We bathed. They dug in their closets and found clean sundresses. Although Alice would not be in a position to inspect their ears, I gouged the wax out all the same. Theresa had given them haircuts recently so they did not look like street children. Claire wriggled with excitement. Emma bounced on the bed. I tried to clip their nails but they couldn't keep still. When I let them go they ran out the door. They went skipping in the dry grass, running back and forth, shouting in a singsong chant, "We're going to see Mama, we're going to see Mama." For the second time that morning I knelt to retch.

At the jail the girls clung to me as we passed through the metal detector. They were terrified by the doors buzzing and the crush of the visitors in the narrow corridor. We sat on the stool at the second station, waiting for Alice to emerge. I had never had to wait much before, but that afternoon there was a delay. We sat, waiting, thinking she was going to come through on her side any minute. No one was let out. The girls were fighting over how they were sitting on my lap. Claire insisted that Emma had more of my body than she did. I spread my legs and put one child on each, so that the territories were clearly fair. Once that was straightened out they began to argue over who was going to talk first. Emma lay out an elaborate plan. Each of us were to have three minutes, then two minutes, and then one minute. We'd start the cycle over and over, until our time was up. Emma, just because, was going to begin. When they began swatting each other I sent them to look through the large glass window at our backs, at what I believe is called "the communication room." There are several computers, switchboards with blinking lights, and two deputies wearing headsets.

Alice was the second out. She wasn't to her station when she saw them. I stood up, both trying to get a better look at her, and trying to block her view. She was wearing a pink bandanna around her head. It was tied up tight, in a way that made her look as if she didn't have any hair. She had a bruise on her forehead, a large purple and black and green circle, like a third eye. She had a panicked, hunted look in her two eyes. I turned to find the girls, trying to think how to keep them from seeing her. They were still watching the operators. I reached for the phone to say something, anything. She pressed against the glass as if she'd forgotten that it separated us. But even as I was yelling, "Pick up the phone," she was backing away, making for the guard. The girls were at my side then, trying to see over the dividers. I thought for a second that she was going to fight the guard, but the minute he touched her she sank into his arms. She was limp, even as he pushed her off. He was shouting at her to stand up, to get moving. She kept sinking back into him. He finally had the sense to put his arm around her and let her out the door. He shook his head. He kept shaking his head as if to say, Not another crazy one.

Chapter Fifteen

─────

THE FIRST TIME I thought we'd have to leave the farm might well have been the day at the beginning, when I called around trying to find a sitter for the girls. I had called Suzannah Brooks and Cathy Johnson to ask them to take the children while I went to visit Alice. I remember standing with the phone in my hand watching Emma and Claire run through the sprinkler. They didn't know yet that they were blackballed. They were skipping like they had nothing to worry about. Emma figured she'd wear twirling skirts to school in the fall and drink milk out of pint cartons. Kindergarten in her book was in the neighborhood of heaven. I guess I'd known as I watched both of them dancing in the spray that we couldn't stay in Prairie Center. Still, it would be a lie to say I had seriously thought of selling the farm before that last night Theresa came down. I hadn't known before just how easy it is to lie. I hadn't known either, what it costs.

We got out of the visiting room at the jail as fast as we could on Sunday. The girls had at the most only seen Alice's form, almost a shadow it was. "She can't come down today," I said, as we tore along the corridor to the outside.

"Why not? Why not?" Emma cried, running along to catch up with me.

"She's sick," I said.

Emma stopped by the locker where we had had to stash the car keys. "She is not sick!" The veins in her slender neck bulged when she screamed. "You made that up. She just didn't want to see YOU!"

I slammed the locker shut. The door buzzed and I got out. I walked down the block to the car without hearing the girls screech after me. There was glass, a condom on the walk, scraps of Styrofoam in the gutter, paper twisted into the metal of the chain-link fence. "You're lying," Emma shrilled at my back.

After we settled in the car I suggested we go find a beach, that we take a look at Lake Michigan. The name comes from an Ojibwa word that means "It is a big lake." I said so, to the girls. I could see Claire in the rear-view mirror, staring out the window. There were tears slipping down her cheeks. Emma had her head down and was crying to herself. What they were learning, what I was teaching them, was to grieve like adults. "We'll find a beach," I said. "We'll hunt for some good skipping stones."

"Shut up," Emma said to her lap.

We did go to the lake, and we did gather stones. We found smooth gray and black and white stones. There was a large sign stuck in the sand that said in red letters, Swimming Prohibited, By Order of the Health Department. The beach was deserted. We walked, choosing stones and putting them in my cap. A few gulls screeched and flapped at us as we picked our way around the dead alewives. The sun was hot and the water looked hot. And the fish bones were baking and the stones in my cap grew heavier and heavier.

On the way home, near the outskirts of Prairie Center, we saw something that you never see in small towns. There was an older man, squatting by the highway. He was too close to the road, on the gravel shoulder. He didn't have anything on his head. Our corner of the state was a prosperous one. There weren't homeless people or poor minorities. There weren't rich minorities either. The guy was squinting into the sun. He was holding up a piece of cardboard that said, I Need Food.

We drove past him and went on home. The girls took a swim and I dunked in and out. I did the chores earlier than usual, and by seven-thirty Emma and Claire were in bed. Emma had been giving me the cold, silent treatment, as so many of her sex have done before her. After they were asleep I sat at the kitchen table to write a letter to Alice, to explain. I must already have known that I would try to sell the farm. Rafferty would be furious. He had often seemed to relish the fact that we had so much property, the one thing that should prove to the judge the quality of our citizenship. He used the words synonymously: upstanding, moral, hard-working, four hundred acres, sixty head of cattle. Our holdings were none of his business. Our life had come apart swiftly in June. We had waited through July and now into August. It had taken time to understand that the damage was irreparable. I knew that the girls couldn't go to school at Blackwell Elementary. I knew that I couldn't farm without a wife, that there wasn't any point in farming without a family. I also couldn't picture living down the road from Vermont Acres year after year. I'd have to sit in our living room reading the paper after lunch, knowing that up the way Theresa was singing in her kitchen.

"Dear Alice," I finally wrote:

> *I think I'd be a good used car salesman. Maybe in the next life. I've lost all of what you used to imagine were my redeeming qualities. Emma called me a liar this afternoon. I am no longer calm or moderate, and despite the tone of this letter, I'm not nearly so senti-mental. I am worried about you. I'm sorry about bringing the girls. It was a mistake. Claire and Emma have learned to cry like adults. They sit by themselves and cry without making much noise. We need you with us, for plenty of reasons, but not least to gently help the girls shake off a few years so they can again have a tantrum. What a relief that will be.*
>
> *Howard.*

That was the best I could do. It took me nearly two hours to write so little. When I was finished I went out to the mailbox and slipped the envelope in the long, silver insides. I wondered if the man was still out on the road. It was the simplicity of the sign that made it effective. I Need Food. When my time came what would my sign say, I wondered. I Need

Work? Jokes? Family? Love? When I came back to the house I set the stones from the beach, one by one, in a glass pie plate. Those were our stones, to put up in the attic, our small, heavy pile for remembrance.

On Monday morning after chores I called Davis Realty in faraway Waukesha. I told the receptionist that I wanted to list the farm with them, that I would like to get the wheels turning as fast as possible. There were cicadas droning away in the trees, the first I'd noticed. They should have been singing for a couple of weeks. The whole place looked different. It looked like it didn't belong to me anymore. Maybe the farm had slowly become unfamiliar, starting to change on the day Alice left, and by now, at this late date, it was finally unrecognizable. She had had a kind of fit that night before she was arrested—she had lost her mind while I made love to her. It was very probable she'd done it. I don't think I would have thought her guilty if dozens of children had come forward with far-fetched stories. She had always spoken of Robbie with an anger that seemed beyond reason. She wouldn't hurt people in mass quantities—but one. She could have hurt just one. It was possible. I didn't have to voice those thoughts to be certain about the farm. There was no point in having it anymore.

Shortly after two o'clock on Monday afternoon Sandy Brickman from Davis Realty got out of her dented Maverick. She tottered up the gravel driveway in her high heels. I had seen her scowling as she removed her keys from the ignition. She tried not to show her disdain for the house, which was visibly tilting to the south, and the outbuildings which long ago should have been burned to the ground. We had no grapevine wreaths stuck with dried flowers at our door. There were no lawn ornaments, no little black Sambos in cast iron, in our burned-out stubble. The place might have looked habitable if the grass hadn't been white. It might have seemed a find if the shutters in the front weren't hanging from one hinge, if the paint hadn't chipped off and fallen like snow to the ground. Our home suggested ruin. Sandy Brickman, with her real estate radar, knew it before she'd even set foot on the gravel drive.

She had too much lipstick smeared on her mouth. She had bad skin, the pockmarked, greasy variety that reminded me of the girls in high school who used to give themselves away to any willing customer. Out of all the surreal characters in our dream summer Sandy Brickman took the cake. She was incongruent in our landscape, as if she'd been set on our driveway as a gag. She stretched her hand out well before she was within seven feet of me. I called to her. I knew I didn't want to get too close. "If we walk up to the plateau we can get an overview," I said. She clasped my hand. She was sweating inside her pink suit. She looked directly into my eyes as if she had a method of measuring what I would settle for. Her rings dug into my skin and no doubt we exchanged something communicable in that shake. She thought that might be a good idea, to start off with the big picture. "The house—well," she snorted.

My urchin children, who hadn't had their hair combed, or a decent lunch, not to mention breakfast, trailed behind us.

"We didn't see our mom yesterday," Claire said, running up ahead and then facing Sandy and walking backwards.

"That's too bad," Sandy said.

I had made a point of calling a realtor in a distant city. Our potboiler was localized and had not, as far as I knew, been heralded more than once on the news at the beginning. There was a fair chance Sandy knew nothing of our misfortunes. She would jump to her own conclusions. She might think that I was the ex-husband who had kidnaped his children. She might take a more kindly view, might assume that my wife had died in a crash, that we had gone to a seance to try to make contact.

Sandy Brickman and I talked zoning. We talked arable land. We talked mound systems and septic systems and sewer. We talked county planning and town ordinances. Another one of my mother's famous sayings that has stuck is this one: "He that is slow to anger is better than the mighty; and he that ruleth his spirit than he that taketh a city." I had the terrific urge to take Sandy by the shoulders and yell in her face.

"I'll be honest with you," I said quietly. "My twin sister is dying of leukemia. None of us have insurance. We've been trying to raise funds for bone marrow treatment by having dances and collection cups in the supermarkets. I'm sure you can imagine what kind of money we're talking."

"Oh, I'm so sorry," Sandy said.

"Selling this place is a shot in the dark, I realize, but it's all I have left now for cash."

I had wanted to spend my life caring for land, being a steward, and raising food. When we moved in, and I walked down to the barn for the first time, I couldn't imagine needing anything more. I had my own barn, a wife, a child. The barn had stanchions, a haymow, a milkhouse. It had stalls down below for sheep, a horse if we wanted. Alice once said that most men must secretly want a barn, even city-dwelling men. She saw how I was about the barn, how at night I'd make excuses to go out one more time.

"I need the cash," I said again. I wasn't sure there was anything in me that went deeper than my stinging skin. I wasn't sure I'd ever felt much more than an animal sensation, a veering toward ruin. Everywhere I looked I kept seeing that sign, I Need Food.

"I can tell already that it's a real special piece of property," Sandy said as we walked along the edge of the soybean field. It was a respectable stand and the only green thing close to the ground. She was probably seeing the place divided up into five-acre lots with dream houses, sprawling brick affairs with hardwood floors and decks, windows and views, stone fireplaces, master bedrooms with walk-in closets and Jacuzzis, family rooms, great rooms, mud rooms, closets, closets, closets. "It's going to take that special buyer. Now, you say that this property, parts of it anyway, cannot be zoned residential, is that right? Is it locked into some kind of conservation easement?" She was huffing and puffing as we climbed the slope to the plateau. "I just gotta get back into aerobics," she muttered. She kicked the ground and the earth rose in a puff of smoke. "Is it dry or what?" When she'd had a chance to catch her breath and scan the horizon, she pursed her lips, as if to whistle. She blew out a silent stream of air as she shook her head.

It is a good place. With your back to the east you hardly notice the greyhound racetrack in the distance. You can see the fields laid out in squares, the pond sparkling in the sunlight, and the old orchard beyond. You can see the cows standing still around the few shade trees in their worn pasture. You can see how far the woods stretch. You can see the marsh with its cattails, and the cranes lifting off into the air, making their guttural trill.

"There's a marsh, a bog, and a fen on this property," I said, which was stretching the definitions of those wet places slightly. We definitely had a marsh, and pretty much had a bog. The fen was questionable.

"No kidding," she said. "I didn't know there were so many things like that." The bog is what had sold me on the place originally. A farm with a barn and a bog. "This is a real special piece of property you've got here," she said for about the third time. "I'll tell you what." She was going to deliver a secret, a Sandy Brickman kind of secret. She put the stem of her sunglasses into her mouth. They hung from her lips like some gruesome piece of orthodontia.

"Yes?" I said, waiting for the revelation.

"We'll have to have the house appraised, do a survey, work up the papers, take care of the business. I'm going to zip back to the office and make a few phone calls." She managed to say that with her mouth full.

"I'd really like to get this going," I said.

She put her glasses back on. "I think I'm having an inspiration, Guy." She called me Guy, as if it was my name and only I hadn't known it. "What you have to do is sit tight. That's all you have to do."

Sandy Brickman, as it turned out, was the answer to the prayers somebody must have been making. Theresa was the only person I knew who prayed every day. It was more than likely that she was praying not only for her damned soul but also for Alice, and for me. I hold Theresa personally accountable for conjuring up Sandy Brickman. In the weeks that followed, the appraiser and the surveyor did their work. Even before Sandy wrestled with the details of our farm, the image of Mrs. Arnold L. Reesman must have risen up in her mind. Sandy had spent much of her professional life cultivating Mrs. Reesman. She must have somehow appealed to the lady not as an obsequious money-grubbing real estate agent, but as a friend, an advocate, perhaps a lover of nature.

It was mid-August when Sandy showed up. Alice had been in Racine for nearly two months. I remember Emma, around that time, wanting to go to the summer library story hour on Tuesday afternoon. She'd seen the banner across the windows, advertising the event. I wouldn't let her. She went to her room and slammed the door like a teenager. Without Theresa we were back to eating cornflakes for every meal. I had dreams that the old man and I were standing out on the road, both of us with our signs held high. I didn't let myself sit still to think. I didn't breathe a word of my plan out loud, even when I was alone in the presence of the barn walls. During the day the girls put on their dress-up sun bonnets and together we hauled stones. They didn't like it much, but they didn't have a choice. They'd get tired and play under the wagon. I cleared about forty acres of stones last summer. One day, in Alice's stead, I made sauce from the early apples. I had to cut around the bad spots in every single wormy apple. There wasn't any sugar in the house and when the girls tried a spoonful of the hot sauce they acted as if I'd poisoned them.

Right after the sign went up Mrs. Reesman came to look at the farm. Sandy, Mrs. Reesman, and Arnold Reesman III arrived in a silver Volvo on a Wednesday morning. The sight of that car almost brought me to my knees. I have never really had a hankering for cars, but that silver auto-mobile, so sturdily made, accident-proof, with the soft black leather seats, was a thing of incomparable beauty. Sandy got out first. She had not learned during the first round that high heels are unnecessary and also perilous when showing country property. Mrs. Reesman followed. She was a small woman, fine boned, with short white hair and a lip that I guess was naturally swollen. It was an enormous upper lip. She was the same vintage as my mother. But she was rich and as a result she seemed less concerned with appearance. She was wearing an embroidered shirt that had come from a poor Latin American country and ordinary white Keds, yellowed with age. She had the deportment of a queen.

I learned that her late husband, Arnold L. Reesman II, had been the Scout master for thirty-five years of Troop Nineteen. She was looking for a plot of land to donate to the Boy Scouts of America—the Arnold L. Reesman II Scout Camp. Reesman, the boys would call it. We stood by the barn, getting our bearings. I handed the county topographical maps to Arnold III and I held out the aerial view photograph for Mrs. Reesman. As I watched mother and son pore over the documents, I felt that I was beginning to see the world through Alice's eyes. She prided herself on her snap judgments. She had always seemed to think that sizing up people was a special talent. It didn't seem difficult to know strangers that morn-ing. It didn't seem like much of a skill, judging character. Mrs. Reesman was old enough to know that rain would fall again. She was talking to her son, asking him to picture with her the place in spring, when the grass is blindingly green. She could imagine the tulips, the first chitter of robins, the leaves unfolding. The spring-fed pond violently appealed to her imagination. When we took the short walk down the lane and stood before the water she grinned, that upper lip enlarging to grotesque proportions as it spread across her face. She could see the naked Scouts running the length of the wooden pier and jumping, arms outstretched, into the clear water. "It is a shame," she said with her patrician, sharp diction, "that inner-city youth have to grow up surrounded by cement and broken glass. They don't know that they, themselves, are of the earth." The boys would study birds as well as microscopic organisms. They'd want to recycle and save the rain forests. The old farmhouse would be torn down, of course, and the barn could be turned into a lodge. They became slightly animated, thinking of the potential. Arnold nodded. Mrs. Reesman raised her eyebrows. He suggested they rent some of the fields to the neighboring farmers. There won't be any for long, I might have said. Mrs. Reesman put her hand to her heart at the idea of the Scouts earning merit badges for detasseling corn.

Although suburban encroachment was fast upon us, to Sandy, and even to Mrs. Reesman, our farm was deep country. For them it was plenty wild enough and so close, only seventy minutes from Milwaukee. The girls staggered behind us as we walked the property. When Claire couldn't cope, I carried her on my shoulders. I held onto one of her legs and with the other hand I dragged Emma along. She poked her fingernails into my palm, trying to hurt me.

Arnold was a thin, clean-shaven man in his early thirties. He had taken over the family business, which I gathered meant managing the money. When we came to the old orchard he took a deep breath and sat on a stump. He pulled each burr from his pant leg and flicked it away. Restored to his original state, he seemed at peace. Mrs. Reesman bent down and picked up a gnarled apple. "Isn't this a Duchess?" she asked. Although I wasn't sure, I said that it was. "We had these at Maud's when I was little, Arnie," she called to him. The Duchess apples were going to snag her in, just as the barn with the fresh white walls had caught me. Caucasian boys, Native American boys, Afro-American boys, would come together to harvest the apples of her youth.

Mrs. Reesman had an old-fashioned graciousness as well as a detachment that befit her wealth. She would or would not have the property, and either way her life would go on exactly as it had before. She seemed not to enjoy shopping, particularly, but she asked me questions about the farm. She did not have direct experience, but she was educated and knew what to ask. "How interesting," she responded, without fail. Her great dignity, her code of behavior, neither required nor allowed her to ask me any personal questions.

Sandy walked me to the front door after the other two were in the car. "She really likes it," she said, in hushed, conspiratorial tones. "She's a lady with a vision, that's for sure, and she's very impressed. She's the kind of person who feels a need to give back to her community. Her grandfather, I believe it was, founded one of the big Milwaukee breweries. Adele has always been so involved." The only thing that kept me from trusting Adele implicitly, was the fact that she had Sandy in tow. "I've worked on a lot of different properties with her," Sandy went on, "and I can tell when she's affected positively."

I'm in a terrible hurry, Sandy baby. I'm about to jump out of my skin. I know you didn't believe that shtick about my sister so I leave it all to your imagination, if you have one. I want cash now, sweetheart, that's the long and short of it.

"People have been stopping at the sign," I lied. "A couple drove in last night and wanted to look around."

"Really." It was a statement of disbelief.

"I told them to call you, of course."

I'm sure that on the way back to Milwaukee Sandy, doing her utmost to represent me, explained to Mrs. Reesman that I was having personal problems and was looking forward to selling my property, that I had, in fact, an urgent need to make a major life change. And that considering my desperate need I might be willing to part with the land at a radically lower price. Not many people in their right minds, after all, would buy a place with a conservation easement.

I don't know if Rafferty had some kind of sixth sense operating. The day after Sandy came to scout out the farm he called me, for a change. And he continued, calling me several times that week, as if he knew he needed to be alert. He phoned with good news once, about a witness he'd discovered that was going to blow up the prosecution. He asked me how I was doing, how I was managing with the farm and the girls—questions he had not asked me at the start, when I could have used someone's concern. I gave him no clues. "We're going along," I said. "Waiting. We're waiting."

On Friday Sandy called to say that Mrs. Reesman was planning to make an offer of three hundred thousand dollars, a substantial cut in the asking price. I had figured what I would need to pay Rafferty, to retrieve Alice, to wrap up my considerable bank debt on land and machinery and livestock. I had hoped also to pay back my mother's loan. Mrs. Reesman's offer fell short. "You can think about it," Sandy said. "You let it simmer and then give me a jingle."

I was standing at the window just the way I had when the girls were running through the sprinkler that morning near the start, in June. Although now they were listless, sitting in front of the television, I could visualize them out in the yard, prancing around in their suits. "No," I said to Sandy, "it will do. I can live with it." I hung up. I announced, "Forty-three thousand minutes. We might actually be able to have Mom home in forty-three thousand minutes, Emma."

"Good," she said, without taking her eyes off the commercial. It was an advertisement for a doll that performed the bodily functions of a real baby.

I took amphetamines in college but that was nothing like the bug-eyed, empty-bellied rush I felt during those days when I systematically got rid of my farm. Soon after the offer was made, I called Dick Smelts, the local auctioneer. He was the only person in Prairie Center, besides Theresa, who spoke to me that summer. When I told him I wanted to have the sale in three weeks he said, "What's your hurry? You can't get it ready that fast." I said I was sure I could. I'd sell the herd, the tractors, the milking equipment, the hen house, the watering tanks, the baler, the combine, the fencing, the odds and ends. Hordes of people, sensing desperation, would come from miles around for a bargain.

"That's going to be tight, buddy," he said.

"Everything's tight," I said.

There was only one person who might have understood my action. Theresa would take the sale personally and think I had overreacted.

Rafferty was going to be livid. Dan didn't seem to care about much of anything. But had Alice been an outsider, I think she would have understood. She was extreme herself. If I'd been in a fiction, the sale would have made sense to her. She must have understood how a thing can be spoiled. If it hadn't been her property, she would see that my course, ditching the place, was reasonable.

On the Thursday after we had all visited Alice, Emma was sick with a sore throat and a rash. I ended up taking her to a doctor in Blackwell's satellite clinic down in Silver Lake. She had scarlet fever. Claire was probably next in line. If I had made up the excuse of illness to avoid visiting Alice it would have seemed flimsy, but our reason had the fortitude of truth. I wrote to her immediately, explaining that the girls needed to be isolated for a few days, that I would see her the following week. It was good to have a reprieve. The girls weren't uncomfortable once they got the antibiotic. They didn't have to suffer too much to accommodate my need to stay away from the jail.

I would have liked to find a way not to visit the following week also. By that time Mrs. Reesman had made her offer. If I didn't make the trip, Alice would know that something was awry. By the same token, if I did come she would be shrewd enough to see some change in my face. There was danger, and I guess the risk made me bold. It was a challenge, to keep her from knowing, to be self-possessed and sedate while my heart raged. I felt strapping and loud and fast and to conceal my secret I had to be quiet and slow and careful. I brazenly parked in the jail lot, in a space reserved for a police vehicle. I locked the girls in the car with candy and crafts, leaving a crack in the window for air. Emma had charge of my old-fashioned watch. "Twenty minutes," I said to her. "When the hand gets to the four. This is the only way. The only way." They were to stay in the car. They were not to roll down the window. They were to stay and keep still. They had learned that I was hard, that nothing would move me.

I thought Alice might not show up when it was her pod's appointed time. I waited, watching the other inmates file past. She was the last one in line. She sidled up to her stool, slid on, and then picked up the phone. She didn't so much as glance at me. Her bruise had turned a pale yellow-green. She was wearing the pink bandanna that made her look bald.

"I'm mad," she said.

"I know."

"Nobody tells me anything anymore."

"What do you mean?"

"Theresa hasn't written to me for weeks. What's that shit you said about her needing family time?" She hadn't yet graced me with her all-knowing eyes. "She suddenly stops taking care of Emma and Claire? She said it was so good for them, she went on and on about the healing process. Why do the girls think that they can only go play up there on Sunday afternoons?"

I did not correct her assumption that Theresa was caring for them while I visited the jail. "I think it's because of Dan," I said. "He's suffering over Lizzy."

She nodded, as if what I had said fully explained Theresa's change of heart.

"What's happened to you, Alice?"

"When my hair grows out a little more I'm going to look like Laurie Anderson. I try to imagine, for fun, that I'm on the last frontier, that this is the kind of place you go to prove yourself. There's got to be a little something here, a lesson, some kernel. At the very least I should feel that I've been on some existential Conradian journey into darkness. And you, having to cope with everything, the farm, the girls, the neighbors, while I'm learning some stupid moral—"

"What happened?" I asked again.

"I bumped my head," she said. "I don't know. I had a concussion and they even sent me to the hospital for a few days. It was a mess. I was really surprised they didn't call you, or Rafferty, for that matter."

"You bumped your head? That's all?"

She looked up then, as if the question was rude. "Yeah," she said. She laughed, not as if it were funny. It was derisive, that Ha ha.

"This is getting long, Alice. It's going on too long."

When I got back to the car Emma was holding Claire in place in her seat. She had her pinned down. Claire was unable to move or make a sound. She was crying so hard her mouth was wide open all the way down to her uvula.

"She wanted to get out," Emma shouted. "I told her she couldn't. She was going to get out."

I yanked both of them by their collars and pulled them to the sidewalk.

"Where are we going?" Emma cried.

"Walk. Just walk. Walk!"

Emma ran ahead. When she was a safe distance she turned and called, "I don't ever want to go back home with you!"

"That's a good attitude," I said. "You keep that attitude. You'll need it."

In the weeks that followed I got up early, as usual. I milked as quickly as I could. The cows were surprised by the way I slapped them around. They turned their heads to look back at me, their eyes wide, as if I was a stranger. I'd go into my study and make my list and then study my list, learn it. I went from one task to the next, no longer thinking about Robbie's doll, or Alice's bruise, or Theresa's sweet voice. Although nothing was further from the truth I told myself that everything was pretty well settled. Right after Mrs. Reesman made her offer, I went to the grocery store outside of Racine and found boxes. I told the girls we were going to pack up everything and then pretend we were hobos, living in freight trains, eating out of tin cans, singing all the day long, sharing one towel, living the carefree traveling life.

"You mean we'll make fires and roast wild animals and eat them with our bare hands?" Emma asked.

"Something like that."

"Will Mom come with us?"

"Sure."

"Yes!" she cried.

Of course the girls had no idea how desultory it would be when the hay wagons were piled high with wash tubs and boxes of nails, old mattresses, picture frames, the broken toys. I walked through the rooms hearing the auctioneer call, "Here'saprettylittlelampshade, takethewholewagonfiftyforadollar, whatthefuck, there'stheladywithsixtydollar—" We would leave with a few suitcases. I would take what I had: two pairs of jeans, three coveralls, a few shirts and sweatshirts, and a brand new suit which would serve us well in court.

There was not as much as I'd thought there'd be to disassembling the life we'd made. I must have had the idea that the job meant packing up the farm from its inception, over a hundred years before. I guess it seemed to me that I was dismantling the history of the place, taking it apart, year by year. Considering the age of the homestead, there wasn't actually so much clutter. And we didn't own much. I realized through the process that we were transients, with our few bags, moving on. We'd always been nothing more than transients stopping by in a tumbledown house.

I didn't let myself think about what the things up in the attic and in the outbuildings had meant, what their purpose was, who had handled them, who would next own them. I went from shed to shed making piles of trash here and auction goods there. Emma and Claire knew they were to keep close, to stay clear of the pond, and out of my way. They were getting to be resourceful, my girls were. They had thick, black dirt under their fingernails and their hair was matted in the back. They watched TV until it made them sick and tired and then they'd go out in the yard and pull a cat's tail and kick at each other. When they got that out of their systems they settled down to make collections of stones and seeds, sticks, and bird berries. They'd build up a city, make it perfect, and then fight about it and wreck it. At night we fell dead asleep. In the morning I woke up and again looked at my list. I dug in with such grim determination it might have been mistaken for zeal.

One afternoon near the end of August we drove to Spring Grove, a small town near Racine, a place where no one knew us. I had told the girls that we might stay in an apartment before we began the rambling life. We looked at a spot above a shoe store for one hundred and seventy-five dollars a month. It had a flea-bitten carpet and the stench of a long history of beer drinkers. There was an appealing cottage that would have been fine if it hadn't been right next to the sewage treatment plant. We went through a duplex, the low-income housing complex, and a group of condominiums along the river. We finally settled on a unit. It wasn't a home. It wasn't an apartment. It was a unit. It was a unit in a whole string of units. Together the group of units was called Pheasant Glade. When we walked in the door Emma, who had not said a word since lunch, sang out, "This is a nice one. This would be okay for us."

Alice used to think that things which weren't at all amusing were in fact funny. That trait in her over the years had sometimes provoked me and driven me into a kind of quiet. But I was beginning to understand how something could be so astonishingly black you couldn't help laughing. Emma's easy pronouncement that the Pheasant Glade unit would do, after living on four hundred acres, was so far from what was true that it was like slapstick. "I'll be able to ride my bike down the driveway," she said. "No gravel." Claire pointed to the corner where there was a station of metal mailboxes. She called triumphantly, "That is where Mom's letters will come!"

I wanted to be out before the closing so that when the cash came through we'd already have made the break. We would go get Alice and hole up in Pheasant Glade, waiting for what came next. I had not yet realized how pitiful our house was until I tried to make a last-ditch attempt to care for it as I packed it away. I caulked around the shower and washed the windows. I tried to scrub the rust out of the toilets and the sinks. Sandy and Mrs. Reesman had not looked inside because the place was clearly in need of the wrecking ball. I had not prepared it for a viewing and now, when it was doomed, I wanted to give it a last token of care. We hadn't ever had time to keep house. We had moved in when Emma was an infant. Alice had gone to school, and found a job, and then had Claire. I worked around the clock. Paint was peeling from the windowsills and the molding. We had never purchased curtains. In the bathroom we had a worn towel that was held up by thumbtacks. We had long ago stopped seeing the rust, the holes in the linoleum, the cracks and water spots in the ceiling. We had grown used to having the spilled milk in the kitchen flow downhill into the bathroom. The house had given us a sense of history and belonging. I had always thought that it was benevolent, sheltering us, exerting a kind of love as we passed through. We had washed the walls when we first moved; that was all we had ever done for it.

I was a meticulous packer for Alice. I put like things with like things. I labeled each box on four sides. Most of the games and toys were missing several pieces. The cane in two of the four chairs my mother had given us had been stood on so much the seats were about to give out. The sifter's handle was bent, the clocks didn't work, the wooden blocks were covered with scribbling, the Magic Markers were dried up, the sofa was filthy, the wing chair was ripped, the stereo was missing half the knobs, the books had been gnawed on, by children, or mice. Our junk didn't deserve my attention. I packed up the money box I had made out of oak for Emma on her fifth birthday. There was also a cherry-wood bowl I'd made for Claire when she was born. Emma might someday give her money box to her son or daughter. He would have no way of knowing what the box meant to Emma, but he might like it. It was a good box, well made, with compartments in it, for jewels, baseball cards, money, coins, dead animal specimens. It, a wooden box, might be the one good thing to survive me.

I hauled down the trunk from the attic. "We're taking this," I said to the girls. "It goes with us." Inside were the farm relics: the stones, the lace, the books, the photographs.

"That trunk is old and ugly," Emma said. She had inherited her mother's habit of quickly judging a thing.

"It's supposed to be," I sniped. She recoiled. I didn't look but I knew she was giving me the evil eye.

I wrote to Alice every day, short notes reiterating my need to have her out of jail. Those letters seemed honest enough. I had told her half-truths along the way. I'd said that I couldn't find a baby-sitter, that Theresa needed family time. I mentioned that no one in town would serve us, speak to us, consider us among the living. Alice would have to understand that we couldn't send Emma to Blackwell Elementary for kindergarten. I laid the groundwork. I would tell her about the sale as late as possible, and when I felt like it I'd inform Rafferty.

It took about two weeks for Theresa to come down again. I let myself think about her for short periods of time. I'd give myself an image, or the sound of her voice, and then let it go. I suppose I was fairly sure that she would weaken first. I could think about her, but taking the walk up to Vermont Acres, knocking on the door, was an impossible step. She came one afternoon when I was sitting on the floor looking over my old record albums by the boxed stereo. There was a rustle on the porch. I assumed it was the cats, trying to get in. I was reading the song titles on the *Tea for the Tillerman* album. I was expecting the appraiser from Mrs. Reesman's bank. Before I could get up to see which it was, Mr. Phelps or Betty the tabby, Theresa appeared in the arch between the kitchen and the living room. I guess she'd done the wrong thing with her hair because it was bushy. It was big and awful. The girls were behind me, making beds for their dolls out of some of the smaller boxes. I didn't leap to my feet. I sat holding the album. She didn't look the way I remembered her.

"It's true," she said. She wasn't out of breath. She wasn't smiling.

"Theresa! Theresa!" Emma cried. "We're playing hobos. My dad says we're going to hop trains and eat rabbits raw."

Theresa nodded, although I don't think she heard Emma. She looked at me, and lowering her voice she said, "I've gotten a letter from her every day this week. She's terrified you're going to sell the farm. She mentioned the possibility to Rafferty and he blew his circuits."

"She always knows," I said.

Theresa put one foot in front of the other and came that much closer. "Even though Rafferty got an extension the trial is only two—two and a half months away. She's dealing with it. God knows how I'm going to explain that I haven't taken the girls. I haven't even made an attempt—"

"I'm not going to explain," I snapped.

"Are you okay?" She came into the room and stood over me. Her eyes welled up with tears.

"Look," I said, "we can't stay here anymore. It's so obvious I don't know why I have to explain to you or to her. People don't recover from this kind of charge. We'll have to sell even if she's acquitted. I think Alice is concentrating on surviving and she hasn't taken into consideration the fact that we're finished here. It's over." I started past Theresa into the kitchen. I turned, took her hand, kissed it. She stepped away and put both her hands behind her back. I shrugged and sat down. "Alice used to be so worried about certain people talking about her," I said. "She used to think that old ladies were going to blab about her. I used to tell her to cut it out, that it was senseless to pay attention to rumor mongers. Now I see what there is to be afraid of: Talk. That's it. Talk.

"And I don't know why we ever thought we could farm here. A person needs community. I call up to Madison every time I think of doing something different. I want to ridge till, or start rotational grazing, I have to call a bloody academic. If we wanted to build a barn there'd be nobody to come for the raising. What am I talking about, anyway? There isn't any such thing anymore. A barn. It would be a pole shed, not a wooden post-and-beam beauty. In Iowa all the farms are owned by about five corporations. There's no future in the family farm. None. All the farmers were moving out of here just about the time we arrived. To this town we're some city people who stepped in where we don't belong. I used to think there were rules of nature. Strict rules. If you broke them you'd pay. But of course nature doesn't give a damn about anything. It's our own codes that are arbitrary, merciless. What's wrong with us, that we don't want a ranch house with a big round metal pool in the yard? Nobody cares that this ground means something to me, that I get satisfaction knowing that below our garden there used to be a path that the teamsters used. They brought their supplies into Prairie Junction with their wagons and oxen. You go out there and squint and you can just about see those fucking oxen."

"If it means so much to you then you should stay," she said. She was leaning over the table, about to take hold of my shoulder. Before she reached she thought better of it. "People have short memories. This will look like you're running. Rafferty says—"

"I don't care what Rafferty says! Do you understand? I don't care what he says!" I was shouting in her face.

"You have a right to be here," she said softly.

Claire distracted us by running into the kitchen and grabbing Theresa's leg. "Is it time to go to your house?"

"No," I said.

Claire, who had always been so even tempered, sat down on the floor and proceeded to bang her head against the cabinet.

"Oh, sweetie," Theresa crooned, kneeling down and putting her arms around her, "it's all right."

"I want to go to your house," Claire sobbed. "It's cold there."

"Let's walk down to the pond," Theresa said, looking up at me, but talking still to Claire. "You and Emma can play in the sand and wade. I can see you need to cool off. Isn't that a good idea?"

"No, I don't think so," I said.

"Look at your girls," she commanded. "They are hot and uncomfortable. Claire has prickly heat on her neck, and down her back. She's dirty,

Howard. The pond shouldn't be shut up, like someone's ghostly bedroom. There's no sense in the girls thinking it's a bad place. There's just no sense in that."

I started to say that it was August already and that we'd used the pond every day to survive the heat. She was herding my children out the door, patting their heads, telling them she'd missed them. How many times, I wondered, had we, Alice and I, and Emma and Claire, walked the lane in the middle of a summer afternoon? We had thought of the pond as our perk. We didn't have jobs that offered health insurance or a lunch tab, a company car, box seats at the sports arena. We had slow time on July days. Hot and sleepy, we used to make our way to the water's edge. In that hour or two there never seemed to be anything to hurry for. I used to trick myself into thinking there wasn't a mountain of work waiting for me at all points beyond the clearing.

Theresa stood, looking at the water while the girls ran to get the buckets we kept stashed in the hollow of a log. They peeled off their clothes, down to their underpants. I buckled them into their life jackets. I made them wear the jackets in spite of the fact that they both knew how to swim. It was ridiculous because they couldn't go under water very well with the vests on.

"This is where she is for me," Theresa said. "I could never explain to Dan that the pond isn't sinister. It's just water. My heart hurts like wild every time I come up from the woods. You know everything—that I feel like I'm going to die with the hurt. But I'm drawn here, too. I have to come. And I believe, Howard, that the place needs to be peopled. I have the feeling she is here and that life needs to go on, in this setting, so she won't get lonely, so she'll be a part of us."

We sat on two rusty metal chairs that had been down at the pond for probably a good thirty years. I knew I should do something to stop whatever she was going to say next. I was leaving Prairie Center. We were going. I should thank her for Sandy Brickman and Mrs. Reesman. She had done a brilliant job, sending down those two women to rescue me. She had also marched into police headquarters and told the investigators to lay off Alice. *Thank you* should have wrapped it up.

I braced myself when she took a deep breath. "Howard." She said my name as if it were an imported chocolate. The sound of it made me cringe.

"At first," she said, "I told myself that that night wasn't important, that it didn't matter."

"Yep," I mouthed, trying to concur.

"No, actually, at first I was scared to death, that I'd broken a Commandment, 'Thou shalt not covet anything that is thy neighbor's.' It was the words that horrified me, isn't that the limit? I'm a good Catholic girl at heart and I guess I always will be. After I'd gotten over the fright of the individual sentences, I kept thinking of that night as a mistake. But I just can't believe it anymore. It was spiritual for both of us, I know it was. The impulse was one of love, of purity. It was a rare sort of intimacy. Rare." She nodded, agreeing with herself. "I'm not going to say any more about it. I believe what I just said and I always will." She was staring at my profile. I could feel her eyes on me while I watched the girls frolicking in a place that seemed polluted. "I'm sorry that I haven't come down, haven't taken Emma and Claire. I felt so mixed up for a while. I just didn't think I could see you.

"Dan came home from his conference the next night. I screamed right away, the second he walked in the door, that either he had to talk to me or I would leave him. We had a fight. He accused me of breaking down everywhere I go and I yelled at him about how he is in denial the likes of which I have never seen in all my professional days, and that one of these mornings he was going to wake up and realize his heart was broken in spite of himself, that that was going to be far worse than knowing you have a broken heart and tending your hurt. I told him we wouldn't tiptoe around him anymore, that we weren't going to pretend we were fine. I said I cried to everyone else because I was scared out of my wits to even say her name, to say, 'Lizzy,' in front of him. I've been afraid that I'll make one slip and he'll break. You know that. I said it killed me to see him suffering, it hurt so much to begin with, and then with his pain on top of it. I feel sometimes, like I'm carrying everyone's pain. That's why I've had to go bawling around." She was so close to my face I could smell her. "My God," she said, "he nearly cracked up at the kitchen table. About all he'd let me do is keep ahold of his arm. Finally, finally he started to talk about it. He said he couldn't stand Lizzy being only a memory. He said he just hadn't gotten enough of her, that he hardly knew her. He has been trying to find some way he can carry her presence forward, trying to connect her with our life now. He hates the photographs because they are so flat and still. . . . With you," she murmured, "with you there was all that sorrow, you know?"

We were going to leave Prairie Center. We'd be gone as soon as I could settle the lease for the unit.

"With Dan there is so much anger. He's still furious with me because I let the girls come down here that day. And of course that makes me secretly fume, because when did he ever have to arrange for child care? He gets himself out of bed and goes to work every day, never even has to think about making time for himself, or planning around the family. There's no point in bringing all that up. Who cares about it anymore? But you see, he's not reasonable. He's mad because I got my tubes tied! I got the ligation after Lizzy was born—I mean, we had both decided two was enough. Well, anyway, it was one of those, what do you call them— What? I'm going senile. You know, one of those—cathartic experiences. I have one more cathartic experience it'll probably do me in. We screamed and cried. The next morning he stayed around for a while, though, and we, all of us, talked about Lizzy. I sat down at breakfast and said, 'Remember how Lizzy called the neighbor's dog, Mutt-we?' Audrey looked terror stricken. And then when Dan started to laugh and say how funny that was, I could see her breathing this tremendous sigh of relief."

She was looking out at the pond now, at the girls instead of at me. "After he left for work I said to myself, Howard means nothing to me. It was a fluke. A dream. I thought of calling my old friend Father Albert and confessing. I'm not sure exactly what I would have confessed, but he always tells me at least one thing that changes my life. He'd probably tell me too, that it was time I turned my thoughts homeward, to draw close to Dan and Audrey. I was pretty sure that you would have woken up and felt as strange as I did—"

"Right," I said.

"But as the day wore on I kept thinking about you. Damn you," she whispered, laughing out at the water. "So, all right, all right, a week, two weeks have passed. I see you everywhere I go. I see you out the kitchen window. I see you in my closet, I see you in the glass of the coffee table. I dream that I'm riding up and down elevators trying to find you. I love you, you know that?" She turned back to look at my profile. "It doesn't matter in our day-to-day life, I know. Maybe it's the displacement of the love I have for Lizzy. Maybe I'm giving that to you. It doesn't matter, because there's nothing to be done. It's just one of those things I want to shout from the rooftops."

I continued to watch the girls' every move.

"So, I love you, Howard," she said again. "You are a good person— you are everything that's good."

I rolled my eyes and snarled. I was about to say that that was the sort of crap sixteen-year-olds drool into each other's ears. I made the mistake of looking at her. Her face was pink, bright. I think it was the hope in her expression, in her half-smile, that momentarily chastened me. "No, I'm not." I shook my head. And then I thought of something that might be true. "When I was a kid," I said, "I used to think that bravery involved action. It took courage, I figured, to move forward, to pursue a dream, to get ahead in the world. Just to get where you were supposed to. I thought having desire took courage. Now I realize that none of that requires bravery. The only thing you really need bravery for is standing still. For standing by."

I put my hand on her cheek. She closed her eyes and gasped a little, leaning into my fingers. She was making her cheek as if to hold my hand. I didn't feel as if I had the strength to stand up. To walk back to the house. To wait and wait for Alice to get out. To wait and wait through the years in some strange town with my daughters and my wife.

Chapter Sixteen

———

THE TRANSACTION WITH MRS. Reesman was not complete until the middle of September. The land had to be surveyed and assessed by the bank. The water had to be tested. The Boy Scout officials and their legal counsel had to give their approval. They came out twice to inspect their future camp. Arnold L. Reesman III visited several times in his Eddie Bauer outdoorsman costume to walk the property. He confided that his mother knew what she wanted within five minutes of laying her eye on a thing, and that it was his job to do the delving. They'd looked at quite a few properties, he said, most of them farther away from the city, in crowded lake communities, or in distant tracts of dense woods that offered little more than ticks or mosquitoes. His mother had a knack for spotting quality, and although she was usually right about her decisions, there were exceptions. Take the row houses on the east side of Milwaukee, for instance, that she was just about to sign on when he'd discovered radon so thick in the basement the air was yellow. I didn't talk much beyond pointing out the interesting geological features of our farm. I didn't say that radon is invisible. The exertion of walking under the summer sun in pants and hiking boots brought color into Arnold's pallid face and left him panting. He had a clean handkerchief in his pocket to wipe the fine beads of sweat from his brow.

He conceded that the farm was an excellent property. He was going to get a lot of enjoyment out of it once he hacked some trails here and there. I wondered how long the land would sustain his interest before he was off on one of his exotic fishing vacations. I had once, in a moment of sentiment, almost told him about the teamsters, about the fellow who built the house, the boy who fell off the hay wagon. I half wanted to show him the abstract and the journal. In the next instant I thought about the trunk. I realized then that those things in the trunk belonged to the farm and that it was only right to leave them for Arnold to discover. He could go down for coffee at Del's and get the whole story. I would leave everything to chance, to what, in my younger days, I'd thought of as, "the Guiding Hand of Chance." Perhaps, if Arnold was subject to whimsy, if he was a closet sap, the relics would tickle his fancy. The objects in the trunk, after all, and the trunk itself, were not much without the associations: the barn, the fields, the hint of wagon-wheel ruts that a person could still make out if they wanted to enough. The trunk was like a fish out of water by itself, something that was dead.

I'd mentioned to Arnold that I had burned out milking cows, that I couldn't make enough at it, not with milk price supports what they were. I lied and said I was going to take it easy for a while before I looked for gainful employment. On the final visit he thrust his bony hand into mine and said, with the heartiness and sincerity of a good Eagle Scout, "Well, best of luck to you."

"Same to you," I said.

In my negotiations with Mrs. Reesman she had agreed to let me use the chicken shed for storage through Christmas. I hauled some of the furniture that was not going to fit in the apartment down there. We might someday want the old dining-room hutch, the extra bedsteads, the mahogany chest of drawers, and the kitchen table. Although the table was as much a part of the house as the trunk, I knew the Reesmans would sell it, or have the help hack it up for firewood. I could justify taking it along. The fact is I needed it. I thought of it as having an eye. It had seen the Indians up in the township of Winston. It had been witness to countless disasters and fewer triumphs. Its virtue lay in its inability to speak.

On the morning of the auction, September fifth, we escaped to Spring Grove and set up house in the apartment. There were fair skies across the state. I guess it's accurate to say that I had been in a frenzy as the sale got closer. I'd packed up in boxes everything we wanted to keep, and organized the rest into categories on the lawn. If it had rained that Saturday it would have been the last bad joke of the summer. Dick Smelts, the auctioneer, had come over twice to help me. I had spoken to very few adults since the end of June. I kept talking to myself, out of habit, even while he was at my side. He looked over our possessions and wrote down figures on his clipboard. He remembered some of the things that were back again on the hay wagons, that had not sold when the former owners had had their auction.

I had gone at my tasks methodically and in high gear during those last weeks. The cows and the girls felt my anxiety. Near the end I did not unwind enough to fall asleep. I trained Emma to answer the phone, to ask, "Who's calling please?" I told her she was my secretary and I paid her a nickel a day. If it was Rafferty she was to tell him I was out working. I kept going over the auction items in my mind. I lay in bed, picturing our things, one by one, as if before me all night long was a great TV auction. I had little doubt that most of it would sell. Smelts knew of two potential buyers for the herd. Each of the parties had come beforehand to look over my Guernseys. When I went out that last morning to milk I didn't let myself slow down once. I didn't walk around the barn, or loiter to admire the weathervane. It was just as well that there hadn't been enough of a hay crop to fill the silo. I didn't speak to the cows as I milked. I kept right on going when I was finished, out the barn door, into the house, up the stairs to wake the girls, down the stairs with our bags, standing up to eat breakfast, and out the front door, Hello to Dick as he arrived, into the Ford. We buckled up and drove off.

I think the girls had settled into a perpetual state of shock. They didn't know what was happening to us. They didn't know either what question to ask that would make me explain the upheaval. I'd packed their beds the day before, but I didn't tell them as we drove off that we weren't coming back to stay. They were often quiet, and I think, scared.

We would go back and forth to the farm over the coming weeks, but we didn't ever sleep there again.

Everything in our unit in Pheasant Glade—the carpets, the cabinets, the walls, the doors, the bathtub, the toilet, the faucets, the doorbell, the molding, the shades, the light fixtures—everything down to the carpet tacks was brand new. I couldn't get used to that. The whole townhouse had the fresh toxic smell of new vinyl. The living room had the all-important cathedral ceiling, a stone fireplace with a small glass door and a grating that barely held one log. The floor was covered with blue-and-gray speckled wall-to-wall carpet. The living room opened into a galley kitchen and breakfast nook. The breakfast nook looked out to a wooden deck that had just enough space for a Weber and a porch chair. Upstairs there were two bedrooms, including the master suite with sliding doors and a deck that faced the highway. There was a bath with a whirlpool tub that was just big enough for two very young children. The whole place was deceptive. Here, it seemed to squeak and stink, is the American dream. Except that everything we were supposed to want, everything that looked so good, was too small or too flimsy to use. I realized as I dragged in our few old scratched pieces of furniture, that even the shabby rooms above the shoe store would have been better than the false cheer of Pheasant Glade.

We did have our own garage and a basement with a laundry room. There was no yard beyond the short deck. The girls sat on the driveway and watched me lug in their beds and the chairs from the U-Haul I'd rented. I managed to move the piano single-handedly, with a lot of curs-ing. Both Claire and Emma seemed to sense right off, in the second viewing, that what they had given up was in no way compensated for by an asphalt driveway and a six-by-eight wooden deck, a whirlpool bath, and shag carpet. I didn't answer Claire when she asked, "We're not really going to live here, are we?" One of the tacky cupboards fell off the wall right to the floor. I hadn't done anything more violent than put a glass on the shelf. As it smashed I wished for Theresa. She would have taken the girls from room to room and made the cheap, ugly things seem interest-ing. She would have feigned excitement over the public library down the block and the A&W beyond the second line of units. She would have encouraged us to go out for breakfast routinely and feed on egg and bacon biscuits. I would have very little money by the time we were through. The bulk of my sudden wealth was going to clean up my debt to the bank, as well as purchase Rafferty's supposed decency and skill. I hadn't spent enough time to work out all the numbers. We could keep body and soul together for a few months before we scratched our messages on our signs and went out to the highway.

For dinner that first night in Spring Grove we had a ground beef and cheese casserole that Theresa had made. She'd left it on our doorstep in a cooler at the farm sometime after dawn. As we were eating in our new kitchen Emma looked at me and said, "If Mom can't ever come home, do you think we could live with Theresa? Could she be like a grandma?"

"I want Mama," Claire protested.

"But I mean, if she couldn't ever come home, ever, ever, could we go live with Theresa for part of the time, so we could be with a lady?"

My daughters were guileless. Out our window, past the deck, you could rest your gaze on the dumpsters. I'm sure all of us were thinking about what it would be like to come downstairs in the morning in that house in Vermont Acres. We'd come down to the kitchen where there'd be so much love in the air it would be visible—yellow, thick, probably exactly how radon looks.

When Alice came to her visiting station the last Sunday she was in jail she studied me before she picked up the phone. I waited for the conversation to begin with the receiver at my ear. She was wearing the pink bandanna on her head. Her face had grown longer, thinner in jail, her blue eyes larger. I didn't think I looked any particular way, but after a minute she grabbed the phone and said, "Don't tell me you sold the farm. Just don't tell me that. I haven't had a letter from Theresa in ages, or one from you all week, and it makes me nervous as hell. Rafferty's even been wondering about you. He says he leaves messages and you don't call him back. There's no law that says Emma has to go to kindergarten. We could teach her ourselves. The farm is the first place I ever felt safe and alive, and—oh Christ—real, and at home. Did I ever tell you that?"

"I sold the farm," I said, as calm as my usual old self. "I'll tell Rafferty when I'm ready. I thought you would want to know." She surprised me by crying. "The auction was yesterday," I continued. "A farmer from

New Derry took the cows. He took the pop-up baler too." The tears were streaming down her face and splashing on the counter top. I wouldn't torture her further. No need to mention how little some of our fine equipment had brought. "I sold it, Alice," I said, "because I want to get you out of here, more than anything." There were elements of truth there. "I sold it, because our life in Prairie Center is over. We'll be guilty even if we're proven innocent. That's what Rafferty doesn't understand. As soon as we close we'll come and get you."

She got up to tell the guard that she was finished. I swore, watching her go, that I wasn't going to come to the visiting room one more time. I swore I wasn't going to leave the girls out in the parking lot again. We'd start up our life fresh, once Alice was out, back along the straight and narrow. If she was proven guilty, we'd try to keep to our rigid path. We'd try to go slowly, creeping, so that after she'd served her term, she'd run only a short distance to catch us.

"Is this what you meant by being a hobo?" Emma asked after a few days in Spring Grove. It was no use drawing the ever-receding future. I didn't know if our fortunes would improve, if I could find a job, if the trial would come out in our favor. If Alice was acquitted then we would take to the road. We could go to Alaska, South Dakota, Australia. We could move to California where I could set up a Dairy Shrine West, to honor the dairy industry that had helped to drain the Colorado Aquifer of her water.

"It isn't exactly what I meant, Emma," I said.

We closed in the late afternoon of the third Friday in September. It seemed fitting that we had to go seventy miles, all the way to Milwaukee, to the twenty-sixth floor of a fancy downtown office building, to give our farm away. The girls had gotten used to tagging along, waiting in reception areas with candy and some new cheap thing, a little doll, a puzzle, beads to thread. They didn't get too excited over treats anymore. While I was signing the papers in the inner sanctum they got into a brawl in the lobby. I could hear Claire's bloodcurdling scream down the hall. I excused myself. There was nothing to threaten them with because they'd already lost everything. They also didn't seem to care if I hurt them. The receptionist saved the day by showing them how her fax machine worked. I took my leave to finish giving over the farm to Mrs. Reesman. When Sandy shook my hand for the last time, she said, "I sure hope that operation goes according to plan."

"What operation?" I said.

"Your sister—the bone-marrow treatment."

"She died," I said, giving her hand a final squeeze.

Through the summer there had been occasional respites from the heat as well as a few insignificant rainy spells. The night we closed rain poured down and cool air moved in from the east. By Saturday morning the crickets had come back to life to sing their farewell song. Some of the maples had turned color prematurely and were beginning to shed their leaves. Families were raking together and burning trash when we drove to the bank in Spring Grove. Smoke was rolling across the streets. We were going to get our certified check for one hundred thousand dollars and then head for Racine. It was Emma who suggested we find some flowers for Alice, that we decorate the unit. Before the bank opened we went along the road out of town and picked a few straggling clumps of chicory and Queen Anne's lace.

We harbored our fears as we drove to get her. Emma fretted that the money wouldn't be enough, that the rules might have changed. Claire wondered if Alice would remember us. Emma called her sister an idiot and insisted that they would never be forgotten. I had plenty of my own worries. I once thought that memory was naturally coupled with under-standing—with perspective. I have found that not to be the case. Despite the distance I can't say now I have a clear sense of what happened last summer. I don't know, either, if you can compare one thing to another, if a specific thing is actually like any other thing. The summer had been a test of some sort. I suppose it was a test of faith. If that was so I had failed. But I also wasn't sure that there would have been any way to win, if it would have been better to look with blind eyes, to be faithful to the ideal. It wasn't apparent that one way was better than the other.

To doubt was not a deadly sin, but it seemed to be as poisonous as any of the seven. Doubt had undermined all that I had taken for granted. I hated the fact that I would never really know what was true. There were reasons not to believe either side. There is no point in fixing the summer in my mind, settling upon a half-truth to satisfy my need to know. It still seems to me now that it is better to be vigilant, to keep those months fluid, never firming up the story, never calling any one person a defining name. It is better, I think, never to finally decide. In a weak moment I once tried to ask Alice, to tell her that I wasn't sure. She stopped me. It is probably for the best that I didn't give voice to my gravest doubt. Because I tell myself that I don't know and will never know, I can almost fool myself at times. I can almost talk myself into believing that last summer didn't take place.

We waited in the entry of the jail while Alice was notified. When the guard let her through she rushed at the girls. I gathered up the things that she dropped on the floor. After a few minutes I made them move to the door. I pushed them out of the stuffy entry, out of that place. Alice knelt at the curb and they alternately held close to her and pulled away to stroke her bandanna, her face, her chest. They touched her shyly, as if she was a wounded animal. She didn't say much. Emma was quiet but Claire fired questions at her one after the next, without waiting for an answer. "Did you miss us? Did you have good food to eat? Was it like a restaurant? Will you have to go back there ever again? Dad got me a Skipper. Why are you wearing that hat?"

After a while I helped her up. It was starting to rain again. She lifted her face to the sky for a minute and opened her mouth. We walked across the parking lot to the street. She carried Claire in her left arm and held Emma by the hand. As we passed the Presbyterian Church the carillons began to chime, a warped rendition of "For the Beauty of the Earth." Each note was in tune as it was played and then went flat as the next one rang out. There were people in their Sunday best waiting in lines on the steps. Emma announced that it was a wedding. Somehow she knew, without being told. "The bride is going to come so everyone can see her dress," she said, in awed tones. We kept walking. Emma pulled at Alice's hand to slow her down. I wanted to leave Racine. I wouldn't have stopped for anything. When they caught up with me on Grand Street Alice spoke at last. "The bride had some teeth missing," she said. "Maybe she'll be covered by her new husband's dental plan. Maybe she'll be able to get them fixed."

She seemed happy at the prospect of the strange girl getting a bridge and a few crowns. I guess I laughed in disbelief at her pleasure. "Maybe she will, Alice," I said.

The sky opened then and rain began to pour down, fresh cool rain falling in sheets. We walked on without worrying. The girls danced at our sides. We didn't quicken our pace or try to cover up. The water struck our heads and flattened our hair and poured down our necks. When we got to the car we were drenched and cold. I turned on the heater full blast. There was a fire engine parked up the block, its revolving light showing red through the rain. It pulled out into traffic right before we did. Emma and Claire didn't seem to notice or care about the general splendor of the equipment. It was in front of us until we reached the outskirts of Racine.

The fire trucks used to drive through the streets after a fire when I was a kid, ringing their bells to let everyone know that all was well. It was too bad they didn't do that anymore. There used to be a collective sigh of relief when those trucks came past our houses, on the way to the station. I wondered if the firemen in front of us were history buffs, like me. Maybe they kept a metal bell in the truck, a relic from the old days, now with a few cracks along the side, and a broken clapper. I turned around to look at Alice. She was holding both girls in her lap in the back seat. She was resting her head against them, breathing heavily, as if their dirty hair and clothes, and the forced air of the heater, was fresh. Claire was sucking her own thumb and Emma was running her finger along the frayed edge of Alice's shorts. I could almost hear the ring of celebration and homecoming from the fire engine in front of us, the ring of that bell's damaged clang.

Alice

———

Chapter Seventeen

WHEN I WAS OUT on bail, Theresa, in her eternal optimism and breathless wonder, pronounced that I had learned to embrace fear. "Embrace?" I asked, laughing. "No, I don't think so," I said, "not embrace, nothing nearly as active as embrace. No," I said again, "not embrace."

But while I was away I did learn again to be quiet and wait. There were days when I felt little different in jail than I had when I was nine years old, up in my bedroom at home, with the tray of colored pencils and the sheaf of papers at my side, at work on my map of the world. All those years ago I used to curl up, secure in my own country, an old stoic in a young body, sure that if I feigned indifference out beyond my bedroom door, I would not be hurt. How many times had I advised Emma to ignore a taunt or an injury, knowing full well that the slightest insult to a five-year-old stings like salt in a wound? I remembered what resolve I'd had after my mother's death, to remove myself to the tropical climate suggested by the green-colored pencil on my map. I was alone and yet never lonesome in a place I think now must have been distinguished from earth by an atmosphere made up of new elements—elements to breathe which filled the inhabitants with a sense of a safety.

I remembered having had such acute and chronic stomachaches

through adolescence that my Aunt Kate finally took me to the doctor to see if I had an ulcer. It was all in my head, Dr. Finnegan concluded after the exam. My father, irritated because my infirmity could not be resolved by surgery or medication, ordered me to be more sociable and then withdrew to his study.

As I got older I wondered how to get into the race while at the same time preserving what I thought of as my soul. I was moved to tears reading the ancient philosophers in my ethics class my freshman year in college. I understood that I had spent my entire young life standing guard, as if my body were a great walled fortress around the small thing, as fragile as a twig on its velvet pillow: my soul. It was a delicate, impossible balance—to see, to touch, to feel, and yet to have nothing penetrate to the inner realm, so as not to twist or crack or break the poor twig. At eighteen I was studious and quiet, staking out a carrel in the library and reading day after day until the light outdoors faded and my reflection stared back at me in the window. I'd fold my arms around my head and sleep sitting up, thinking, as I drifted off, that I could feel my pith growing stronger even without the aid of strangers and lovers. I would occasionally find myself out on cold starry nights, right by the railroad tracks, standing close to the trains as they streaked past. I wanted the cold to pierce me, wanted to feel the tremor of the earth under the train, wanted to stay awake in the snow until every part of me was aching with fatigue, and all so I'd know I was alive. Years later, with several experiments in sociability under my belt, Howard had come to me like some exotic remedy, that rare extract calibrated to produce sensation without harm.

Sometimes I couldn't think exactly why I was in jail; I'd lose track of the reason. I was locked away, I'd think, to test my liberal upbringing, to measure just how deep my muddled convictions went. When I was in high school Aunt Kate used to read aloud from her holy books, from E. M. Forster's novels, over our oatmeal and stewed prunes. Where Aunt Kate professed that despite our differences we are one, my father meant me to understand that other people, not our sort, are the ones who starve, who suffer indignities.

I don't think I'll ever be able to see a piece of playground equipment rising up from the cement at the park or the zoo without my heart convulsing at speeds that are not recommended on exercise pulse charts. In our living unit at the jail there were two steel tables that had been cast into concrete and looked to be growing out of the floor. While I was locked up I cleaned my plate and changed one pair of tube socks for another without having tremors. When I was out I could not abide the sight or smell of American cheese between two pieces of soft white bread, scalloped potatoes, fried chicken, Tater Tots, fruit cocktail, and canned peas. I bought expensive cotton socks with textured flowers in bold colors.

Emma asked me repeatedly what the jail was like. Should I compare it to a day at the baby-sitter's, I wondered. Or to the cow comfort stalls Howard had built for the Guernseys with staggering results in milk output? In their new quarters the cows had remained cleaner and spent two hours more a day lying down and ruminating. In jail I had been leagues away from the air and the sky, so perhaps it was like spending months near the ocean floor in a submarine. "It was like being one of a large litter of hamsters in a small metal cage, Emma," I said at last.

"Really?" She looked out the window for a while, surely imagining living flat up against everyone else's wet hairless skin. No privacy for the most basic, the most intimate functions. Finally she turned to me and said, "You mean you had one of those wheels to run on?"

"What's so funny?" Howard said, coming into the living room where I was huddled into the sofa, clutching my stomach. Before I could explain, Emma said sternly, "It's a joke I have with Mom."

He raised his eyebrows and backed off. "Wouldn't ever want to get between a private joke."

She came to me and whispered in my ear. "Did you have a water tube, and the green pellets to eat, and sawdust on the floor?" To gratify her, to keep her beside me, I spun out my laughter, trying to keep it even and continuous, relishing our first little confidence.

I had wittingly hid from the terrors of the world in the bosom of our farm. I had been grateful not to worry about crossfire on my way to the grocery store, grateful about not having to lock our doors, grateful there weren't yet signs of gang activity in the high school. I had known that a person's place in society was precarious, that an ill wind could push you across to the other, the wrong, side. Theresa carried on at length in her letters about how difficult it must be for someone such as I to deal with the horrors of jail. She meant well, I know. And while jail is a shock to a middle-class person—more so than for the drug addicts and prostitutes who regularly come in off the street, I came to think that for the common good everyone should spend a little time reduced to a hamster, that incarceration should be mandatory, like jury duty. Lynelle, a prisoner who was dying from AIDS, said, "Bein' cooped up make a person feel, I don't know, real churchlike after a while. Your big old body ain't nothin' but shit, so it make you think about whatever else is kickin' around. I sees visions, I hears words. And then, when you gets out, don't the air smell good? Damn, even the cold smell good."

Howard, like Emma, curious about places he'd never been, at first seemed to have an urgent need to know all about my experience. I understood that he wanted to relieve me of the burden of it, to feel as if he had somehow shared in my misery. I think he must have thought I was bent on denying him the opportunity, that I was holding my trials close to my chest as I made my way to martyrdom. For the longest time I couldn't speak of what it had been like to be locked away, partly because it was only afterward that I registered fear. I'd start thinking back and break out into a sweat. I sensed that what he really wanted was a neat package, a summary which concluded with the assertion that I was well. It wasn't as simple as telling the family a narrative about a trip downtown. Jail is one of the last holdouts on earth, a place where there is still an oral tradition. Sometimes I think the inmates made trouble not only so there'd be a story to tell, but so there'd be five stories to tell, each rendition becoming funnier or more grotesque or outlandish. There were stories to tell, certainly, but there were also stories to tell about the telling of the stories. Although I long ago lost faith in the idea of Truth, I knew that once I spoke, the stories would take on their own shape, their own truth. In my darkest hour I doubted that there was even a lesson to take from that rubble of time. But whatever the moral was, I knew I needed to fashion the pieces together, and to myself, before all of it came tumbling out, the essence drifting heavenward, gone before I understood what it was.

Plenty has been recorded about the violence, the foulness, the utter uselessness of jail life. A great deal more will be said as the years wear on, with the present trend of sentencing criminals without the opportunity for parole. The Racine Jail was a relatively mild place and I should count myself lucky that I wasn't part of a larger, poorer system. It is marvelous how few details there are in jail; it is a feat, that in a world so various men can pare a place down to hard steel and dull, ungiving concrete, a few thin blue blankets. The grease ant has more color and variation than did our pod on the fourth floor. Everyone wore the same Day-Glo orange shirts and pants. Everyone ate the same food, and had the same space under the unrelenting sameness of the fluorescent lights. It was the small things I sometimes let myself mourn for: sunshine; shadow; the dark of a country night; the thick, hot air of summer. We could never get away from our own smell, or anyone else's smell, or the noise of the television or the noise of angry talk. So that after a short time we began to hold like fury to ourselves, because our very distinctness seemed endangered. In that struggle some of us took ourselves to extremes; we became caricatures, shrill and distorted.

I had felt, from the first mention of Robbie Mackessy, that the mess was so much bigger than all of us put together. Not long after my arrest I woke up knowing that I couldn't fight. It wasn't that I didn't have the strength. Howard, white with fear, tried to feed my anger, so that I'd be fighting mad. I couldn't explain to him that it was beyond fighting, beyond requiring strength. He thought I had given up, but that wasn't right. The die was cast; that's what I knew. It wasn't a matter of hoping or praying, or even deliberately working hard in order that justice could prevail, because already each of us, Howard and I, Emma and Claire, had lost so much. I came to know that Robbie would suffer most from the process. It was he more than anyone else who gave me the face of resignation. I did not want to lose the case, and yet winning would be a somber victory, no grounds for rejoicing. I told Rafferty that I thought the stocks were a good idea after all, that I wouldn't have minded people coming and hurling things at me for a limited time. Howard, in many of his history lessons, had once told me that in the American colonies women used to be punished if they were considered "common scolds." Surely that was my crime. I could have easily granted anyone who wanted a few pitches of a tomato, a rotten egg, a small pebble below the waist. Everyone would feel better and then we could go home.

"How did you spend your days?" Howard wanted to know. He asked me in letters, he asked me on our Sunday afternoon visits, and he asked me after I got out. In my blackest moods I might have told him that our mission in life is not to discover our fate as we go along, or even procreate, but rather to fill up the endless gray void that is time. "I didn't do much," I used to say. "Read. Take naps." He thought I was responding like a petulant teenager. I couldn't explain that I was in a way being honest and yet there was a—texture, I'd say it was, beyond activity, that preoccupied us even as we slept.

Our existence was pared down to three meals a day and a shower. And it wasn't so much a question of what did we do all day, but how did we pass the night as well. Because there wasn't much difference between the two. At 10 P.M. we were locked in our cells and the day-room lights were dimmed. But it was never dark and the fighting didn't stop. I have heard enough racial insults to tide me over well into the next life, where I have no doubt the battle will wage on. The only thing I told Howard right off was the amusing dream I'd had my first night home, the waking dream that our pod had become a miracle of harmony, that I was like Anne Sullivan, heroic after all, giving the girls new words in their own hands.

When I was brought into the pod for the first time, the five or six women were milling around, looking at TV, playing cards; one was lying on the floor of her cell shaking uncontrollably. They stopped their games and even the sick girl raised her head. They stared at me with what seemed at the time to be identical expressions; the narrowed eyes, set in their faces, it seemed to me, for the sole purpose of expressing hate. They watched as I walked across the room. They were poised, perfectly still, as if they might spring when I made a false move. I was white, weaned on the stuff of Western Civilization, and to them old, someone they figured who would topple over if they as much as spit in my direction. My skin had turned from a healthy brown to a light shade of gray in the previous weeks and the pockets around my bloodshot eyes were sagging and mottled. I knew that people were raped, knifed, driven mad in jails. I tried to swallow, tried to choke down what I knew was the fully substantive thing called fear. While I was in my cell fussing with my bag of books they began to talk quietly among themselves, trying, I assumed, to think what to call someone as improbable as I was. I lay down on my mat and covered myself with my blanket. If I was going to be like the old hen in the yard, the bird that the others try to peck to death, then I was going to need some rest.

I wasn't in the cell for more than fifteen minutes when one of them came in and stood before me. She thrust out her right hip and put her fisted hands to her waist. If I'd started reproducing at the onset of puberty she could have been my daughter. She was a slight girl with hundreds of braids coming from a middle part and falling to her shoulders, and skin that was naturally the burnished unreal color of a woman in a Coppertone ad.

"What'd you do?"

Dyshett had the uncanny ability to find out just what she wanted to know. I never did understand how or where she got her information, about forty percent of which was accurate, and I often imagined her reaching into the air and grabbing a handful, and then looking at it, at thin air, to learn the secrets. She was unlike so many of the girls who had no concept of life outside of their own neighborhood, who could not have said who the governor was, who assumed that everyone spent their lives living off welfare. Dyshett knew far more than the others, and furthermore she had a vocabulary to talk about what lay beyond her own horizon. When I didn't answer her she smiled in a way that I nearly mistook as genuine. "How exactly do someone like you fuck a kid?" She smiled even wider. "I know about the birds and the bees but I just don't get how someone like you do it. You got nothin' to put in, far as I can see. What ch'you use, broom stick, flashlight, a big ole banana?"

I was surprised by her frankness. I tried to think quickly. I didn't see much point in answering, but I knew that if I didn't respond I'd be in trouble. Either way I guessed I was in trouble. "I've been accused of sexual abuse," I said. "Is that what you mean?"

"Accused?" She nodded slowly as she studied me. "You nothin' but a pervert."

"Accused," I repeated.

She reached out and twisted my braid around hard in one hand, so hard my eyes smarted. "You probably think I should be showing you some respec', since you an old lady by now. But I don't take too kind to people who mess wid others. You sit and wait, Granny," she said, twisting harder. "You sit and wait for me." She let go, sashaying into the day room, singing out in a rich, clear voice, a number about coming into the promised land.

I remember Howard wondering on the first visiting day, in a muttering way, how I could be so sanguine. My attitude was to become a source of irritation to him as the summer wore on. Surely he knew me by now, knew that I was someone who did not thrive on danger, who could not live happily on the edge, who did not seek out risk. I had married him for plenty of reasons, but not least because I thought he offered safety. "I'm not really sanguine," I had said, feeling that any explanation was futile. *I'm only trying to find the way, Howard, trying to figure out if I should shut down and play dead, or rise above, like a bony ascetic, waiting for grace.*

At the beginning I spent most of my time in my cell with Debbie Clark, who at eighteen had had the misfortune to bear twins in her mother's car and then accidentally do away with them. She whimpered for most of the thirteen weeks we lived together. It was helpful to me, to be cooped up with someone who was so extravagantly sorry for herself. Not that she didn't have good reason. She had been charged with the murder of her twin infants shortly after she delivered them, by herself, in her mother's dusty blue 1985 Bonneville. She had never used birth control for fear her parents would discover the pills. Because she was a large girl and always wore oversize shirts no one realized her condition. She hadn't been sure herself, although she had an idea that a change had occurred. There had been a thing inside of her, she said, punching at her heart. She was peculiarly unattractive, primarily because she had no eyelashes or eyebrows and because of an ailment which made her skin ooze and flake. She had the scruffy sick look of a neurotic zoo bird who's lost interest in preening. It didn't help matters that she grew heavier by the day in jail as she worked her way through bag after bag of Doritos from the vending machine. Although her lawyer told her not to talk to anyone about what had happened the night of the "accident," she swore me to secrecy and told me everything she believed to be true.

It all started with Jesse O'Leary, the boyfriend, who had skin the color of milk chocolate from his Jamaican mother, and from his Irish father, pale green eyes, the beauty of which was not readily apparent behind his thick lenses. He worked for the electric company as a meter man. She had first seen him when she was fourteen. She had blocked his way on the basement stairs, begging him to show her how to read the meter, as if she'd always had a burning interest in energy consumption. Sometimes I had the urge to shout at her, to tell her that she was the most magnificent human being I'd ever met, in her own terribly bungled, absolutely narrow and tortured way. In the first three meter checks that year she garnered his full name and the location of his barber—more than enough information to track him down. He lived on Quincy Boulevard in Racine, not too far from her home on Russet Street. She used to ride her bike to his apartment and sit on his doorstep waiting for him to finish work.

When I finally was able to tell her story to Howard he said he found it unlikely. But I have come to believe in all manner of things, natural as well as supernatural. It was astonishing, Howard, yes and true, that an ungainly fifteen-year-old with the nervous habit of plucking her own eyelashes and eyebrows, had had the confidence to sit on Jesse O'Leary's welcome mat. Who can say anymore what is unlikely? It was nothing short of a miracle that he eventually returned her affection. That he had forsaken her was certainly the most credible aspect of the romance, but ultimately the least important.

At any rate, she hadn't meant to leave the babies under the viaduct in a grocery bag. It had nearly killed her, giving birth, not to one but to two extremely scrawny brown babies. When she was pushing she prayed that she was just passing kidney stones. She continued to pray even after she heard what sounded like snorting. What overtook her next was the deep and terrifying anxiety of a child: What would happen when her mother found out? The shock of one white baby would have been enough to give her mother palpitations. Consider then, the shock of two—and brown! As far as she could tell under the viaduct and by the dome light in the car, which she turned on and immediately switched off, they were the color of horse chestnuts. They had big round eyes like chimps. There was the terrific mess in the back of the Bonneville to consider as well, the car Debbie wasn't even allowed to drive. She had set out along the highway when she couldn't stand the pain. She said driving always made her feel better, although that time proved to be the exception. She meant only to leave the babies by the interstate for a little while; she had planned to come back for them after she'd gone to the Stop & Shop for diapers and

T-shirts. But she was so tired and needed to rest, and she knew for a fact that Linda Brewster's parents never locked their basement door. It didn't take long for Mrs. Brewster to put two and two together. There was an inordinate amount of blood in the basement bathroom, a solid line across the laundry room to the storage room, the phone call from Debbie's mother—she was wondering if anyone had seen the car or her daughter —and the news reports on television concerning the dead twins. When I mentioned to Debbie that coping with post-natal blues was bad enough, she continued to produce her seemingly endless supply of tears. "I know," she sobbed. "I wish there was something here I could kill myself with."

She used to kneel on her mat with her hands clasped, and rocking up and down on her heels, she'd keen: "Jesse! Jesse! How could you do it? How could you do it to me?"

I had my own sorrows but hers were so noisy and continuous that her specific grief was contagious. I used to sit on the floor and hold her. I found myself crying easily for the babies, and for Debbie. At eighteen she should have felt that the possibilities for her future were before her in a stunning array. She probably would never again have much expectation or hope. I didn't assure her that she wasn't going to die for decades, that the present misery would probably change through the years and deepen, that the grief would always be with her, like some unwanted person holding her at her elbow, guiding her down paths she hadn't planned to take. She never wondered why she didn't love the babies, but given time she might ask herself who they had been and what they meant to her. I think she believed that they were still out by the freeway, somehow warm and taken care of, waiting for their shirts and diapers.

She never did heave up out of her own mire to ask after my particular brand of trouble. She assumed that I had been set down in jail for the sole purpose of listening, again and again, to the fairly consistent versions of the same sad story. We were all shut off from the world, but she was especially so because she couldn't get beyond the horrifying details of that night; she couldn't begin to be quiet and think about the nature of her own calamity. If there was one lesson she might have learned, it was that each of our stories was singular and so riddled with pain many of us became dull.

There were several others in our living unit who were in for at least three months. Dyshett had been charged with scratching a police officer while she was being booked for possession of cocaine. Sherry had been an accomplice in an armed robbery. Janet, a large white girl with curly blond hair that came down in front to the end of her nose, and a mouth that hung open, had charges too numerous to count. There were up to sixteen at any time, some in for an hour or two while their bond was being paid, some for a day or a week while they awaited their transfer or a hearing. When anyone new came in Dyshett, if she didn't already know, bullied their charge from them and then she sang out into the day room, as if the felon were a beauty queen coming down the ramp, "Here she is, Debbie Clark, she do in her little tiny hepless twin girls under the viaduc'." She often pointed out our cell to a newcomer. She'd say, "Don't you get too close. The baby killers, they sleep in there."

The first trouble took place not more than a few days after I began my stay. I tried very hard to think breezily of my term there as "a stay," as if it were a nineteenth-century trip to the sanitarium up in the mountains, a little room from which I would emerge cured. We were eating lunch off of the yellow sculpted trays which were plate and tray in one. A slice of American cheese between two pieces of white bread, yellow applesauce, two flabby carrot sticks, and one chocolate chip cookie. Despite the fact that we had many of the major food groups, everything was of the same doughy texture. Dyshett came to the table wrapped up in her blanket and sat hunched over her tray. "What this shit?" she said. Without looking up, she said, "Did you know you was about to have them twins?"

When Debbie tried to whimper and eat at the same time there were often disastrous results. She choked regularly, even on soft foods, donuts and Jell-O, so that I, or later Sherry, would have to pound her on the back until the chunk went down.

"Hey, girl," Dyshett said, reaching over and prodding Debbie on the chest with the flat of her hand. "I be talkin' to you." When she was frightened, Debbie's bald eyes glazed over and she breathed through her mouth like a snorer.

"You such a fat girl. Was you so ass fat all the tahm you can't tell what's what? You thought them kicks was your stomach grumbling? You got so much flab in them juicy pink thaghs, in your sweet little ole stomach, pink as a pig. Ain't she jus' pink, Sherry? What you give to be fine and sweet and pink?"

For a small, thin person, Dyshett had a surprisingly deep laugh. She sang in the shower, couldn't help it. We used to stop to listen, stunned by the beauty of her voice. She sang old Motown hits, songs that were on the charts long before she was born. We were determined to listen, determined not to let on that we knew she could charm us. I used to imagine that all of us shared the secret of Dyshett's true power, possibly the one thing she herself didn't know.

Sherry was six feet tall, with a large frizzy orange ponytail, and skin that was a deep, glistening black. She said to Debbie, "I bet your man thinks you one choice cut. He a fatso like you?"

"Oh, oh," Dyshett moaned, "oh, my blubbery little ole elephant, you got such a sweet, greasy, tight pussy for a fat girl. What can I do to make you satisfy?"

I ate. It was difficult to concentrate on my sandwich in the midst of so much gaiety and mirth. I wished Debbie would finish her lunch and leave them to pick on someone else. Her head was bowed so low she was in danger of thunking over onto the table.

"You makin' her cry, Dyshett," Sherry said, when she'd recovered herself. "Poor baby, she ain't ready to get took from her mama yet." She reached over and pinched Debbie's arm. "We your friends, honey bun. We here to teach you about all the big do-do that goes on in the world, so you be ready."

"We want to know more about Mr. Dick, Your Man," Dyshett said. "He handsome and strong? You always available?—like, 'Over here, Mr. Dick. Yoo-hoo, right here,' wavin' your arms? He a nice white boy, goin' off to some hot shit college? You get outta here, you come to Dyshett for a little somethin' to ruin his career."

Debbie was under the impression, short-lived to be sure, that crying was a kind of defense. The more Dyshett talked the harder she cried.

"You!" Sherry said, turning to me. "How come you don't stick up for your sistah? Here we teasin' her to kingdom come and you jus' sit there like she ain't no relation. What's matter w'chyou?"

Dyshett only glanced at me, muttering "pervert," and then she leaned down under so she could see Debbie's face. So softly she said, "Or is it your daddy did it to you? Hmmmm? Your daddy visit you in the night?"

Debbie's mouth opened to its astonishing limit by degrees. It took her several seconds to understand what Dyshett was saying. "No!" she cried at last, in horror.

"Whoa, we thought it was a whale comin' up out of the ocean there for a minute," Dyshett said, sniggering.

"You awake now, girl, that's for sure!" Sherry bellowed.

At night, when I couldn't sleep, I'd try to think of all of us in some larger context, in allegorical terms. It was Howard who taught me to look at a patch of ground, a terrible day, the befuddled irrigation rig, our Holy Roller neighbor, as something more than just the sum of its parts, so that a thing at once is curiously both diminished and enlarged. Dyshett had so many qualities it was hard to pin her down; she was Joy and Beauty, Rage and Cruelty. I finally settled on Nature. The rest came readily: Lynelle was Wisdom. Sherry proved to be Compassion. Janet was Stupidity. Debbie was Shame.

"Your mama know your daddy visit in the night?" Dyshett asked. She was still leaning forward over the table so that the applesauce, which seemed to effortlessly issue forth from Debbie's mouth in a single clot, went right into Dyshett's eye. Sherry was so astounded she laughed. It took Dyshett a moment to register the enormity of Debbie's reflex action. She blinked, putting her fingertips to the substance dripping down her cheek. Debbie herself looked right and left, unsure that she'd done what she was afraid she'd done, hoping that she dreamed it, that she could slip away. She let out a high-pitched whine as she cowered, sinking down and down into her stomach. Dyshett licked her lips slowly, luxuriously, as the grainy yellow sauce came toward her mouth. She stuck her tongue out, trying to reach her cheek. She made a smacking sound. Only when Debbie glanced up, wondering if, by any chance, the worst had passed, did Dyshett dive on the table; she slid across it on her stomach, upsetting our trays and our milk cartons. "YOU MOTHERFUCKING FAT ASS WHITE PIECE OF RATSHIT, YOU—" She struck Debbie and pulled her along onto the floor.

"My boyfriend, he's black like you," I heard Debbie scream from under Dyshett. Sherry grabbed my shoulder, "What she say?"

"I didn't hear," I replied, certain that the news of Jesse O'Leary's racial composition was not going to provide the sudden spark of camaraderie and affection Debbie hoped for, that Dyshett wasn't going to make peace because they liked the same sort of man. I slipped to the window of our pod and beat on it, so that the guards, a hall and a window away in their control room, who were standing with their backs to me, might come and rescue my white sister. Two of them came running in a flat-footed vertical way that didn't gather much speed. By the time they opened the door another girl, Rita, was on the pile, all of them grunting and clawing. The fight was broken up and the girls were handcuffed and taken off to solitary confinement. Debbie's nose was bleeding and we were given surgical gloves and towels and told to wipe up her trail.

Sherry turned to me as we swabbed the floor. "How much time we got without Dyshett?" she asked.

"I don't know," I said.

"That's how much time we got to breathe easy. Any time without that girl is easy time."

We were more like rats, than hamsters, to tell the truth. Sometimes I don't think it would have much mattered who we were; we would have fought in the end because we, unlike the cows, did not have comfort stalls. At 6 A.M. the cell doors were opened and the lights were turned up in the day room. The guard, from her panel of switches in the control room, also turned on the television to the channel of her choice. We never knew if we were going to wake up to the CBS morning news, or "To Life! Yoga with Priscilla," or "Woody Woodpecker." There was always noise and sickness, and always light, so that it was impossible to sleep deeply. We stumbled about as if we were perpetually hung over. Because the jail had not been remodeled to accommodate the multitudes of unoccupied and dangerous citizens of Racine county, we did not have double bunks. I slept on my mat, which was on top of a cement block, and Debbie had her mat on the floor of our cell. When there were more people than cells they slapped down mats out in the day room.

I tried at first to find some sort of routine so I wouldn't so easily lose track of time. It seemed of the utmost importance to mark time, to keep my place so I'd know where I was when, like a shade, I came back to the world. I did sit-ups on my mat first thing every morning. There was no outside courtyard for fresh air, no exercise room, no place except the day room to run in small circles. I read after breakfast and wrote letters after lunch, like a scholar might. I read the books I'd brought along with me. I had thought in those moments while the officer stood by in our living room that I'd need books I loved, books to keep my mind alive, books to let me escape and not think, books I'd always wanted to read. I had handed my full bag to the police that Tuesday morning when they came to the farm, imagining the quiescence and time before me like a wide road that narrows and narrows until it is nothing but a dot forever going into the distance.

In the jail I was often so tired I'd fall asleep mid-sentence and then wake up feeling drugged and wrenched. I read the Laura Ingalls Wilder books again, for solace, for the company of old friends. When the good dog Jack was left behind, across the swelling Missouri River, I threw myself under my blanket and sobbed. I knew I was crying out of proportion to the dog's bad fortune and ill treatment and yet I couldn't stop. The tears kept coming even as I beat my fists on my mat. I was still hitting the mat when I realized I was asking a question: It had nothing to do with the dog, not at all. It was Howard; it was about Howard. Why hadn't he come after me at Lizzy's funeral? I hadn't ever wondered before, and I had to sit up with the asking. Why hadn't he tripped through the crowds and tried to help me? It had seemed, in the aftermath of the funeral, noble of him to remain and cover for my inexcusable blunder. It was a difficult job, a terrible position to be in, but he had risen to the occasion admirably. I had mortified Howard. I was far too much for him, like a daily dose of strong medicine that makes a person sputter and gag. He had had to stand in line at church, shamed, while everyone stared at him. How like him to take the blows without batting an eyelash. But if he had come after me— if he had caught up with me, and if we had climbed into the woods and lain in the dry earth together, disregarding the community that was set to pillory us; if he had been able to apologize for the thousands of times he had unthinkingly belittled me, made me feel that he knew best, that I was just off center, just enough to the left to be—and he never would have said, but he had thought it—unreliable: How different the summer would have been! He had thought I was one way when we first met, and I had gone and surprised him by being someone altogether different. He had luck on his side, however, because by the merest chance I turned out to be exactly what he wanted, someone who would show him his own strength and honor that strength. I was increasingly sure, as I sat and clutched my pillow, that the rest of our lives would have been transformed if we'd held each other and wept, if he'd been able to make some sort of offering, some token, a chink from his armor, a word, a shoring up. He was so methodical and even-tempered and in his shadow anyone would have been erratic and moody. There was nothing for me to do in his presence but sit and yap at the moon, go mad periodically, run around with a sock in my mouth, jump on him, naughty, knowing better, but feeling it was worth it if I could once or twice actually lick his face. He had been betraying me all those years, in small insidious ways, leeching from me what was my strength.

"Do you think I should call him?" I didn't have to look to know it was Debbie, back from her self-esteem class. She was oblivious to the fact that I was under my blanket. "Officer Stephans says we have to take responsibility for our actions. Does that mean I should call him instead of waiting? Jesse said he didn't want to hear from me again, but if I don't call I'm not taking responsibility for my own feelings."

"It means you're alone," I said without moving. "It means you go on without Jesse." It was the harshest thing I'd say to her.

"Oh God," she cried. "Don't. Don't tell me that."

"It just means that it can't be different," I said. "It means that until you're forgiven the trouble is yours. It means you have to hope for exact justice, which is probably the most merciful."

"Stop," she moaned. "Don't talk to me!"

I hardly knew what I had said, or if it was true. I was confused and enlivened with the kind of pure rage Emma showered upon us on a daily basis. Howard could never have come after me at the funeral; it wasn't in his constitution. He had had to make excuses for me ever since we'd met, and standing in line, representing the family, was no different from any other day. He seemed never to have forgiven me for myself; he had led me to believe that I was unforgivable, that there was no hope for change. I had thought all along that it wasn't in his nature to judge, and yet in his silence he was judging continuously, always standing back with his arms folded, looking askance. It was so convenient to be quiet, to let others fill in what they wanted about you while you stood mum. I was sprawled upon our life, gibbering like a monkey, spilling myself out like oil from a troublesome bottle that doesn't have the right lid.

I did one hundred sit-ups and stretched my limbs on my bed, stood and touched my toes, did forty jumping jacks, jumped up and down, did an abbreviated version of a Rumanian dance I'd held on to through the years, and lay down. I suddenly felt weak with too much inactivity and self-pity and the aftershock of hatred. I remembered Howard cutting a rope that was wound around a tree, setting the strange dog free. He had made us climb a cherry tree first, in case the dog was rabid or fierce. I had loved that in him, that instinctual man-force, protecting us, taking the fire. I wondered how he was faring, what measures he was taking to feel that he was still protecting what was out of his range.

The television was on all day and into the night, and it was by osmosis that I partook of endless reruns of "Cheers," the "Bob Newhart Show," "M*A*S*H," "Dobie Gillis" and "Star Trek." The one happy constant in my life, however, was the "Oprah" show at three o'clock every weekday afternoon. Lynelle, a twenty-two-year-old hooker, used to say, "Oprah, she the fairy godmother, don't take crap from nobody." Although I have trouble now, remembering the sequence of my jail highlights, Lynelle must have come in during the fourth or fifth week of my stay. Ordinarily she lived on the streets of Chicago or very occasionally in the county hospital where she was treated for AIDS-related symptoms. She had somehow landed in Racine, in the company of a brother, or a pimp, who'd been up to no good and dragged her down along with him. "You real lucky to be in a place as fine as this," she said of our jail, which had been built about ten years before. "You come to Chicago, they don't give you no clothes to wear."

To Lynelle the week in the lockup was a welcome respite, three square meals a day, medical care, a bed with sheets, a pillow, and a blanket. She was wise beyond her years, and I sorely regretted that whatever she'd done required only a week's stay. "I like Oprah," she'd say. "Much better than them others. Oprah, she could be me. I could be her. She start with nothin' and work her way to the top. She over the top, Oprah is. She out in the atmosphere, ain't nobody can ever reach up to touch her. She done fine for herself and I enjoy that. I look right at her, then I close my eye, and it seem like it don't take nothin' to be her. Poof, I be Oprah, jus' like that. Sometimes it seem like her—success, you know what I be sayin'? Her success is my success. I tell that to anybody else they get they mouf right up to my face, open it wide, and they laugh half a day. But you know what I mean, you sure do. Oprah, she got fancy things, but I know if she could, if she could do it, she reach out her hand and pull me up too. She can't because she ain't God, no sir, not yet! But you know, if she could do it, jus' reach out and pull me up, she would. She want to do that but no people is strong enough to take the weight. She want to and she would if she could, yes Ma'am, uh huh, she sure would."

I sometimes could not keep from staring full on at Lynelle as she spoke. She was nothing but hollows and joints, her few long teeth spaced apart, looking, set in her translucent pink gums, as if they were about to fall out. The others knew that she was untouchable and wouldn't have thought to strike up conversation or sit close. I tried to believe that it wasn't her illness but her mantle of wisdom that made them stay away. Whenever I began to ask Lynelle about herself, her circumstances, she'd say, "What ch'you bother for? I be dead before too long. I be dead before Christmas." She said so, not in a self-pitying way, but as a fact. If I pressed her, she'd wave her hand in front of her face, slowly. "There more to us than our bodies," she'd say. "It just the husk for something that—*fffzzzt,* fly into the air the minute my heart stop. Oprah, she outlive all of us, she my shining star."

I used to think that I would go and find Lynelle on the streets of Chicago, and take her to see the "Oprah" show. I still dream of her sitting on the set, smiling, those long teeth flashing at us in the light, telling the millions across America, "Your big old body, it ain't nothin' but shit." I used to wake up in the night, my heart racing, wondering just how long I'd have to walk before I found her.

"Let Oprah be the judge," I said to Rafferty at one of our meetings. "Let Robbie and me, Mrs. Mackessy, Howard, Theresa, Dan, Mrs. Glevitch—let all of us come before Oprah. Let the studio audience decide. They're nice suburban women, many of them, dressed for a lark. They have common sense and speak their minds." I remember how he looked at me, as if I'd found a new voice, as if I had been altered more than he'd thought by serving time. Although I didn't know Lynelle for long, she raised me up. I often wanted to wake her, in that short week she was with us, to sit by her side, but she seemed to want to keep to herself. She sat, day after day, on her mat with her bony knees bent, nearly up to her ears, mumbling to herself. I waited for three o'clock when together we got lost in what seemed the simple problems of the estranged daughters, the celebrities after privacy, the sexually wayward, the overweight, the under-weight, the shoplifters, the cross-dressers, the sick in body, the sick at heart.

When someone down in Chicago paid Lynelle's bond and she was getting ready to leave I went and stood by her cell. I started stuttering things such as, "You take care." She was trying to fit her long feet into her tight jail shoes, her Keds, so that she could go to the holding room and put on her street clothes. She looked up. "What you say your name was?" She waved her hand in front of her face in that particular fanlike way she had. "Oh, it don't bother. You keep the faith." She handed me a worn book-mark, with the words of the Twenty-third Psalm typed in a column. At the bottom it said, Presented to Lynelle Duchamps, November 12, 1974. First Baptist Church, Chicago, Illinois. "You keep the faith, you hear?"

The minute the door had closed behind her Dyshett shuddered. "That nigger," she said, "give me the creeps."

I remember clearly when Dyshett got out of solitary confinement the first time, after she beat up Debbie. She came waltzing into my cell while Debbie was taking a shower. "Come on in," I said, after she was already well into the middle of the room, right on Debbie's pillow with her dirty shoes. She assumed her characteristic pose, one hip out, her fists at her waist. "You some kind of smart-ass professor, always readin' like you the Queen?"

"I read about other things besides horses and dogs," I said. "So who's next? Do you systematically work your way through everyone here? I've never been in before and it would be nice to be able to plan. Are you going to go from cell to cell and insult us and then beat us up?"

"Oh my," she said, her eyes wide, her nose in the air, her lovely long neck extended. "If she ain't going to figure me out, mother fuckin' an-a-lyze me." She called out across the day room, "Hey, Sherry—she one

of them mind doctors, tell me your problems, your dreams, all that shit."
She turned to me, coming closer, squinting at me so that I couldn't see the
least shine of her eyes. "It kill me, you know that?" She spoke in the most
dulcet of tones. "It just drive me crazy, how you can't tell nothin' by
looking at it. I'd walk down the street past you, think you was the perfect
person, you know, wid the house, the two-car garage, the country club,
the maid to wipe your ass. I see people like that and part of me is saying, 'I
hate that bitch.' Another part says, 'How come I can't be her?' And now
come to find out you nothin' but a pervert." She shook her head once,
back and forth, her right nostril hiked up in a sneer. "That make me
crazy, when things turn out so different from what I see."

I regret that I didn't have the sense to realize that she was speaking as
much about herself as she was about me.

"You look like a princess wid your pretty braids, and deep down you
a creepy little man after some pussy. That all you thinking about. You got
the idea you sit in here and keep your mouth shut, ain't nothin' going to
happen to you, but you got that wrong. The stink a you is flowing out and
getting in my face. You jus' got to sit there and your stink come and get
us, make me want to stab somethin'."

I was relieved of her because someone new came into the pod, someone whose life history was surely already on the tip of her tongue. I knew
from the talk that went on most of the day and night that Dyshett had
moved up from Illinois with a cousin and the cousin's boyfriend, in search
of a better life, but bringing along with them their drug connections,
reinforcing one of the many crack spokes that fanned out of Chicago. I
had heard her brag that she didn't have children yet because she'd had the
brains to get Norplant. She wasn't going to be a welfare mother with ten
kids in a project and she wasn't going to die from any virus. She was
everything the others thought they wanted to be: She had knowledge, and
strength that went beyond theirs, and she had beauty. She had the singing
voice that was as potent as love. In addition to her natural gifts she was
rich. She spent a major part of each day cataloging her possessions. She
had furs, TVs, diamonds, shoes, earrings, silk underwear, alligator purses.
Any item mentioned at table would trigger her memory of her wealth at
home. When Sherry said she loved toast, Dyshett put both hands to her
head and said, "I got me a toaster in every room. I jus' love toast too."

It was those scores of toasters that made me start to think that there might be common ground for us. She was still a child at heart, dreaming up her house, believing in it, committing to it as it became more and more fantastical, with a toaster at every turn. She was all nerve, so energized by rage she had a hard time sorting out what she most hated. I understood right off, after she'd left my cell, that I'd missed my chance with her, that if I'd been quick enough, smart enough, I might have been able to begin to know her. Perhaps it was odd, that it mattered to me. I wanted her to realize that if she could channel her energy she could actually make a path for herself. I often had the sensation that nothing else was real but the confines of the jail and the enraged and hopeless girls who passed through. My family existed only in a dream. I came to think that it was there, in the jail, that action counted for something. And although Dyshett was far stronger than I would ever be, I understood finally that in many ways we weren't so far apart. When she had stood on Debbie's mat I hadn't been able to listen to anything but the drone of myself, in order to remain steady and fearless. For a good part of my stay I tried to think how to get back to the conversation that would reveal and instruct.

She told different versions of a particular incident, as if it were a favorite bedtime story. She used to tell it to whomever was currently sharing her cell, and so I heard it several times over that summer. It was about the time she was raped, depending on her mood, by an uncle, a stranger, a half-brother, an old boyfriend. In some of the tellings she pulled out a knife she happened to have in her shirt and stabbed him as the rape was in progress. She waited for the perfect moment so that he would "be dyin' and comin' at the exac' same tahm." When she first said that line it naturally got a big response and so she included it in the following versions, repeating it several times in the course of one telling. Sometimes she'd weave Debbie's story into hers, telling her captive audience that Debbie hadn't been so fortunate. "That girl, she couldn't kill her daddy now, could she? And how could she take the poor little babies home to her mama when they look jus' like her ole man? That night I kill my Sidney I stole all a his diamond rings off a his hands. Poor Debbie, poor, poor Debbie, she didn't get lucky and kill her dirty ole pappy. The police, they can't never get me now because of the statue of limitations."

It was Sherry who told me what I took to be true stories about

Dyshett, about her being passed from foster home to foster home because her mother was a heroin addict, about how Dyshett had been abused by relatives, sent to the Audi home as a teenager, sent to a group home, waived into adult court, booted out into the world. "I keep tellin' her," Sherry said, "I say, 'You be one maaaad Sistah,' and she jus' look at me, real proud, tossin' them braids. She give me that superior look—you know the one—she say, 'Don't no one mess wid Dyshett. Don't no one ever mess wid me.' "

Every day I waited. On Sundays I waited for the afternoon visit with Howard. I waited always for Rafferty to either save me or send me to my doom, and I waited, hour by hour, for the impending explosion. I thought of Job and how what he feared most came upon him. I had never thought to be afraid of any of the things that happened to us during that summer. Through my life I had trembled before the prospect of numerous dangers and potential disasters. Never before last year had I even vaguely considered the misfortunes that sometimes seemed to be of biblical proportions and at other times seemed like the sort of thing that could easily happen to anyone, as ordinary and expected as a leaky pipe or a stalled car. There was no sound in the large institutional electric clock in our pod, but I watched it occasionally, sure that I could hear the ancient ticktock, ticktock, the useless noise of time passing. I often felt like an old woman at the end of my life, sitting on a strange bed in a nursing home. I used to close my eyes and think of the beauty of Emma's long, smooth limbs. I think when I am old I will dream of the pond more than anything else. In my sleep I used to see the sun shining down through the warm green water, shining on Emma's creamy, wrinkled hands and feet as she paddled in her inner tube. Even in sleep I couldn't consider such a scene for long before the waves came up, dark skies, forty-foot breakers, gray bodies drifting like sacks to shore, their gauzy souls sailing up over the water, up and up.

I'm not sure I'll ever be able to tell anyone much about the day that started as every one of the others had started, with the lights coming on and the click of our cell locks, the bright chat of the television. Although I had managed to keep my distance from Dyshett, staying in my cell and watching where I tread, I was sure I was not afraid of her. I remember

Howard asking me in the visiting room once if I would let strangers into the yard, if I would stand by while they pummeled the girls. "No," I had said, "of course not." He was implying that I was doing just that, by lamely sitting in my cell. I didn't know how to tell him that I hadn't lost the instinct to survive and yet at the same time I didn't feel much need for self-preservation, that somehow there was a distinction between the two.

That nameless day I sat up on my mat and began my exercises. Despite my efforts I had lost both weight and strength. After fifteen sit-ups that left me exhausted, and a few idle stretches, I rolled over and began pawing through my books, trying to determine my appetite. There was nothing exceptional about the morning. Janet, the hulking white girl, had joined us the week before. "You," she used to boom across the room, "what ch'you—" She rarely had to say more because the offender abruptly dropped whatever she was doing and scuttled away. Janet, like so many of the others, had already spent half her life in juvenile detention centers or prison. That morning she and Dyshett were playing cards at one of the tables, shouting at each other when their luck turned. Debbie sat on the floor eating Doritos and watching television. Sherry slept. I read *Franny & Zooey,* and then I brushed my teeth for a long time, thinking about the Buddhists, trying to enter the moment, entering the pleasure of Mint Crest toothpaste, and knowing it, and experiencing it fully. Next I took a short nap. In fact, I slept through lunch. When I came to I wrote a letter to Emma and Claire, dredging up yet another episode of the life we had lived together. As usual, at three o'clock, I went out to the day room for my program.

"How come you always watching Oprah?" Dyshett called from her cell. "I got my eye on you." She snapped her fingers, swaying to her own music as she moved toward me. "You always waiting for the magic hour. You put them books away and hop out here like some little ole bunny rabbit, your bushy tail all quivery." To demonstrate, she bent her knees and wiggled her behind. "You think," she made her voice go higher, 'I'm not a racist, no sir, because I sure do like Oprah.' She make you feel real tolerant, don't she, like a do-gooder pervert. Now, Debbie, I understand her likin' Oprah because they both the same size. What you got going wid her? Who she have on today, some queen about to die? Oh, oh, I know, you hoping Oprah announce at the end of the show, you hoping she say,

'Any white trash out there in TV land who do the nasty wid boys behind the bushes, anyone like that want to come on my show?' You could go on there, looking so fine, so in-tea-llectual—'I read books, but I don't know shit about real life.' The psychiatrist lady on there will say, 'How long you had this problem?' "

I knew all of a sudden that I wasn't feeling right. It wasn't anything specific, wasn't nausea or hot flashes, wasn't prickling skin, nothing even close to boiling anger or clutching fear. The room was closing in on me, getting smaller, all of them getting closer, everything slowly coming nearer and nearer.

"You get teary, wipe your eye on a hanky, tell her when you was a chile someone hauled you out by the braids, laid you out on the fence—"

She would go on for the rest of the afternoon by herself, and to stop that I said, "One of the reasons I like you so much, Dyshett, is the fact that you do all the talking. It's very restful."

Of course she wouldn't like me saying that. I saw her and Janet coming for me, and that's when the room got so close it started to go around and around, inch by inch at first and then faster, faster, the walls, the orange of our clothes, the table, spinning and spinning. It was like the old movie technique to take the viewer back in time, the frames whirling around into a kind of vortex before everything firms up again in the peaceful days long gone. I was trying both to think and to keep from reeling; I was saying to myself, I guess I'm going to let this girl hurt me, if that's what she wants to do. It was the queerest thing, how I felt my head come down hard on the steel table and all I could think was this: It's important for Dyshett to understand that it doesn't hurt me.

When I felt the heat on my face I was sure at first that I was lying in the sun by the pond. It was summer, I knew, and so there was every reason to be stretched on the sand in the nearly fragrant warmth of the sun. I opened my eyes and I saw before me windows, and through them the golden light of the evening. Even before I realized that I was in a hospital it came to me fully, that last waking moment. I had sat on my stool at the metal table watching Dyshett rush at me with her teeth bared. She had done something to me, beaten me, maybe, cracked my head down on the table. I had let her do that, sitting serenely on my stool. As I woke I panicked right away, trying to think what it was we had fought over. Never mind the name of this new place or who had taken me away. I would have to know about the fight so that I could explain it to Howard. I had enough clarity of mind to know that the reasons were myriad, that he of all people could trace our conflict back to at least slave time, that he could speak of impersonal forces, of Manifest Destiny, the industrialization of the North, the cotton economy of the South, the balance of power, supply and demand. Theresa, on the other hand, might say simply that our struggle was as old as cats and dogs. I would have to explain to Howard why I had let Dyshett beat me, why I hadn't at least screamed for help. I would argue in vain that I did have the survival instinct, but that unlike Napoleon I had chosen not to fight back. Theresa was the only one, I thought, who would understand, who would know that I had begun by good measure to pay my pound of flesh for Lizzy.

Chapter Eighteen

I CAME BACK INTO the fold four days after the struggle and they still had not settled on the authentic version. The contest was recounted to me plenty of times with more fire and detail than I'm sure there actually was. Debbie said I threw up before I passed out. The next time Rita told the story I was vomiting blood and then bile. When I questioned her she said, "What do you know? You wasn't even there!" Hilda, a woman who passed through briefly, spoke with a certain authority because she had two bullet wounds on her thigh. "You didn't hear Blondy moanin'?" she'd say. She was incredulous at the group's poor observational skills.

"She wasn't moanin'," Rita called.

"Shut your face! I was right there with my ear in her mouth."

In Hilda's version Dyshett came at me, we wrestled, I was brought to the floor, and badly beaten. The others for the most part did not try to hide their confusion about what had taken place. I had ended up in the hospital, in surgery, because a blood vessel had ruptured in the crash and was leaking blood into my brain cavity. That, at least, is how I understood the problem. I had been unconscious and apparently the doctor tried to call Howard, only to leave messages, he said, with a young girl. The jail authorities did not knock themselves out to inform either Howard or

Rafferty. I knew nothing about the specifics for a few days because no one told me anything. I was shackled to my bed and there was a guard outside, one of the larger men, just what you'd expect, hairy, with unclad women tattooed up and down his arms. I knew my head hurt, and that in all probability I would live to go back to the airless vault from which I'd come. On the last day, an Iranian doctor explained in the Queen's English just how they had put a burr into my skull to drain the fluid. He comforted me with the fact that it had been a serious procedure and that I would mend. I did feel, as Hilda later remarked, that I hadn't really been present for much of the trauma.

When I finally saw myself in the bathroom mirror at the hospital it wasn't the bruise on my forehead that startled me as much as my cropped hair. I had always had thick, long hair. I had been vain about my braids, but I also believed that it, the hair itself, was somehow the truest, the best part of me; I liked to think it was the feature which described me.

"Too bad they had to go so close," the nurse said from behind, as I stared at myself. "It's a shock, isn't it? I've got a scarf you can have, if they'll let you, an extra pink thing to cover all that up when the bandage comes off." By "all that" she meant my head. She didn't seem to notice my manacles and she made conversation as if I was an ordinary person who'd had an accident.

I was in the hospital a short time, but in that brief interim I tried to fill up on air and light, silence and darkness. Lizzy's death seemed close again in the hospital setting, and I found myself welcoming the familiar oppressive images only to then fully remember their content. I sat up when I could manage and watched the sky. Despite the constraints I felt free as a bird, being able to look out a window. The blow seemed to have shifted the contents of my brain, so that the heavy portion was up front, the fluff in the back. The dull continuous ache left me dizzy. If I didn't consciously hold my head straight I had the feeling it would fall forward to my chest. In addition to the work of balancing the new weight, I couldn't keep from thinking about Howard. I was sure that he would have been notified, and that at any moment he would walk through the door. I kept waiting. I wanted very much to see him without the barrier of the Plexiglas. I wanted to lay my hands on him; I thought that with touch, only with my fingers on his skin, would I know clearly what I felt.

During my time in jail I wasn't always sure that Howard and I would weather the storm, and I often tried to think what it was, a single thing, that went deep enough to hold us. I knew that what had brought us together in Ann Arbor was the mysterious chemical bonding that is not rational, eyeball to eyeball, so that we both went to our respective apartments and dreamed each other up, yearning, never straining against the force that drew us right against each other. Emma had been conceived shortly after we met, we had bought the farm, and then Claire came along. There were children and real estate to bind the ties. His parents, Nellie and Walt, had had a strong union, and Howard believed, with a kind of fervor that seemed nearly Christian, that there was a sanctity in marriage to uphold, that the husband and wife were to make their way through the world, shoulder to shoulder. I hadn't known anything to speak of about marriage when we met, but I had found his aspirations impossible to resist. Lying in the hospital bed I thought to myself that my passion for Howard had soon been replaced by something that was stronger than respect, or habit, or maybe even need. It wasn't a simple connection like affinity, because there had been periods when I felt as if I was living with a stranger, that I didn't know or particularly like the man asleep beside me, the man who always got up so early. There were dozens of feelings that came to me in varying strengths as I lay still. I recalled my affection for Howard, my admiration, the attraction I felt to him, and the way he could take me by surprise and amuse me. Those feelings were on the side of what I called love. On the other side there was rage, irritation, disappointment, boredom. Somewhere in the middle was endurance, stolid and essential as air. I wasn't certain the group of feelings wouldn't cancel each other out, if any of them could possibly be powerful enough to carry me along by his side, shoulder to shoulder.

Because I couldn't make out the blur of the next week, or month, I tried to see through to the end. I would die, and if I was still married to Howard I would be buried next to him. Where would we rest our useless bodies? We might not be allowed a plot in the Prairie Center Cemetery, but it would be of little matter, save for our hurt feelings, because Howard would want to be buried with his relatives in Minnesota. Imagine lying down near Nellie, having, even in death, even as a pile of bones, to feel her approval. Howard would want to be laid between the two of us, for old time's sake. "Look on the positive side, sweetheart," Nellie might say over Howard's bleached carcass to me, "the worms need to eat too." I would never feel at home in the Goodwin plot outside of Hastings, Minnesota. In the end maybe what marriage offered was the determination of one's burial site. We would be laid to rest and little children would come along in the fall and kick leaves around and jump off the stones while their parents reprimanded them. Emma and Claire would grow up and die and go off and be buried with their husbands—oh, it was too lonely, too desolate to think about.

I sat in my bed while my head pounded and the guard sat outside chewing his gum. I thought of a time right after we'd moved to Prairie Junction. Emma was a baby. We had put her in her crib in the otherwise empty nursery. When she was sleeping soundly we went out, locking the swollen door behind us. Howard assured me it would be all right. We would be gone for just a minute. It was so hot and she was asleep. We had run down the lane in the dark and yanked off our clothes, dropped them in the sand. Howard carried me in the good, cool water, kissing my neck and my breasts. He had let me go and we had swum side by side, going under, opening our eyes to the darkness. And I wondered, as I came up into the air, if my mother and father had ever done anything of the kind, swum naked together on a sweltering night, stroke after stroke, going down together into the darkness. I had hoped so hard my teeth began to chatter, and then I hoped, most certainly in vain, for my mother's mother, and her mother before her. I had stood in the water, catching my breath, throwing my head back, hoping beyond all the other hopes, that my daughter would someday know that particular joy.

Lying between the cool hospital sheets I tried to remember, to feel, the black water on my skin. I remembered being afraid that night at the pond, that Howard, the Howard who was so sure of animal husbandry, auto mechanics, and history—his beautiful face, his hair wet and slicked back, his marmoreal torso—I remember fearing that he was bound to go up in flames with no notice. That night I had wanted to swim to him and yet I wanted to think of him always there on the dock, safe and waiting for me. I had fluttered my hands and kicked my feet trying to stay in place, out of my depth.

Always my thoughts of the water, of Howard, led me to the farm itself and the worry I had that he might try to sell it. It was irrational, I knew. Rafferty had explained to me that the farm was what we had in our favor, the thing that rooted us to Prairie Center. Howard wasn't prone to impetuous behavior and he would be able to keep the faith, I always told myself, keep the faith that we could outlive everyone in Prairie Center, closed up in our house, secure in the woods. I was sure we could outlast everyone, until all the faces pressing against the glass were nothing more than a mild, unpleasant dream. It was impossible to imagine Howard without the farm. I couldn't think what would fill his days and his nights. What would replace the map that was securely lodged in his brain, a weather map complete with every weather possibility? Clouds: cirrocumulus undulatis, stratus uniformis, a plain old cold front floated before his eyes even as he looked at the night sky. In my worst moments I pictured Howard coaxing the shy postmistress down at the Prairie Center P.O. out of her cage with a pail of fresh warm milk only because he knew that if he merged their stamp collections they would make a fortune. Helen, that was her name, and Howard! They belonged together. Emma and Claire would have brothers and be blended.

I had learned as a child that it is foolish to take anything for granted, and so I knew that it was possible that in my short absence Howard could fall blindly in love with Postmistress Helen. He would do well with someone who liked to weigh concrete objects and count out change and deliver goods. Mrs. Glevitch would say that it served me right, that that's what happened when you let a decent man out of your hands. I tried to imagine taking up with Luther Tritz, the band director, once I was sprung, living a life of exile like the Duchess and Duke of Windsor, quarreling in between our games of blackjack, and all on Luke's meager allowance. A fly had somehow made its way up the stairs in the hospital and was buzzing near my tray. I gave it a second look, one of God's creatures, a dirty insect that we took for granted and treated with contempt. How charming he was, washing himself with his feet, how dapper the gray stripes were, running down his body. I might take him back to the jail girls as a token from my trip abroad.

While nothing was impossible, nothing, not life imprisonment, not ᵗth, or the keeping of a fly in a shrine, I wondered if it was remotely ᵗle that something, a shred, to be sure, of the old life, could be salvaged. The old life: Howard, arms bronzed up to his T-shirt, cultivating the corn, thinking about his cows, the storm systems, the farmers who'd come before him, the Blackhawk War, the wonder of growing vegetable matter from a place as unlikely as the ground. And I, upstairs on the porch, with the shades drawn, dancing by myself. All the while our girls would grow up, making their lives out of the pieces we'd given them. Ordinary life was laced with miracles, I knew that, had read enough poetry to understand that we are elevated with the knowing, and yet it was difficult to notice and be grateful when one was continually fatigued and irritated. I suppose that unquenchable sense of wonder is what separates us dolts from the saints and the poets. This was the lesson, perhaps, that I was sent to learn: The old life was worth having at any expense. Had Theresa been imprisoned, she would have guessed the moral after five minutes. I would know, wouldn't I, when I got out, what things were worthy of complaint? Maybe there was value in going to jail to weigh the feelings I had for Howard, to determine if the scale would tip one way or the other. I thought so often last summer of the pond all those years ago, when Howard and I swam back and forth that first night in Prairie Junction. I couldn't make heads or tails of the last year, but I could remember and find sense in that single evening in the past. At face value it had been a dip on a hot night. But it was something else too, I could see that now, something on the order of a baptism, a kind of blessing. It had been impossible to see at the time, to understand what was taking place right under our noses. Without minister and feast and candlelight and absolution, our swim had marked a beginning.

When I returned to the pod after the incident an unexpected change had taken place. I came through the door, and just as happened on my first entrance, the girls stopped their talk. They stared unabashedly as I made my way to the cell with my white bandage wrapped around my head like a squashed turban. I looked beaten, my hair was gone, but I did my best to stand up straight. I moved slowly across the floor without looking to the left or to the right. They watched me walk. I had lived, presumably still capable of telling the story, whatever it was, while Dyshett and Janet scratched at the walls of their cells across the corridor.

It was Sherry who came to my side just as I got into bed, who gave me a hand. She may have known that I had doctor's orders to rest and as much Demerol as I wanted. "She don't know what hit her," Sherry whispered.

"Who?" I said.

"Dyshett," she answered. "You took it, like a sponge or somethin', you jus' soak all a her—" She wasn't sure what to call Dyshett's fury. "She screamin' at you somethin' fierce after you knock over—she screamin' at Janet to kick at you. Big dumb Janet was like, 'Huh?' But you, you was somethin' all raggy on the floor but we knowed you got strength inside a you. You wasn't using it except you was too using it. We been tryin' to figure that out ever since."

She held my stiff back as I eased down into the mat. "Thank you," I said. "I appreciate it." She squinted at me as if my halo was hurting her eyes. "I don't have any idea what happened," I mumbled.

"Some of them, Natasha, Hilda, Rita, they say Dyshett and Janet beat on you. But the way it happens—and I seen it, I seen every move— Dyshett jus' about ready to get you and you do it for her, you take all a her and dump over wid it. I tell myself, don't get involved with this scene because there ain't nobody goin' to see it the same way. I tell myself, the Almighty's takin' over this picture. I seen you, with the grin on your face like you at heaven's gate. And then you bump over, slam, head goes on the table, and then you fall to the floor, smack, head goes on the cement. The way I see it the whole story is one big trap, only I can't figure out who got caught."

"Dyshett didn't hurt me?" I said. "Is that what you're saying?"

"Let's put Debbie's pillow under here too," she said, lifting my head and sliding the flat pillow under me. "She don't need it with all her padding. No, it make Dyshett lose her mind a little. She not used to people jus' takin' her, right in the face. She been fighting her whole life and people been fighting back. You sat like you some dead sponge, soakin' her up. Maybe you got so full a her you can't take it no more, you jus' drop over with all that shit she give off. When the guard ax what happen, she look at him like she a poor little lost lamb who accidentally kill her best schoolteacher. She don't even know if she did it. She don't even know he didn't do it. Dyshett, she never been in that spot before. I love seeing girl all confuse. That the most beautiful sight, that girl mixed up so she don't know if she going or coming." She spread my blanket over me. "You got to get comfortable and rest. No more talkin' right now. You need somethin', you call."

Afterward it was dismaying, that jail life should just continue. Sometimes I felt as if I'd been on a rocky, slightly dangerous flight. I should have felt relief, maybe a little bravado, laughing off how rough it was, how much worse it might have been. I had apparently won something in the process, and yet the days went on, time went forward in its indefatigable way, as it had before. Although for a while afterward the girls occasionally argued over the finer points of the mystery beating, they seemed to believe that Dyshett was responsible for my bruise and my bandage. Sherry privately assured me that neither Dyshett nor Janet had ever touched me. I wanted to believe her version, because in her absurd and compelling story I was delivered from Dyshett's blow by my own failing body, a body that seemed at once weak and wise, knowing to give way at an opportune moment. I was sure that Howard and Rafferty, too, would find it implausible. I had bumped my head hard on the metal table and passed out, and then I fell to the floor and banged it again on the cement. Howard might find certain aspects of the narrative perfectly in character, in particular, the fact that I couldn't bump my head without inciting a race riot.

For the most part the others gave me a wide berth, as if I were someone unpredictable, saintly or loony, they weren't sure which. I didn't show myself much, didn't let on that curled up on my bed under my blue blanket I was nursing my wounds. When Dyshett returned to the pod I was dimly aware that she was subdued, and that the old order had crumbled. Janet was packed off somewhere else, four of last week's inmates had moved on, and with a new lot Sherry came into her own, ordering Debbie to get a Band-Aid if anyone so much as had a hangnail. She was matronly, firm, her generosity expanding by the day in her self-appointed role. She gave Dyshett Valiums from a stash she had hidden in a sock, and advised her to behave during her sessions with the public defender. She seemed to take it upon herself, for the good of the group, to occupy Dyshett by playing endless games of rummy. If Dyshett were out at a meeting or asleep, Sherry would visit me as if she were a minister making her rounds. It was more fellowship, certainly, than the Reverend

Joseph Nabor from Prairie Center had been able to muster on my account. Sherry routinely saved half of her sandwich from lunch and brought me candy bars from the vending machine. "You got to keep up your strength," she'd say. "You look like somethin' plucked with that new hairdo, so the least we got to do is fatten you up."

I mentioned at one of those bedside chats that although I was sleeping through the daytime drama I was well aware that she was now the undisputed leader.

"Jus' wait till we get a new warrior in here," she said, shaking her head and laughing. "Jus' wait till Dyshett perk up a little. She depressed about her life right now, and she droopy from my medicine cabinet, you know, a little a this, some a that, to calm her down. Once she get back in gear we can kiss the peace good-bye."

"What's the matter with her?" I asked.

"She lookin' at five years for scratching that cop," Sherry said. "That ain't cheerful news. And you, layin' in here all day. I think that sort of spook her. She watchin' you for signs of life. You some big mystery to her, she don't know if she be afraid, or how much she hate you, or what. It some big mystery, and she don't like no mystery. That old man she kilt in Chicago, he dead, and now she can brag about him. But you, you still layin' here, and she don't know if she should brag and strut. She want to, but I think she afraid a you, she afraid you planning to voodoo her again. She one jumpy girl. I think everything that ever happened to her in her life is catching up with her right about now."

"Would you mind telling her that I have not and will not voodoo her," I said.

She leaned over and whispered, "I tell her I ain't sure about you. I tell her you laying in here whispering to yourself, seems like you saying your spells and mumbo jumbo. That girl, she jus' about eatin' outta my hand these days."

I prepared for Rafferty's occasional visits by taking a shower, pinching my cheeks, and putting on clean socks. I remember once, as I was getting ready, Sherry, in her capacities as doorman, minister, nurse, and gang leader called out, "Where you going?"

"My man is here," I said.

"Your man?"

"My man."

"What he look like?"

"He has a chronic sinus condition," I said dreamily. "He wears terrible suits of the cheapest magnitude. His hair is slick, like Elvis's, only it's speckled with gray, and his goatee has tobacco stains."

"You sick?" she asked, coming closer with a look of motherly concern on her face.

What I loved about Rafferty, what I felt I surely must have loved about him for all of my life, was the fact that he never once doubted me. When I was taken down to the conference room to meet with him the first time after my arrest, he looked at me and then he shut his eyes, as if for some reason he hadn't expected to see me in my orange togs, as if they were indecent and offended his sensibility. "I'm sorry," he said.

"No," was all I could say, laughing a little at his surprise.

He spit, "I despise these cases," as if the words themselves were venomous and he wanted them out of his mouth. He was agitated enough to have trouble snapping open his vinyl briefcase. I knew right away that he had the anger Howard wished for me. "I thought these cases were over, a thing of the eighties, but they keep coming on. They keep coming." Of course, he never looked me in the eye and asked me to say if I'd done it, but I felt that his capacity to know and identify was exact, that he could look at a rare coin and right off say its worth, just as he could quickly size me up and understand that I would never have hurt Robbie or the other boys as I stood accused. "I hate to see you in here," Rafferty said, as if we were old friends and my condition pained him.

I never asked him if he was going to win my case, or what he thought my chances were. He was an eccentric man, whose personal effects looked to have been frozen about 1957. It was illogical, I knew, but I also felt that he was someone who never passed judgment. I realize now that I always sense that quality in people about whom I feel rapturous. In our meetings I tried to look clearly back over the last year, to tell him everything in proportion. I had hit Robbie, and in my mind both he and I had grown monstrous. Although he was a thin, undernourished child, in my dreams he often had the constitution of a punching bag, something you can knock down all you want and it will always pop right up again. Mrs. Mackessy, in my mind's eye, was golden, all flickers and dazzle, slithering down the hall to get her son. For Rafferty I tried to draw them as I had first seen them, nothing more nor less than the sick, neglected boy and his preoccupied mother.

Although Rafferty felt that Robbie Mackessy's case was relatively simple, there were three other boys who had come forward: Norman Frazer, Anthony Jenkins, and Tommy Giddings. There were also several other children who were being evaluated by the child welfare agency, although Rafferty did not tell me just how many until later. My records showed that I had seen the three boys once or twice during the school year, but I didn't remember them without some prompting. There were seven hundred children at Blackwell Elementary, and I had never thought that I might have to keep them straight.

"Is there any procedure you do that could be misconstrued?" Rafferty asked, his hands folded, his Bic pen at rest on his empty legal pad. In all those months he worked on my case I only remember him writing something down once. I may have misjudged Rafferty, investing in him qualities that were no doubt preposterous for any criminal lawyer. It doesn't matter now. I liked the way he was not afraid to watch me. He kept his eyes on me as I tried to think, not as if he were a vulture, waiting for me to stumble, not as if he was trying to determine innocence or guilt, but as if it was his duty to fix his loving gaze on his clients. I think I believed in him, just as a young child believes in his father. He would be there—I was sure of it—keeping watch even if the sky fell down and covered us like a tarp.

"If they're sick I have them lie on a cot," I said. "Theresa says that when she was in school the nuns used to warn the girls not to go on a date to a restaurant where white tablecloths were used, because it would remind a boy of bed sheets and drive him wild with desire. Do you suppose a cot is suggestive to a six-year-old boy?"

Rafferty rolled his eyes and threw his head back as if he was gargling.

"I really don't do much," I continued. "I'm only a nurse. I can take temperatures and look down someone's throat and see if it's red, and then if they say it hurts I send them home. If the parents are at work the children spend the day on the cot or return to class. During health week they all come in and get weighed and measured. The scale is one of those massive upright contraptions with ominous black weights waiting to fall on someone's toes. I don't know, maybe everything is frightening. Last year for health the eighth-grade science teacher wanted me to come in and talk to the class about how AIDS is transmitted, as if the uniform gives me the authority to speak about disease. Sometimes I'm in a hurry; I have a lot to do in the three hours I'm there and I'm sharp. I tell them to hold still, to be quiet, to watch their manners. Maybe anything can be misconstrued, so that one thing eventually becomes another, I mean in such a way that it's completely changed."

Down in that barren cubicle it seemed that Rafferty would sit across from me and listen for as long as my mouth opened and shut. "Maybe it isn't possible to move an inch without being misunderstood. That must be a relief in law, that for everything there is a rule."

He laughed out loud and then said, "Yes, right, Alice, a relief, all those rules, oh, absolutely."

"But you see the entire spectrum in school," I went on. "That's what's good about it. We have the undeclared lesbian gym teacher, the homophobic principal, the bleeding-heart liberal teaching social studies, the right-wing Christian sneaking in his stuff in earth science—"

"But can you think of anything specific?" Rafferty prodded.

"Yes! Yes—I can think of thousands of specific things, some I did, some I dreamed, some I feared. I lie quaking when I remember certain days. I was walking down the hall last spring, and the gym teacher, as a matter of fact, Miss Orin, called me in to take a look at a girl's back, a junior-high girl who was changing in the locker room. Miss Orin was concerned about this girl's spine. She was having them parade around for some kind of posture exam but you have to understand, I'm an LPN: I don't know anything! I just ran my hand down the girl's back, the way I would if it were my daughter, to see if I could feel ribs in the wrong place. I only know about scoliosis because I was evaluated for it when I was a teenager. My father may have thought that I was so isolated and withdrawn, like a Victorian heroine, that I probably at least had gout. I remember leaving the locker room, feeling the girls' eyes on me, knowing that they were going to start whispering about the homo gym teacher, the homo nurse. Junior-high girls are like savages, you know? I tried to wave my left hand with my wedding ring around, to remind them that I'm *Mrs.*

Goodwin. But I knew they'd talk about us all the same. Sometimes I used to have the urge to crack up in front of those girls, to rave about the passionate crushes I'd had on women teachers when I was young, but how as I grew older it was the dear, ecstatic act of copulation that spurred me on— Do you see what I mean, they were so snide and sure in their disgust that one somehow wanted to knock them off their perches?"

Rafferty nodded, blowing his stuffy nose into a red bandanna.

After I looked at the records I remembered that Norman Frazer, a kindergartner, had come to my office, because of a very loose and bloody tooth. He seemed to be one of those volatile children, like Emma, who can not take the unexpected in stride. His tooth was hanging by a thread, his bloody saliva slipping down his chin as he howled. I'm sure the teacher sent him to me because he was disrupting the class. "Am I supposed to go find a picture of a tooth, show him the roots, try to educate?" I asked Rafferty. "One child is on the cot throwing up, another is waiting for medicine; I don't have time!

"Norman was hysterical, nothing to do but hold him around his stomach with one arm and, reaching around with the other, pull out the tooth. It was so loose it came away with a pluck. It was a pluck, not a pull. I didn't even wear my gloves as I should have, to protect myself from his blood. He was so surprised he stopped in the middle of his screech. We put the tooth in an envelope and he went back to the classroom. Howard thought it was terrible, that I had violated the child's body. Once he made some comment to Emma and Claire, that they should watch their teeth. The remark bothered me more than I let on. Norman was so busy screaming he hadn't really noticed, until I had the tooth in my hand."

"That's all you know of him?" Rafferty asked.

"Yes," I said.

The only thing I remembered about Anthony Jenkins, another of the boys, was that he had skinned his knee and I had poured disinfectant over the gritty wounds. He had trembled with the pain and growled deep in his throat. Rafferty got a hold of a class picture so I could see what the third boy, Tommy Giddings, looked like, and still it sparked no memory. According to my log I had given him a dose of Amoxicillin for an ear infection in October. They all claimed that I had shouted, spanked, hit them across the face, held them down, that I was pernicious and preyed upon them with the greed and toothiness of a shark.

At one of our meetings, when we were trying to find any possible association between the boys and Robbie Mackessy, Rafferty leaned over the table and asked me if I was ever afraid. It was an early session, before my run-in with Dyshett. I looked to the pale yellow cinder-block wall, wondering what I should say, and also relishing, for a moment, his steadfast attention. Did he mean, I wondered, was I afraid of death? My girls have an animal terror of death, as I did at their age, but I had begun to think that I had lost that particular instinct. I wanted to avoid dying not least so that Emma and Claire wouldn't have to go through the trauma of having a dead mother. I had seen enough death to know that it isn't anything more startling than taking a next breath. My best and fondest hope for the hereafter was that there was some kind of design and that it was trustworthy. Life on earth, filled with uncertainty and change, seemed far more difficult than what lay beyond the grave.

"Not afraid, exactly," I said to Paul. "There's so much good, and it's been taken away."

I may have been whispering because he said, "What?"

"I miss the farm," I said.

Rafferty's clerk spent several weeks digging up information on the boys, trying to find out if they'd been in the same class, or the same neighborhood, or day care or church school. I don't know how he discovered that the four of them were on the same T-ball team during the month of June, and that it was highly likely that they occasionally spent time at one another's houses. Tommy Giddings's mother was a waitress at Dolphin Bay, the restaurant Carol Mackessy managed. Anthony's mother was the sister of Mrs. Mackessy's hairdresser. It seemed incredible that even Robbie could have fanned the flames and turned the boys against me. That Carol Mackessy could have done so was another matter all together.

"Can you think of a common thread with the boys?" Rafferty asked me. "Something that would have pulled them in the same direction?"

I imagined Carol feeding Norman and Robbie, Anthony and Tommy, hot dogs with Day-Glo orange cheese spread from a can in zigzags over the wiener. She might think that she was a good mother, to be able to reproduce, exactly, down to the last zig, the picture on the can. Although she could well have had a bright kitchen with an island, sparkling copper pans, framed prints of fruit, I pictured her in a poorly lit room with dark cabinets and a red sheen, nearly a glow, coming from a fake brick wall. "What do you boys think of the school nurse, that Mrs. Goodwin?" she might have idly asked as she poured them Hawaiian punch on an afternoon only days after Lizzy's funeral.

"She's mean!" Norman would say. "She pulled my tooth out."

"She pulled your tooth out? She went in and yanked out your tooth?"

"She held me hard around the stomach, I couldn't get away, and then she reached in and dug my tooth out. It wasn't even loose, she probably would have taken all my teeth if I didn't scream and run away. She has a pair of pliers, a gigantic pair of pliers in her desk drawer."

"I always kick her," Robbie might have offered.

"Does Mrs. Goodwin do the same awful things to you that she does to Robbie?"

"She rips my pants off of me," Robbie would have shouted, giving them a quick demonstration. "My mom says we're going to get a pile of money from her because she did that. She killed a girl, too!"

"Put that thing back in where it belongs!" Mrs. Mackessy might have said, in anger, before she realized that the school nurse had made a little exhibitionist out of him. "Come here, Pumpkin," she said, going to him, putting her arms around him as he stiffened.

"She did that to me once," Anthony Jenkins cried, remembering the time his sweat pants were torn clean through and I had him take them off so I could clean the wound.

"More chips, boys? Soda? Anyone ready for a Twinkie?"

Robbie, still within the circle of his mother's embrace, said, "We're going to be so rich, my mom says we'll get a sports car, the kind with a roof."

"What did she do to you, Anthony? I can't believe this— She's hurt other boys too—"

Robbie burst from her arms, charging at the back door, shouting, "Them cars go ninety miles, *varoom*—"

"Slow down, tiger—"

From the porch, through a small window, he called into the kitchen, "She licked my pee-pee!"

"Did she do that to you boys?" Mrs. Mackessy asked. "You don't need to be afraid to tell. When someone touches you, and hurts you, like Mrs. Goodwin has, it is so important to tell someone. We know it's happened. We know what she is. You only have to say one little word and we'll know the rest. There were days"—she was getting upset now, having to blink away the tears—"when she wouldn't let me take Robbie home. We all know what she is! Only you can help do the important job of making sure Mrs. Goodwin never sees another boy, never hurts another one of you. It's your job to help us get her. This town will be so thankful to you four boys because you saved us from a person who is disturbed, twisted."

"It's starting to make sense," I said to Rafferty, knowing that as far as proof went, Mrs. Mackessy in her kitchen was as solid as a hallucination.

"Do you think Lizzy's death tied into the charge?" Rafferty asked. He always waited for my answer with his chin resting on his folded hands. I never thought, until afterward, that he was getting paid for his time, that my reveries were costly. Still, his questions, his watchful eye, forced my memory.

"Was it something specific that triggered the charge?" he probed.

It was as if he had the power of the hypnotist, that he need only snap his fingers to make me sleep or wake. I could see into the hospital lounge right after Lizzy had been brought to the emergency room; I could see Mrs. Mackessy in her chair leafing through a magazine. I had forgotten that she'd been there. She had been with me, like a shadow, while I waited to hear. I had been dripping wet, and I had sat on the edge of the sofa, doubled over, praying. I must have looked as desperate as I felt. I remembered, too, that I had run right past Carol and Robbie at the funeral as I fled. Was it Carol who put it into his head just as I streaked past them; might she have mused aloud, "Is that woman out of her mind?" She might have realized it was I, and said to Robbie, "Mrs. Goodwin looks as if she'd killed the girl. How can they let someone like that work at an elementary school?"

"So much of all of this, I'm afraid, is a feeling," I said to Rafferty.

Instead of looking at me with contempt or scoffing, he nodded, saying, "It's only taken me about ten years to understand that that's where every case begins, not with facts or a body, a few tattered pieces of evidence, but with a couple of people and then a whole range of possibility: their pride, their love, their lust, their sense of injury, vengeance, greed, despair—you name it."

"This is what I think might have happened," I began then, "not too long after the funeral, in Mrs. Mackessy's kitchen."

When Rafferty and I met about a week and a half after my fainting spell he took one look at me, and with his normal adenoidal fire and indignation, declared that we had reached the limit. "Why didn't they call me?" he shouted, beating the table with his fist.

I shrugged and said that I thought they'd tried to get in touch with Howard. But he knew as well as I did that they didn't go out of their way to keep the families up to date. My bruise was not as colorful as it had been and I assumed I could just say, "I bumped my head," and leave it at that. "You don't get a bruise the size of a grapefruit from bumping your head," he protested.

"It's funny," I said, cutting him off, "about being afraid? You asked me about that a couple of weeks ago. I thought for a while that I was going to get pounded. It wasn't that that I feared. What's frightening is that I can't—love those girls."

"For God's sake—"

"No," I said, "Theresa would find it within herself to love them. She would understand what they were given at the start, understand why they're so angry. I'm more afraid of what I don't have, that deep down, you know, way down, there isn't really much of anything."

"You're reading the wrong novels," Rafferty said. "You are not required to love your fellow inmates." He went on to lecture me at length about how we have to protect ourselves against those, who, for whatever reasons, are barbarians. "Save your love for your daughters," he ordered.

I said that of course Emma and Claire gave me reason to be afraid. I had wept when they were born, each in their turn, because of semiautomatic weapons on the street, stockpiles of hazardous waste, terrorist acts, hatred—all of the horrors which we bequeath to our children. My general sorrow in relation to the human condition was nothing compared to my new and specific grief over the fact that my daughters' lives were forever changed. I had sworn I would never do to my children as my mother had done to me, that I would never abandon them, and yet I had, for all intents and purposes, left them. Even if I was let go, even if we moved to Australia, they would always know that I had been responsible for something that permanently altered each of us. They would always feel, even if no one else knew, that they carried with them a stigma. There wasn't really any place we could go where we wouldn't suffer from the knowledge that evil had been done to us, and that we, in our turn, had injured those around us.

It was nearly a week after my hospitalization that Debbie came out of herself long enough to ask me a personal question. It was a relatively quiet morning, each of us at the work of holding ourselves together. Debbie shuffled into our cell after breakfast and stood, staring at me while I read. When she realized I wasn't going to look up she said right out, "How old are your children?"

That she might ask me something was so uncharacteristic I found at first that I couldn't answer. "What?" I finally said.

"You keep getting letters from your girls. They draw you pictures. I just wondered how old they were."

I had not, up to that point in my stay, showed much emotion in front of Debbie, except in relation to her own troubles. I felt my mouth start to move. I wanted very much to control myself. Debbie had the sense to avert her eyes while I tried to master my poor trembling lips. For several minutes she stood looking out at the day room, pulling on her nose. To my dismay I found myself sobbing into my lap. I was apparently making enough noise to attract attention because pretty soon Sherry was poking her head around the corner. "What this fuss about? What you be doin', Debbie girl, goin' on and makin' her cry?"

"I just asked her a question," Debbie squeaked.

"You missin' your babies? That it?" Sherry asked, sitting down next to me. She pointed at Debbie. "Go get some tissues." Sherry was nineteen years old. She had been driving the get-away car when her boyfriend held up a Handy Pantry. He'd wounded two people and nearly gotten away with six hundred dollars. I couldn't stop crying. I felt as if a ball bearing had come loose inside my head, that it banged from side to side, every time I blinked. If I was sent to prison and my children got a stepmother in due course, I would still be a blight to them. If there was a plea bargain and I pleaded guilty for a lesser sentence, Child Welfare might barge in and take the girls away from Howard. If I lost the trial, I would be in prison for years. My absence was a wound—I might just as well have cut off a limb or put out an eye.

"I miss my babies too," Sherry said, slipping her arm around me. I was rigid in her arms as she moved back and forth, trying to rock me. "I got my three little dickens at my mama's house."

I remember wanting very much to protest, to insist that someone nineteen years old couldn't possibly know my pain, that our ages, our experience, our upbringing were so dramatically different we were virtually not of the same species. I remember trying to say that. My head was throbbing and I couldn't make the words to tell her that she knew nothing.

"You have three babies?" Debbie asked.

Sherry stared at her. "You in awe today or somethin'?"

"Well, I—"

"Ain't she though?" Sherry said, trying to draw me out. "It's like she noticing we made of bones instead of cee-ment. Congratulations, girl. Three babies, that's right, Dante, Jamella, Michael J. One, two, three. They always say jail ain't no vacation, but for me it is, that's for sure!" She laughed her big belchy laugh. "Don't let Dyshett fool you," she said. "She had a baby boy when she was fourteen, a baby girl a year later, but they both got took away to foster care. She say she don't mind, but that ain't no shit but talk. She go out and bust herself buying fancy presents for their birthdays. She got her girl a gold necklace with a diamond the size of my butt."

I stood up then, dried my eyes on my sleeve, and thanked Sherry. My head hurt so much I couldn't see. I needed my children not to know me, not to remember that it had been I who made their world smash, as much as I needed to breathe near them, to encircle them, to keep them safe. I leaned over the toilet trying to choke down the grief, as if what was inside was likely to come ripping up my throat, as if it was something that could be purged and flushed away.

After Debbie and Sherry went into the day room I lay on my stomach and looked at the stack of drawings the girls had made. Claire made scribbles and Emma drew stick self-portraits in triangle dresses with funny little club feet pointing in the same direction. I smelled the drawings and I held them to my cheek because the paper always seemed as if it should be directly related to them. If I only could look more closely, or read in a way that was just beyond my ability, the girls would be there, underneath the paper. I didn't ever seem to remember the keen disappointment I always felt, and each time there was mail delivery I opened their letters with great expectation. As I lay in bed I tried to study the pictures objectively, to see if I could tell if the girls were scarred in any way. Emma's portraits included feet and fingers, and I tried to remember if that wasn't a sign, that a child was well adjusted, had a sense of self-worth. Claire's lines had been made with a free hand, and she used a good deal of color. I thought that a child who was suffering would surely use somber tones, and draw spirals that circled into a tight knot. I tried to will the girls to be fine and well and unscathed and unharmed. I closed my eyes and assumed the tense prayerful attitude I'd used to no avail in the hospital.

The following morning we were eating our scoop of oatmeal with milk and sugar prepoured, a dirty slice of cantaloupe, orange juice, and cold coffee. For some reason Dyshett had already been out of the pod. No one looked up or paid any attention when she was buzzed into the day room. She sat down at her usual place at the other table. She seemed to take care to keep her distance, to avoid eye contact. After the meal she went into Sherry's cell to play cards. I had a headache and spent most of the morning lying on my bed trying to sleep. Debbie sat on the floor cross-legged, rocking forward and back as she listened to music on her headset.

At lunch, Dyshett sauntered over to the table where I was eating and straddled the stool, her side to me, her profile obscured by her mass of braids. A woman named Carla, who was in for fraud, was explaining how her boyfriend's credit-card scam worked for years before he got caught. I assumed that Dyshett was interested in how to go about the business. I was nibbling at my hamburger, reading my college alumni magazine, which Howard had sent me in a brown envelope along with the *L. L. Bean* catalog. A man named Robert J. Harrison, class of '67, had figured out how to grow plastic by genetically engineering a potato. The potato itself produces plastic, in the ground. One of the problematic aspects of making the technological wonder a reality is the fact that the plastic could get mixed up in the food chain. I dabbed a French fry into a puddle of ketchup, imaging our Golden Guernseys putting their heads down in their pasture to graze the perfect lush green grass, only to find that it was fake.

"How many kids you got?" Dyshett asked, turning around to face our group, looking straight at me.

"Why is everyone asking me that question?" I whined into my hamburger bun. I wished to continue thinking about the tuber that was going to be genetically engineered to grow vinyl tablecloths with or without flower patterns. I didn't want her to know that I had been diminished by our fight, such as it was. The others thought I had come out ahead, but they were mistaken. I didn't want her to know that there were days I couldn't see straight. And I didn't want her to know that I loved Howard in a way that I was sure she would never love anyone. I had a life full of marvels and she wasn't going to get so much as a glimpse of it. He and I had mapped a course in which work and love were to go together. She wouldn't be able to conceive of such a commitment. We had invested our lives in our children and the gifts we were giving them were for their heads and their hearts. Emma and Claire were not merely showcases for expensive jewelry.

"I don't want to talk about them," I said.

"Escuse me," she said, bending her arms so that her hands, palms up, came to her shoulders.

"So, like stores had his name on their lists," Carla was saying, in her lesson on fraud, "you know, how they do for people who write bad checks?"

I felt a violent shudder in my abdomen again, and I swallowed my hamburger as fast as I could in hopes that the bun would stanch the sobs.

"What's their names?" Dyshett said. "You can tell me that." She was blurry across the table from me. "A boy, you got, or what, a girl?"

"No," I said, the awful sharpness and heft of the thing in my stomach lurching up, falling back, lurching up again. "NO," I said. I left the table and went to my cell and I sat on the bed, doing breathing exercises meant for giving birth. I tried to focus on a speck on the wall, to feel as if I was pouring what was inside myself into the black dot on the cinder block, filling the infinite space behind that smallest of portals, until I was empty.

It was as I tried again, and then again to focus on the speck, that I recalled the day and the time. Howard was going to come soon for his weekly visit. He too would see my pink bandanna and wonder why it fit so snugly over my head. I would try to distract him by saying, Remember the night we swam together in the pond, Howard? Remember how we moved so effortlessly through the water, holding each other as if we were one body? That was the beginning, wasn't it?

When I went down to see him that afternoon, and when I came to my station and reached for the phone, I saw in that instant behind him, Emma and Claire looking into the communications room. Without thinking I tried to get through the window, as if I thought the girls being there meant the glass would dissolve. They were so beautiful. They were wearing new sundresses and their clean hair was shining. I hadn't, for a month and a half, been able to count on the fact that they were real, and now there they were, wonderful and alive, curious about the operators, as if the outing was a trip to a museum. I was so glad and I felt a rush of gratitude toward Howard, for knowing, despite my command, that I needed to see them. He was standing up, shouting into the phone, trying, it seemed just then, to keep me from seeing. I couldn't think why he was blocking the view. He was wearing a blue shirt, looking like a dark shadow in the window, like some ominous figure coming down the street in a cartoon. I was going to say so, into the phone, and then I was going to shout how glad I was to see the girls. I needed to look beyond him, if he would only get out of the way, and I needed to say the lines I had been working on: Remember the pond that night, Howard? Is it love that connects us, is that what it is? I never knew that the feeling I have is regular old love because it's so—intricate. Perhaps there is another name for it, one we don't yet know. I used to think that love was simple and noticeable, like rain falling, so that just as you'd look at your skin and say Water, you would also wake in the morning and say Love. But it has been underneath, this new and old thing I feel, subterranean, silent and steady, like blood, rushing along and along without often making itself known.

When I looked at him he was jabbing his finger at the window, as if he meant to poke me. His face was red, bilious. I had never seen him with such an expression, his frown running all the way into his neck. "I love you, Howard," I tried to say into the window, but he was spitting and frothing, erupting into what looked very much like anger. The room began to lean and spin, slowly, like a merry-go-round just heating up, going at a drowsy pace so that you could still jump aboard if you had your ticket. I wasn't sure then that the girls were really there, that they weren't some kind of mirage. I had to get out before I tipped over. The guard tried to make me go back to my station, but he finally let me out when I said, "There is no one here I know."

Chapter Nineteen

———

I NEVER DREAMED THAT Howard would actually sell the farm, that he could part with the barn, and his cows, upon which he lavished what seemed a maternal care. I remember a day long ago when I looked out to see him shining the four-paned windows that are set into each side of the barn near the roof. Our house was falling to pieces and was unclean from top to bottom, and he was polishing the windows up in the haymow, where the dust was thick, like haze.

It was not clear to me that Howard meant to sell the farm, but near the end of the summer his letters became infrequent, short and full of gloom, and, to make matters worse, Theresa stopped writing altogether. There was no balance, no yin for the yang. I was mystified: One day she was telling me how delightful the girls were, how much they meant to her, how stoic I was, and the next day there was nothing. A postcard trickled in a week later, saying that they'd been sick, they were busy: I could practically hear her making the feeble excuses, and yet I couldn't think what she was trying to hide. I was writing to her several times a week, first of all because I was so thankful she was caring for Emma and Claire, and second, because I thought that as well as nourishing Howard she might be able to keep his spirits up. Theresa's letters were unusual because she wrote just as she spoke, bubbling along about her mother, the girls, the flower borders, an epiphany, a recipe for shortbread. I appreciated her trying to keep me in touch with ordinary life, a place where one fretted over shoddy merchandise and strained relationships. After her communications stopped I knew that something had happened, and that she, even with her considerable talents, did not know how to tell me.

When the call came through that I could go, everyone stopped what they were doing. They gathered in the day room to watch me pack. Sherry asked me what I was going to wear home and I described, as best I remembered, the khaki shorts and the gray T-shirt that I'd worn the day I was taken.

"You jus' as well keep the orange shit on," Sherry said. "That sound bland as mud."

"You are so lucky," Debbie whimpered. "I wish someone could get me out of here."

"You try to keep the faith," I said.

"You going back to the farm?" Sherry asked. When I didn't answer she said, "I couldn't stand to live out there in all that dark empty space. I'd feel like somebody was lookin' at me all the tahm."

A woman who was new called from across the room, "Like there ain't nobody lookin' at us right now?"

"Let's not have long faces!" Sherry shouted. "You know we'll be back here someday. You know we was meant to be one happy family."

Dyshett stood just outside of her cell and watched. I gathered my books in the grocery bag and went quickly for the door without any personal good-byes. It was possible we would meet again, that we might spend the prime of our lives together, if we were convicted of our various crimes. As the door buzzed and the guard came through to get me I turned and waved. "Be good," I said.

"Keep in touch," Sherry yelled.

I could see them soundlessly repeating both jokes as I was led along the hall and out a series of doors to the elevator.

I felt as I'm sure that dog must have felt, the dog we came upon in our woods one day, wrapped around a tree by its own leash. It was barking and barking. And after Howard carefully unwrapped the leash and it was free to go, it still stood there, barking and barking. Even when it took one step, and another, it couldn't believe that it was no longer bound. It barked at us, at the tree, at itself. It barked as it ran off, astonished all the way through the woods.

Before we went to our new town we stopped at a county park to walk along the nature trails. We didn't talk much, except to point out a turtle, a kestrel, a great blue heron. There had been a short spate of rain and the trees dripped their water on us. I had missed a season, one dry summer; I had gone in when it seemed the heat would never abate, and come out to find a wet, cool September day. It had rained in my absence. Howard had told me about the first storm in July, and then the few showers that came after. I hadn't heard the thunder inside our pod. The rain hadn't been enough or come in time, and many of the farmers in the southern part of the state had lost their crops. One summer wasn't much to lose over a lifetime, a season blotted out. There might be others to follow in some new place, lush wild summers, with cicadas, fireflies, mosquitoes, fish jumping, sunsets, and northern lights. There was no telling where we might go. I felt weightless walking along the trail, as if I might drift up to the sky like a helium balloon if I once let go of Howard's hand.

I was standing in the brush looking over the cattail marsh when he told me that school was starting on Monday. There had been a teacher's strike for nearly a month. The girls had seemed so far away while I was holed up, and I had somehow not been able to absorb the fact that Emma was going to be a schoolgirl. She was looking at a nest that Howard had found along the path. I wondered if he'd thought to enroll her at Spring Grove Elementary. We'd have to write down our names and addresses on a registration card, as well as our occupations, our home and work phone numbers, someone to contact in case of an emergency. We wouldn't have much information to give. We had nothing permanent except our tarnished name for that card. I wondered if we had money to buy Emma crayons, a paint smock, a pencil case, a folder, new shoes. I went and knelt down by her, pretending to look at the nest. I won't let her go, I thought. I'll hide her away, or pretend that she's sickly.

Howard set the nest back in the thicket. I remembered how lovely he used to look with a small wet lamb in his large splayed hands. He looked tired and unhappy, and I kept glancing at him to see if I was only imagining that he looked so tired and unhappy. It was nice of him to bring me to the park, and I said so. He smiled a lame smile. The girls ran alongside of him, by habit now. I was like a guest.

I had decided, once I knew about the farm; I had resolved that I was not going to be ungrateful about my freedom. We left the park after we'd had some peanut butter and jelly sandwiches on doughy white bread, the cheapest brand there is, the same kind they served at the jail. Howard occasionally used to make bread with our cow's milk and with flour which he ground from the wheat he'd grown. I used to tell the girls that it was the best bread in the world and they called it that, "The-best-bread-in-the-world-bread." We stood up and ate because the picnic tables and benches were wet. We were like acquaintances, standing and eating, not quite knowing what to say. Even the girls were subdued, staring up at my bandanna.

When we were finished we made our way to Spring Grove. We drove into the garage that was attached both to our apartment and to the next apartment in the Pheasant Glade development. Howard unlocked the white door and ushered me into the small vestibule. Never, not in our strangest dreams, would we have seen ourselves in a place so new, a place that smelled as if air freshener were somehow built into the very walls. Howard's jaw was clenched, his eyes narrowed as he moved quickly to open the sliding doors off the kitchen. He had warned me that the place was only temporary and that it was not something we would have chosen under normal circumstances. He and the girls had picked goldenrod, Queen Anne's lace, black-eyed Susans, and chicory from the side of a road somewhere, and put them in jars in the living room and kitchen. I sat down in the sagging wing chair we'd had on the farm and took the girls on my lap. I began to talk with them about the time my Aunt Kate moved in with me when I was a little girl, about the day she came to the door with her suitcase, how she led me right out into the yard and began planting tulip bulbs. "We'll ask if we can plant some tulips in the back," I said.

"There isn't a back," Emma said.

"The front then."

"That's the driveway."

"A window box. We'll make a window box."

"I don't think you should put bulbs in a window box. There's not enough dirt in a window box."

She was right. "We could color tulips," I ventured, "and tape them to the walls in a border, and then we'll have them all year around?"

"If you want to," she said, slipping off my lap, defeat in her knock-kneed walk, resistance in her hunched shoulders. She was choosing isolation; it was all hers as she made her way up to her room and closed the door.

"What's under your hat?" Claire asked.

I untied the bandanna and showed her my very short, soft hair.

"You're not so pretty anymore," she said, matter-of-factly. "We'll pet you." She nestled into my chest and I read her *Blueberries for Sal.* When I was finished she said, "Can we go visit Theresa soon?"

"We'll have to call her one of these days."

"When?"

"One of these days we'll give her a call."

"This house is sticky," she said. "I think it smells bad."

I wouldn't let myself think that "the unit," as Howard called it, with no space to breathe, was the price we were all paying and paying for my release. That first night Howard sat me down at the kitchen table in the breakfast nook and showed me his accounts. He was going to be able to pay off his debt to the bank if he could get a job. He had paid my bond, money which we would get back when I showed up for my trial. There was enough to pay Rafferty for the time being, a meager amount for food, insurance, rent, taxes. Nellie would have to wait for her portion. I think Howard was trying to show me that the reason for everything was in the account book. "I see," I said, although the numbers ran together into one big blot of ink at the edge of the page. I am sure I will never understand what moved Howard. He said that our life in Prairie Center was tainted. It was a defensible excuse, and yet I had always felt, as he did, that the place was ours in a way that went beyond ownership. When Howard farmed he looked as if he didn't have to do anything much more than pick up a shovel and start digging to be a part of the landscape. I don't mean in a pictorial way, but actually a part of it, part of the dirt, the sky, the growing things. Away from home I had realized that the farm was not as dear to me as flesh, but nearly so, that the ground was something that I could very easily have knelt down on and kissed, tried to embrace. Perhaps it was Lizzy's death that had given new meaning to the word "ground." It, the ground, the shabby buildings, the shoots in spring, the pond, the garden, began just where our bodies ended.

Sometimes his letting the land go seemed as if it could only have been an extraordinary act of kindness, that he assumed the months until the trial were going to be my last chance in a long while to be with the girls, that even Rafferty's reason would not prevail and I would be proven guilty. Sometimes, it seemed another punishment for something we didn't even know we'd done.

We were sitting on what he used to like to call "the davenport," that first night, after the girls were in bed. He set his muscled arm around me. It didn't seem to weigh much more than a stick on my back and shoulders. My head was thrumming, something it did when I was tired. I could tell he was nervous; I was going to ask him about the farm, he thought, or say something about the apartment or Rafferty. He was sitting with a terrible erectness and formality. We must have looked as if we'd been positioned, like mannequins, as we tried out various topics, all of them running aground before we touched on anything difficult or meaningful. "What about Nellie?" I finally asked.

"She'll be back soon," he said.

"She always knew you shouldn't have married me," I said lightly.

"I haven't told her much. She's pretty involved over there."

"We still owe her quite a bit, don't we?"

"Yep," he said, "we owe her."

We were quiet for a while. "Thank you, Howard," I said. "Thank you—" He sprang up before I could finish.

"We tried to have a fire one night when it wasn't so hot," he said, looking at the fireplace, "to roast marshmallows. The girls wanted to," he added, perhaps to make it plain that there wasn't much he wanted anymore. "You can hardly get a log in the grating, it's so small. What'd they make the thing for if you can't use it?"

"It doesn't matter," I said.

"But what'd they make it for?"

I followed him up the stairs to the master bedroom. I wanted to lie down with him and cry or laugh or be sick, shivering under the covers, partners in misery. He had put the futon on the orange-flecked carpet, the old lump we used to haul out for guests. Our clocks were there, the Big Ben and the Little Ben, ticking away as always, both of them keeping the wrong time. From storage Howard had pulled together a box of essential things for me, not unlike jail basics: underwear, socks, T-shirts. I was trying to think what to say beyond, "Thank you," when he said, "I'm tired. Could you get the light when you're done?"

I climbed in and he turned over and kissed my cheek, mumbling something about how much they had missed me. When I was sure he was asleep I crawled out, pushed open the sliding door, and stepped onto the rough planks of the small deck that faced the highway. The air smelled of fry from the bar and grill down the street. It wasn't the chintzy carpet, the newness all around that made me feel that I'd just been born and had neither a past nor a sense of the future. It wasn't the street lights shining in over the bed, or the fact that we didn't have one speck of dirt for a tulip bulb; it wasn't any of those things that made me feel as if I had cracked. I got back under the blanket and tried to pull close to Howard. He was asleep and his jaw was still clenched.

He found a job at the Motor Vehicle Registration Office that's right next to Shopko on the outskirts of Racine. He had to take the Civil Service Test and the fact that he scored off the charts temporarily bolstered his spirits. He gave people eye exams, did the paper work on title transfers and registrations, and processed driver's licenses. His starting salary was twenty-one thousand dollars with benefits. It was the most he had ever commanded thus far in his life. He stood at a booth like a bank teller, all day long, and was courteous and helpful. They told him that if he stayed a year he'd most certainly rise to the rank of Team Captain. I had become maudlin, sentimental, as temporarily bright as a new penny. One of those oppressed and hideously cheerful Victorian children heroines, Sara Crewe or Pollyanna, kept a running list of reasons to be thankful. Emma and I had a notebook where we wrote down the good things that had happened to us. Howard's success on the job market was the first entry in our book.

It came as no surprise to us that Emma was reluctant to leave home in the mornings and go to school. At 8:20 every day Claire and I walked her to her kindergarten room in the old schoolhouse that had high ceilings and tall windows and a musty charm. We left her in the hands of Miss Smucker, promising, crossing our hearts, hoping to die, that we'd be waiting by the door at 11:36 when the bell rang. I hated to promise on the off chance that I might get carted away. I had come to think, while I'd been in jail, that I deserved to be there, a normal reaction, Theresa later assured me. I couldn't see a squad car go down the street without thinking that I'd better hurry and get my things.

After we dropped Emma at school, Claire and I used to walk to the playground. We'd swing, take the trip down the slide, and then head over to the A&W. We always split a sweet roll and had a glass of water each. She prattled on and on and I'd close my eyes and listen to the pure sound, the cadences of her three-year-old speech, trying, somehow, to etch the music into my brain.

Not long after my release Theresa called, saying that she was so anxious to get together. I remember thinking that it was both a curious and appropriate word choice: anxious. I had not yet felt ready to talk to her. I wasn't ready to feel so vividly, as I would in a meeting, the void. Theresa may have begun somehow to adjust to Lizzy's death, but my time in jail had not made me know more deeply that it was real. She suggested that we meet for breakfast on a day three weeks away. It seemed so agreeably distant, far enough in the future that it might never come to pass. But the morning arrived and Claire and I stood on the sidewalk outside the A&W, waiting, knowing from experience that she'd be late. When her blue van came along the block I wanted to run, and I had to breathe hard to get an adequate supply of oxygen, and I had to hold the metal outdoor menu post to keep myself from giving into that old habit of fleeing. As she turned into the driveway she stuck her head out the window and called, "It's so great to see you!" She rolled up onto the curb and rocked back into the parking space. "God," she cried, trying to untangle herself from her seat belt, "it's so good to see you."

She turned off the engine, and jumped to the pavement, talking as she hugged me and talking as she held me at arm's length. "I like it! I like your hair. It's so comfortable. It's chic. Did your long hair get to be too much? You look younger—it makes you look like you're about twenty, no honestly. Come on, Audrey, honey, come see Claire." She stooped down. "Hi, Claire. Give me a hug. Ummm, I've missed you. Audrey, do you have the little present you were going to give Claire? There you go. God, Alice," she said, taking hold of my sleeve. She hadn't really looked at me yet. She was buzzing and flapping, all movement and noise.

"It's good to see you," I managed.

We admired the children and expressed astonishment at their growth. Inside, the girls went directly to the play corner, where they had old-fashioned desks and a pot full of coloring books. Theresa settled herself into our booth, first smoothing her skirt over her rump and then sitting down. She leaned forward and said, in an undertone, "Can you believe what happened? Aren't you still in shock? Sometimes I just can't believe it. Sometimes I say to myself, No. I just have to say No!"

At first I thought that what was different about her was her new feverish pitch, her record-breaking speed. Other than that it seemed as if she was rattling on in her regular old way. She was working twenty hours a week, she said, and no more, because she meant to devote herself to Audrey. "You can't get the time back," she said, looking at her menu. She was going to have her tubal reversed at the beginning of November, with a doctor in Milwaukee who had a ninety-percent success rate. Dan was making an effort to be at home more and they'd been planning a lot of family activities. "I've got my hopes pinned on a baby," she whispered. "Maybe I shouldn't, but I do. We'll heal faster with new life, I just know we will."

I said how nice that would be.

I could see by the way she kept turning the pages of her menu without reading that she wanted to move away from the subject of Lizzy. Lizzy was near—we both felt it. As we talked of increasingly smaller and smaller things, the thick hovering form of the little girl became more oppressive. Theresa understandably would certainly have rather been at home; she wasn't quite engaged, going through the motions of breakfast and friendship. When our food came and we had the business of eating to preoccupy us she casually asked, "Will the whole—deal take up your time now?"

"I think Rafferty's trying to leave me alone for a while," I said. "He was so angry at first. Howard didn't tell him about the farm until after the closing. Rafferty always maintained that the property was our anchor, our greatest asset; it proved we were not going to turn tail and run. Howard went over to the office the Monday morning after I got home, to break the news. I've gathered that Rafferty gave him a dressing-down. Paul and I talk details and stay away from the farm issue. I think he's worried that Judge Peterson is going to be against us. He's always very reassuring, but all the same I know he thinks that the judge might bar our key witnesses."

"Oh God—"

"No," I said. "I don't worry much. I've always, from the start, felt that the thing just had to play itself out, that Howard and I are only two of the many powerless players."

She sat across from me eating her bacon biscuit with the sort of intense concentration that's required for taxes and higher math. She had her head bent over the plate and she chewed as if she was inspecting her food for something that might better have been observed under a microscope. "I've struggled a lot lately to keep from feeling helpless," she finally said.

I nodded, knowing that it must require tremendous energy to keep up her unfailing good cheer. I nursed my coffee along staring out the window and she continued to work at eating. We had suddenly and unexpectedly fallen into a silence. We had run out of material, gone dry. We used to tell each other the kinds of private stories I had never planned to tell anyone. We didn't know how to start up again; we didn't know what to say. The silence had descended upon us like a hex.

"God," she said, for filler, shaking her head.

I racked my brain, trying to think of something that didn't point to Lizzy. Later I came up with numerous topics we could have spent hours belaboring, but at our booth I was sure we had lost our bearings, that we had somehow forgotten crucial information about each other. We both went at our breakfasts as if we were actually hungry. When we were finished Theresa cleared her throat, and wiped her mouth carefully, and I blew my nose. She picked up a sugar packet and read it, and I motioned Sharon, the waitress, for more coffee. "Those girls sure are busy," Sharon said.

"Yes," I nearly shouted. "Aren't Claire and Audrey doing a good job?"

"Oh, they are," Theresa cried. "They really are! They are so good."

We turned to look at them over in their corner, sitting at the desks, scribbling in their books. Emma always used to play with Audrey; Claire was the one who had been Lizzy's friend. "I was really impressed by how well the older girls included Claire when they were at our house," she said. "Alice, oh Alice, was it awful in there, in the jail?"

We had come through. We had passed the doldrums, found wind for our sails. I shook my head first and then nodded. "I don't know." I laughed at my own confusion. "I read a lot. There's a poem, *'No worst, there is none. Pitched past pitch of grief, More pangs will, schooled at forepangs, wilder wring.'* The last line too especially spoke to me: *'All life death does end and each day dies with sleep.' "*

"That sounds good," Theresa said faintly. "I'll have to look it up."

"One of the funny things I finally figured out," I said, "was that the need for stories was so elemental—the jail girls could turn the smallest happening into something supernatural."

"Oh God, Alice," she groaned in her good old way.

"Any longer in there and one of us would have turned into a top-notch orator, a little Homer, a Homerette, reciting the long list of inmates as if they were ships going to battle." I put the warm coffee cup to my cheek. "I'm still pretty disoriented. I'm mixed up about the whole experience."

"Of course you are."

"Take Sherry," I said, "the one I told you about who was driving the get-away car. She was nineteen years old, had two or three children. At first I thought of all the girls as wayward kids, but by the end I realized that Sherry, in particular, had a dignity, a nobility, that I will never have, no matter if I live to be ninety. I don't even know how to talk about it without making that nobility sound like some ridiculous racist stereotype, the Noble Savage idea. I don't know how to talk about them. Maybe there isn't any way to talk about them. Even Dyshett, the other girl I wrote you about, tried to bridge what seemed to me an infinitely wide, an unfathomably deep gap. When I was in my do-gooder phase several years ago I used to think I might volunteer at a prison, tutor someone toward their high-school equivalency test, but now I don't see how I could teach those girls anything they don't already know."

"Can you imagine having to take them through something like the—

the Boston Tea Party?" she said, laughing. "All of that seems so irrelevant to street kids."

I started to tell her that that wasn't exactly what I meant.

"What they need is life skills, birth control, nutrition, that kind of thing," she interrupted.

"I-I-I don't know," I faltered. "I think Dyshett would have understood, 'No worst, there is none.'"

We ate some more. Everything had changed: I had been carted away, her daughter was still dead, we no longer lived close by, I might end up locked away for the next several years. I had been naïve to think a friendship could be maintained on a different plane from circumstance.

"I should visit them," I said, "but I'm not sure I could face it. I'm working up to sending them something, a care package."

"Give it time, Alice."

"I feel—"

"You don't have to ever visit them. You don't have any obligations to those people."

"Obligation," I said. "I don't understand the first thing about obligation. Howard's mother called the other night. 'Alice, dear,' she says so sweetly, 'how are you?' 'Fine,' I say. Bear in mind that I haven't talked to her in almost three months. Three tumultuous months. She says, 'Could I speak to Howard?' He's been in a sweat for weeks because he hasn't heard from her since he wrote her about the farm. We owe her so much money. The failure to pay your mother back is one of those primal failures. I listened while they talked and he kept saying things like, 'That's great, Mom. It sounds like you did a good job over there, Mom. We're fine, yep, the girls are terrific.' When he hung up he looked as if he'd been run over, back and forth; I was sure he'd pull up his shirt and there'd be these great tire marks going every which way." I used my arms to demonstrate the random course of the four-wheel drive that had flattened my husband.

She covered her mouth in that delicious familiar way of hers and laughed in spite of herself.

"Nellie is relieved that our 'farm adventure,'—that's what she calls it —she's relieved that our farm adventure is over, and that now Howard can get a real job. Isn't it fantastic how little she knows him? She knows nothing about him! Maybe I'm the only one who can really know that he'll never be as happy again as he was with his barn, his barn with the beautiful, clean, four-paned windows up in the dusty haymow, and down below the Golden Guernseys chewing away on their cuds."

Theresa turned her head and I went on quickly to spare her the embarrassment of her tears. She had always been one to cry easily, an ability I had at times envied. "But back to obligation," I said. "I would have thought that Howard was obligated to tell me that our children were being interviewed by the police. He mentioned it recently—as if it was nothing. He told me after dinner, 'Ah by the way . . .' I was incensed. I couldn't get him to say more than a few monosyllables about it. 'No big deal.' The girls could have been put into foster care! 'No sweat.' I asked him if he was trying to punish me, by not talking about it. He looked at me uncomprehendingly. 'It was short,' he said. 'The girls were fine. It lasted five minutes. It turned out to be nothing.' "

"I think he was wanting to keep you from worry," Theresa said.

"I suppose. But it feels like, well, like something on the order of betrayal."

We didn't talk too much longer after that. She said we should get together more often. I said I was pretty busy, with the trial coming up. I didn't have transportation either, so it was hard to plan for anything more than five blocks from home.

"I'm so busy too," she said. "It's just terrible." When she was buckling Audrey into her car seat she asked—maybe to prove that we actually did have more to talk about, that we hadn't exhausted our subject matter— "How is your place? Is it all right?"

"It's—incredible," I said.

"That's great."

We made the obligatory embrace and she leaped into the van, turned it on, and promptly backed into the dumpster. She smacked her palm to her forehead and laughed. I watched her go, wondering why she had called in the first place, if she needed to see me because she had been well brought up, because she felt it was the nice thing, the proper thing to do. We had survived the breakfast, and we had found, after the slow start, that there was enough to say. But standing on the curb, watching her fly off, I felt the oddness of it. The compulsory meeting had taken place. It had felt stylized, like a Kabuki version of a women's breakfast. There wouldn't, in the future, be much reason to see each other.

I bought tubes of paint with money from the change pot, and to Howard's horror, I painted flowers at waist level all around the living room. Perhaps the Pheasant Glade life was what I was secretly yearning for back in the old days when I used to get mad at Howard for dragging us into the dairy business. He didn't look like himself in his dark blue dress pants, his light blue shirt, his crimson and blue tie, and his dark blue jacket, the official uniform of the Motor Vehicle Registration Worker. Sometimes it seemed that he could hardly stand to ask me for the smallest thing, that it was difficult for him to get out the words, "Please pass the salt."

I bought Emma some clothes at the Goodwill store, and with Vaseline I polished up a pair of patent leather Mary Janes that I'd found at a rummage sale. She is a very particular child, and I was grateful to her, another for our list, for not turning up her nose at most of the things I put in her closet. She had grown up over the summer, grown up and gone into her own world. She spent a lot of time lying on her bed, listening to books on tape from the library. She couldn't yet read herself, but she listened to *Heidi, The Little Princess,* and *Charlie and the Chocolate Factory,* over and over again. She didn't want me to read to her anymore. In the evening I'd lie on the floor or on the bed and listen with her. Sometimes I'd fall asleep and stay there all through the night. When I was small, I used to listen to my tape in the dark, to my dead mother reading *Little House in the Big Woods.* I used to try to believe that she was sleeping right beside me.

Chapter Twenty

————

THE LEAVES IN THE park turned color and fell and we walked through them, scooped them up, pressed them flat in the dictionary. Emma found a kitten and I agreed to take her in, which overnight changed the smell of our unit. We had long since forgotten what it was to have a weekend and we were taken by surprise by the sheer fact of Friday, by the prospect of liberation. Even Howard's heart finally temporarily eased at five o'clock every Friday evening, at the thought of two blank days. We had the habit of getting take out fish fry from the bar down the street. Howard usually managed to jam a log in the fireplace and we'd sit on the hearth with our dinners on our laps watching the flames. Over the course of the fall we went to Old World Wisconsin and watched women make butter and spin wool. We went to the science museum, the art museum, the lake front, the movies, the botanical gardens, the children's museum, the state capitol, the train museum, the circus, and the wax museum. Howard was a working man and I spent his money without thought of tomorrow. What we were experiencing, I believe, is called Motion. I watched us in the reflection of the store windows in downtown Milwaukee, Howard pushing Claire in a stroller, Emma and I, hand in hand. We looked fine. We looked like perfectly regular people who were having a weekend. At the end of the day, we always came home exhausted, hungry, the four of us snapping at each other. I warmed up the brand-name supper the girls insisted upon: Kraft macaroni and cheese, and hot dogs to go along with it. They ate noisily with their faces right down in their bowls. Howard read the paper over his peanut butter and jelly and carrot sticks. Because of his job we not only had major medical insurance, but we also had dental insurance and ocular insurance. We had never before been so secure, so prepared for failure.

The trial was set for December second. At the end of October the three boys, Anthony Jenkins, Norman Frazer, and Tommy Giddings, dropped their charges. The whole story was like a carefully wrought pile of sticks, and it was Norman who began pulling out the supports at the bottom. He made half the structure cave in. He apparently started naming everyone at school, saying that the gym teacher had put a gun to his head, the art teacher made them drink paint, the classroom teachers put aside numbers and letters in favor of what sounded like Satanic rituals. When the investigators tried to pull him back to the original perpetrator, he remembered nothing that he had said before. Anthony Jenkins had also been giving inconsistent statements, and it was determined that his story would not hold up in court. The Giddingses decided that it was going to be more damaging to Tommy to have to testify than the already substantial harm that had come to him, and they reluctantly withdrew the charge. The older children who had been assessed were said to have grievances which would have required disciplinary measures by the school, and termination of my contract, if they'd come to light while I was still an employee. They were not serious enough to warrant criminal charges. My case then, was a small one, contained after all. It had been front-page news for a few weeks at the beginning, and later was occasionally found near the back of the paper, a short paragraph about the trial again being postponed.

If I had a meeting with Rafferty, I'd take Howard to work and in the same shopping center I'd drop Claire off at Happy Haven, a day care that had previously been a Fashion Bug store. Claire didn't mind the atmosphere of commerce, the fluorescent lights, the shiny linoleum. She had a friend named Brianna and she loved the applesauce that was white and came from a jar. She was the family member who had been serene before and had remained so, who seemed to have come through unscathed. I waited, watching for signs of disturbance, for sleeping or toileting problems. I wondered if there was something wrong with her, to have been untouched by our troubles.

It seemed strange at first, to walk, on my own power, to Rafferty & Finn, to climb the stairs to what had once been a bedroom, and sit with Paul in his mess. He was good about explaining what he meant to do in the trial. "Think of it this way," he said. "The prosecutor's case is a dot-to-dot puzzle. If she connects all the dots she has a beautiful picture of a guilty defendant and she gets her conviction. My job is to mix up the dots so that no clear picture emerges, so that there is a jumble. My job," he said, making mock diabolical hand-washing motions, "is to sow seeds of doubt." We sat on the sofa and he scrawled on his paper, showing me some of the things he expected to get out of the witnesses in his cross-examinations. Under Robbie's name he wrote, "Provoke him, by my mere presence, to be disrespectful and rude. Show the jury he's a temperamental, unreliable, violent kid. Ideally, get him to admit he's seen Mom in compromising situations."

"Are you sure?" I asked.

"We have Mrs. Sheridan. Wait until you see her. You are going to love Mrs. Sheridan. If Judge Peterson denies me Mrs. Sheridan I'm going to lie down on the carpet and bang my head. I'm going to file appeals until we get Mrs. Sheridan. Mrs. Sheridan is going to be our star witness, with higher billing than even you. I'll never forget that day I knocked on her door and she looked up at me with her runny eyes as if I was the Angel of the Lord."

I said, "I think you're having fun." The Paul Rafferty I had known when I was in jail, the fatherly, concerned man who would restore my life, occasionally let down his guard in the privacy of his boudoir, to reveal a slightly effeminate character, an eccentric who was in no way embarrassed by the pleasure his job afforded him, who was concerned, but not preoccupied, with the players' pain and suffering.

"Of course I'm having fun. I wouldn't be any good if I didn't have fun, you know, the kind of fun a person has on Outward Bound, killing yourself so that afterward you feel great. That's what we're talking about here, the kind of travail that brings reward. However, a work such as

Mrs. Sheridan is more than fun: It's downright exhilarating, like hauling in the prize fish. You don't get a witness like Mrs. Sheridan hand delivered more than once in a lifetime." He adjusted his tie, put his hand on my shoulder, affected his sober Father expression. "I'm not having fun at your expense, Alice. Is that how it seems? You can be sure I'm enjoying the prospect of getting the real story out. Susan Dirks is going to be doing a lot more homework on the next sex-abuse case she takes, and so are the investigators, I can tell you that much. We're shedding light into dark corners, into places most people don't go. I am always respectful of serendipity in my cases, and if I am having fun it is only in isolated moments, getting my kicks where I can. I've had my share of disappointments in this case—you know the score. I've had a hell of a time getting a hold of the boyfriends and the one we needed, the primo beau, doesn't want to cooperate. So, we do the best we can. You have to realize that it is the judge who will shape the outcome of this, depending on how he sees it. I could be brilliant. Susan Dirks could be the genius prosecutor of the century. If Peterson isn't on our side it doesn't really matter how good we are."

He told me that often in cases like mine his hardest decision was whether or not to have the accused testify. "There's no doubt here," he said. "We'll put you on last. We'll leave the jury with your honest, forthright, and indignant denial."

I had several sessions with Rafferty in which we rehearsed his direct examination, and then a friend of his, a lawyer named Ross Gryle, cross-examined me, firing dirty, abusive questions, one after the next. Rafferty had filed a motion asking the judge to prohibit any cross-examination on the subject of Lizzy's death, because it was not relevant to the case. The accident would serve, he said, only to inflame the passions of the jurors. Judge Peterson had written a stern letter to both Rafferty and Susan Dirks, granting the motion, and instructing both of them to keep their witnesses from including Elizabeth Collins in the testimony.

When I answered Ross Gryle's questions, Rafferty would say things like "Yes, Yes! Beautiful!" and "Deliver it with more punch, Alice," or "You have talent, my dear!" Once he said, "You look like Audrey Hepburn in that movie where she plays the blind girl. You know the one I mean? *Wait Until Dark*. Helpless, so pure and unsuspecting. The audience knows the killer is in the room and she is saying so sweetly, 'Is anyone there?' "

When I thought I might lash out at him, or cry; when I protested that I did in fact feel that I was on location, Rafferty said, grand in his humility, "I'm sorry. I'm terribly sorry. I'm getting carried away because I know you, because you're my friend, because we share certain sympathies. I'm very sorry. You have to understand that this is where it comes together. We're getting down to the last few pieces of the puzzle. It's intense, I know. You'll do fine. You're doing just great. You're wonderful. Say, Ross, do you remember the time you tried that guy for rape, and the girlfriend had the monkey, no, it was a parrot, wasn't it?"

I'd leave them to remember their early glory days. Sometimes I'd walk over near the jail and I'd look up to the fourth floor, wondering if they were all still there. I'd go so far as to slip inside the courthouse and study the trial lineups, the arraignments, the motions, the hearings, to see if any of them were on the schedules. Afterward I always made myself go outside and sit on the steps. I had a ritual: I had to stay put for so many minutes and think of them, think of what TV shows were on, how many card games they'd been through. I had to put my time in, sitting, as if it was church. It was silly, I knew, to think I was doing them good by having a moment of silence in their honor. When I'd done my small penance I turned around and drove away from the city. I picked up Claire, and if there was time we went in the Motor Vehicle Registration Office, to watch Howard guide illiterate customers and old ladies through the paperwork of title transfers.

For the first time in their lives the girls had an old-fashioned Halloween. They got to walk through the town streets in their disguises, trick or treating. They opened their bags and strangers dumped candy in, telling them they looked precious in their St. Vincent de Paul kitty costumes. No one ever used to come to the farm for either pranks or sweets, and we had managed to keep Emma and Claire in the dark about the treat aspect of the holiday. In Spring Grove you could take the candy to the hospital to have it X rayed, but we chose instead to rely on blind faith. When we got home the girls poured their stash onto the floor, drew a circle on the carpet beyond which no others could come, and began to eat and trade and eat. Howard and I did not have the heart to stop them, and they neither turned green nor got sick. They seemed healthy, peaceful, happy, drowning in sugar.

Nearly a month later we solved the dilemma of what to do for Thanksgiving by all of us, one by one, coming down with the stomach flu. Nellie had invited us to Minnesota for the long weekend. I don't think she really understood that I was going to be standing trial days later for something that could put me away for years. I don't know that Howard had ever fully explained the fact that I wasn't allowed to leave the state.

"Could you tell her we need family time right now?" I asked him. "Could you say it's been a confusing season and we need to have a day alone?"

"Would it be possible for you to come to us?" I heard Howard say to her on the next call. "We've got the sofa bed in the living room." That alternative was not what I had had in mind. They phoned back and forth and she finally settled on driving to Spring Grove early Thursday morning, bringing her homemade cranberry sauce, and making stuffing when she arrived. Emma got sick on Monday, Claire went down on Tuesday night. It was only a matter of time before Howard and I capitulated. He was stricken on Wednesday and I held out all the way to Thanksgiving morning. "It's your fault," Emma said to me as I squatted by the toilet. "It's your fault that Grammie can't come for dinner."

When I came downstairs midafternoon the girls were on the floor putting together a puzzle that Theresa had sent them, and Howard was sitting on the sofa staring out the window. There were a few saltines in a package on the kitchen counter, a six-pack of Seven-Up, and in the refrigerator the thawing turkey and the makings for coleslaw. I shut the door quickly, plunging the big, dimpled bird back into darkness.

As the trial got closer, Rafferty predicted that it wouldn't last more than a week, two at the outside. When I sat through the jury selection and then the trial itself, I tried to hear a melody, to find a sense of music in that mournful room. The story was so old I was quite sure there had to be music running along somewhere, through the benches, up through the heating ducts, out of the worn woodwork. I once tried to explain my feeling to Rafferty; I tried to say that despite all of his careful tactical maneuvering, in spite of his knowledge of the rules, the new rules, the newest rules, there had to be something lyrical in the game, had to be something on the order of music.

"I don't quite follow," he said, looking mystified. "Music?"

My head was hurting quite a bit back then and I could only put my hands to my crown and wonder if something had in fact come loose.

"No, I like that," he said after a minute. "I'll have to listen. I like that. Music."

The day of the trial I closed my eyes at the sight of the jurors filing in. There was already a feeling of weariness in the courtroom, and if, as I had hoped, there was music to be heard, it was the slow occasional twang of a music box winding down. Rafferty had said that there were conflicting strategies for choosing jurors for child-abuse cases. Some lawyers believed that women were more sympathetic to children; some believed, as he did, that senior citizens didn't generally believe that adults were capable of abusing children, that a child's testimony often seemed preposterous to them. Rafferty also thought that men were more tolerant of abusers. Although I had sat in a pretty dress watching the interminable selection process the day before, it was quite different to have to watch them move in together. They seemed connected, something on the order of a centipede in the school play, minus the blanket thrown over them. At first glance, they all seemed to be aged, overweight, stone-faced. They wanted to be in their beds, in front of their televisions, crocheting, fishing, anything but this at the end of their lives. They slumped down miserably in their chairs as if they thought they were going to have to do something unpleasant in a few moments, something that required exertion. When the testimony began I was able to observe them, sneaking looks periodically, and they soon came to be individuals, to have definite personalities. But as they settled themselves that Tuesday morning I found myself turning to Rafferty, grabbing his forearm.

"What?" He cocked his head so he could hear my complaint.

"They don't look equal to the job," I whispered.

"You'd be surprised what people can do," he said. "Eight times out of ten they rise to the occasion." I swallowed, believing.

Judge Peterson sat up at his desk reading and biting his nails. He had the thick, dark hair of a youngster, but his face was deeply lined. He looked as if he'd grown old prematurely, as if he'd prefer not to hear another cross word, as if his job no longer taxed him, but instead, only irritated him. My future was in his crabbed hands and I tried to look as if I trusted in goodness, the way Theresa would have if she'd been in my position. Howard was taking unpaid personal days to sit behind me in his handsome suit. That suit, which had proved so useful, was another thing for which I was grateful. Nellie had been right: It was important to have one garment you could count on for certain occasions.

I had dressed according to Rafferty's specifications. I had taken the last hundred and sixty dollars in my checking account and at the Laura Ashley store in the mall I had purchased, on sale, a light pink angora mock turtle sweater and a Viyella skirt with small pink and blue flowers. My hair had grown out to a point where it could have looked corporate chic, but Rafferty didn't approve that style for me. "As vulnerable, as feminine, as soft as you can get that butch cut to look," he said. I combed what there was back from my face and secured it with a pink velvet headband.

I had thought there might be a crowd at the proceedings, but when we came into the courtroom there were only a handful of Blackwell women. Rafferty reminded me that Christmas was coming and that people were busy.

"They've gone on to consume other things," I said.

"Yes, that's about the size of it."

Although Howard insisted that the case was over the second day of testimony, that Susan Dirks's primary witnesses cut their own throats, I knew he was only trying to be helpful, that there was not sound basis for relief. What I had been worrying over in particular was the fact that earlier in the summer Rafferty had lost his motion to suppress the admission I'd made to the investigators. He had argued that I should have been read my rights that night of the school-board meeting, that I was actually a suspect, that I was being interrogated rather than questioned. Mrs. Dirks maintained that I had been free to leave, as in fact I did, that I had not been forcibly detained, and that therefore there had been no legal requirement to read me my rights. When Mrs. Dirks, in her impassioned opening statement at the trial, made reference to my confession, Rafferty objected with his finger, the way a seasoned bidder makes himself known at an auction. "Objection, your honor. Will the word 'confession' please be struck from the record?"

In her mauve linen jacket and white wool skirt, black high heels, and a smoky gray silk shirt, she was far more beguiling than Rafferty could ever hope to be, even if he replaced his cheap plaid suit coat with something more fashionable. At the very start she advised the jurors that where there is sexual abuse there is often no physical evidence. "When we are listening to a child testify," she instructed, "we must listen very carefully. It is not necessary to believe everything a child says. We must take into consideration the details, but in abuse cases we must also listen for the emotional truth in the child's telling."

Rafferty objected, and the judge slowly rubbed his mouth from side to side before he declared that Mrs. Dirks should continue. When it was his turn to speak, Rafferty explained to the jury that Mrs. Dirks had as good as advised them to forget certain democratic values, values such as the critical importance of the evidence in a criminal trial. He asked them if they could suspend their belief in the Constitution. He said that historically we were a society that seemed to go through a self-cleansing exercise every fifty years, and that the jurors were witnessing just such an exercise, that similar cases were going on all over the United States. Dirks objected, and the judge informed Rafferty that he was out of line, using closing-argument material.

It was all such a far cry from my office at Blackwell Elementary, so far from the day I slapped Robbie and he stared back at me, seemingly unaffected. "Mrs. Dirks told you," Rafferty said, "that my client made an admission, but what she hasn't told you is the circumstance and the context. Fortunately I am here to tell you more about my client's statements, to draw a complete picture. Thank goodness I will be able to give you the all-important context, ladies and gentleman, the context."

I took in the jury with sidelong glances. There was a pair that intrigued me: one, a stout woman with jowls and a mouth that had petrified into a scowl, and the other, a gray-green, tall, thin lady with penciled eyebrows, arched in perpetual wonder. Both of them had identical blond beehives, nominal hair teased up into the magnificent fluff of what looked like cotton candy. They sat next to each other, the one surly, the other astonished, thinking—what? I longed to be ridiculous, to sing to them, "Beau—ootful Soo—op! Beau—ootful Soo—op! Soo—oop of the e-e-evening, Beautiful, beautiful Soup!" Next to them sat a young man who stocked dairy products in a grocery store, perhaps a soulmate of ours, in love with yogurt, cheese, butter, cream, eggnog. There was an aging hippie with white hair flowing down his back, the face of a Greek god, and eyes that looked from a distance as if they were golden. He climbed telephone poles for a living, and I imagined him with a houseful of colored-glass insulators, his wife in despair at the collection that was growing beyond their storage capacity.

Robbie was the first to take the stand. Again, he sat on his mother's lap. He'd lost a front tooth so that in some ways he looked more childlike than he had before. I wondered how he'd spent the last several months, how it felt going to first grade as the little boy who'd nearly been done in by the school nurse. His mother was exquisitely sad, her luster slightly faded, though nothing that couldn't be polished up at a moment's notice, brought back to its former gloss and shine. It was my fate being decided, and yet the words of the hallowed court fell away as I watched the darling gestures mother made, the tilt of her head, her little caresses, the smallest kiss at his ear after they were excused. She herself seemed to me like some golden, steaming, delectable, irresistible potion that is held out, that one is urged to Drink, Drink! And only when the liquid has irretrievably slipped down the throat does one know what one has drunk. I couldn't help thinking of her in immoderate terms. Rafferty's protestations did not in any way move the judge to order Mrs. Mackessy down from the witness box.

Robbie had grown up enough so that he no longer required the doll to demonstrate my torture. His long, serious face and the baby language he used for his private parts did not match. The words were those that Miss Flint had perhaps suggested. Against his glimmering mother he was nearly invisible. But what I saw was a tired boy, someone who looked as if he didn't want to play anymore. He was going through the motions but it was as if he could hardly muster the energy to do much damage. When Mrs. Dirks requested a recess until the following morning, due to the witness's apparent fatigue, the judge, to our amazement, rumbled that we were all tired, that we'd all been waiting, that the thing had been postponed twice, and that we had to move along. He granted her thirty minutes for rest.

Out at the far end of the hall, during the break, Rafferty hugged his appointment book and simpered, "He likes me! Judge Peterson really likes me!"

Howard was standing by the water cooler and when he heard Rafferty he turned and gave him a withering look, the sort that makes a person feel that it might have been better not to be born. I hadn't realized before just how very capable Howard was of conveying disdain. "The judge is on our side this time," Rafferty said, taking fast sips of hot coffee, oblivious to my husband's disgust. "He's going to let it go wide open for us, that's my sense."

Robbie more than fulfilled Rafferty's hopes during the cross-examination. Rafferty stood with his arms bent, his hands clasped at his chest. He asked Robbie ever so gently the most probing, and occasionally indelicate questions. More than once he said, with a lush softness, "You didn't say that at the preliminary hearing, Rob." Rafferty only grew more kind as the boy glowered and shouted. My first-rate criminal lawyer displayed the paternal care that had drawn me to him in the first place. For an hour he questioned the boy, repeatedly asking him about the material of his pants, who unbuttoned them, did he have a belt, was there a snap at the waist, and a zipper. Robbie became so irritated part way through that the judge ordered another short break.

Close to the end of the questioning Rafferty said, "Did you have a neighbor when you lived on 372 Main Street, Robbie, in your old house, a kid by the name of Jack Sheridan?"

Robbie said, "So?"

"Jack was a little bit older than you, wasn't he?"

"I don't know."

"Mrs. Sheridan didn't baby-sit you, I know that, but she looked out for you, didn't she?"

He shrugged.

"She came to your house once, on May twenty-third, last spring, just before school was out. Do you remember that night?"

Anyone who had watched Robbie before would have known that he was thinking. He didn't move or blink. It was impossible to say if he was wondering how to respond, or if the question had carried him back in time.

"Mrs. Sheridan came to your door. She asked if Jack was at your house. You wanted her to come in, to see something. You had something to show her."

Mrs. Mackessy shrank into her chair; it was as if she faded away, as if her lights went out. Her boy came into focus: the dark circles under his eyes, his unnerving stare, his unhealthy complexion, his skin pale and taut as the hide over a drum. There, the jury must see, was a sick boy. The blond beehive of the taller juror was bobbing with her touch of Parkinson's, and she had such wide, wondering eyes she seemed to be willing herself to stay awake. Mrs. Dirks was objecting loudly and asking for an offer of proof. The two lawyers and Judge Peterson trooped into the inner sanctum. After several minutes they returned, and Rafferty continued his line of questioning.

"Mrs. Sheridan came to your house on May twenty-third, Robbie, and you told her you had something to show her. Is that something that you remember?"

He didn't answer, which Rafferty noted to the court reporter.

"Is that something that you don't want to talk about?"

Still no answer.

"It was just getting dark that night, and you said she had to come look in the den. Do you remember that, pal?"

Rafferty quietly asked that it be entered into the record that the witness sat expressionless and refused to respond.

Later he asked, "Wasn't Mrs. Goodwin's job, her main job, to give you medicine when you were sick?"

"No."

"Did Mrs. Goodwin ever give you medicine when you visited her in your office?"

"No."

"You never got Suprax, that yellow medicine which comes from a bottle and tastes like strawberry syrup? You never got that medicine from Mrs. Goodwin?"

"I said no."

"Were you scared when you showed Mrs. Sheridan in the den?"

There was no music in the courtroom after all, nothing but dull questions, shouts from Mrs. Dirks, the tired judge paving the way for justice. The one time I looked at Susan Dirks she had her entire bottom lip drawn into her mouth and she looked to be biting down fairly hard. Her pen was between her second and third finger and she was beating it on her notepad.

"Did Mrs. Goodwin give you your medicine with a spoon?"

"Yeah."

"She gave you that yellow stuff, Suprax, with a spoon?"

"Yeah."

"So sometimes you went to her office and she gave you your medicine?"

"Stop asking me that," Robbie cried. "You're so boring! You hurt me when you're that boring."

"I'm hurting you?"

"I SAID, 'YOU'RE HURTING ME.'"

There was a hush over the room. "No further questions, your honor," Rafferty said, after a decent interval.

Over the noon hour Howard and I sat by the lake in the cold and I wondered out loud what the jurors were eating, and were they bonding over their boxed lunches, and had the leader already emerged? I tried to flesh out the few I'd taken an interest in, tried to imagine their home life, but Howard wasn't listening. If I said much more, he would ask me how I could be detached at a time like this. And I'd have to say that if I thought about the trial too hard I'd be so nervous I'd have to consider drastic alternatives. I'd be seriously tempted to flee. There was among the jurors a woman with graying curly hair and half-glasses, who always seemed to be paying attention, who looked intelligent. Perhaps she would be the one to guide the group to an informed decision. Howard and I had ham-and-cheese sandwiches, which we ate in the bitter wind. We passed the Thermos back and forth, clutching the cylinder for the last warmth of the coffee. We were out of sync with our surroundings, having the kind of picnic people have when they are in love, when it's worth braving the cold, when you're so happy you don't notice the stale bread or the temperature of the drink. I stopped talking and we ate, watching the gulls.

Mrs. Dirks called the child protection worker that first afternoon. Myra Flint was a broad woman with a turned-up nose, nothing like Mrs. Mackessy to feast our eyes upon. She clumped to the witness box in blue clogs, the noise of which somehow penetrated the carpet. A good deal of her testimony was about interviewing techniques she had used to elicit Robbie's confession. The technical nature of the questions may have disappointed those few observers who had hoped for the lurid stuff of TV dramas, but I found that I could fasten on her, that for the most part I could follow the concrete and suffocatingly tedious and repetitive questions and answers. The judge had to reprimand one of the jurors, an older man, because he was snoring.

"Children's memories," Myra Flint explained, "can become locked inside their minds. One possible key to unlocking those memories is to ask very specific questions, or even leading questions. In the legal context, of course, we are not allowed to do so. Consequently, one set of techniques I use provides children with retrieval strategies and cues, while at the same time steering clear of leading questions. The cognitive interview is a technique I use on older children, but with some modifications it is also useful on someone Robbie's age.

"Context reinstatement," Myra droned on, "is another technique I use, when appropriate, for improving children's recall. Taking a child back to the scene of an event helps to reinstate, if you will, the child's memory."

"So you helped him, didn't you?" Rafferty asked at the start of a series of questions. "Spent quite a lot of time with him? In fact, this is how you make your living, in part, helping children to recall?"

"It can be a long process, Mr. Rafferty, helping children through the trauma of abuse."

"It takes many sessions to enhance their memories?"

"That is not what I said."

"In fact, isn't it fair to say that oftentimes it is your work that allows someone like Robbie to recall enough to allow him to testify at all?" He was always hinting at, but never asking the question: Without your work, Ms. Flint, Robbie is like a ventriloquist's dummy? "Isn't it right that without your skill in memory enhancement children would not be able to come up with the specifics necessary for believable testimony?"

The accusations had been shocking in the beginning, but they had lost their sting the second time around. The details seemed flat, without meaning. I tried again to think what the trial was actually about. I had thought that it was about hate, pure, undiluted hatred: hate for the joyous sake of hatred—but I wasn't sure anymore. It was peculiar, that I couldn't very well remember how Robbie used to affect me. We are told when we are growing up that Hate is a strong word, that we should save it for the despicable things in life. In quantifying my feelings for Robbie I had to strain to remember back all those months, to gauge the intensity of my anger as he came scraping along the hall. He'd stand at the door, staring me down. He always looked as if he knew full well that he had far more knowledge than was appropriate, or good for him. I used to try to keep in mind that I hated what had made him foul-mouthed and cold-hearted. But I remember the sinking feeling I had when he appeared in the doorway of my office, the feeling that there wasn't anything beyond him in the moment to hate. Now those violent sensations were no longer with me. He had made me feel small and empty. In a way it was an immense relief, to know that a boiling rage could leave one, that emotions were temporary, that they could chase away, like rats scurrying down the gangplank, evacuating the ship.

Myra was an able and committed therapist who clearly cared about the children she treated. She was convinced from Robbie's acute symptoms of post-traumatic stress syndrome, from his reporting to his mother and to herself, that he had been sexually abused by the school nurse. In the cross-examination she did not let Rafferty rattle her. She never became belligerent or wary or defensive, although the temptation must have been considerable. When Rafferty asked, "Isn't it true that all children lie at times?" she said, "Yes, of course! Adults do too. Children, however, generally lie to get out of trouble rather than into trouble."

"Isn't it true that Robbie is a known liar, Miss Flint?"

"I am well aware that he has had problems at school. It is all the more important that Robbie be assessed by experienced clinicians who are trained to tease out truths from falsehoods."

"Isn't it possible for lies to become set in concrete as a child repeats them, so that a child believes the lie to be true?"

"Yes, indeed. For children and adults." She went on to discuss how the clinical data in Robbie's case included his spontaneity, his sexual knowledge, and the fact that he did not retell his stories in a rigid manner, which would have suggested rote memory.

"Would you say that young children have active fantasy lives, Miss Flint?"

"Yes, often."

"Isn't it possible that this accusation of sexual abuse is nothing more than wishful thinking or a fantasy based on a sexual scene from television, or parental behavior?"

"I would say, Mr. Rafferty, that that is an unlikely interpretation. Fantasies tend to be oriented toward positive experiences. Very few children or adults daydream about being assaulted. Fantasy is directed toward solving problems—not creating them, which is certainly what happens when an allegation is made."

"What, Miss Flint, do actuarial studies prove about the frequency of sexual fantasies and abuse in young children?"

"I haven't recently read up on actuarial studies on that subject, Mr. Rafferty. I'd be happy to go over the evaluation of Robbie specifically and tell you again what I discovered about his fantasies and how they fit with the overall clinical picture."

She was not behaving the way Rafferty would have liked. Although she was not charming or attractive, she was never evasive or defensive. Her sensible skirt and sweater, her short easy-to-care-for hair, her sturdy frame—everything about her, except her clogs, suggested sound judgment.

He later tried to trip her up when he questioned her about anatomically detailed dolls. "Isn't it true that many different anatomically detailed dolls are manufactured?"

"Yes, it is," she said.

"Isn't it also fair to say that the anatomical detail in the doll, the design and sexual nature, differs markedly from one manufacturer to another?"

"Yes."

"Are there published and accepted standardized procedures for using anatomically detailed dolls?"

"None exist that I know of," she answered. "And it's just for that reason—that standardized procedures are not available—that interviews using anatomically detailed dolls call for experienced clinicians, who know how to be objective and who over the years have developed practical norms."

"Isn't it true," Rafferty persisted, "that the Board of the American Psychological Association has determined that these dolls cannot be considered standardized assessment tools?"

She pushed her hair behind her ears with both hands before she began to answer. "There are indeed experts who have criticized the dolls as inaccurate tools that lead to false conclusions of child sexual abuse. However, the statement written last year by the American Psychological Association's Committee on Children, Youth, and Families, judged that doll-centered assessments may be the best practical solutions in the hands of competent psychologists and social workers."

"How many articles have you written for professional or scientific journals?"

"None."

"Not even one, in any journal, anywhere?"

"That's right. While some of my co-workers spend their careers writing for publications, my focus has been on helping and evaluating people."

"You are not a medical doctor, is that correct?"

"As I told the court, I have a masters in social work."

"Have you had graduate-level courses in memory and perception?"

"I've not had formal courses on those subjects, Mr. Rafferty, but every social worker is required to take psychology courses, classes which stress the fundamental role those factors play in people's lives."

"Have you ever misdiagnosed a client, Miss Flint?"

"A medical doctor can look at an X ray and be sure that the diagnosis is a broken arm. Evaluating people for emotional trauma does not always produce a neat diagnosis."

"I understand that. Have you ever had a client, a child, who you thought had been sexually abused and then later recanted?"

"Yes, I have, Mr. Rafferty."

"Some of your colleagues believed that you had so aggressively questioned the girl she confessed the abuse in order to placate you."

"Objection," Susan Dirks called.

"Could you give us a profile," Rafferty later asked, "of a character-disturbed or unattached child that a social worker such as yourself would find in the *Diagnostic and Statistical Manual of Mental Disorders* and in the book called, *High Risk, Children Without a Conscience?*"

"I'm not familiar with that second publication. I don't know the comprehensive list by heart, Mr. Rafferty, but some of the symptoms an unattached child might exhibit are self-destructive behaviors, ah, the inability to give and receive affection, various types of learning disorders."

"Isn't also included in that list a particular pathological type of lying —'primary process lying,' I believe it is called."

"Possibly."

"As well as abnormalities in eye contact, cruelty to others, a lack of long-term friends?"

"I haven't recently studied the list in depth."

"To refresh your memory, manipulative behaviors, phoniness, superficial attractiveness, and friendliness with strangers, are also included as symptoms."

"Again, I haven't studied the list lately."

"Would you like to review it?"

She looked over the sheet he handed to her.

"Did it cross your mind, as you examined Robbie, that he had some of those characteristics I just mentioned, that he was manipulating you and his mother?"

"No, it did not, Mr. Rafferty."

"Did it ever occur to you that he might have the profile of the character-disturbed child."

"Most definitely not."

"Did you interview Robbie's mother?"

"No."

"Did you not think it might be important to interview the child's primary caretaker?"

"In a case where a child reveals abuse the child is our focus."

"Keep your chin up," Rafferty said during the break. "We're doing great." He was whacking his letter opener against his pant leg. "Heard anything from the girls over in the jail?" He was someone who didn't often make small talk or show signs of nervousness. Perhaps Myra Flint had not been as pliant as he'd hoped. I reached over and touched his hand, to still him. "Keep your chin up, Paul," I said.

Howard and I drove home without saying too much the first afternoon of the trial. When we parked the car outside of the day-care center Howard lingered in the driver's seat, absently knocking the key chain against the steering wheel. I put my head back, knowing he would say something worth hearing. "I wish," he began.

I waited for him to develop the thought and when, after a few minutes, I could no longer hold out, I said, "What? What do you wish?"

"Why couldn't he have been the one to drown? He might as well have. He might be better off if he'd died."

"Robbie, you mean."

"Why have we let this go on? The questioning was the devil's version of Simon Says. Rafferty baited Robbie and then trapped him. There must have been something we could have done to keep that poor kid from getting slaughtered."

"I know," I said. "I've felt that all along, that he is the one who will suffer more than anyone, more in a way, than we have. I still have music and words, our children—"

"Rafferty is—I've never met someone before who made me sick, who made me think I was going to vomit."

"I have to get Claire," I said, "or they'll charge us for the next hour."

"You never listen to me," he muttered. "Did you know that?"

"Howard," I said, "I am listening. I just don't know what else to say. Robbie didn't drown, Lizzy did. If not Rafferty, who? Maybe I should have copped a plea and served a sentence, and then we wouldn't have had a trial. But that didn't seem the right thing to do, not for me, and not for us, in the long run. I could say I'm sorry for the rest of my life, every day, every minute for the rest of my life and it still wouldn't exhaust all the sorriness I have inside me. I'm sorry for Lizzy most of all. I'm sorry for Robbie, I'm sorry for Theresa, I'm especially sorry on your account, and for Emma, and Claire. I'm sorry specifically, and I'm just plain sorry. I'm sorry Rafferty makes you sick. Maybe, just maybe, he'll get me off, and then we can somehow try to begin all over, or back in the middle, or go forward from this ending place."

He stayed in the car, clicking his key chain against the steering wheel while I went for Claire. We drove back to Spring Grove, picked up Emma at the school after-care program, went to the A&W, had the salad bar and bacon burgers, which even Emma had grown tired of, and finally made our way home. Many of the Pheasant Glade units had not been sold and the few that had been set aside for rentals had not been snatched up either. The two blocks of apartments had the feel of a ghost town, particularly at night. By the time we left it, it had begun to fill up, but we often felt, coming home, that we were driving into a place where nobody else wanted to be. All those nights during the trial we'd eat out or scratch up a supper, put the girls in the whirlpool tub, tuck them into bed, and then, because there didn't seem to be anything we could talk about, nothing to say until we knew one way or the other, I'd rearrange the cupboards or play solitaire until I figured Howard was upstairs fast asleep.

On the third day of testimony for the prosecution, David Henskin, the principal at Blackwell Elementary, and Robbie's teacher, Mrs. Ritter, both took the stand. It seemed a ridiculous exercise, both of them saying that I was sullen, that I was somehow sinister, Rafferty protesting at every turn, valiantly trying to keep character assassination out of the evidence. I was wearing an old quilt jacket I'd made years ago and a green corduroy skirt, which Rafferty had the nerve to pronounce bookish and eccentric. "Don't wear it again, all right?" he ordered. Mrs. Ritter said that she realized now, with hindsight, that Robbie was always disturbed after he'd been to see me, that his artwork was violent, that his behavior was problematic only in relation to his visits to me. As an aside she mentioned that she frequently saw me out in the hall doing some kind of strange dance. She had always had such faith in the staff at Blackwell Elementary, she said, and she had never thought to suspect any of the employees.

Rafferty did not bother to cross-examine her because he thought her worthless. He explained that the jury would think so too, when they saw that he would not dignify her by asking a single question. He had had a floor plan of the school blown up to fit an easel so that the office spaces were visible. With his pointer he took Mr. Henskin through the various hallways and offices asking as he went: Did Henskin often leave his own door open to encourage students and teachers to seek him out? Did the secretary leave her door open? He rarely had to use the intercom, she was so close? His schedule was varied and unpredictable, wasn't it? Did he have to leave his office to solve a problem in another part of the school? Several times a day? And when he so frequently left his office he walked right past, or even through the nurse's office?

Rafferty had told me that the jurors would ask themselves how in the hell the abuse had taken place with Henskin in and out a dozen times a day. After Paul had gotten his point across, he said, "There has been a great deal of publicity about sexual abuse in the last decade. Have you ever been concerned, yourself, about being accused of sexual molestation?"

"It's something that crosses your mind, as an educator. I think anyone who works in this climate with children is aware of what care must be taken."

"What climate are you speaking of?"

"People are sensitive to the issue of child abuse."

"It is a climate where anyone on your staff could be charged with abuse?"

"We have an excellent staff at our school, overall."

"I agree your staff has always been excellent, but my question to you, sir, is given the climate, as you say, a sex-abuse charge is a real fact of life for any of the district's employees and yourself included."

"Any person who works with children has to be exemplary."

"Because of the hysterical climate—"

"Objection," Susan Dirks shouted.

Rafferty rephrased the question. "Would you say, Mr. Henskin, that an employee at your school has to be beyond reproach, because there is a heightened awareness about sexual abuse?"

"Yes, I'd say so."

"And a fear about sexual abuse?"

"There is new, general knowledge that child abuse is pervasive in our culture."

"Would you say that many parents are afraid for their children?"

"I couldn't say specifically, but I suppose that's true."

I scanned the jury, trying to see if they were getting the idea, that they, too, could be accused. The Greek God had been wearing Hawaiian shirts all week, in spite of the fact that it was December. I dressed in particular for him every morning, wondering if he would think better of me if I was wearing the pink sweater or the blue cotton shirt. In addition to the blond beehive ladies there were two other older women who had become individuals as the week wore on: Grace and Bette, I called them, the type of women who went home to put on their aprons and knit by the television. They were both plush and grizzled, unpretentious, surely satisfied by their lot. I imagined the big crystal jars on their end tables filled with hard candy, homemade afghans draped over their chairs and sofas, a cherished little dog. I thought of them in the evenings, both of them widows, home alone, heating up supper, thinking as they waited for their food, of me. They would both be overwhelmed and saddened by the case. They wouldn't know what to think. They would sit at the table over their beef stew, thinking not of the words of the experts or any of the witnesses, but of me, and the single question: Did she do it? Could that girl with the handsome husband in the back have done it?

On Thursday Susan Dirks called Dr. Eugene Bailey, a psychologist from the University of Wisconsin. He was a frail-looking man with small round glasses, thinning red hair, and a cyst on the bald part of his head. Rafferty had never seen him in court before. He had told me at the break that he nearly felt sorry for the professor. "The guys Dirks usually haul in must be out of town. I can't imagine how she dragged this poor mole away from his books, unless he's a relation, a brother-in-law. I bet he's been in the tower for the last forty years, going back and forth on the path between his office and the lecture hall. I felt like asking him if we should call his mother, that we permitted our witnesses to sit on their mother's laps."

Dirks questioned Dr. Bailey primarily about post-traumatic stress syndrome. There was the litany: bed-wetting, aggressive behaviors, nightmares, detachment from others, recurrent and intrusive recollections of the event. By now so many of the questions seemed formulaic that I felt that I could have asked them myself. "Dr. Bailey," she said, "you have told us that Robbie Mackessy suffers from PTSS. Have you formed an opinion based upon your training and experience and based upon your evaluation of the child, to within a reasonable degree of psychological certainty, as to the cause of PTSS?"

"Yes, I have."

"And what is that opinion?"

Again I watched Bette and Grace, the Greek God, the Dairy Man, the intellectual woman, while Dr. Bailey declared that I had both physically and sexually abused Robbie Mackessy. My favorite jurors had settled into their duty. Some of them rocked a little in their comfortable chairs. They were all listening, but their faces were placid, unruffled. They were saving their judgment, their emotion, for the deliberation perhaps; I couldn't have begun to say what any one of them was thinking of Dr. Eugene Bailey's partially audible, careful testimony.

Rafferty began his cross-examination by saying, "Let me ask you, Dr. Bailey, about the so-called trauma of the primal scene. By the primal scene I am referring to sexual intercourse. The orthodox psychoanalytic notion I believe is this: A child who witnesses the primal scene is deeply traumatized. Is that correct?"

Dr. Bailey was wearing a turtle neck and sucking on lozenges. It was good to know that his voice may not normally have been so thin and reedy. "That is Freud's general interpretation, yes," he answered.

"When a child witnesses the primal scene does he not frequently interpret sexual intercourse as a cruel, destructive act?"

"That is one of the possible misinterpretations on the child's part. The psychic content will vary according to the child's age and previous history."

"Uh huh. But what is almost always present in the young child, the four-, five-, six-year-old, who witnesses intercourse, is the linking together of sex and danger. Is that not true?"

"The content varies according to the details that have been witnessed."

"But if a young child does witness the act, it is possible for that child to be traumatized?"

"Yes."

"Traumatized to the degree that he may develop subsequent neurosis?"

"Freudian scholars would certainly agree with that statement."

"Other psychoanalysts, not only Freud, but Róheim and Ferenczi, for example, talk about the identification with the mother, who represents the support of the child, and the child's inability to deal with the mother's relation to other objects, such as the father. Ferenczi says, if I recall correctly, that the child is overwhelmed by emotions that he cannot yet organize when he witnesses the primal scene. Is that a reasonable statement?"

"Reasonable, yes."

"We all understand that there is enough literature on this subject to more than fill this courthouse. Would you be so kind as to briefly tell us what effect the primal scene has on a young child in your view?"

Dr. Bailey cleared his throat. "When a child sees that his parents cannot transcend the body in their most intimate relations, the child naturally has anxiety. The child is in the process himself of trying to work out the problem of the body, trying to overcome the horror of the body."

It wasn't difficult to understand why Dr. Bailey could speak to the horror of the body, when his own form—his sunken chest, his slim waist that required a belt for which he likely had to make extra holes—might alone have caused him plenty of trauma and subsequent neurosis. I liked Dr. Bailey, felt his sensitivity, his probable fondness for moss and lichens, wild flowers, Debussy.

"If the child then sees the parents in conjugal relations," he was saying, "he can well feel betrayed by them. He sees the adults keeping the relationship, an obviously special, deep relationship, of the body, away from the child, in fact denying it to him. The child will undoubtedly experience alarm and confusion, but as I said before, the trauma is dependent on what he witnesses, how much, how long, and so forth and so on."

"Is it possible, Dr. Bailey," Rafferty said, walking along the jury box and tapping it with his pen, as if he meant to wake them up, "is it possible that when a child sees his parents having sex he may feel betrayed?"

"I believe I just said so, yes."

"What would you say are typical reactions to betrayal: If a person feels that he has been betrayed how might he act, in general?"

"Well, I'd say that typical responses might include anger, despair, perhaps vengeful feelings."

"And could that feeling of betrayal in a child make him exhibit some of the symptoms of PTSS that we've been talking about?"

"Hypothetically, yes."

"Did you ask Robbie if he'd witnessed the primal scene?"

"No, I didn't."

"And yet you just said that a child who sees the sex act may exhibit some of the symptoms of PTSS, did you not?"

"We are speaking hypothetically."

"So you did not think it necessary to ask a child who has sexual knowledge and symptoms of PTSS if he had witnessed the primal scene?"

"Not in this case, no."

"And from your description of the primal scene am I correct that this is usually presumed to be the sexual act between the child's parents?"

"That's the presumption."

"Now, Doctor, if that child were to witness the primal scene, but let us imagine that the sexual act was a violent one, involving bondage, or whipping, would it be fair to say that this could cause an even more severe reaction?"

"Yes, that's fair."

"And suppose further, if you would, that this scene is not only violent, but is between the child's mother and a veritable stranger—not rape, but a man who does not know or care to know anything about his paramour's child. Couldn't that result in even more pronounced symptoms of PTSS?"

"Undoubtedly."

"You stated in your report that Robbie's nightmares, his acting out, his regressive behavior were pronounced symptoms of PTSS, did you not?"

"If it's in the report, then I did."

"You stated in your report and in your testimony that Robbie had pronounced symptoms of PTSS."

"Yes—as a result of—"

"That will be all my questions, your honor."

The last person to testify for the prosecution was Officer Melby. He was put at the end so that the jury would be left with my own words, my admission, the "I hurt everybody" line. It began to snow while he described my conduct at the school-board meeting. Susan Dirks asked him several different questions about my admission, so that he kept repeating the incriminating sentence. I watched the flakes come sifting down past the windows. It was going to be Christmas soon. Dan and Theresa had only had two Christmases with Lizzy. There would be milestones every year: the day of the drowning, the day of her death, Christmas, Easter, her birthday. The years couldn't ever simply go forward because of the cycle that would keep them anchored in the past: the day of the drowning, the day of her death, Christmas, Easter, her birthday. I didn't dare think about Christmas, about where I might be. I had thought that I should buy a few things in case I wasn't with the family, so that Howard wouldn't have to brave the mall. If I'd been fanciful, I might have felt Lizzy's presence because of the snow; I might have thought it was her way of being with us, assuring us with the soft, white cover.

I couldn't listen anymore and Howard had to tell me on the way home that he thought Rafferty had sufficiently clouded Melby's case. Howard didn't sound entirely convincing. He said that Rafferty had forced the officer to admit that he hadn't investigated any other explanations or any other possible suspects. Rafferty had moved for a directed verdict at the end of Dirks's case for some technical reason I didn't want to understand. He knew the judge would deny it, but it would be necessary to have made the motion in the event of an appeal. We stopped at the hardware store outside of Spring Grove and bought two plastic green sleds. It was Thursday and we were set free until Monday, sent out into our new world like moon walkers on a tether. After dinner we turned on the spotlight outside and we all took turns sliding down our driveway into the empty street.

Chapter Twenty-one

————

THE TEACHER FROM ROBBIE'S preschool, Rafferty's first witness on Monday, was a tall, graceful woman named Linda Gildner. Her brown hair was done up in a French braid with pretty, tightly curled tendrils framing her face. She was wearing a navy dress with a scooped neck and a dropped waist, speckled all over with light blue birds. Howard, during the break, in a moment of surprising levity, said that she looked like a Disney version of the caretaker, the sweet nanny who had magical powers. I said that she could probably make the birds in her own dress come to life and fly around to amuse her charges. He snorted and his lips widened. Although as a family we hadn't gone anywhere over the weekend, he had disappeared for several hours Saturday afternoon with the car. I suspect he had driven to the farm. It had been a long, quiet two days and the girls had bickered quite a bit. Although our joke wasn't too funny, it nonetheless gave me a sense of relief. It was communion, of sorts. Howard and I had been in a holding pattern, like two aircrafts circling each other, around and around in the fog, the heavy weather preventing us from landing or straying from our loops.

Linda Gildner spoke about Robbie as if she didn't want to mention his bad behavior, that it wasn't her nature to squeal on people, but of course she had sworn to tell the truth and must please the court. Rafferty managed to act as if he also was suffering throughout, as she quietly explained that Robbie had been a belligerent, troubled child two and three years before, and that her staff had repeatedly suggested that the Mackessys have him evaluated. Rafferty nodded periodically and then shook his head slightly, saddened, shocked, that one so young had gone awry. I thought to myself, Oh, but Robbie wasn't that bad. Truly he wasn't so awful. They were drawing him as a budding psychopath, based on his performance at preschool. It disturbed me that both the Gildners and Rafferty belonged to the Yacht Club and had spent vacations boating together. Linda told the court that even at the ages of three and four Robbie had had a pattern of lying, and not lying about isolated things here and there as all young children will, but deliberately telling falsehoods so that others would get into trouble. He lied to place blame elsewhere, and while that is not an unusual practice in three- or four-year-olds, Robbie, she said, had carried the tendency to extremes. He was a bright boy, sensitive to group dynamics, further along cognitively, she thought, than other three-year-olds in terms of knowing how to manipulate an adult. I wondered if it was evident only to me what gestures and phrases Rafferty had suggested she use in her testimony.

When Robbie had held a little girl's arm on the jungle gym, and wouldn't let go, so that the arm was broken, in full view of his teachers, Linda said that he vigorously denied having done so. He lied in the face of reality, she added, pursing her lips and nodding. He hadn't been withdrawn or frightened, the way so many other children would have been, when he was gently questioned about the incident. He stormed and shouted, blaming the other boys, calling them by name, saying that they all had been on the jungle gym with him, that everyone but himself had twisted her arm.

It was one thing to be on trial as an adult, to have every past act come bubbling up and held to the light as a misdeed, every poor judgment fitting so nicely into the desired profile, but it was altogether different, shameful, to do the same for a boy of six. I should have been grateful for Linda Gildner, but I thought she rang false, coached to death, exaggerating the few naughty pranks that Robbie had pulled as a three-year-old.

Susan Dirks, in her cross-examination, asked why Robbie had been allowed to break a girl's arm when the teachers were looking on. "That sounds like negligence to me," Dirks said quickly, before Rafferty protested.

"How many teachers were watching while the girl's arm was broken?"

"Three."

"Three teachers standing by while a girl broke her arm on the jungle gym?"

Later Dirks said, "In your testimony you spoke about the cognitive abilities of Robbie Mackessy at three years of age. Do you have your Doctorate in Psychology?"

"No, I don't, but I—"

"Do you have, at the very least, a Master's in Social Work?"

"No, but I—"

"A degree in education, Mrs. Gildner, hardly qualifies you to speak with authority about childhood psychology. Isn't it true that it is normal for a three-year-old to lie to get out of trouble?"

"Yes, but I said—"

"You said that he had a pattern of lying, Mrs. Gildner, and yet you've only mentioned one incident."

"I—I remember that he had a pattern of lying, but now, with the years passing, and all the children I see, I can't tell you more about that. I mean, children lie about little things, about toys and food, so that for me to bring back a specific—"

"You don't remember other incidents?"

"Well, I—I know they happened, but like I said—"

When we were leaving the courtroom after her testimony Rafferty whispered to me, "Don't look so glum."

"She was a disaster," I said.

"No, no she wasn't at all. The jury will remember how mild she was, and that Dirks preyed upon her. They'll remember that Robbie broke a kid's arm when he was three."

"Did he really do that?"

Rafferty's chin shot down to his chest and he looked severely up at me over his glasses.

"I don't think the boy is as bad as you've made him out to be," I said. "I'm not sure it happened like that."

He drew me to him as we walked down the hall. "This is stressful," he said. He was still whispering but his hold was firm; the pressure from his fingertips on my arm was almost painful. "You have to understand that I would never put a witness on to lie. Never. And it's not going to do you much good at this juncture to start feeling sorry for Robbie. It's admirable but beside the point right about now. Go get yourself a drink and let's keep calm."

I heard Dyshett, heard her loud and clear, her voice nearly strong enough to make my own tongue move. She was saying, "I'd walk down the street lookin' at ch'you, Mr. Raff-er-ty, thinkin' you was a smart-ass lawyer, but you nothin' but some kind of pop-eyed, mangy half-breed dog, rippin' that boy limb from limb, chewin' him up, spittin' him out, and then you expect us to study what's all over the floor and say, 'Yes sir, that pile of shit is a boy.' "

That first afternoon Rafferty called James "Grinder" Perkins. He worked as an office manager at the Oscar Mayer plant in Madison, overseeing those who process beef and pork into hot dogs. He was a fine-boned man, not much taller than Mrs. Mackessy. He had expensive-looking hair, layered and conditioned and blown dry, and blue wire-rimmed glasses. No one around Prairie Center, except Dan, wore skinny ties and designer glasses. Shortly after he took the stand the judge summoned Rafferty and Dirks into his chamber. Howard and I waited out in the hall. He was trying to study his vehicle registration handbook so that he might soon advance to Team Captain, and I looked out the window wondering about the girls across the street in the jail. Rafferty had expected that the judge would ask for an offer of proof that his witness was not collateral to the case, that the witness would provide relevant information. Howard was unable to stop jiggling his foot, what for him could pass as hysterics. I had to say his name three or four times before he looked away from his manual. "I just wonder," he said after a while, "I just wonder what makes Rafferty think the judge is going to take our side."

"Judge Peterson promised when he took office that he would treat those who appeared before him with fairness and impartiality," I said.

"Oh, please." He had his hand at his throat. "You sound like you're reciting a Scout's oath."

"There is still hope," I said.

He sighed. "What I find hard to believe is that she actually dated a man who makes hot dogs. Someone called 'Grinder.' Did Rafferty assume she'd fall for someone who made hot dogs and brats? Did he go to the Oscar Mayer plant and ask all the workers if they'd gone out with her? Why does it have to be hot dogs? Why couldn't she go out with someone who works for the Sierra Club?"

"Howard, I don't know," I said. "He works in an office, anyway. Rafferty said he wasn't the first choice, that there was some other boyfriend, a real piece of work, who the neighbor lady saw. At least Grinder's not down on the line, pulling the wieners out of a machine. He's not some big, beefy Neanderthal guy who can't speak in complete sentences and wears a loincloth. I was surprised that he's a white-collar worker, not some awful redneck—" I heard Dyshett again, talking to me this time. "You always sayin' things like you think you God, lookin' down at the half-ass work you made, like you don't like nothin' you spent all that tahm makin'. You always sizin' people up and you don't know shit about them, girl. You don't know shit!"

"Who knows," I said. "Who knows about any of them."

When Rafferty and Dirks and Judge Peterson reappeared, the trial resumed.

Jim Perkins wasn't harsh or vulgar in appearance. He was a quiet, well-mannered, well-dressed citizen. It would have been easier for the jury to understand him if he'd seemed stupid or coarse. Later Rafferty articulated so well what came across about Perkins, what the jury, with a bit of luck, may have perceived and found distasteful beyond the prurient details of his sex life. "Did you notice," Rafferty asked me, "how earnest Perkins was about his pleasures? He takes himself very seriously. He didn't have any qualms about getting up in front of us to tell us about his mastery. And he made it clear that his recreation was his constitutional right, and that he was proud of his potency. Perkins wasn't my first choice but he did all right. He was better for us than I'd hoped."

"Did you usually stay the night at Carol Mackessy's?" Rafferty asked him during the questioning.

"Maybe once or twice. Not usually."

"Where was Robbie when you had your trysts at her house?"

"He wasn't around."

"Do you know where he'd been sent?"

"We didn't talk about him."

"He wasn't a concern?"

"He was hers."

"I see. So you were not involved in her personal life."

"That's right."

"And if Robbie had been around you might not have known it?"

"I never thought about it. I didn't know she had a kid until pretty near the end."

"Did you meet him?"

"I saw him a couple of times."

"Did you see him at the house?"

"Yes."

"Were you ever at the house for a social visit?"

"Ah, we always met for a purpose."

"For what purpose?"

"What I'd advertised for."

"So you came to the house for sex?"

"Correct."

"And you saw Robbie, a couple of times, you said."

"We had a meal afterward a few times and he showed up."

"Where had he been?"

"A friend's."

"Who told you he'd been at a friend's house?"

"Ah, I assumed it, I guess. She didn't say."

"Robbie showed up, you said? He was suddenly just there in the kitchen to eat the meal?"

"As I said, I didn't think about him."

Howard was silent on the way home that night. It is one thing to be in a car with someone who is quiet, and another to be with someone who is silent. I couldn't remember the last time I'd seen him look anything but grim. I made a few observations along the way. I wondered what it meant that Dirks hadn't chosen to cross-examine "Grinder." I thought Howard might answer, but he got out of the car when we pulled into the driveway and walked into the house, shutting the door before I got there.

Mrs. Nancy Sheridan, Rafferty's dream come true, appeared before us on Tuesday morning. She sat down, wiping her runny eye with her ironed white handkerchief. Theresa, who had been unable to come to the proceedings the week before, because of work, was sitting behind me, next to Howard. When she said later in the hall, that she had prayed for a witness like Mrs. Sheridan, Howard looked down and his mouth curved slowly into a smile.

Mrs. Sheridan was a good Catholic who had been bearing children since 1960 and had only recently, three years before, finished with the stillbirth of her eleventh baby. Her tailored maroon suit had been out-of-date for so long it had come back into fashion, and it still fit reasonably well. She wasn't any taller than five feet and she had short, dull black hair. Robbie and his mother had lived next door to the Sheridans, in a rental house, for three months the previous spring. Mrs. Sheridan deplored the fact that Mr. Gillis, the landlord, always had undesirable people as tenants, and that he did not keep up with essential repairs. Rafferty did his best to hold her to the subject, but with a captive audience she couldn't seem to help making asides about the ills of society.

There weren't any boys in the neighborhood Robbie's age and Mrs. Sheridan told us that for a while Robbie latched on to her eight-year-old son, Jack. After a few weeks, however, she had had to prohibit Jack from playing with Robbie because of the child's foul language, the likes of which had never before reached her ears. "I'm not inclined to repeat any of those words," she asserted, "even for the benefit of the court."

"That won't be necessary," Rafferty assured her.

With Rafferty's prodding Mrs. Sheridan related an incident that had taken place in May. She had gone looking for Jack at about 7:30 in the evening. She had called first, and then rung the dinner bell several times. He was ordinarily reliable, and she began to worry. Some of the older children had gone with Mr. Sheridan on a fishing trip and it was just going to be herself and Jack for dinner. It was a rare occasion to have one child at home, and she was going to take him out to Taco Bell for a treat. She walked down the block, down Main Street where they lived. She turned the corner and followed the path to the subdivision where he sometimes went to play with school friends. There was a group of boys skateboarding in a driveway but he wasn't among them. They said he hadn't been around for an hour or so, that they thought he had gone home. She became very anxious. "We all know what the world is coming to," she said, looking at the jury for confirmation. Although Jack was her tenth child, she didn't feel that she was overprotective, due to her long experience. There had been recent rumors of a man in a green pickup truck harassing young girls. The year before a Walworth County boy had disappeared, plucked off the street, no trace. Even a seasoned mother worried.

I don't think there was any one in the room, not Rafferty, not Susan Dirks, not Judge Peterson himself, who wanted to endanger their reputations by interrupting Mrs. Sheridan, or objecting to her statements, or telling her to hurry along.

On the evening of May 23 she stopped in front of the Mackessys, having decided she'd check at their house before she walked all the way over to the playground. She had told her son not to play with Robbie, but Jack was a kindhearted boy who might have responded if Robbie had been in need. It was not impossible, she thought, that Jack had gone into the house to assist him in some way.

"Wouldn't Carol Mackessy have been on the premises," Rafferty asked, "to put a Band-Aid on his knee or pour a glass of milk?"

Nancy Sheridan shook her head and again wiped her face. She seemed not exactly to be crying, although there was a steady stream coming from her right eye. "She often left that poor boy at home by himself," she said. "Jack would go over there and come back and tell me that Robbie was alone eating from a box of Froot Loops." While Dirks was making a hearsay objection Mrs. Sheridan went right on talking. "It's bad families that are spoiling it for everyone else. I found it impossible to believe that a mother would leave a kindergarten-aged child alone for more than ten minutes—"

"Sustained," Judge Peterson said.

"He never looked me in the eye." Mrs. Sheridan wasn't hearing either the judge or Rafferty, both of whom were trying to get her to stop. "A mother doesn't raise ten children without knowing that that boy was afraid to look up and see that no one was there to love him."

Mrs. Dirks made a number of objections during the testimony, and she asked that certain asides be struck from the record. Although Peterson granted her some small victories, he was clearly disposed toward the star witness, who Rafferty referred to in private as, "the mother of us all." Mrs. Sheridan didn't know precisely how often Robbie was left alone, but it seemed to be on a regular basis that he was at home when Mrs. Mackessy's car was gone. As far as she could see, there was no baby-sitter watching out for the child. It was none of her business, she said, but it was hard not to notice him looking at her from his dining-room window. She'd wave, she said, but he wouldn't wave back. She could feel him watching her so that sometimes, before she looked to see if he was there, she went and closed the curtains.

On the night in question, however, when she was out looking for Jack, she went up to the Mackessy's door and was about to ring the bell. There was loud music coming from the back of the house and she thought it might be a party. "I was about to go," she said, "because I knew my Jack wouldn't have come over to the house under those circumstances, when Robbie appeared at the door. He was usually, a—well, angry-looking little guy. He seemed to want to take on the world, by himself, bless his heart. You could see all that's tender in that child just hardening up."

"What happened next?" Rafferty asked.

"I hadn't ever spoken more than two words to the mother," she said, in no relation to the question. "She probably didn't think that someone such as myself had anything to offer." She took a deep breath and felt her collar to make sure it was still in place. "Robbie said I should come in. He said, 'You—you should come in.' I said, no, no thank you, that I was looking for Jack. 'You have to,' he said. He insisted. He was stuttering and he was looking at me for once, with those great big eyes. I was surprised by his familiarity. It frightened me, because he looked—"

"How did he look, Mrs. Sheridan?"

"His eyes were huge, as I said. He was so pale. He was scared, Mr. Rafferty. His little body was quivering. I didn't know what to think. I was afraid for a minute, for my Jack, afraid there'd been an accident. 'What is it, Robbie?' I asked him. He said, 'Come and look.' 'Is it Jack?' He said no, he hadn't seen Jack. I didn't want to go inside that place but I followed him."

"Where did he take you, Mrs. Sheridan?"

"He took me to the back of the house, to the den. The door was closed most of the way." She bent her head, apparently unable to continue.

"What did you see, Mrs. Sheridan?"

"This is not easy for me, Mr. Rafferty."

"I appreciate that."

She gripped both armrests with her hands and sat straight. "I looked."

"And what did you see?"

"It was dark, and the music was loud."

"What could you make out?"

"There was something adult going on, something a child shouldn't have seen. The music was so loud it made your heart beat hard."

"What was happening in that room?"

"It was dark, like I said, but I could see her, Mrs. Mackessy, on the sofa, with one of her men. They were like animals, Mr. Rafferty. That's what it looked like. She on all fours. He biting at her neck. Robbie had to scream at me, 'My mama's getting hurt.' He took my hand and pulled me away, into the kitchen. He was crying, saying something about how it would happen to us too. The music stopped then, and that child barreled into me; he said I had to get out of the house. He as much as pushed me out the back door, Mr. Rafferty."

"Did you see anyone besides Robbie on that evening?"

"No, I did not. I was extremely upset. I wanted to take the boy, but he closed the door. I ran from that house as fast as my legs could carry me. I ran straight upstairs in my own home and saw that my Jack was in his bedroom after all. I was so relieved. I should have called the police, I know that."

"Did you tell anyone about your experience?"

"That's a very good question, Mr. Rafferty." He didn't flinch, didn't as much as crack the slightest smile. "My husband was on a fishing trip and would not be home until the end of the week. I felt that I needed to discuss with him any action we would take. I did not feel that I should take steps without my husband. I was aware that my neighbor entertained men, and they were often large, burly fellows. You can't be sure if people are on drugs, can't be sure of their condition. You can't be certain about anything in these times. I was not prepared to call the police myself and possibly place my family in danger. I am not proud of my inaction, but I felt that I was safeguarding my own children. I know that Robbie trusted me and that by not calling for help I violated that trust. It's something I live with."

"When did you next see the Mackessys?"

"I saw Robbie out in the yard fifteen or twenty minutes after I left him. His mother called him in a few minutes later. To be frank I was upset enough so that I began to wonder if I'd been dreaming. As it turned out, the boy and his mother disappeared a few days later. I heard that they were evicted, but I don't know. I came home from a meeting and their curtains were down, the car was gone. Everything looked empty. It was a tremendous relief to me. Someone on the block said they'd rented a house in the country. I decided that I would continue to pray for them, but that I would otherwise put them out of my mind."

When Rafferty finally sat down, he shifted his eyes in my direction and raised his eyebrows for a fraction of a second. As Susan Dirks got up, Sherry, from wherever she was, home with her three dickenses or still in jail, shouted, "Oh boy, she in DEEPshit." I wonder now when Susan Dirks knew that Mrs. Mackessy was either grossly deluded or lying. I wonder if she realized she would lose badly when the other boys' charges were dropped, when even Myra Flint could not get them to say the same thing twice. Rafferty had said many times that mine was the sort of case that should never have come to trial. He placed the blame solely on Susan Dirks. I know very well the urge to protect your failings, a need so strong you make up a different world to inhabit. Mrs. Mackessy had had a need to think differently about her life. Perhaps there was enough force in her need that even Susan Dirks had been convinced.

Whatever Dirks's true feelings at the time of the trial she gave Mrs. Sheridan her best shot. If the room was dark, how could she have seen anyone? How long did she look? Four seconds? Five seconds? How could she tell there were two people? "I know what I have seen," Mrs. Sheridan said. She was not going to be undone. She had God on her side. She was not going to let an infertile woman lawyer who was too big for her britches diminish an incident that had changed her own life, that had made her scrape up thirty dollars she couldn't really spare to send to a senator she felt had the right beliefs. "Miss Dirks," she said, "Mrs. Dirks, whatever you are. There were people in that room. They were hurting one another for, for reasons I am not going to attempt to understand. The life was scared out of that boy. There was evil in that house, and your insinuations, that I have somehow invented a story so beyond my ken, are sorely trying my patience."

After Mrs. Sheridan's testimony, Rafferty and I went into the holding room. Howard trudged off to find us some sweet rolls. Rafferty put his hands to his wide open mouth and wiggled his hips in a way that did not become him. "I'm gloating," he said, "I'm gloating. I'll pay for it someday, but I can't help it right now. I can't help it!"

"Stop," I said.

"Look!" He grabbed my shoulders and shook me. "When some maniac from Hollywood comes knocking at your door for your story, okay? And you sell it for a million-five, and you and Howard buy a ten-inch parcel in Montana, right next door to Tom Brokaw and Brooke Shields, okay, you with me?"

"Would you please stop," I said, laughing uneasily at his bulging eyes and the spit that was foaming around his mouth.

"As—as part of the deal you have to insist that Mrs. Sheridan play her own part. Not even what's-her-name, Streep, could get that accent down, you know how flat Mrs. Sheridan's Wisconsin, Catholic vowels are, and with just that touch of whining in her voice. It's so fabulous. And no amount of onion balled up in a hanky could make just one eye run so righteously."

"Please," I said again.

"I know, I know. But she is such a work of art, like the Virgin she was, appearing at Lourdes."

"Be quiet," I said.

"All right, okay. I hope Howard gets something sinful, something chocolate and very sticky, made with cream and butter and several eggs."

By the time we were called back Rafferty had collected himself. He cleared his throat, smoothed his plaid suit coat, put his head down, so humble, so manly, and walked into the courtroom.

I have often thought about both Carol Mackessy and Mrs. Sheridan, together, as if they belonged in the same photograph. I persuaded myself that in a sense they needed one another. Carol had brought a suit against me without thinking about her past. Had she believed that modesty or politeness would keep her unconventional behavior out of the evidence? Did she believe in Dirks the way I believed in Rafferty? Our lawyers, we thought, would present us as our best selves. Or did Carol feel secure in her right to entertain her own friends in her own home? Theresa maintained that Carol's maternal instincts had finally kicked in, that those strong feelings overpowered her, and made her take action. Theresa said that she probably had deep-seated guilt about Robbie, and in pursuing the case she was overcompensating.

Carol hadn't imagined there could be anyone quite like Mrs. Sheridan. Was the lady too good to be true, I often wondered, or was it rather that in all of our lives there is a Mrs. Sheridan, seeing something in the dark, and translating it into something fully formed? Mrs. Sheridan was perhaps Mrs. M. L. Glevitch's beautiful and good sister. Mrs. Glevitch stood in funeral lines, grocery-store lines, listening, spying, talking, talking, the words running out of her mouth like ink, leaving an indelible trail behind her. Mrs. Sheridan stayed at home, shut her curtains, and still truth came to her. She kept quiet until she was called upon by the mighty forces of civilization, the court of law, where she believed justice was carried out.

On Tuesday afternoon Rafferty called Theresa to the stand. I had asked him several times if it wouldn't be better to hire someone else, someone who hadn't known me, who didn't have the complication of our particular relationship. Each time he insisted that she was perfect for us, not in spite of our friendship, but because of our association. "She's a great expert too—she's always lucid, human, commonsensical. The jury deep down doesn't care how many degrees a person has if he's compelling and speaks their language."

I had talked to Theresa on the phone since our meeting at the A&W,

but I hadn't seen her. I had always envied her fair skin, her long eyelashes, her curly hair, as well as her sunny nature. In court she was virtually unrecognizable. She'd lost some weight so that her round face had become angular; she had planes and cheekbones, what she had always wished for. She'd taken her glasses off, or gotten contacts. She had previously had a schoolgirl sort of charm, an adorableness, but in the witness box she looked as if she'd grown up, come into her prime. She was dressed simply in a blue sweater and a dark blue and crimson skirt.

Rafferty asked her to explain the guidelines she followed for sexual-abuse cases. She moistened her lips and smoothed her skirt down her lap. I found it painful to watch her in the beginning, in the same way it will be difficult to watch Emma or Claire play an instrument at a recital. I'm sure I was more nervous for Theresa than she was for herself.

"First of all," she said in a loud, clear, unfaltering voice, "I always err in favor of the child. What do I mean by that? I don't think that children are capable of lying about their feelings. In other words, I always believe a child's feelings. It is essential to listen very carefully to a child, but it is just as important to be sensitive to details, to be aware that children often mix fantasy with fact. I have myself seen children, in my own practice, elaborate and get carried away with details, especially as they get further from the incident. I have seen child protection workers get into trouble because of various approaches that are still advocated and widely used, and which often mislead a victim."

"Could you describe those approaches, Mrs. Collins, which you believe mislead children."

"The dictum 'Children never lie' is often taken to extremes. I have found, in my practice, that children are often fanciful, that they sometimes say outrageous things that I'm certain have no basis in fact. In courts of law we often establish that the child can distinguish between the truth and a lie. But that is a very different issue from whether or not the child will actually lie or embellish."

I had never seen Theresa before in her professional capacity. She was capable, articulate, and impassioned without appearing rabid. "One of them mind doctors," I heard Dyshett say. "Tell me your dreams and all that cockshit."

"Second," she went on, "anatomically detailed dolls sometimes startle a child because of their unusual genital features. They invite a finger into their gaping holes. Give a child a wooden donut and he will invariably place his fingers in the holes. I have seen professionals jump to conclusions based on a child's natural curiosity. The child often senses the importance the examiner places on the doll. He or she wants to please or possibly get a reaction from the examiner.

"Third, there is a real problem, in spite of the fact that we know we should not, of the examiner asking leading questions. I myself have been guilty of asking specific questions, such as, 'Does your daddy put his fingers in you just like that?' "

"What she talkin' about?" It was Dyshett again, zinging through my mind. "What this motherfuck lecture?" I had tried to tell Theresa, that day at the A&W, that the girls in my pod had gotten inside of me, that they were real now, more real to me than they had ever been in jail, in person. And there wasn't much good in feeling that I was one of them, from a distance, from the safety of the outside world.

"Fourth, there is a danger that the examiners selectively ignore the impossible. Let me give you an example. If the child says, 'My uncle abused me,' we say, 'Oh my!', and we probe and set the wheels in motion to charge the uncle. If the child then says, 'My uncle abused me during a family outing on the picnic table where everyone was eating,' we, as examiners, tend to say, 'Oh, Sally's tired out. We'll let her rest.' "

"So in your opinion examiners hear only what they want to hear," Rafferty said.

"I'm saying that's a danger, yes. Another typical problem in the field is the failure of the child protection worker to interview the accused or the adult accuser. We tend to take at face value the accusations, and we do not consider that there may have been fabrication. We think we do not need to hear another point of view because the child has told us everything. That is not always the case."

"Mrs. Collins, there is, in the *Diagnostic and Statistical Manual of Mental Disorders,* a list of telling characteristics of what is known as the unattached child, or the character-disturbed child. Another name for the disorder is the antisocial-personality disorder. Could you give us a profile of the character-disturbed child?"

"A young child with APD will not look you in the eye. The only time such a child has normal eye contact is when he is trying to manipulate and when he is angry. Character-disturbed children are quick to tell outrageous lies. The child may have a preoccupation with fire, blood, or gore. Many of these children have not bonded with their parents, as infants. They will exhibit aggression and have marked control problems. In fact, the parents are often also angry and hostile people."

"Dr. Eugene Bailey told us that when a child is afflicted with Post-Traumatic Stress Syndrome, often that child's basic assumptions about his surroundings and himself have been upset. The child's belief in his personal invulnerability is shaken, he no longer has the perception of the world as meaningful, and he can also no longer see himself as positive," Rafferty said.

"I agree with that assessment," Theresa said.

"Mrs. Collins, I realize that you are not a psychologist, but I respect your twelve-year career as a family therapist. According to the state's expert, Robbie was suffering from PTSS. Having read the case records, and in your experience, knowing Robbie and his family as you do, would you agree with Dr. Bailey's diagnosis?"

"Yes."

"Based on your training and experience and your reading of the court record, would you also say to within a reasonable degree of therapeutic certainty, that Robbie Mackessy exhibits some of the symptoms of a character-disturbed child?"

"Yes, I do, Mr. Rafferty."

"Unattached children lie even when caught red-handed, do they not?"

"Quite often, yes. It is as if the child confuses the way he wishes life were with the way it actually is."

"In your experience, Mrs. Collins, do you think it likely that a six-year-old boy who'd seen his mother engaged in sex would experience trauma?"

Mrs. Dirks objected, and for the first time Rafferty raised his voice. "Your honor," he shouted, "I am asking a hypothetical question!"

"Yes. Quite definitely," Theresa was able to answer.

"Is it your opinion that the child might experience terror not only for himself, but also for his mother. Might he be afraid for her life?"

"Absolutely."

"Is it possible that a young boy might imagine himself in the same danger as his mother? That a young boy might have the fear of that danger?"

"I think it's possible, Mr. Rafferty."

"If that boy, in his worst fantasy, imagines himself in his mother's helpless position, might he invent a situation in which he triumphs over the danger, the evil?"

"Children often fantasize about conquering robbers, bullies—the bad guys."

I wondered if the jurors were thinking about what it must have been like for Robbie to come up the basement stairs, when his mother called him, coming up the stairs and sitting down at his place. Maybe they were imagining prim Grinder in the den, trying to figure out how to rewind the VCR. Mrs. Mackessy might have had her robe on while she fried up hamburgers on the range. The fan wasn't on, and the doors were closed, and the room smelled of grease and cigarettes. Were they going to force him down on his knees? the boy might have wondered. "Where've you been?" she might have barked at him. "I thought you were over by the Sheridans." She didn't look as if she'd been hurt. He couldn't tell, exactly, if she was angrier than usual. "Look at me when I'm talking to you!" He wanted to tell her that, if it would make her feel better, he'd kill Grinder for her, that that's why he showed Mrs. Sheridan, so that Mrs. Sheridan could call the police and take the stranger away. He thought they'd be arriving any minute, with sirens and flashing lights. But when Grinder came into the kitchen, she started slamming down plates in front of the man, as if she wanted to feed him up. He couldn't tell if she liked him or not, the way she was slamming the plates down. He didn't understand it, any of it, and he wondered if someone did those terrible things to him, if she'd feel worried about him, and afterward slam plates down in front of him and feed him full of good things. He remembered the time he got his hand stuck in the car door. She'd been mad that he'd been clumsy but she'd also sat with him at the doctor's office tickling his ear. It was confusing, the way she was being so nice and noisy, and smiling at Grinder, and he wondered if that's what grown-ups did, hurt each other.

I looked out the window while Rafferty went on with the questions, trying to think about Mrs. Mackessy, trying for the millionth time to imagine her side of the story. She had grown up with deaf parents, and might have run wild with bad girls, coming home late and signing lies, squandering her promise on men who ill-treated her. She would probably always think of me as someone who was without question thoroughly evil. She wouldn't care that we'd lost a way of life; I had deserved my misfortunes and so did my family. I wondered if she could ever begin to bring any of Robbie's tragedy back to herself.

Before Rafferty finished with Theresa he asked her, as I knew he would, about our friendship. I remember how she looked out at us, first at me, sitting at the table alone, and then at Howard, who was behind me. She studied us, as if she was evaluating our bonds. I thought she was going to get choked up. "Yes," she responded, "we were neighbors and friends."

"Did your children play together?"

"Very often. Several times a week."

"Did you ever suspect my client of neglect or foul play?"

"No," Theresa said.

"You never saw anything, any signs, any flares to alert you?"

"Never."

"Your daughter was always happy to go to the Goodwins?"

"Yes. Thrilled."

"Would you allow your daughter to stay unchaperoned with the Goodwin family at this time?"

She was crying now, in her good old way, her professional mantle at her knees, revealing the woman, the mother. She was weeping so affectingly some of the juror's were dabbing their eyes. "I can't impress upon you enough," she said through her sniffles, "that Alice never would inflict —that she never did any of those things."

I'd like to say that I was not afraid when I took the stand. I wished for the convictions and confidence of Mrs. Sheridan, and the dignity of Theresa. I could not remember anything about our rehearsals except Paul's flatulent praise. I took a moment to pray while he gathered his papers. I prayed that I could stand up to the assistant D.A. as well as Theresa had, even though Dirks trashed her credentials. I sat with my shaking hands in my lap, feeling as if my mouth had been stuffed with sawdust. I looked at Paul, who had job happiness, who would go on to save someone else after he was through with me. We had gone through the questions several times. We had agreed on certain wording. It would all flow he said, like a piece of cake.

He began by asking me what I had been charged with that had been the occasion for my spending nearly three months in the county jail.

I remembered my line. "Sexual abuse, reckless endangerment, child abuse," I said.

"And how did you plead?"

"Not guilty."

"And how did you find the jail?"

Dirks objected.

"Your honor," Rafferty said, "I think my client deserves to say a few sentences about her time in jail as a result of this charge. She was beaten and had a serious injury, so serious she was hospitalized."

Peterson nodded his head. "And how did you find the county jail?" Rafferty asked again.

I knew what he wanted me to say, that it had been the most difficult period of my life, that it had been sorely trying being in an overcrowded facility with seasoned prisoners, that as a result of my beating I had to have major surgery at St. Luke's hospital. The words failed me. But I could see the girls plainly—Lynelle, Dyshett, Sherry, Debbie—sitting in the back, watching with hope, scorn, affection, disinterest. "I was in awe," I said, under my breath.

"You were what?"

"I was in awe."

"Not something you'd like to repeat, I take it?" he said quickly.

"No."

He carried my log around in his hands, opening it, reading from it, as he asked me at length about specific visits Robbie had made in the previous year. Finally he asked, "In all of the, what—twenty-five visits—we have recorded here, Mrs. Goodwin, did you ever touch Robbie in an inappropriate way?"

"Yes," I said.

"What did you do to Robbie that you shouldn't have?"

"I hit him."

"How many times did you hit him?"

"Once. I hit him once on the face. I slapped him."

"Did you notify the principal that you'd hit the boy?"

"No, I didn't."

"Why didn't you?"

"I was ashamed. It is awful to lose your temper."

"What made you 'lose your temper,' as you say?"

I closed my eyes, trying to fasten on the correct sequence. "Robbie was a difficult child to treat," I said. "He was often verbally abusive to adults —he seemed not to have any fear or respect. There was a pattern in his office visits. He would come to the door and stand and stare at me in a way that was extremely unnerving, and then he often made personal remarks. I had tried to get some guidance from both the principal and the school counselor—" I was not answering in the succinct way we had practiced. I couldn't recall how I had justified the slap. "His derision and his contempt overwhelmed me one day," I mumbled. "And I slapped him."

"Is striking Robbie one of the charges that has been brought against you, Mrs. Goodwin?"

"No."

"Why didn't Robbie tell his mother you hit him?"

"I suppose Robbie may get hit at home. It may not have been anything out of the ordinary in his life."

Mrs. Dirks objected on the grounds of hearsay, and the judge ordered the statement struck from the record.

"What did you mean, Mrs. Goodwin, when you said to Detective Grogan and Officer Melby, that you'd hurt everybody. What did you mean by that?"

"Our neighbor, a two-year-old, had very recently drowned in our pond." I looked at Theresa as I spoke. I said again, "She was two years old." Rafferty had told me I should not under any circumstances volunteer that information. The judge had written a letter advising that both

Dirks and Rafferty keep Elizabeth Collins out of the testimony. But it was important, wasn't it, that the jurors know the context; Rafferty himself had said as much. I no longer remembered what I had been supposed to say. I was under oath to tell the truth, and Lizzy's death was a good portion of the truth. "I was—stricken by that accident. It was an agonizing period. I didn't feel that I was taking good care of my children, my family, my friend. Everything fell apart for those few weeks after Lizzy drowned. I had no idea what the officers were asking me about that night, but my guilt was considerable."

Dirks was standing up and yelling as to be expected. Even Judge Peterson was on his feet. I guessed that he called a recess because Dirks was running into the judge's chamber and Rafferty, head down, hands behind his back, was following. Rafferty said later that he'd never seen the judge so angry, that he shook the air as if to throttle Paul, and shouted. "I granted your motion to keep Elizabeth out of the testimony, and *you* brought it up! Were you playing games with me, Paul? Because if you were you'd better tell me, and I'll declare a mistrial right now and we'll start this thing all over again." To Susan Dirks Judge Peterson said, "Now, Mrs. Dirks, your colleague opened the door and I want you to know that you can have as much latitude as you want to explore that drowning on cross."

Rafferty didn't look at me as he finished his questions. He said simply, "So you felt that you were causing harm?"

"Everything feels hurtful, still. This trial has hurt all of us, my children and my husband, and also the Mackessys."

In his most slow, solemn tones Rafferty asked, "Did you ever sexually abuse Robbie Mackessy, Mrs. Goodwin?"

I shook my head. I was supposed to be honest, forthright, and indignant. He was waiting for me to use words. He tapped his foot four or five times.

"No," I managed to croak. "No, I did not."

I knew that Susan Dirks could now ask me about the drowning. I waited for the questions that would turn the jury against me. "Did you like Robbie Mackessy?" she asked as she began her cross-examination.

"No," I said. "He was a difficult boy."

"Is that reason for a professional health-care worker to dislike a child? Because they are difficult?"

"It wasn't necessarily right for me to dislike Robbie," I said. "I guess our reason isn't always responsible for our inclinations. It's a fact that I found him difficult, and that I didn't like being with him."

"You hit him?"

"Yes."

"Are you aware that it is against the law for a school employee to hit a child?"

"Yes, I am."

"And still you struck him?"

"Yes."

"Where did you hit him?"

"On the cheek."

"He was sent to the nurse, to you, and you struck him across the face."

"That's correct."

"You knew it was against the law."

"Yes."

"Did you report your conduct?"

"No."

"Did you notify anyone that you'd broken a state law?"

"No."

"So you lived with the knowledge that you hurt Robbie Mackessy, just as you lived with the knowledge of the other abuse."

Rafferty rose with his objection.

"Stick to the facts," Judge Peterson muttered.

" 'I hurt everybody,' you said in your admission to Officer Melby. That to me suggests something very active."

"For a parent," I said, "not taking action, not doing a certain thing, can be just as damaging as willfully striking a child. Not paying attention when they are taking a sharp knife off the counter, turning your back just for a minute when they are in the bath, letting go of their hand when they need you. Sometimes it seems that every minute, every second, there is peril. The officers and I, we were having a general conversation, so I thought. I meant that I was human, and that I had therefore hurt the people closest to me."

She was about to speak, but I think I'd caught her off guard. " 'I hurt everyone,' you said."

"Yes, I did."

"Did you tell your husband that you'd slapped Robbie?"

"No."

"Did you tell your best friend, the social worker?"

"No."

"You were secretive about it."

"Yes," I said. "I was."

When I sat back down next to Rafferty at our table he kept his eyes on his legal pad. I didn't care if he was infuriated, didn't care if I would always receive a chilly reception at his door. If he had misjudged me, and my acting capabilities, he had only himself to blame. I didn't know why Dirks hadn't asked me about Lizzy, and I wondered briefly if it was something again that I had only thought I'd said. But when she mentioned the drowning in her closing statement, Rafferty nodded. It served me right, he seemed to be saying, to have Dirks throwing the accident in the jurors' laps. He didn't lean over and whisper in my ear the way he had through-out the previous days. I was certain that for everyone in the courtroom Lizzy was suddenly the only presence. How could the jurors think of anything but the girl who should have been among us? I wanted to stand and do my own part, stand before them and tell them exactly what had happened: I had gone upstairs to look for my swimsuit, and I couldn't find it, and I had stopped to look at some old pictures from my childhood, and all the while Lizzy was on her way down the lane.

I remember only bits and pieces from Rafferty's closing statement. After he'd admonished the jury about their duty he said, "All right then, let's go right to the meat of the prosecution—let's go down, as the great poet Mr. William Butler Yeats once said, to 'the foul rag-and-bone shop of the heart.' Let us see what, if anything, has been proven beyond a reason-able doubt. Mrs. Dirks has shown to my satisfaction, and I suggest to yours as well, that Robbie Mackessy has been abused by someone."

I prayed while he spoke. I stopped listening and prayed for strength and heart. When I was very young I used to sit before my map of the world imagining myself in an ideal country, alone and at peace. Now, if I could make the world over, I said to myself in my prayer—and as always, to Howard—if I could make an impossible, new world, Howard, this is who you would see: You'd see Emma, and Claire, and you'd see yourself, and me, all together, dancing on the porch with the shades down, outcasts making a perfect circle.

Chapter Twenty-two

IT HAS TAKEN ME a long time to know how to remember last year. I've wondered if I should go back to the newspapers and clip the articles, put them in a scrapbook so that when they get older the girls can see for themselves what happened. It is tempting to want to brush the whole thing under the carpet, hoping that none of it in any form will resurface. But for the most part when I catch myself in the mirror and see that my eyes look different, the scars of last year so evident in my face, I know that I can't forget and that, in truth, I don't want to forget. Howard has suggested, reluctantly, it seems, that we go to family therapy. My guess is that Theresa put that idea in his head. "Give me a little more time," I keep saying. "A few more weeks." He always seems relieved when I put him off.

He manages the dairy animals in the Lincoln Park Zoo in Chicago now, what we laughingly call "the herd." I cannot tell anyone what my husband does for a living without also wanting to tell them that it is absurd, what he does. The six cows are Holsteins, a word nothing at all like Golden Guernsey, a word you cannot say without looking as if you're masticating. We can go out on the flat of our apartment roof near Wrigley Field and watch the Cubs play ball. Howard watches the game raptly from his lawn chair, not because he likes baseball, particularly, but because we have the best seat in the city. If I am awake in the early mornings I watch him down the hall, sitting by himself in the kitchen, running his hands over the table we brought from the farm. His hands move in swirls, as if the table is a Ouija board, about to give him an important message for his future. He has grown quieter, something I used to think impossible, like a turtle evolving into an animal that makes less noise. I don't know if he is raging or if he is merely resigned. If there is one thing I've learned over the years, and learned well, it is how to be still and wait. Periodically he is so fiercely merry, determined to have a good time, that the rest of us, Emma, Claire, and I, slink away to our own corners. And yet once in a rare while Howard and I are able to reach back to the quality of the old days, to sit at our table after the girls are in bed and talk into the night. It is as if we've somehow been, as Theresa would say, "blessed with grace."

On occasion I have thought that we are where we belong, city people returned to the city. We have a sunny apartment, Howard goes off to work, and I am a full-time mother. We have Dan Collins to thank for Howard's job, for pulling strings with the director of the zoo. We have tried, halfheartedly, to incorporate a few details from Prairie Center into our urban landscape. Howard has built walnut shelves in the kitchen with wood from the farm, from trees he felled himself. Lynelle's bookmark is on the floor by the futon, the first thing I see when I wake up. We had rolls of film from our farm life, which I recently gathered together in an album. After it was done I put the thing out of reach, out of sight. As for city dwelling, there is the homeless man on our block, the Waldorf school Emma attends with children of all races and creeds, for which Nellie pays. There is the feeling of being in the midst of noise and trash and people and life. What throws me off, every night, when Howard comes home, is the fact that he still smells like cows, like silage. He spends a fair amount of time at a desk, but he is also involved with the animals' daily care, and therefore, of course, he smells. Even when I am prepared for his entrance I have to brace myself against the fragrance of grain and hay and manure, against all that those smells conjure, against hot summer afternoons and the marvel of the pop-up baler throwing a bale of hay onto the wagon.

We have apparently left Lizzy behind. She is, Reverend Nabor said at one point to Howard, "forever young." I wrote Theresa on what would have been Lizzy's third birthday, and she wrote back, a short note thanking me, telling us that she is pregnant. We are no longer friends, really, and yet I know that we are a part of each other's lives in much the same way a dead parent, or lover, is only slightly beneath one's consciousness by day, and always behind closed lids in sleep. I walk Claire to the park on nice days and I sit on the bench reading a magazine while she plays. Sometimes I talk with other women who are also sitting on benches with magazines on their laps. And if we discover that we have more in common than location and ages of children, and if she is lonely too, and invites me for a cup of coffee, my heart races and I try to get away before the exchange of telephone numbers. I'm not sure, I might tell her, how to be friends a little bit, and I don't have the strength to be friends at full tilt. I don't have the stamina for the obligation and trust that's required. I am still preoccupied with the old life. I might tell my acquaintance that I have not yet fully moved into the present. I find myself lingering in our last days in Spring Grove because it was there, and then, that Howard and I, each in our own ways, began the long process of making peace.

The Saturday after the trial I asked him if I could use the car, that I'd like to run a few errands. I think he knew where I was going because he stood in the middle of the kitchen floor pondering my request before he dug in his pocket for the keys. I drove out of town slightly under the speed limit, inspecting the Christmas decorations and the fields, beautiful in their drabness. I imagined I didn't know I was driving back to Prairie Center.

I had always liked December because it was the beginning of the quiet season. The crops were in, the house was full of food, we were ready for any siege, and we could rest. In the mornings before Howard went out for chores he'd start a fire in the stove, so that when I came down to get breakfast there was always the good warmth and smell of wood burning. Although I had had to go to work I often felt, just for a moment, that we were all shut in, in the glow of the generous hearth, in the house where there was color and music, the thick smell of our life that would go on and on despite the naked trees shivering, the bare, cold world outside. Then of course I had to chase to get dressed, to wake the girls, to stir the oatmeal, to pack lunches, to find mittens, to make a grocery list. But there was often that moment, coming down the stairs, turning on the dim yellow light over the stove, loving our shelter.

When I got to Prairie Center I parked up the way by the old Kresler place and then walked along the road the quarter mile or so to the farm. I had wanted to come back since I'd been let out in September, but I hadn't had a way to get there during the week, and I wouldn't have had time anyway, with Emma gone for a short morning at school. I knew that Howard had driven over on the weekends a few times, to get lumber and furniture, but I had not had the nerve to ask him to take us. It was clear that he hadn't wanted us to come.

He had mentioned that the Boy Scout people were going to take the house down. It didn't look like much, and it would require more money to make sound than it was probably worth, and if it stood empty it would only invite vandals. I walked in through the woods by the road. The house had been a good place, but I had been trying to tell myself, day after day, that we would find another. The woods were a different matter. I used to come out on winter nights, when the sky was heavy with stars. The shadowy trees, dignified and knowledgeable, seemed as much a part of the heavens as of earth, and I'd get the feeling that it wouldn't take much of anything to step into the blackness of the sky, that there wasn't any magic to becoming a part of it.

On that December day I walked over the carpet of wet brown leaves, touching the gray trunks, one after the next. I could see the pond, dull and still, in the distance. I leaned against an enormous burr oak and it came to me then, not only in my intellect, but also in my limbs, my blood, my skin: Lizzy wasn't here in Prairie Center anymore. It was a comfort to feel the tree's cold, spiny bark through my sweater, to feel my own fingers in my mouth. The grief, I knew, wasn't really ever going to go away. I leaned there for a long time, feeling the sharpness, the weight of the thing that was Lizzy's absence. We would never understand what she had become. She probably wasn't anything independent of us anymore, and in each of us she was evident in different ways: in Dan's graying hair, his slow smile, in Theresa's faraway look, her nervous laugh, perhaps in a deeper tenderness.

The pond had meant various things to all of the people who had lived on our farm—and it would be the Boy Scouts' best place—but for us it would always be more than just what it was, a shallow hole filled with water, a few cold, nearly dead fish on the bottom. The water was motionless. It looked, through the trees, as if it was a large eye that would have been grateful for a lid, for sleep.

The terrible thing, I wanted to tell Howard, the terrible thing is that there is so much good, and gradually it slips away from you. I had not believed until last summer that loss is determined, charted in us from the start, as inevitable and fixed as blood type and eye color. As I stood against the tree I remembered only days before, after the verdict was read, after I was acquitted. The jury had deliberated for two hours, while we waited in the courtroom. The words, "What say you?" and "We find the defendant not guilty" rang in my ears and the room began to reel around me. I didn't cry. I must have stood up because I found myself in Rafferty's plaid embrace. He had not spoken more than five words to me since my testimony. Howard was putting his arms around the two of us. The judge in his imposing desk, the jury members, the spectators, were slipping back and forth. I looked out over Rafferty's shoulder and I saw, in one fixed place, Mrs. Mackessy. Susan Dirks was patting her hand and talking at her. She was pale and dead-still. Theresa stepped forward then, blocking her out as she grabbed Howard and hugged him, weeping into his neck. When she moved away, still keeping hold of his hand, Mrs. Mackessy had gone, vanished. Having an enemy is a strangely intimate affair, and I felt, even while I was hanging onto Rafferty, that already something was missing, the canker to which I'd grown accustomed.

Rafferty grasped my wrists and adjusted me to face him squarely. "I have to rush off," he said. "We'll talk in a few days. We should very seriously think about suing Mackessy for damages."

"No," I said.

"You feel that way now, but you let it settle. You think about it."

"No."

"We'll talk," he said, leaning over to kiss my cheek. "Good-bye, sweetheart." He whispered, "You threw me for a goddamn loop but you pulled it off. It couldn't have gone better; I couldn't have designed it more perfectly myself. Dirks knew if she brought it up in the cross the jurors would feel even sorrier for you. It probably made her blood pressure go off the charts to pass up the opportunity. Did you plan it? It was a coup, my dear, a coup."

"No," I said to his back.

That morning, walking in our woods, it seemed as if everything had been out of focus all year and gradually, very slowly, the lens was being turned, the picture coming clear. For Theresa, God was something that was outside of her, some unfathomable being who made the highway radiant. I thought in the harsh December wind that for me God was something within that allowed me, occasionally, to see. Theresa had forgiven us, forgiven me—she had done so not long after Lizzy's death. I hadn't known that a person could so willingly forgive, didn't know what it meant, how it could be, what it was made of, the strange stuff called forgiveness. She had forgiven me nearly as soon as she thought to blame, so that her forgiveness was allied with what seemed a holy sort of understanding and love.

They had looked as if they belonged, Howard and Theresa, when they walked out of the courtroom together, side by side, shoulder to shoulder, as if they were the ones who lived together and were going home to their supper. And I thought how much easier it would be for Howard to love someone like Theresa, someone whose trouble is clear. My misfortunes were messy, hard to pin down, brought upon me by my own hand. In the woods it seemed to me that Theresa represented the world as a wholesome, good place, and that she must seem so for Howard too. I walked around the marsh, scaring up some ducks and a few geese that had not yet gone south. I would someday soon try to tell Howard more about it, all of it, I said to myself. I didn't know who else I would live with if it wasn't Howard, who else would understand the strangeness of our life. But I also knew that we might go along and along, that we might come to a point where we'd look back to find that the relationship had disappeared.

I had walked out into the old orchard, looking at the brown, hard, rotten apples still hanging on the trees. I remembered the night, after the funeral, when I'd run into Theresa and we had stood against the trees, talking. I was grateful for that accidental meeting. As much as it pained me to think of it, I loved that night, too. We hadn't realized it at the time but the conversation had been our chance to make an ending. It had been a suitable and good end.

I stood looking out across the fields, knowing, I thought, every stone, each clump of dirt, calling all of it ours. I wanted to take something, but I couldn't think what it should be. In the end I looked, and closed my eyes, holding it, keeping it. I had driven home then, back to Spring Grove, and we had spent the afternoon in the kitchen, cooking our long overdue Thanksgiving dinner. Howard had thought of it, had thought to haul the turkey out of the freezer compartment of the refrigerator. I made one of Nellie's famous Jell-O salads, and pumpkin pie with the last of Howard's wheat flour. He peeled potatoes and, with Nellie's blow-by-blow instructions over the phone, pulled together her sacred stuffing. Shortly before the food was ready the girls became insufferable. We fed them hot dogs and put them to bed. We came back downstairs, and by the light of two candles we sat before our feast.

We ate in silence for a while. We both knew we weren't going to be able to talk about the farm for a time; we couldn't talk about the future because we had no idea what or where it was. The present itself had for so long been uncertain, and we weren't ready to rehash the details and the chance that had brought us back to solid ground. We tried to find our way. I told him a few more bits and pieces about Dyshett and Sherry and Debbie, and he told me about the dream life of the Indians who lived a billion years ago in Wisconsin. After the meal we put the turkey and Jell-O and stuffing into the refrigerator, and blew out the candles, leaving the entire mess of the afternoon and evening in darkness. There were no lights on in the house anywhere and we fumbled up the stairs to bed.

I had gotten down under the covers and was waiting for him to wind his clock and slide in next to me. He sat, his elbows on his thighs, his head in his hands.

"What is it?" I asked. "Is it the farm?"

He shook his head. "That's not what's bothering me. I don't know, Alice. I don't know."

Although I couldn't have said what it was he needed to tell me, I had the sense of its color, its shape; it was like a small black haze hanging over him. It was something that he would say that would change us, again. I thought of what he had come through, losing what he loved most, and I thought too of the separate journey I'd taken, the anger I'd felt at him in jail for the hundreds of little betrayals, and then how I'd come to have faith that at some point those feelings would be washed clean. For him, perhaps nothing had come clean. He lay down with his back to me. I could feel him shaking. I cried some, too, then, holding him in my arms, kissing his hair, feeling what for Theresa came easily, and what for me had always been difficult. All the same I knew I was forgiving him. I had that miraculous clarity for an instant and so I understood that the forgiveness itself was strong, durable, like strands of a web, weaving around us, holding us.

ABOUT THE AUTHOR

Jane Hamilton lives, works, and writes in an orchard farmhouse in Wisconsin. Her short stories have appeared in *Harper's* magazine, and her first book, *The Book of Ruth,* was awarded the 1989 PEN/Hemingway Foundation Award for best first novel.